Spirit Legends

of ghosts and gods

Edited
by
Christopher Ficco

Cover Art
by
Laura Givens

RuneWright, LLC Publishing
Aurora, Colorado

ISBN-10:   0983278237
ISBN-13:   978-09832782-3-8

contents

Spirit Legends

of ghosts and gods

ᏟIntroduction

hen I put out the call for submissions to *Spirit Legends*, especially with a sub-title of "*ghosts and gods*, I felt a tinge of trepidation that I would receive a plethora if zealous, pro-religious dogma rather than thoughtful and entertaining fiction. It's not that I have a bias against dogma... well, actually, I do, but that's a different topic... but when you have a finite amount of time to read submissions, and you're looking for solid, creative fiction, the last thing you want to read is how utterly amazing God, Jesus, Buddha, Yaweh, Jehovah, Allah, Muhammad, Gaia or whatever is and how much we should take him, her or it into our hearts.

Certainly there's a place for all of that and more in this world (and beyond), just not in an anthology of this sort. I was both delighted and relieved when I finally sat down to read through the slush pile. There wasn't a single story that crossed the line. What I did get was a marvelous assortment of predominantly speculative fiction with some genre horror, sci-fi, paranormal and fantasy mixed in for good measure.

What you'll read in *Spirit Legends* is the best of the bunch, and I must say there is some really wonderful writing and some fantastic stories contained within these pages. I tried to cover as many pantheons as possible as I went through my acceptance process. There are Greek, Incan, Norse, Celtic, Christian and Native American tales as well as a fictional pantheon that caught my eye and an invented deity that really puts a different spin on the notion of what god is.

I was a little disappointed that I didn't get any stories from the Asian cultures, but, like any editor, I can only work with what I'm given. I've always had a keen interest in the world's religions and spiritual philosophies—even studied them in college—so I guess I was hoping for a much wider representation. However, what's here is definitely a mish-mash of Western belief-systems, and every one is both entertaining and thought provoking.

I supposed that's part of the reason I decided to do this particular anthology. I was curious to see what kinds of things were being written about in this arena. A *Spirit Legends II* is not on the list for next year's production. I've had to limit things down to four rather than six in order to get my own writing done. However, I think there is value for almost everyone to explore the myriad faith-systems and philosophies that exist or have existed. Ultimately, the relationship sentient creatures establish with what they perceive as their creator or as the sublime connection to that which lies beyond this mortal coil—or absence thereof—can say more about the "human" condition than anything else in our experience.

I encourage everyone to take time out of the daily grind, at least every now and again, to extend understanding beyond the confines of what you've been raised with; explore what other peoples and cultures believe and open your mind to the limitless possibilities of that which you do not yet understand. I'm not suggesting that you adopt a different belief-system. What I am suggesting is that you endeavor to understand better those belief-systems that exist around you and discover the commonalities that you will inevitably discover between yourself and the people you meet each day. I can honestly say that if the human populace did more of this, there would be less strife and suffering in the world.

Be that as it may, what you have in your hands is what I hope you find to be an enjoyable collection of short stories. In small doses or large, I think you'll find yourself exploring and discovering new possibilities... and even if you don't, I'm confident that you'll come across a few yarns that speak to you in ways you didn't expect.

So sit back, relax and dig into *Spirit Legends*. If you find a story that touches or even offends, hit me up at www.Diascribe.com and we can talk about it. I love hearing from my readers, and I'm always open to both praise and criticism.

INTRODUCTION

The Muse's Inkpot

by Harris Tobias (Virginia, USA)

People often ask me where all my ideas come from. It's a question we successful writers are frequently asked, and since my writing has received a modicum of popularity and won a handful of cherished awards, it's a question I am pestered with all the time. I have developed a glib rejoinder to those critics and fans foolish enough to actually pursue this line of questioning.

I usually respond with a clever remark like, "Oh I get them from my notebook." That sounds farcical but is, in reality, the god's honest truth. That is exactly where my ideas come from.

If the questioner persists and says that my answer begs the question, "How do your ideas get into the notebook?"

I always answer, "From my pen."

"So how comes the pen by these ideas?" they often cry out in amused frustration.

"The ink," I say.

And there the game stops, because to continue would reveal matters I have sworn never to reveal. I usually shrug my shoulders and put a dumb smile on my face and say "Ahh, that is the mystery." Everyone laughs, and the subject of ideas is dropped. No one really expects a serious answer to so ridiculous a question anyway.

Now that I am old and my writing days are done, I feel it is time to answer more fully that most asinine of questions. What difference does it make now if the real answer is known? My good partner, the famous portrait artist Jethro Montague, is long gone to his eternal reward. I am old and failing. I have written my last novel and told my final tale... almost. Perhaps this last story will enlighten and amuse those aspiring artists who will surely follow in my wake. Besides, no one will believe it anyway. But here for posterity is the true story of the source of my inspirations. I give you the story of *The Muse's Inkpot*.

*   *   *

As a young man I was a rapscallion, a hell raiser, a party boy, a good for nothing ne'er-do-well. I'd spend my nights drinking and my days sleeping. I was a witty lad and a boon companion, at least as long as my coin held out. I dabbled at poetry and comic essays for the amusement of my friends, and I had acquired the reputation as a modestly talented writer. My literary efforts had thus far not yielded any monetary reward, however. Fortunately, I was lucky at cards, so I usually had a good supply of silver with which to buy wine and keep the whole jolly cycle going. As a result of this lifestyle, I believed I had plenty of friends. As for women,

I had plenty of those as well, although I cannot say that I found any real happiness from either quarter.

One of my companions was a student of the magical arts, a young fellow named Jethro Montague. Jethro was a contemplative lad of a far more serious nature than any in our group. When I drank too much, which was often, Jethro would often take me to his tiny room and lay me out on his threadbare carpet to sleep it off. Many a morning I would awake amidst a clutter of papers and old books in Jethro's ratty attic.

I remember waking one afternoon on Jethro's floor with my host absent, at class somewhere I assumed. I was alone and badly in need of a drink of water and something for my throbbing head. My mouth felt like a dry hole and tasted of last night's carousing. I staggered about the tiny apartment, looking for the tap or a cup and bucket with which to slake my thirst. I could find neither. However, while looking in every corner and shelf, I chanced upon a dog-eared and tattered old manuscript titled *The Muse's Handbook*.

I put the ratty old book on a table, expecting to examine it further as soon as my immediate needs were satisfied. By the time I had drunk and refreshed myself, Jethro was back and, when he saw me, gave me a hug so fierce you'd have thought he had just discovered his long lost brother.

"Jethro, my friend!" I exclaimed when I could free myself from his embrace. "Why this display of emotion?"

"The book," he stammered. "I saw that you had found the book and feared you'd opened it. When I saw that you had not, I was overcome with joy."

"How could you tell I had not opened it?"

"Because, my dear friend, had you opened it you

7

quite likely would not be here now."

"Where, pray tell, would I be?" I snatched the book from the table and pretended to open it.

Jethro blanched. "Some things are not for the uninitiated. Please, if you love me, if you love life, if you wish to die an old man in your bed, keeping your senses to the end, you will put that book down unread."

Now I don't have to tell you that there is no better way to induce desire for a thing then to forbid it. Jethro's admonitions only made me want to see what this strange little book was all about. But I thought poor Jethro would burst into tears if I did not stop toying with him, so I gave him back the book. I did, however demanded an explanation.

"You've heard of the Muses?" he asked. I nodded that I had. I may be poorly educated, but I knew that the Greeks attributed the creative sources of music and art to semi-mystical beings called Muses.

"There are a half a dozen of them, if I recall, and they have the power to inspire or deny inspiration to the artist. It's all a bunch of mumbo jumbo, if you ask me."

"There are nine of them, and I assure you they are quite real. They are also quite powerful and, like all women, jealous and fickle creatures." Jethro prattled on about the Muses as he prepared tea and some bread and cheese for our lunch. It was obvious he had been studying the myths and legends of the Muses for some time. His knowledge of them was extensive. My head was hurting, so I was only half-paying attention.

"The most common question people ask is where did the Muses come from?" He poured me a steaming mug of tea and added healthy measures of butter, honey and brandy to it. It was most gratifying, and I sipped it while he continued his lesson. "According to the ancients, Zeus seduced the beautiful Titan Mnemosyne, the goddess of memory. Zeus slept with her for nine consecutive nights. The results of these encounters were the nine Muses, all similar to each other in their beauty and their love of the arts.

"Legend has it they were not interested in human affairs. They cared only for the arts. Apollo noticed this and encouraged them by taking charge of their education. He brought them to Mount Elikonas where an older temple of Zeus used to be and taught them all he knew of music and dance. As their powers grew, the sisters invented new forms of poetry, drama, comedy and music. Ever since, the Muses have supported and encouraged artistic creation, enhancing the imagination and inspiration of artists. They alone have the power to grant an artist inspiration and make him great or to withhold it and make him fail. The Muses attend the festivals on Olympus and entertain and inspire the other gods with their wit and charm. Apollo puts aside his bow and plays the lyre as the Gods join in the dance of the immortals."

"That's all very interesting," I said as I stuffed my face. I was hungrier than I thought. "But what's it got to do with that book?"

"Why, that's what I've been trying to tell you. The Muses are real, and this book is the way into their world."

"Why would anyone want to bust in on them? Isn't it dangerous?"

"It certainly can be. Historically, the Olympian Gods haven't taken kindly to strangers, and they have been known to be vengeful. One story says that a singer and poet named Thamyris challenged the Muses. He mocked them and made light of their skills. For his insolence,

Thamyris was blinded and his memory taken. He could no longer remember his songs or his poems. The Muses can bestow the gift of talent and insight, but they can also viciously revoke their blessings. King Pierus boasted that his nine daughters rivaled the Muses in beauty and talent, and they were turned into magpies."

"Why would anyone want to mess with them?" I asked.

"Why? Just think of it man! You would have the ability to write immortal poetry or music that would inspire an age. Your compositions would be inscribed on monuments, your songs sung for a thousand years. Your name would live forever!"

I shrugged. "A fat lot of good it will do me to be famous long after I'm dead."

"Then think of the immediate rewards," Jethro said. "Crowds would pay to hear you speak or sing or purchase your volumes of verse. You would live like a prince, be welcomed to perform at the great houses of the rich, be pampered and fed, a welcomed guest among the powerful."

"How about girls?" I asked warming to the subject.

"Women beyond reckoning," Jethro replied. He was up and pacing the tiny room. "Your songs would pierce their hearts and open their skirts. I'm reminded of the story of Aristarchus of Thebes whose poetry is said to have seduced a thousand princesses in a single night. It ultimately killed him, or so the legend goes."

"What a way to go," I sighed in sympathy with that long lost brother.

"Through my studies I have learned a great deal about the Muses." Jethro was slipping back into lecture mode, but this time I was more inclined to listen. "There are nine Muses according to legend." Jethro dutifully counted them off on his fingers.

"First is Calliope; she is considered the chief Muse. Her domain is epic poetry, but her influence extends far beyond that narrow discipline. Homer called upon her for inspiration, if you recall, but so do all modern writers. She attends the birth of kingly nobles and decides what talents to bestow, not only artistic talents, mind you, but gifts from the other gods as well.

"Next is Clio, the Muse of history. History was named Kleos by the ancients whose view of history was much different from our own. She is also purported to have invented the guitar.

"Euterpe's name means "giver of delight" and is the Muse of music. She is credited with discovering several musical instruments and is seldom depicted without her flute. Somewhere along the way she became the Muse of lyric poetry.

"Thalia is the Muse of comedy. It is said that she actually invented comedy. Imagine how dreary the world must have been before that. She's also credited with discovering geometry, architecture and agriculture, though none of those pursuits have much humor in them.

"Melpomene, Thalia's opposite number, is the Muse of Tragedy and protects it fiercely, often depicted holding a bat. She is also credited with the art of rhetoric for reasons known only to the Greeks.

"Terpsichore, Muse of the dance, invented dancing, the harp and education. She is generally considered the liveliest and good humored of the Muses.

"Erato, as you might expect from the name, is the Muse of love poetry and matters erotic. She is the protector of love, weddings and lovers. She's often depicted holding a lyre and a quiver filled with love's arrows.

"Polymnia's domain is sacred music, hymns, that kind of thing. It's believed that she invented grammar and is also credited with inventing geometry. Maybe she and Thalia invented it together.

"Ourania is the protector of celestial objects, and her domain includes the stars and astrology; she is the one who gave us astronomy. She was always depicted bearing stars, a celestial sphere and a compass."

When this long recitation was complete, I was half-asleep. I snapped back to attention only when Jethro tweaked my nose.

"Oww! What did you do that for?" I complained, rubbing my insulted appendage.

"I suspected you weren't listening."

"I wasn't listening. I don't need to know about the Muses in such detail. I'm not a student. Why do you persist in boring me to death?" If my words hurt Jethro's feelings, I was sorry, but I was finding our discussion tedious, and sounds of laughter were wafting up from the tavern across the street.

"Because I want you to come with me," Jethro whispered in reply.

"Go with you where?"

"To Mount Olympus or, more specifically, Mount Elikonas to see the Muses and steal Calliope's inkpot."

I stared at my friend open-mouthed for what seemed like several minutes. "Are you mad?" I finally managed to ask. "Studying ancient myths is one thing. Believing in them is quite another."

"If it's not real then you have nothing to fear," Jethro said calmly.

"I didn't say I was afraid. I said that believing in fairy tales is madness. But let's assume it's all real. I see two rather large problems, getting there and getting back alive. You said yourself they're vengeful and nasty. You want to be turned into a magpie like that king?"

"It was his daughters that became magpies," Jethro said pedantically. "Anyway, we have a secret weapon. I have been delving into the old records and discovered something quite extraordinary—a tenth Muse."

"You discovered a tenth Muse?" I asked, incredulous. Suddenly I was interested again.

"Yes, my friend, it's really quite amazing. I won't bore you with the details of my research, but it is one of history's great cover-ups. I expect Clio had much to do with it, but there was a tenth Muse born to Mnemosyne, fathered by Zeus and named Cacophony. She wasn't like her sisters. She wasn't beautiful, and her talents were so far beyond the taste of the time that she was shunned and eventually forgotten. She, of course, hates her sisters and will surely be our ally should we need assistance, as we almost certainly will."

"Cacophony?" I said. "As in *noise*?"

"That's what it's come to mean, but that's just part of the smearing of her reputation. On a list of Muses, Cacophony would be considered the Muse of the avant-garde, the modern, the misunderstood, the underappreciated. She'd be the Muse of percussion instruments and bagpipes… something like that, anyway."

"Oh, I get it. Like that strange impressionistic art that we've been seeing?"

"There's strange and misunderstood art in every age, sometimes only appreciated centuries later."

"And this book of yours? You think it's our way

in?"

"That's what I believe. All we have to do is plug Cacophony's name into the spell, and it should deliver us there. So what say you, are you with me?"

Poor Jethro, he looked so earnest and sincere. He'd always been kind and descent to me. Hadn't he taken me in just last night and fed me this morning? And wasn't it all a lot of hooey anyway? So I gave a merry laugh, clasped his hand and gave my word.

Jethro beamed. "Marvelous. There's a full moon three days hence. Meet me here in this room by ten."

*　　　　*　　　　*

In those days, three days of merriment and debauchery could seem like a year, and so by the time the third evening rolled around, I had forgotten all about my promise. I was deep in my cups, playing dice with a group of friends, when I reached for my wallet to buy a round of drinks and purchase a pile of tokens. I had been losing steadily all night, which was most unusual for me. I noticed that my entourage of friends had shrunken along with my fortune. No one, it seemed, likes the company of a loser. I didn't like losing either and was not feeling very convivial toward my fellow man. As I was saying, I reached for my wallet only to discover that my pocket had been picked and my cash stolen.

I looked to my companions for some sympathy and perhaps an offer of some credit, but there was nothing of the sort forthcoming. When I offered to write a check, no one would take my marker. I felt hurt and alone. Where were my so-called friends? I realized then and there that my lifestyle was unsustainable, and if I wanted to keep myself in the style I had grown accustomed, I could do worse than earn a living. I did a quick inventory of my marketable skills and understood that writing verse was the one talent I possessed that I actually enjoyed doing. Of course, making money from one's pen is no sure thing. Only the top tier of writers can live off their writing, and you can count on one hand the number of poets that make their living versifying. I recalled Jethro's words about the riches one could expect from a truly Muse-blessed writer, and I vowed to stop drinking and join Jethro in his quest for the Muse's Inkpot.

I excused myself from the gambling table and returned to my room where I thought I'd take a nap and clear my head. When I woke it was a quarter of ten. I scrambled around thinking of what I might need for questing on Mount Olympus and threw a few necessities into a sack. I took a knife and fork, a sewing kit, my hunting knife that I used for cutting string and my last two gold coins that I'd been saving for my retirement. I knocked on Jethro's door a quarter of an hour late. He didn't mind. We had to wait until the moon was three hands above the land.

I noticed that Jethro had been consulting the manual. The handbook was opened to the first page. "Is this where you got that three hands stuff from?"

"It looks like another hour before the moon is that high. In the meantime help me with these candles." He chalked a pentagram on the floor and put a candle at each point. The moon was bright and shone a patch of silvery light on the floor. As the moonlight crept toward the pentagram, we busied ourselves with our preparations. "I doubt if you'll be able to bring that," Jethro said pointing to my sack of useful items.

When the moonlight touched the pentagram, Jethro lit the candles and began to chant something from the book. I thought it was in Greek. After I heard it four times, I learned it and, although I didn't know what it meant, repeated the two lines over and over again.

Aouwey Cacophony aouwey borough
Aouwey aouwey tim come torrough

In retrospect, I realize how childish this entire description sounds. Moonlight, magic signs, chanting in an occult language, but who are we to say how the ancients called their gods? Their myths survive by little else. Men encountered the gods much more directly in those days. Maybe they knew how to summon them or to travel between worlds better than we.

I learned years later what the words meant. It wasn't Greek at all; it wasn't any human language. It was Enochian for:

Hear this, hear this, Cacophony, I am coming
Welcome welcome I'll meet you there...

Or something to that effect. The long and short of it was that we were engulfed by a swirling mist and transported to a marble palace with tall fluted columns capped with gilt capitals. Black marble floors and sumptuous rugs completed the picture of classic beauty. The beauty of the scene was marred by fearful pounding, twanging and crashing noises coming from another room.

We were met by a strange creature that appeared to be part cat and part woman. Her lithe body was covered with a golden fur, and her tail swished beneath her filmy dress with a life of its own. She bowed before us and bid us welcome. "I am Caterwaul, your guide. My friends call me Cate, and you may do so as well. We have been expecting you. My mistress will be with you as soon as she has finished practicing." She listened to the crashing and banging, smiled and added, "She's very advanced."

"What is that racket?" Jethro yelled over the din.

Cate looked shocked at the question. "You are ignorant of our customs, mortals, so we'll excuse your bad manners. What you are hearing is a musical form that won't be heard in your world for at least another century. I think my mistress calls it *Rock & Roll*. It takes some getting used to, but don't judge what you see or hear in this place with your current standards. Art is a living, growing thing. Ah, I think the session is winding down. If you come with me, I'll present you."

We followed our guide through a hallway lined with the most curious statuary and paintings I had ever seen, strange shapes that exist nowhere in nature, paintings of nothing but splatters, or if there was a recognizable shape, twisted and distorted as if in a fun house mirror. It was ghastly art, but I remembered to keep my opinion to myself.

Caterwaul stopped outside a closed door and waited until the last screechy chord died away, then she rapped lightly. We were admitted to a small room. Four musicians were putting away their instruments, and what strange instruments they were! We beheld triangular objects with wires attached and a set of drums of various sizes, all with the same a garish outside. As weird as the instruments were, the musicians were even weirder. They wore leather costumes that revealed their chests, and their faces were painted with outrageous designs like nightmare clowns. Cate went up to a large woman sitting behind the drums and whispered in her ear. The woman must have told her assistant to offer us refreshments while she prepared herself for visitors. She gave us a little wave as

Cate led us out of one room and into another.

This next room had an enormous table spread with all manner of food. We were hungry and ate our fill. Everything tasted better than any food either of us ever had. Think of the best meal you ever had on Earth, multiply it by a factor of ten, and you would have a fair approximation of what we ate. I asked Cate how it was possible that food could taste so incredibly good.

"Oh, does it?" she asked and looked at it quizzically. I suppose even the food of the Gods can become dull and routine after a few centuries. We were saved any further embarrassment by our hostess's entrance into the room. Cacophony was a large woman with stringy brown hair and the face of a German housewife. She held out her hand and spoke to us for the first time.

"Welcome young mortals. I hope Cate has been treating you well." We both nodded and mumbled that was indeed the case. "Allow me to show you around. I have an extensive collection of modern art, much of it quite inventive." Cacophony took us on a tour of her galleries. There were miles of them. Much of what we saw entailed drawing, painting and sculpture Cacophony claimed was centuries away from being accepted. To tell you the truth, I couldn't make heads or tails out of any of it. The sculpture was artless shapes, some of it of monstrous size, and the paintings looked like they were made by children with little aptitude for the form. Aside from the occasional eye-roll to Jethro, we got through the tour in pretty good shape.

"And that's just the visual arts," Cacophony said with obvious pride. "I also have a very complete collection of music and poetry you simply wouldn't believe. And you want to know the best part?" asked our hostess, looking us in the eye so we could not answer. "The best part is that my sisters hate it—every last bit of it. Ha! It gives me pleasure encouraging young artists but even greater pleasure making my sisters squirm. They can't deny that its art, yet they are so stuck in the past they can never expand their horizons and embrace it."

Cacophony showed us into a private chamber, a much smaller room with a low ceiling and a long table. There were chairs enough for twenty people, but there were only the three of us. Cacophony took her chair at the head of the table.

"Let's get down to business," she said. "Why are you here?" I was about to answer, but she held up her hand to stop me. "I know why you're here. You want to steal something from my sisters, something you can use to improve your life in your world. It's always the same. How tedious you mortals can be."

I was remembering the magpies and stayed quiet. Cacophony continued. "I don't care what you take from them. They have shown me no love and no respect. I owe them nothing. They turned my father against me, and they don't value what I do. Whatever diminishes their power benefits me, so steal what you will. If you are caught, well... I certainly wouldn't want to be in your shoes."

Jethro spoke up and in a frightened voice squeaked, "Is there any way you can help us so that we won't get caught? We are not professional thieves in our world. I'm a student and quite clumsy actually."

"We're only looking for a little fame," I added, "just enough to pay the bills."

"Just a little fame, huh? I can help you to a limited extent," Cacophony said, "I cannot directly intervene. Certain protocols make that impossible. I can, however, draw you a map and tell you what to steal for fleeting fame."

"We've come for Calliope's inkpot," said Jethro with newfound authority.

Cacophony threw her head back and laughed as only an immortal can.

*   *   *

"The inkpot is on Calliope's desk. She writes her epics with it, so there's always a good supply." Cacophony pushed a button on the desk and swiveled her chair around. Behind her a white screen unreeled from the ceiling. She pushed another button, and the lights went dim. Then pictures appeared on the screen. They were like magic lantern slides.

"This is Calliope's palace. It is two days walk from here." The picture changed.

"My sister," –slide– "her writing chamber," –slide– "her desk. Can you zoom in?" The surface of the desk increased. "That's the inkpot." A small object on the desk blinked. "Just a few drops of that and you'll have all the fame you can handle."

I tried to get Jethro's attention. This adventure was turning out far more dangerous than I expected. Not that I knew what to expect, but Jethro was not paying me any mind. He was enthralled by the fact that his magic actually worked—that we were sitting here in the land of myth about to embark on a dangerous mission. I made a mental vow to never go on an impossible quest with a hopeless romantic. He appeared oblivious to the dangers we faced. The book we used to get us here didn't follow us, and I wondered how we would ever get back. I was going to ask Cacophony about that very thing when she answered the question before I could give it voice.

"In the unlikely event that you succeed in getting out with Calliope's inkpot and make it back here in one piece, I will see to it that you are returned to your proper place and time, although why you would want to go back there is quite beyond my understanding."

She was right, of course. Why would we want to return to that squalid life? But for the fact that it was all we knew, anything else was too frightful to contemplate. Besides, we had to make it back here first. Living in our world with wealth and fame wasn't such a bad prospect. Cacophony pushed another button, and her assistant Caterwaul appeared.

"Arm these gentlemen, give them the maps and send them on their way. Goodbye boys, and good luck." Then she swirled out of the room and left us with Cate who asked us to follow her. She strode down a long hallway with long, cat-like strides, clutching a stack of papers to her chest while her tail occasionally whacked the wall.

*   *   *

A few hours later we were walking along a forested trail trying to follow a poorly drawn map to Calliope's palace—a two day march south and east. We were armed with chain mail, a lance, a broad sword and a short sword, all of which made enough noise as we marched to signal our approach to every living creature. I wasn't sure of the purpose of all that armament or what possible use it would be against immortals and mentioned this to Jethro. He walked in silence for a while before answering. "The only possible use I can see is that there are creatures dwelling in this forest that we might need to defend ourselves against."

We each carried a sack containing the papers we were given and food enough for four days. The sacks were heavy and uncomfortable to carry. Add to that that it was a warm spring day, and you have some idea of our discomfort. Little by little we began to shed our gear. First the chain mail was discarded piece by piece along the trail. A few miles later I leaned my lance against a tree and left it there. I noticed that Jethro did the same. After that it was the broad sword's turn. I stuck it into a rotting stump where I could retrieve it on the way back. A few leagues further on, Jethro did a similar thing with his sword. We kept the short swords, as it seemed prudent to have some protection in case the forest harbored unfriendly beasts, although signs of that menace we saw none.

That first night we slept under the stars. We heard much roaring and movement in the brush near where we lay, so neither of us slept a wink. When dawn finally broke we saw the spoor of a large animal not five yards from our camp. I wished I had my lance, and I'm sure Jethro felt the same, but we conquered our fears and soldiered on. We stopped for lunch on a high promontory overlooking a vista of endless woods and hills. There was a sparkle of white marble in the distance.

"Is that...?"

"Calliope's palace. Yes that's it." Jethro sat down and dug in his pack for the papers we were given. There were pictures of the palace, a huge expanse of gleaming white marble in the classical Greek mode. It looked like the Parthenon only bigger. There was a picture of Calliope herself. She was stunning. More beautiful than any woman I had ever seen, all the more amazing considering her age. She had piercing gray eyes, wavy bronze hair and perfect features like the image of Helen of Troy I had seen once on a Grecian urn.

"She looks nice," I said, already in love with her.

"She's not that nice. She's jealous and quick to anger. You especially don't want to challenge her in any way. She hates losing, but she can be kind and fair. She's wise, and the gods use her to broker disputes. It would be best if we gave her a wide birth and didn't encounter her directly."

Jethro shuffled through the papers and came up with one titled *Calliope's Schedule*. It showed the Muse performing music in the evening and writing poetry until midnight before retiring. "It looks like we need wait outside the palace until after midnight, make our way to the writing desk and slip out before she wakes." It sounded too easy, but I kept my mouth shut, not wanting to jinx our enterprise. We trudged on until we were just a few hundred yards from the palace. We could see groups of toga clad people playing music or dancing.

The sun was sinking, and we were tired after our long trek and lack of sleep the night before. We settled in to wait for midnight but promptly fell fast asleep. When I awoke, I checked the time. It was 4:30 in the morning, less than an hour until dawn. We had overslept. I shook Jethro awake, and we made our way to the palace as fast as we could. In our haste we left the map of the interior along with our packs behind. Jethro assured me he had studied the map and could guide us to the Muse's desk unaided.

We approached the front door. It was as tall and as wide as the mast on a sailboat and made of solid bronze. We heaved on it with all our might, but it wouldn't budge.

We proceeded to walk around the palace looking for an easier way to gain entrance. We found a small door in the rear, probably for deliveries, or perhaps it was the kitchen door. It was locked tight when we tried it, but it soon opened with a bang, and a curious looking half-animal, half-human creature with the ears and legs of a donkey carried a heavy bucket of kitchen scraps away to a distant barn. He didn't seem to notice us standing there or, if he noticed, didn't care. The kitchen door was ajar, so we entered into a stone passageway. We walked past a brightly lit kitchen bustling with activity. Bakers baked bread and pastries for the Muse's breakfast. Sleepy-eyed cooks stirred pots of porridge, and pancakes sizzled on the griddle.

"We better hurry," I whispered to Jethro. "It looks like the palace is waking up soon."

We blundered onward. I don't think Jethro's mental map was much use as we padded through endless corridors past innumerable doors. Fortunately there was no one about. Once, when we passed a window, I saw the first blush of dawn color the sky. I was about to abort the mission when Jethro suddenly got his bearings. He brought us to a halt before a door and stood there frozen.

"This is it," he said and pulled on the handle. The door opened on a dark, wood-paneled room. There was just enough light in the dawn to see the outlines of Calliope's writing desk. There on her desk was the draft of her latest epic poem, a quill, a blotter and her inkpot, a round silver topped container filled with her special ink.

"Did you bring the flask?" Jethro whispered in my ear. I hadn't. I assumed he had brought it. There was no use arguing about who was responsible. I grabbed the whole inkpot and stuffed it in my shirt. The second my

24

fingers closed on it, a cock began to crow, heralding the sun. We dashed out of the room and down the hall the way we had come. When we neared the kitchen, the passage was alive with servants carrying breakfast trays and steaming pots of coffee for the household. We couldn't slip out the back door unseen. We ran back into the house in hopes of finding the front doors. We could hear the servant's voices behind us as they scattered throughout the palace, bringing breakfast to Calliope and her guests.

The big front doors were barred with an iron bar. We struggled to remove it from its keepers and pushed the huge doors open without any trouble. We were outside when we heard the first cry of, "Hey you! Stop!" We ran for the woods, the alarm already raised.

*   *   *

We ran until we could run no more and lay panting by the side of the trail some distance from Calliope's palace. We could hear dogs barking and expected a troop of horsemen to descend on us at any moment, but we were too flagged to travel another step. All those years of dissolute living had taken their toll on my physique. I vowed to mend my ways in the future, if only I had one.

We thought it prudent to leave the trail and bushwhack our way through the undergrowth where our pursuers would not have such an easy time of it. We crashed our way through brush and brambles, fell into streams and pools, but we kept doggedly on, fearing confrontation with Calliope's minions at every turn. We lost our packs with our food and gear. We lost our maps. We lost our way in the tangle of forest and bush. Night was falling, and we were at the end of our strength. We found a small clearing and lay down, exhausted, wet, cold and hungry. All we had was Calliope's little, silver inkpot, and much of its precious contents had spilled or leaked away. I held it up to the dying light and saw less than an inch of liquid remaining. I smelled it, and it smelled of satisfaction, of romance and adventure and long nights curled by the fire with a good book. It smelled of stories around the campfire that make you look behind you in the dark to see if the demons were really there.

I passed the ink to Jethro, and he too smelled the possibilities in that mysterious liquid. I don't remember who suggested it, but we decided that rather than risk spilling the rest, we should drink what we had and see if its magic would transfer to our blood. We made cups from a giant leaf and filled them with water from a spring. Then we divided the precious ink between them and drank to our success.

The ink was the deepest blue and, when added to the water, colored it as dark as paint. It tasted like all the best fruits I had ever eaten. I tasted juicy pears and tart tangerines; there was the sweetness of melons and the bitterness of lemons, the mustiness of grapes and the clarity of apples. It quenched our thirst and satisfied our hunger. That night I dreamed of Hercules and Achilles. I dreamed whole epics in rhyming couplets.

I could feel Helen's hot breath as I kissed her on the walls of Troy. Of course, it might have been the hot breath of a wild beast sizing me up for a meal. I was too frightened to look, which, in retrospect, was probably a wise decision. Instead, I feigned sleep and forced my racing heart to slow its panicked beating. Whatever it was, it must have found us unpalatable and wandered back into the forest in search of tastier fare.

There was no use trying to sleep after that. We resumed our aimless walk-about, hoping to stumble on something familiar. By noon we were reduced to eating berries and boiling bark for tea. We stumbled ahead blindly, hopelessly lost, cursing our fate until we were forced to stop and rest yet again. Our strength was failing and our situation grave. We sat on a mossy log, lost in thought. With a start I jumped to my feet. There in a stump not six feet away was the broadsword I had left just two days before. Jethro insisted the broad sword was his, but it hardly mattered. We were saved. We found the trail and followed it back to Cacophony's palace without further ado.

We told Cacophony about our adventures. I offered her the ink well that we had stolen.

"What happened to the ink," she asked.

"We drank it," Jethro said.

"Very resourceful," Cacophony played with the stolen object.

"You can keep that," I said, referring to the object. "We were only interested in the ink."

"You boys amaze me. Drinking the ink is not something I'm familiar with. There's no telling how it will affect you. The last time any mortal used the ink, he wrote the Iliad. You'll either be geniuses or drunks in your world."

* * *

Cacophony sent us back in a similar manner as the way we arrived. She and Caterwaul chanted some Enochian words as the band played some god-awful noise, bringing forth a swirl of mist that engulfed us. We were back in Jethro's room in Cambridge before we knew what happened. My ink-stained shirt was the only proof that we had ever been there. We took an oath never to tell anyone about our adventure. We shook hands and went our separate ways. *The Muse's Handbook* was never seen again.

Jethro soon developed an overwhelming urge to paint and immediately made plans to study art. That was how the ink affected him. He changed his major from magic to fine arts. I understand that he was an excellent pupil. Now he paints portraits for the well-to-do and has made quite a name for himself in France.

As for me, well I wish I could tell you that my writing leaped from the page into history, but that is not what happened. From the start I could experience marvelous ideas in my dreams. I saw plays and heard poems that would have been the envy of any writer, but when I went to write them down, I was not adequate to the task. The skill to find the words worthy of the Muse-inspired ideas was simply not there. The satisfactory transition from inspiration to execution was still a painful and difficult process. I persevered, and slowly the world came to know my name and read my words. But in the end, history will judge me a minor figure. My words will not be carved on monuments nor recited by orators and schoolchildren for generations to come. I have, however, written some fine things and had the reward of a good review and a bestselling work. It was a slow and painful education. I have learned to write, it's true, and while I still mostly enjoy it, it has not been an easy road.

So that's how the Muse's ink has worked for me. It gave me great insights but not the talent to express them.

It gave me dedication to my craft but not instant success. The modicum of fame I have achieved has come at the expense of hard work, and maybe that is the way it should be. If there is a lesson to be learned from all this, it is that there are no shortcuts. You can drink the Muse's ink, but talent is still hers to bestow.

I will die soon. All I leave behind are these few pages of thought. I wanted fleeting fame, and that is exactly what I got.

The End

About the author:

Harris Tobias lives and writes in Charlottesville, Virginia. He is the author of two novels and dozens of short stories. His fiction has appeared in *Ray Gun Revival*, *Dunesteef Audio Magazine*, *Every Photo Tells*, *Quantum Muse*, *Thrillers, Killers & Chillers*, *Eclectic Flash*, *E Fiction* and several other obscure publications. You can find links to his novels at:
http://harristobias-fiction.blogspot.com/

Return

by Rick Coonrod (Idaho, USA)

The inner chamber still reeked of blood, and for good reason. The blood grooves in the floor leading away from the now crumbling altar had seen their share of it. Even still, a thick layer of black gore flaked from their sides and collected at the bottom of each groove. Centuries of abandonment had only dulled the heavy, metallic smell that still hung in the air.

Accla leaned against the doorway, steadying herself with one hand and holding the other to her chest. The climb up the mountain had almost been too much. Her shoulders heaved as she tried to steady the breath that came in gasps. Below, macaws fighting over fruit screeched in the jungle canopy. She tried to focus her eyes as sweat rolled from her forehead, tried to focus on the patch of sunlight that streamed through the hole in the partially collapsed roof. Four hundred years had taken its toll on the temple.

She remembered the screams most of all. Sometimes she connected the screams with a contorted face or a young body pulling against the bonds at wrists and feet, but she knew that it was just her mind filling in the gaps of memory. For most of the sacrifices she had her eyes closed while she chanted, and she kept them closed as she plunged the long, copper knife into their abdomens, sliced them open and pulled their intestines free. It was interesting how long a person could live without their intestines, but many had simply died from fright before they bled out. The memory of the warmth of the organs, the blood washing over the altar, and the screams caused her to smile, and she closed her eyes, reveling in the smell that she now realized she missed. Her breathing slowly steadied enough for her to draw in a deep breath, and she felt her youth again for a moment.

She was the only one left. Four centuries ago she was a priestess of Inti. Each day, with her sisters of the order, they spoke the sacred incantation of *qqii isa imi xaxiq xaxiq isa imi qqii*—flesh made fire, fire made flesh—as they set human entrails aflame, bringing forth the earthly form of Inti to consume the human sacrifice. In exchange for Inti's meal, he preserved their bodies, and they aged slower with each sacrifice. Then the Puccas to the south had overrun their city. They slaughtered the priestesses and sacrificed them to their god Supai. To escape Accla was forced to abandon her robes as she left the temple, fleeing into the jungle with only the copper sacrificial knife hidden in a bundle of sticks.

She presided over the sacrifices for decades, so Inti had extended her life into the centuries, but now her body was near its end. When she felt strong enough again, Accla staggered out to the middle of the chamber. Every part of her body ached from the climb. Hunching in the swirl of dust her motions had disturbed, her withered lungs burned, and she collapsed on the floor in a fit of coughing. Flecks of blood from her lungs spattered the floor. She knew she was running out of time.

While still sitting on the floor, she took off her leather pack. Climbing the mountain with its weight had only added to her struggle, but its contents were necessary. She pulled the sacrificial knife out first. For four centuries she polished the hilt and kept the blade sharpened in anticipation of this day. It was a trinket to the people that knew her now. They had no idea it was forged and tried in the fires of human blood. With her other hand she pulled a bundle of pitch and kindling from the pack.

Accla pushed herself up and stumbled to the altar. She set the bundle in the brazier at the altar's foot and laid the knife next to it. This was her time, and she savored the smell once more as she pulled a flint from her pocket.

A few quick sparks set the dry kindling smoldering. Accla climbed up onto the altar, pulled her shirt over her head and plunged the sacrificial knife into the soft flesh just below her sternum. The pitch in the bundle caught and flared as she pushed the knife downward to her pelvis. The hole in the roof was too small to let all of the smoke out, and it hung low in the chamber. She fought the need to scream. She whispered the incantation, tore her intestines from her body and threw them into the fire.

The fire sizzled from their moisture. Her breath came in quick short gasps. "Flesh made fire...fire made...flesh" she repeated, wheezing in the smoke. The pain was like the fire itself, but she would not allow herself to pass out, not now.

The fire rose higher and formed into a hulking shape. Inti stepped from the fire and stood on the altar above Accla. Slowly the fire covering his body subsided, and his massive, leathery body took its earthly form. His eyes, like two black saucers, surveyed the chamber and then looked down at Accla.

"I have missed you Accla." His voice was like gravel. "Where have you been?" he asked.

Between gasps she stammered out, "I tried... the temple... was lost.... I am here for you now... my master."

Inti leaned down and caressed her head with his massive hand. "You are my sacrifice?"

She nodded. She could feel her limbs getting numb. "Take the last ....of my life force... return to this world... devour them all." Her vision was starting to cloud.

Inti smiled. He opened his mouth and bit down over her head. He didn't stop feeding until she was gone.

Inti stepped down from the altar. The last of the smoke rose through the hole in the roof as the fire burnt down to smoldering embers.

Outside he heard voices and scuffling. "Does everyone have their cameras ready?" a female voice asked. After more scuffling and some murmuring, she said, "Good. Now, this ruined temple was just discovered last year. We think it was used for human sacrifice."

There was more murmuring. "I know, exciting, huh?" The female voice said. "Please be careful not to step in the grooves on the floor. Yes, Mr. Thompson, we'll have lunch back on the bus. Is everyone ready?"

Inti sniffed the air. He could smell their blood pumping through their intestines. Salivating, he wiped Accla's blood from his mouth and moved to greet them.

The End

About the author:

Rick Coonrod is an android from the planet Zarkon. When his star cruiser returns in the year 2035, you will all be destroyed.

RICK COONROD

Horror House

by Neil Riebe (Wisconsin, USA)

he morning was cold and damp. Derek liked it that way, because cold and damp equated with peace and quiet. People tended to stay indoors. Reaching from his easy chair, he pushed open the window. As he took in the smell of the curling autumn leaves in the chilled outdoor air, he reveled in the silence.

Turning to his book, he slid his finger between the pages where his silk bookmark draped and immersed himself in words. A set of footsteps interrupted his reverie. His expression soured as he looked up. There in the doorway of his den stood his brother Allen.

"I'm leaving," Allen announced.

"For God sake's, Al, this is the third year in a row. I don't even have to look at the calendar to know it is October 12. Why do you insist this house is haunted? Nothing happens when you're gone. Nothing!"

Allen put on a petulant frown. "You forget about my experiences."

"Yes," Derek crooned, "your experiences." He put

his book under his chin and moved his free hand over it as though he were playing the violin. "Let's say you did see a ghost. It didn't hurt you, did it?"

"I sensed something malevolent on the landing as I was going up the stairs. Then I heard it, the ghost, walking up the steps ahead of me. It sounded like it was walking barefoot with thick nails on its toes clicking on the wood. I stopped, then it stopped, and as it stopped," Allen paused, trying to contain himself as a tear glistened in his eye, "as it stopped," he tried again, forcing the words in a loud voice, "it materialized just as it turned to face me. It looked exactly as Mary Whiteheart described!"

"Mary Whiteheart! Thank small mercies that shriveled up crone is dead and buried. I couldn't believe she wanted to tear down this beautiful house. She had to be nuts."

"Or damned certain of what she believed."

"It's a good thing," Derek leaned back, speaking with an air of superiority, "we made a killing in our respective businesses, or this house would certainly be gone. It goes to show, when money talks even the decrepit and insane can understand."

Mary Whiteheart, the prior owner of the house, had claimed that something not exactly human and not quite dead was buried in the basement. That was about as coherent a description as anyone was able to get out of her, doctors or otherwise. Derek had brushed her off. "Not only has her body gone," Derek had said, for she was confined to a wheelchair, "her mind's gone, too."

Allen was Derek's opposite. Softhearted, "a ninny," as Derek put it. Allen believed something real had disturbed her.

"Besides," Derek interjected, "I thought hauntings

were supposed to happen in old, old houses. Ours was built in 1891. That's just twenty years ago."

"Apparently that's more than enough time."

"Allen, most psychologists today say ghostly appearances are mental projections imagined by people when their emotions are at a peak. In other words, it's all in your head!"

"You forget the scratching I heard at the door."

"Yes, the scratching at your door."

"No! Your door!"

"Yes, my door," Derek corrected himself. "Funny how I didn't hear it."

"That's because you are hard-headed and insufferably callous. That is why you're divorced. That is why when your children call they ask for me, their Uncle Allen."

"And that's the way I like it. I put up with you because you are my brother. Of course, after all these years, I don't know why that should matter either. I guess something should be sacred."

"And that is about the only reason why I tolerate you. It is a good thing this is a big house." Allen tightened the belt for his overcoat around his waist. "I'm going to find help. If it means anything to you, I hope you will be safe."

"I'll be right here, reading."

Allen departed.

Derek returned to his book. Out of the corner of his eye he saw his brother outside plop his derby on his head and survey their Queen Anne house with dismay. Their eyes met. Allen looked hurt. Concern underscored his pained stare. Derek raised his book in a show of being preoccupied and didn't lower it until he heard Allen start down the walkway.

Allen was forty-eight. Derek would be damned if he was going to coddle his younger brother's feelings anymore. If Allen wanted an excuse to be scared, he should stare down the business end of a loaded gun. Derek had that experience when he moved out west thirty years ago. He wanted real work, work that would make him break a sweat, not juggling numbers at their father's accounting business in Manchester. Derek started out as an extra hand on a ranch. Harley Johnson, one of the men on the cattle drive, thought it would be fun to spook the "greenhorn from New England."

He remembered Harley well, his pockmarked face and the tobacco juice splotched on the front of his shirt.

Derek had his share of fisticuffs growing up, but staring at the hollow eye of a .45 Schofield's muzzle was another matter. His will to live scrambled to find a way out. Then he realized that he wasn't dealing with the revolver. He was dealing with the man, and not a bright one, with the weapon being held within reach.

The thought cleared Derek's head. He snapped hold of Harley's firing hand and twisted down. The Schofield went off. A sensation of heat and pain slashed across his hip, but Derek kept swinging. In one blow he pulped the man's nose, sending him sprawling onto the hard, Texas dirt. In the same move Derek wrenched the gun free and put the sights on Harley.

"All right, kid." Harley held his hands up. His purpled nose made him wince as he spoke. "You proved your point. Hand back the gun."

Derek fired between Harley's legs, sending him scrambling away. The other cowhands laughed.

"You're lucky I'm a bad shot," Derek called after him, "otherwise we'd be calling you Miss Johnson!"

The hip wound turned out to be grazed skin. It didn't even keep Derek from work. As for Harley Johnson, he never came back for his gun. Just as well, because Derek didn't intend to return it. He still had the Schofield to this day, so, noises upstairs weren't going to frighten him, not after being a moment away from having his head blown open to the hot sun. Derek wet his finger and turned a page.

The clock ticked on the wall.

The floorboards creaked in the hall.

October 12...

Derek looked up from his book. Something had caught his eye, as if something had passed through the doorway.

Then the clock stopped ticking.

Derek frowned. He decided to fix it later.

The room turned cold. He shut the window, but the temperature continued to drop.

He set his book down and rubbed his fingers.

Coffee would hit the spot.

He brewed a pot in the kitchen and came back to the den with a box of matches. Setting the steaming mug on the fireplace mantle, he struck a match.

The instant the little flame touched the wood, a fireball blasted out in a shock of heat. His reflexes saved him from being burned, but the fireball leapt up over the mantle and set fire to his father's portrait on the wall. To keep the fire from spreading, he wrapped the throw rug around the painting and threw it to the floor. The flames lashed at him as he stamped them into submission. Stepping away, he wiped his face with a handkerchief. The veins in his neck pulsed from the excitement.

Glaring at the ruins on the floor, he noticed an orange

glow creeping through the fibers in the rug. The fire burst back to life and leapt out of the rug to the middle of the room, burning bright and hot on the hardwood floor.

Even though taken by surprise, Derek held onto his wits. He pulled the rug from the portrait in a clatter of broken frame and smothered the wily fire yet again. To be sure, he fetched a bucket of water and doused the rug.

The fire remained extinguished. Derek opened the window to clear the smoke. Worry lines furrowed his brow when he examined the damage. He had to admit he was at a loss to understand what happened.

October 12...

*　　　　*　　　　*

After his father had passed away, Allen took over his father's accounting firm. Henry Saward, a prominent industrialist and long-time client of the firm, heard about Allen's problem from the chatter among the secretaries. He had recommended speaking with his daughter, Marcella. Ghosts were her hobby.

As a rule, Allen started with the cheapest services, and since a consultation with Marcella was free, he accepted Mr. Saward's offer. The old capitalist gladly arranged an appointment. October 12, today, was the agreed upon date.

At the Saward's sumptuous estate, a butler led Allen to the library and announced him through the open doorway.

To be honest, Allen expected to meet a bookish schoolmarm with spectacles. Her father had confided that she was unmarried. The fair-haired woman proved to be quite the opposite when she looked up from the work on her desk. Her features were as alluring as a Gibson Girl illustration, while her eyes gleamed with intelligence.

The state of the room, however, fit the description of a rat's nest. Books crammed the shelves to overflowing. Boxes of photo albums and stacks of old newspapers covered the floor.

"Mr. Peterson," she left her desk and strode up a path through the stacks of printed material, hand extended, "thank you for coming."

"No. Thank you." Allen shook her slender palm. "Forgive me for being so forward, but you make me wish I was a young man again with a full head of hair."

She laughed. "Since when did anyone need a reason to wish to be young?"

Allen refrained from making any comments about the room and took the chair in front of the desk to which she indicated.

Marcella sat down and pulled out a folder from a stack of papers. The label on the folder had Mary Whiteheart's name and her address, 2102 Cathedral Lane, which was now his address. Taking the notebook, Marcella flipped to a clean page.

"Mr. Peterson," she began, getting down to business.

"Please, call me Allen."

"Certainly," she said, pen poised and ready. "Tell me about your haunting."

Allen related the scratching at the doors, the feelings of an invisible presence watching him and the heavy-footed lumbering through the halls upstairs.

"Any physical evidence? Marks in the wood? Damaged property?" Marcella interrupted.

"No." Allen then told her about the ghost appearing on the second floor landing. "Ever since, I refuse to be in that house come October 12."

"Only on that date?"

"Only then."

"Interesting…. How long have you been vacating the house?"

"This is the third year."

"Anyone in the house when you're gone?"

"My brother Derek."

"Does he have any complaints?"

"No."

"Really?" Marcella sounded disappointed.

"You need to add a postscript where my brother is concerned," Allen explained. "He refuses to acknowledge anything is wrong. He's dead set on being indifferent."

"In-dif-fer-ent," she pronounced as she wrote. "If these noises are as loud as you say, I find it hard to believe anyone can be that obtuse."

Marcella asked more about Derek. Allen would rather talk about his problem. He shrugged, humoring her anyway.

"He has been in constant conflict, partly thanks to me. I was a magnet for bullies when I was a boy. Derek was always dishing out black eyes and bloody noses in my defense. He moved out West where he started a barbwire business. I thought it was ironic, prickly as he is, but it was a shrewd move. He got into the business when it was the latest thing, but he caught several junior managers embezzling the profits. Since he had made more money than he could ever spend, Derek decided he didn't have to put up with crooked employees and sold the business.

"That infuriated his wife. Her motto was, 'It was the duty of a man of means to expand his means to the fullest of his ability.' She divorced him and took their two boys.

Now he lives with me, which is little consolation, I'm sure. I think he's so fed up with people that if he admits there is a problem in our house, the word will get out and attract attention. I hope I didn't bore you," he ended with a sheepish grin.

"Not at all!" Marcella set her pen down and shook the cramp out of her hand. "I need to be sure your brother's experience in the house can't be used to discount yours." She cleared a space on the desk and slid forward a fresh sheet of paper and her pen. "What I would like you to do now is draw a sketch of your ghost."

Allen took the pen then sat, tapping the page, leaving ink dots.

"I'm sorry," he said. "I can see that thing in my mind, but not well enough to draw it."

"Start with an outline. Did the ghost have a head?"

"Yes."

"Arms?"

"Yes, yes, arms, head, torso." He pursed his lips. Digging up the bones of his unpleasant memories unnerved him. Persevering nevertheless, he set his hand to the task.

He created a half circle with little dashes, suggesting a head of wild hair. Wild-haired shoulders and arms formed. Large knuckles capped the hands. He drew a long loop for the nose, extending down to the chest, and scribbled in the eyes. Lastly, he marked a series of dashes for the cheeks.

Trembling, he shook his head and threw the pen down. "No more. This is as much as I want to remember."

"This is amazing." Marcella studied the drawing. "You don't have a ghost, Allen. You have a goblin!"

"You can't be serious," Allen chuckled anxiously. "As in ghosts and goblins, except, instead of the former it's the latter?"

Ignoring his quips, she fetched a leather-bound tome from the top shelf of the bookcase behind her. She blew off the dust, waving her hand to thin the gray cloud. Her pert nose wrinkled.

"I received this book on sprites from the renowned Baron Vordenburg of Styria. Since he specializes in the undead, he thought I would find more use for it. Personally, I think the baron was enamored with me and hoped I would be charmed." She paused as if recalling a wistful memory of the baron.

"Anyway," she opened the book before Allen, "this is what I mean. Goblins are akin to elves, fairies and pixies—sprites. However, goblins are the black sheep of their kind."

The book was in German and well illustrated. Many of the images were of mischievous little characters smiling toothy grins. Their noses were exaggerated, their ears pointy. Others were frail-looking girls sitting on toadstools, sporting butterfly wings. The next page revealed a picture that turned Allen's insides. The picture depicted a man working by candlelight. In his humble surroundings was a black shape peering at him from a dark corner with glaring eyes. The creature had the same wild-haired outline as Allen's drawing.

Allen snapped the book shut. "How do you get rid of such a thing?"

"I'll cable some friends for their input," Marcella answered. "Your goblin has chosen October 12th to work its magic. We need to find out why the goblin is aggravating you and to what end." She tore her notes out of the notebook and slid them into the folder. "In the meantime, go home. Write down anything strange you hear, see or smell. To dispel an intruding spirit, knowledge is essential."

Allen agreed to her instructions, albeit with reservations.

The overcast broke at sunset, and the spire capping the corner tower of their Queen Anne stood sharp and black against the pumpkin-orange glow on the horizon. A single light shone inside the house. Allen regarded his home with resentment. A home—*Hah!* he thought to himself before going in.

Derek told him what happened in the den and showed him the scorched remains of their father's portrait lying on the dining room table.

"I told you!" Allen burst out.

Derek pinched the bridge of his nose, appearing strained. "I don't want to hear anymore about ghosts. I'm not happy about losing our father's portrait. It's irreplaceable."

"I'm more concerned about losing my brother who is still alive. You expect me to believe what happened to you was a freak accident? Wood doesn't catch fire that fast no matter how dry it is."

They broke off arguing, scowling at each other from either side of the table.

Allen breached the silence. "At least show me the den."

Derek led the way to the room and turned on the light.

Allen examined the smeary smoke stains on the wall where the painting had hung. So far the portrait of their mother was unharmed. Allen noticed the throw rug lying in a charred heap on the floor. He swept the rug aside with his shoe.

"Ah-hah! What do you make of that?"

Derek knelt down on one knee to examine what Allen found under the rug. "Those are an odd pair of burns."

"Oh, please! Anyone can see those are footprints." Allen knelt beside him and pointed out the two oblong blotches, the heels, soles, toes—and claws. "I said the footsteps upstairs sounded like they had thick nails. See those barbs at the end of the toes? This spirit was trying to assume a form in which to harm you. Look! It was facing your way when you were at the fireplace."

"Enough! Do you believe if we brought in a couple of men from the fire department," Derek said, his voice rising, "they are going to look at those burns and say, 'Oh, yes, you had a hot-footed ghost standing in the middle of your den.' Do you?" Derek stormed out of the room.

Allen stood, thrusting his hands into his pockets. Frustrated, he kicked the damaged rug.

Looking back at the strange burns, he compared them to his foot. If these burns were footprints, the goblin's feet extended three inches longer than his. A shiver skittered up his spine.

"And I thought goblins were supposed to be small," he muttered.

After dark the brothers sat in the parlor. Derek was making up for lost reading time, concentrating on the pages with his usual studied frown while Allen detailed in his journal his brother's experience in the den.

The clock chimed. It was nine o'clock.

Allen sighed. Three more hours to go before midnight, and another October 12 would be over. Settling back in his chair, he let his gaze roam around the parlor at the ornamented red carpet and the maple-varnished wainscot.

While he relaxed, the floor creaked. A cold presence pressed upon him, and a moist breeze brushed across his cheek, as though someone exhaled with powerful lungs. A feral odor followed, like that of an animal mixed with the pungent scent of loam. Allen went rigid.

Mercifully, the chilly air and sour smell dissipated as the floor creaked again further into the room, and then once more near his brother. Allen prayed the spirit would not show itself. He could not bear its horrid visage a second time.

Allen got a hold of himself. He decided this time, come what may, he would not fall apart.

"Phew!" Derek exclaimed, covering his nose. "Was that you?"

Allen rolled his eyes. "Didn't you hear the floor creak?"

Derek shook his head.

"Well, that stink didn't come from me," Allen said.

"It isn't coming from me, either." Derek then reacted with a start. "I can feel a draft, like someone is breathing on me."

"That's because our friend is standing right in front of you."

Derek reached forward, feeling for something he couldn't see. His hand jerked back. "You know," he intoned cautiously, "you might be right."

He slammed his book shut and swung it through the air above the spot where the floor creaked, hollering "Scat!" The oppressive presence evaporated.

"The spirit is gone!" Allen exclaimed. "You

dispelled it! You, the skeptic." He sank into the chair. "It hardly seems fair."

Derek got up and searched the room with his hand extended, circling back to his seat. "Hah!" he snapped his fingers triumphantly. "So much for Mary Whiteheart's vaunted ghost. Your spook is more scared of us than you are of it."

"If you are going to admit I'm right," Allen replied, "please don't gloat."

"Oh boo-hoo! You're upset because I don't get worked up like you do."

"It did try to kill you this morning," Allen reminded him.

Derek tossed his hand at him, dismissing the notion.

The clock chimed. Derek declared the matter settled and headed for bed. Allen closed his journal on his lap. Once again his brother had proved to be the stronger.

*   *   *

The next morning Derek came down to the kitchen to heat the coffee and fry some bacon and eggs. He could tell by the way his brother was hunched over his oatmeal that he was in low spirits. He asked Allen what was wrong.

Allen stirred his soupy oats, gazing into the swirls. "I imagine after last night you respect me less than ever before."

"You really were hoping that I'd get scared," Derek said with a chuckle, "so we would be on equal footing, weren't you?"

Allen sat with his hand around his bowl, as though his breakfast were his only friend.

Derek pulled up a chair. He set his chin on his fist,

staring at Allen, wondering what to do with him.

"All right," Derek rapped his knuckles on the table. "Let's face facts. We are never going to get along in any perfect sort of way you want. It's not worth sulking over. We are what we are."

"That doesn't leave much room for self improvement," Allen noted.

"We're too old to change."

In the evening, when Allen came home from the firm, they went through their routine of recapping their day over supper and then turned in for bed. Things seemed to have resumed their normal rhythm.

Allen was in his room, asleep, and Derek was about to turn off the light when he had this sensation well up inside him that someone else was close by.

His door was open a crack. From the hall the silence was disrupted by what sounded like a large paw scraping down the face of the door to his brother's bedroom. The bedsprings crunched on the other side of the wall from Allen, making a sudden jolt of movement in his room.

The scraping then erupted into a cacophony of wood being bashed to pieces. Allen screamed.

Derek leapt from under the covers. He bolted to the bureau where lay an electric flashlight and then to the closet where his Schofield revolver hung from its holster. Slamming several rounds into the cylinders, he rushed into the hall with the gun ready in one hand and the flashlight blazing from the other.

There in the flashlight beam was a wild-haired, obscene melding of man and beast. It was like a huge mole with well-muscled arms and hands. Its snout was long and narrow like a fox's, and barbed with a battery of savage teeth.

The creature crouched on the floor, voraciously chewing the door—an inch and a quarter thick slab of solid oak—to pieces like it was a cracker.

"Hey!" Derek yelled to draw its attention.

The beast looked at him for a moment and then ran for the stairs, making not a sound.

Derek stopped at his brother's room. Allen stood in his pajamas against the far wall, clutching his chest and panting. Before Derek could ask Allen if he was all right, a crash resounded downstairs in the den.

Leaving his brother, Derek ran down and burst into the room, scanning all four corners with the flashlight. All appeared undisturbed, but their mother's portrait was now missing.

A deep-throated snarl emitted behind him. He spun and heard a series of padded footsteps thump out into the hall.

He pursued the noise into the parlor where he found the creature facing one of the windows, crouched on all fours. It swiveled around on its haunches toward Derek. Its lips peeled back in a toothy leer, reminding him eerily of a card shark who still had one more trick up his sleeve.

This time Derek did not hesitate to fire. The gun boomed. Glass shattered. When the glare from the muzzle flash cleared from his eyes, he saw the shattered fragments of the window glittering on the floor. The mole-thing had vanished.

*   *   *

Allen phoned Marcella. She assured him she would be there shortly after sundown. True to her word, she came motoring to the house in her white-polished Pierce

Arrow.

They gathered at the kitchen table where, at Marcella's request, he and Derek set down the burnt remains of their father's portrait and the un-chewed portion of his bedroom door. She raised a fragment of the door to the light.

The brothers watched her scrutinize the woodchip with her magnifying glass. Derek had the Schofield belted to his waist while Allen had a Remington hunting rifle cradled across his lap. His knuckles stood out on his hands from clutching the rifle tight.

"I wish I had a microscope handy," Marcella remarked. "This piece of chewed wood may have traces of saliva stains."

"Saliva?" Allen reacted in disgust. "I never thought that while we were sweeping up the mess we could be touching the monster's spit!" He got up to wash his hands.

"How are you going to get rid of the goblin?" Derek asked Marcella. "I hope you don't plan on hanging garlic flowers in all the rooms."

"Only if it pleases you," she retorted. She chucked the gnawed piece of wood into the paper bag containing the rest of the fragments. "I want to explore the premises first, get a feel for the goblin's presence."

Opening her journal, Marcella recorded the date—October 14, 1911, time—8:40 pm, and wrote, "Quiet. No peculiar sensations. Room temperature—comfortable."

"Right." She slapped her pen down on the open journal. "I need one volunteer to keep watch downstairs and one to follow me upstairs, carrying my camera."

"We should stick together," Derek advised. "If the goblin comes back, we'll have a better chance of blasting it before it can disappear."

"Guns will do no good," Marcella shook her head.

"The beast ran when it saw mine," Derek said. "If it runs, it can be hurt."

"The goblin is a spirit, Mr. Peterson," Marcella explained. "Deceiving is as much its modus operandi as haunting. Now, Allen, would you be a dear and carry my camera?"

Derek snorted. "You said you wanted volunteers."

"I guess she doesn't like you," Allen said softly in his ear.

"Then you and your date have a nice time," Derek rejoined.

"I only work with open-minded men," Marcella clarified with a smile.

Rifle slung to his back, Allen joined Marcella at the stairs leading up to the second floor. Derek remained at the kitchen table, occupying himself with a deck of cards. His revolver lay within reach on the tabletop. Marcella handed Allen a Kodak Brownie from her leather satchel. She also drew from the satchel a crucifix, which she hung about her neck. Its metallic surface caught the light as the cross swung low about her abdomen from a long chain.

Marcella began her investigation at the bottom of the staircase, running her fingers across the wood, searching for any unusual marks or scoring. She banged the handle of the magnifying glass here and there all the way up the steps. At the top of the landing one of the floorboards made a hollow reply and showed the slightest bit of give.

"Did you know about this?" Marcella asked.

Allen shook his head.

"But here at the top of the stairs was where you witnessed your first manifestation."

Allen nodded.

"Interesting." Marcella lifted the hem of her dress and unsheathed a dirk that was strapped to her shin. In one flick of the blade she popped the board loose then slid the dirk back into its sheath.

Allen blushed at the sight of her exposed leg, yet he buried his guilty feelings so as to appear composed.

"Let's see if anything intriguing is in here," Marcella remarked as she reached inside. Her expression turned downcast when she withdrew her arm from the hidden compartment empty handed.

Then Allen smelled that familiar brew of pungent loam and beastly musk. A sultry breath brushed the back of his neck. Fear bound him in its emasculating grip.

Marcella's eyes went wide as she looked past his shoulder. "My God," she said in a soft tone, as if to a pet, "you are big." She stood, slowly. Not for a moment did she take her eye off her quarry.

Allen spun around and dropped back to Marcella's side. Hunched on all fours, the goblin glared up at them. The charcoal-gray hair was thick, flecked with ochre-hued strands, and stood out on end all over its body, except on the snout. There the hair was short and smoothed back. Every aspect of the creature spoke of a big animal, bar the eyes. Those glistened with some sort of unearthly, non-color, as if they were little portals to the ethereal realm from which the spirit came.

"When I give the word," Marcella instructed in a hushed voice.

"Run," Allen concluded for her, equally hushed.

"No!" she hissed. "Take pictures."

He looked down at his hand. The camera had escaped his mind. Even so... "You're crazy!"

The goblin clenched its forepaws, digging ruts into

the floor with its nails. It bared its teeth. A hiss reverberated within its throat, hinting at the viciousness pent up as a pressure cooker inside its muscular frame.

Before it could spring Marcella thrust the crucifix into its fox-snouted face. "Take pictures!" she yelled and then chanted in what sounded to Allen's ears like a Celtic verse.

He stood rooted where he was. Everything was happening too fast.

The goblin coiled back from the cross. It appeared Marcella had the creature at bay. Then in one swift move the goblin rose to its full height, its head brushing the ceiling, and swiped a small table off the floor, sending a vase and a collection of knick-knacks flying. The table struck Marcella in the side of the face. Her head snapped back as she tumbled down the stairs.

Allen popped to his senses. He rushed down to her inert body at the foot of the stairs and grasped her wrist to check her pulse.

Derek came running from the kitchen with the gun in hand. He looked down at Marcella and then up at the second floor landing. A mixed reaction of awe and anger crossed his face. Before Allen could stop him, Derek rushed upstairs. Shortly he came back down without firing a shot. The goblin had disappeared.

They gently moved Marcella to a guestroom and called their physician, Dr. Morrison. She came to by the time Morrison arrived. He said at worst she suffered a mild concussion and asked her to stay put until he checked on her again in the morning. After Morrison left, Marcella sighed.

"It's a shame we didn't get a picture of the goblin," she said. "Collecting photos of spirits is a lot like collecting trophies."

"I'm not putting up with this another night," Derek said. "Whiteheart said something was buried in the basement. You said yourself this thing is deceptive." He jabbed a finger at Marcella who was holding an ice bag to the swollen bruise on the side of her face. "Why else does it keep appearing upstairs but to draw us away from the basement?"

Marcella agreed with his reasoning.

"But we can't fight an evil spirit!" Allen bleated.

"On the contrary," Marcella said, "I think you two are the only ones who can. The goblin shrugged me off. It knows I'm not an occupant, and therefore it knows I have no right to tell it what to do."

"That's all you have to do?" Derek asked. "Tell it to scoot?"

"Exorcising spirits is a battle of wills," Marcella elaborated. "If you know where you stand, you will win. That's the game it has been playing with you. The goblin wants a toehold in the material world. It chose this house. In the spirit plane emotional attachment is equivalent to legal ownership. All the goblin has to do is break your fondness for this place to take possession. That's why you are being harassed—to make this house no longer seem like your home."

What she said made sense. Allen asked Marcella what would happen if their bond with the house were broken.

"You will be driven out," she said, "maybe even killed."

"We should abandon this place," Allen suggested to Derek.

"No," his brother said. "My wife drove me out of

my last house. I'm not going to be driven out of this one, and neither are you."

Marcella offered her crucifix. "My crucifix is made of iron. The iron will repel the goblin from touching you, and the symbol of the cross will remind you that you have a higher source of strength to draw from. Find the goblin. Command it to leave. Be firm. If you harbor the slightest doubt, you give it license to rebuff your command."

Allen took the crucifix and stuffed it into his waistcoat pocket.

For her comfort they left Marcella a glass of Brandy and her journal before going downstairs.

Searching the basement presented one important question. How much damage were they prepared to do to the foundation to find the goblin's lair? They didn't notice anything out of the ordinary when they moved in. Nevertheless, behind a rickety bookshelf they found a crack in the foundation wall that began about waist high and continued in a jagged line all the way to the floor. The noxious loam odor wafted in their faces as they slid the shelf aside.

This was as good an indication as any.

Grabbing a pickaxe and shovel from the shed outside, they set to work. The cement proved to be brittle and broke away as easily as chipping teeth from rotted gums. The ripe stench worsened as they uncovered a four-foot wide hole.

They filled empty jars with kerosene. Allen fetched the acetylene lamp while Derek jury-rigged a torch. When they were ready, Allen wiped his hand on his trousers and extended it to Derek.

"This time I won't fold up on you," Allen said. "I promise."

Derek didn't say anything reassuring, but did shake Allen's hand. "Just pray that whatever we find burns nicely." He struck a match and lit the torch.

Allen picked up the lamp, and they descended one at a time down the hole.

Their feet went splat when they hit the earthen floor. The loam odor ripened into something that smelled fruity and thoroughly retching. All about them gooey globs of dun-colored weeds hung from the walls, looking as though they were about to drip. Allen and Derek stepped carefully and found their mother's portrait on the ground among the jelly-like flora, smashed.

"This may be our hairy intruder's nest," Derek remarked. "Whiteheart was right."

"If this is the nest," Allen said, "where's the goblin?"

Without comment, Derek pointed further into the underground. The hole had emptied them into a tunnel.

They proceeded with caution. The earthen floor was hard packed, as though the passage had seen a lot of use. Its alkaline tang tweaked their sinuses, and the damp air turned their skin clammy.

Up ahead a hulking figure approached them. Its footsteps seemed human, seemed to be shuffling forward, as if the individual were heavily burdened. One foot slid forward in the dirt, followed by a pause, and then the other foot slid forward. Allen set the lamp down and shouldered the rifle while Derek readied one of the kerosene-filled jars. They waited for the creature to come into the light to get a clear shot. Each of them hoped this confrontation would be decisive. For the elder brother, he hoped to end the haunting of his home. The younger wanted something more.

As the shuffling figure drew near, the lamp revealed

a disturbing sight. Tentacles squirmed about its torso like earthworms. Its head sagged, as though the bones had gone soft, and stared with hollow eye sockets. Once in the light, the beast didn't stop. It kept coming!

A battle of wills, Marcella had said. Allen dropped the rifle and fished out the cross. Shooting would do no good, because even if the bullets killed the fiend, he would not be any braver in his brother's eyes until he conquered his fear.

Derek pulled back to chuck the jar with its flammable contents when Allen charged, screaming, "Go! In God's name, get out of here!"

One of the quivering worms snapped around Allen's throat, choking his words. The tunnel monster snatched the crucifix with a second wormy tentacle and popped it into its mouth, swallowing the crucifix, chain and all.

Allen didn't give up. He grabbed its throat. His fingers sank into the folds of its skin. The slacked jaw kept mouthing its wheezy cries over the top of his hands. He spat curses out between clenched teeth as his cheeks puffed up and turned red. With blood and air pinched off, Allen's body went flaccid in the tunnel monster's grip. It released him, letting him fall to the ground.

Derek didn't dare throw the kerosene. His brother lay too close. Instead, he drew his revolver. The Schofield was as deafening as it was blinding in the tunnel. Derek unloaded all six cylinders to no effect. It was like hitting dead meat. No blood drained from the wounds. All the Schofield achieved was to force the monster back a couple of steps.

The beast narrowed its vacant gaze to a malignant glare and lashed its ropey limbs in rapid strikes. Derek evaded the best his fifty-one year old body allowed, which wasn't good enough. The monster snatched him by the ankle and yanked him to the ground.

Unlike Harley Johnson, he had no idea what he was dealing with. Did the fiend have any weaknesses? Was it mortal? The monster's strength awakened Derek to his human frailty.

In a panic he groped for the rifle. It didn't lie where Allen had dropped it. Instead, he found the hem of Marcella's dress. She stood over him, her eye peering at their common enemy through the sight of the Remington.

Marcella fired, cranked hard and fast on the bolt and fired again, and again. The blows from the rifle rounds sent the monster reeling, releasing Derek.

He scrambled to his feet. "I thought you didn't believe in guns."

"And you want to argue about it now?" she replied incredulously.

Marcella had driven the creature far enough away for Derek to drag his brother back. Once Allen was clear, he and Marcella smashed the jars against the monster's body. Kerosene splashed all over its skin. Derek threw the torch, igniting the combustible juices.

Flames roared to life!

The tunnel monster flailed, wrapped in a consuming blanket of fire. The beast retreated and dropped from sight. Derek rushed to bring the acetylene lamp forward. In the floor of the tunnel he found a hole. Marcella joined him at the rim. The depth of the hole was beyond their imagination, for the flaming monster was still falling, plumbing the depths toward an unknown oblivion.

*   *   *

Allen nursed a cup of coffee at the kitchen table. He looked world-weary. Derek stood by with the pot ready to give him a refill. Marcella sat across from Allen, suppressing a yawn while the morning sun peeked through the window.

"You probably think I am a fool," Allen said, his throat smarting from speaking, "rushing that monster the way I did."

"Yes, well," Derek set the pot down on the table, "there's proving yourself, and there's being stupid. Last night you did both."

"Oh?" Allen straightened up in his seat. "When, in your estimation, did I prove myself?"

"Not once when we went down to the basement did you make one peep. You didn't whine. You didn't complain."

"You know," Marcella said while examining her reflection in the coffee pot, poking gingerly at the bruise on her cheek, "your goblin friend is probably still at large."

"We set that creature on fire," Derek jabbed the tabletop with his finger. "It fell down that hole."

"That creature was physical," Marcella countered. "It cried out in pain. A goblin would not do that."

"You mean," Allen said, "we have a whole host of monsters down there?"

"It figures we'd kill the wrong one," Derek snarled.

"You may stay at my place, if you like," Marcella replied. "I'm sure my father wouldn't mind putting you gentlemen up for a few nights while I try a few things here. First I want to examine the nest of brown goo and then explore that tunnel."

"No," Derek said. "We're not leaving. We'll show those critters who haunts this house. Right?" He patted

Allen on the back.

"What? Yes, that's right." Allen smiled. He heard respect in Derek's words. Their fight in the tunnel must've helped his brother understand that fear was not a sign of weakness. "In fact," Allen said to Marcella, "we'll go back down into the tunnel with you."

His spirit surprised Derek. Not to be out done, his elder brother said, "Right!" with as much vigor.

For once Allen felt equal to his brother.

The End

About the author:

SF, fantasy, horror, fan fiction, dinosaurs, role-playing games, my work has stretched across a wide spectrum of subjects. I've been writing since high school. It failed to make me rich, but it has been enriching. Recently I've taken up illustration and did my first book signing at the UFO festival in Roswell, New Mexico. What I love most about creative work is the feedback. Shoot me a comment or two. You can contact me at: neilriebe@yahoo.com. You'll find more of my work on my FaceBook page. Just search for me by name: Neil Riebe.

Safely Home

by Elizabeth Inglee-Richards (Delaware, USA)

The original Northeastern Center had been built as a cathedral to the Hockey Gods. At least that was what my grandfather always said. He had loved hockey and played until he died.

I had been to the Old Center with my grandfather and my brothers a few times. What I remembered about the building was that it was foggy inside and felt like the seats were stacked right on top of each other. It wasn't comfortable and it was loud.

"Branna," my grandfather told me—he always called me by my given name even when others called me Anna—"this place is special. It holds the spirit of every past player and fan."

"Then when you are gone I can look for you here, *Daideó*?" I had asked him at the time, calling him by one of the many Irish words for grandfather.

"I'll never be gone from you, Branna," he told me at the time. "But that isn't the way the world works." His gravestone read *Brian Flynn - Athair Críonna*—Father of the Heart—a fitting description of him.

My father hated all sports and tried to raise us as far as he could from that world of long nights, crazy fans and the heartbreak that goes along with loving sports in the Boston area. I stayed mostly shielded from that world in the time between my grandfather's death and meeting my boyfriend, Arttu, who played for the Nahant Nor'easters as a professional hockey player. My Grandfather would have loved Arttu, even if the rest of my family looked at him as a bit of an outsider. I didn't know if it was the way he made his living or the fact that he was a Finn—as in, from Finland.

I made a point of never going back to the Old Center after my *Daideó* died, not even for concerts if I could help it. I didn't want to know if he was there, or if he was gone for good. I couldn't tell Arttu why I wouldn't set foot in the building, because he thought of me as a very pragmatic person.

The New Center was a lovely, modern building. The ice stayed frozen, and the fans didn't freeze. There was no fog, but I had been told it lacked soul. It also wasn't in Nahant, even though the team was still the Nahant Nor'easters. They now played in Lynn, a difference of about half-a-mile, but for Arttu the New Center might as well be on the moon. I loved the New Center and not only had season tickets to watch my boyfriend, but also went to concerts there as well.

Arttu loved the old building, though, and would tell me from time to time that the reason he had wanted to play for the Nor'easters was so that he could play in the Old Center, but the team had stopped playing there two years before he came to Boston.

Arttu's jogging route took him by the Old Center every day, and I knew he longed for the chance to skate there. He believed *firmly* that skating there would get him the attention of the Hockey Gods.

I believed *firmly* that if there were such things as Hockey Gods, he already had their attention. I was raised Irish-Catholic, but I have nothing against Hockey Gods. There is a lot of space in a Catholic mind for Saints and whatnot, and it seemed to me like most of the people who talked to me about Hockey Gods were Catholic.

Arttu was raised believing in the traditional Finnish Gods, and for him the Gods of Hockey had names and faces: Tapio, God of the forest; Meilikki, the mother of bears; their son, Nyyrikki, God of the hunt. Other than Nyyrikki, I couldn't make the connection between hockey and his gods, but that wasn't my place to say, just like he never commented on the oddity of a Christmas midnight mass. We had agreed to give each other's faith, or in my case lack thereof, the space it needed.

As part of the announcement that the Old Center would be torn down, a special game was scheduled for the Nor'easters at the Old Center. It would be against their long time rivals, the New York Locomotives, and would be the last event held at the old Cathedral to Hockey before demolition started. It was the game Arttu had been hoping for all of his life, and I had expected him to be overjoyed. What I hadn't expected was the way he had fallen apart as the game drew closer. He did have a tendency to get obsessive-compulsive during play-offs, but I wasn't used to it so early in the season. It was only November. For weeks everything in Arttu's life had to be just so. Any deviation could send him over the edge. Even some of his teammates were worried about him. Arttu was, by nature, fairly laid back about anything that was not a play-off game.

The day of his game at the Old Center started well before the sun was up. I hadn't wanted him to get up and go jogging in the dark, but he insisted. My begging and tempting him with more amusing pastimes didn't sway him, and I hadn't really thought it would. I had been quite surprised that he asked me to stay over. Even though I knew Arttu never bought into the "abstinence before big games" thing, I thought he would want his bed to himself. But Arttu didn't always do what I expected.

I fell back to sleep when he left and woke up again when he was in the shower. I knew he had been gone for some time already, because the bed was cold. I stayed curled up until he came and sat down next to me. He rested a hand on my shoulder and I snuggled close to him.

"Do you have a practice today, or is it just the game tonight?" I asked.

"We have practice at ten," he said with a shrug.

"Time for breakfast?" I asked him.

"Yes. There is always time for breakfast."

Later that day I sat with the wives and girlfriends of the other players and watched the Nor'easter's practice. It was an open practice, and there were fans just sort of everywhere, but we sat in a self-contained knot of women. We watched our husbands and boyfriends and brothers and sons as they ran drills. None of the fans came anywhere near us. I wondered if it would have been stepping over some invisible boundary that I didn't know about. We watched mostly quietly until the team was split up to scrimmage. That was when Arttu's nerves got the better of him. He started pushing people around and shooting the puck too hard.

"Wow, Arttu is really bringing it, isn't he?" one of the defenseman's wives said after Arttu sent a slap shot sailing at Vále hard enough that the young goalie fell to the ice to get out of its way. "Shouldn't he be saving it for the game tonight?"

"He's just nervous," one of the other wives said. Some of the wives had known Arttu a few years longer than I had, and they had seen him play a lot more hockey. "He always brings it too hard before a big game," she concluded.

I barely noticed the scrimmage. I had been looking around the Old Center, hoping to see some sign of my grandfather. It was the first time I had set foot in the building since his death, and I knew that if any fan would have found a place in this building, it would be my *Daideó*. I didn't see any signs of or feel my *Daideó*, but the whole building felt creepy... haunted.

I listened to the wives go on about Arttu and the other players during the practice and then for a while after as Arttu got ready to go home. Arttu's house was only a half-a-mile away, and we had walked to the rink together, so I didn't run down to the player's parking lot like everyone else. Instead, I stood in the hall outside of the dressing room and watched the media go in to talk to the team as the players dribbled out, some alone, some in small groups. Only a few of the guys came out before Arttu. He wrapped his arm around my shoulders, pulled me close and we walked quietly, wrapped up in each other for a few minutes. It was odd to have such a private moment in the midst of all the hoopla surrounding the game and the closing of the building.

When we got back to his house, Arttu padded quietly into the kitchen and made a sandwich, then he came out to the living room where I sat watching the news.

While he sat with me, his eyes kept darting to the

alcove where he kept his altar. In any other area of the country, it probably would have been a mammoth closet, but in Massachusetts it had been designed with no door, leaving it open to the rest of the parlor. Arttu had fitted it with a screen that he could close and lock if he had guests. The area didn't just hold his altar. It held all of the little things he held precious: all his memories of home. The alcove was his most private area, much more so than his bedroom.

"It's alright," I said to him, "I can go upstairs if you want time alone."

"No," he said, kissing the top of my head, "you can stay."

I watched him as he moved away and sat in front of the low table that served as his altar. I couldn't see all of him, and couldn't see most of what he was doing, but I did see him lean forward to light his candles. I could hear him speaking and feel the weight of his prayers.

I tried to go back to watching the news, but my eyes kept drifting back to Arttu. I was fascinated. He almost never did this with me in the house. This was probably the most open my Finnish boyfriend had ever been with me.

After a time he leaned forward, blew out his candles and walked back to me. The necklace he always wore was outside of his shirt. It was a bird of some sort, its golden wings extended so it seemed to be flying against the blue of his sweatshirt. He said it was the spirit who protected and guided him through life. I had always equated it to the Saints' medal my grandfather had worn all of his life.

When Arttu sat down next to me, I bent and kissed the necklace, in my mind holding a fierce wish that he would be safe and skilled that night, that his gods would see him and love him like I did. A few of my thoughts were for my grandfather, but I didn't think Arttu or his gods would mind. Arttu smiled at me, as if he could read my mind and knew what my thoughts held.

We spent the rest of the day together. Mostly resting, or trying to rest. Arttu was agitated, and I thought that maybe a roll in the hay would take the edge off his nerves. I was right, and he napped for part of the afternoon.

He left for the rink around three for his six o'clock team meeting, so the edge of his nervousness may have been blunted, but Arttu was far from calmed. Shortly after, Kaija, Vále's wife and my closest friend involved with the Nor'easters, showed up with a bag of groceries for a victory celebration that she planned.

The Nor'easters had three Finns, two Swedes and an Estonian who had set aside their national rivalries to form a sub-team based on loosely similar culture and food. Kaija had become their den mother, and it seemed to be Arttu's turn to host the after-game festivities.

We cooked and prepped a few things that needed forethought and left everything else in the fridge. After all, grilling sausage is simple, and Kaija had actually bought a few fish pies from a place in Cambridge. She also brought a huge amount of liquor. I had the mental image of Arttu's house being full of either angry drunk men or overly happy drunk men. Either way the house would probably be a wreck in the morning.

On our way out I closed Arttu's alcove off and turned the lock so anyone trying to get in would need a key. After all, nothing in there was anyone else's business.

When we got to the rink, it took a little while to find our seats for the game. At the New Center we knew exactly where we always sat and could get there with blindfolds on, but the Old Center seemed strange and alien. I was glad that no matter how much Arttu loved the Old Center, I would never have to see another game there. Being in the building made the hair on the back of my neck stand up. I had no problem believing that it was full of ghosts or sprits *or* gods.

When the puck dropped I noticed that the only seats still open were the three directly behind Kaija and me. For reasons I hadn't been told, we weren't sitting with other wives. I assumed that we had been spread through the crowd so any number of fans would get to sit with player's families.

The Nor'easters came out to a flying start. They were really taking the game to the Locomotives. Arttu scored in the first five minutes, and everyone in the stands surged to their feet, hugging and giving each other high fives. That was when I noticed the seats behind us had been filled by a family, or I thought it was a family. They looked enough alike to be a father and mother and son, but the ages were off. The son was too old to have parents so young. The mother of that little group wrapped her arms around me and spoke to me in Finnish. The odd thing was that I understood what she was saying.

"You must be very proud of him," she said. Her voice echoed oddly in my head. I could tell that she was speaking a language that I didn't speak, but the echo in my mind was in English. It felt like magic.

"Yes," I replied, "I am."

This drew an odd look from Kaija, but then she smiled at me. She had been trying to teach me their language as long as I'd known her, saying it would be important if he were hurt or sick. I figured that she felt he would want to go home at some point, and then I may need to know their language. I didn't relish the thought of living in a country where I couldn't speak to anyone, or at least had to depend on them having learned English in school. I knew how bad my high school French was.

The game went on, and I had to admit I was intrigued by the people sitting behind us. My interest in them even helped me ignore the fog that had filled the building, giving the game an ethereal quality that hockey should never have. The men on the ice looked like the ghosts my *Daideó* had always said inhabited the building.

The family behind me began talking amongst themselves, and I couldn't help but listen in on what they were saying.

"He is one of ours," the son said, gesturing to Kaija's husband Vále.

"He is a hunter by birth," the mother said, "but he has no faith in us."

"He didn't call us," the father agreed.

They worked their way through the whole team before they got to Arttu. My guy was zipping down the ice with a partner. They were passing the puck between them and totally skunking the opposing defenders.

"Him," the mother said. I had begun thinking of her as Meilikki.

"I think you may be right," Tapio said.

"Yes," Nyyrikki agreed, "he is the reason we are here."

"So what do we do about him?" Tapio prompted.

"And about the girl as well?" Meilikki added.

"What does she wish?" Tapio asked. There was a long pause before Meilikki answered.

"She just wants him to be safe and happy," she said with a shrug.

"And she is not one of ours," Nyyrikki said.

"She loves him and does not interfere," Meilikki said, "and I think she called us, not the boy."

I turned to the family, who I realized had to be the Gods Arttu had talked of and said, "I want him to be happy, and he wants you to bless the new rink."

"Is that all?" Meilikki asked.

"I want the sprits that are held here…" I paused. Would my request be too much? "I want the ghosts to go to the new building as well."

"Even if it will make that building 'creepy, '" Tapio asked me gently with a smile.

"Yes," I told him firmly. "I want my *Daideó* to see Arttu. I want him to know I'm happy."

"Easy," Tapio said with a nod.

"He just never asked, and I doubt he would have thought of the ghosts," Nyyrikki told me. Then the three of them disappeared in a flash of light that only Kaija and I seemed to see; everyone else in the building was too distracted by a goal scored by the Nor'easters. Kaija looked at me for a few heartbeats before she said anything.

"When did you learn our language?" she asked.

"I haven't. They did it," I told her, gesturing at the suddenly empty seats. Kaija nodded and went back to watching the game, but something about her posture said she was still weirded out by what had just happened. It made sense. How often do you get to talk to a God? Or have a God talk to you?

We cheered as the Nor'easters clenched a definitive win over the Locomotives. The game seemed hard fought, but I couldn't help but wonder if the Locomotives didn't play with all their heart, or maybe the Gods of Hockey really were smiling on the Nor'easters.

Kaija hadn't settled, even when we got back to Arttu's house, but she didn't bring up my short conversation with the Gods.

A little while after we got to his house, Arttu and the others showed up. They were all in high spirits. I thought maybe they had started imbibing at the rink.

They came escorted by their wives, girlfriends and, in the case of one player who had just gone through an ugly divorce, a random pretty girl who he had probably met outside the dressing room. Arttu looked flushed with joy, but I noticed as he came close that the tips of his ears were red, a sign of stress in my boyfriend that wasn't reflected in his calm blue eyes or his face.

He glanced around at everyone in the kitchen and, one by one, they all trickled out and away. Arttu loved his kitchen, and if he wanted to be in it with his girlfriend after winning a big game, then no one associated with the team would stand in his way.

Arttu was the cook in our relationship. He had been raised by a single mom who worked too much, and he had started taking care of himself way too early by American standards. He was very domestic and would make someone a fine wife one day. I hoped I could make him a fine husband.

I thought that maybe when he retired he might open a little restaurant or coffee shop. He glanced down at the sausages, turned off the heat under them and then turned to me.

"Where you at my stall?" he asked me. He meant his dressing area in the dressing room. The equipment was too big for lockers. Instead, they had stalls, like horses.

"You know I don't go in the dressing-room," I told him. The only time I ever ventured in the room was if

Arttu was hurt, and I needed to come get him. That would normally be the training room.

"Pete said no one came down during the third. He said a wife came down during the second, but I know it wasn't there during the second intermission."

"What?" I asked. I was alarmed that someone would go and mess with Arttu's stuff.

"I felt them tonight," he said, his eyes sort of going unfocused. "That last shot I took? It wasn't on net in the least. It should have gone wide by about three feet."

"Ah," I said.

"The Gods were there looking out for me, and they left this." He reached into his pocket and pulled out a carved bear. He looked at the bear with wonder, and the wood in his hand seemed to glow a little, I couldn't tell if it was a trick of the light, or if it was the power of the Gods at work in the thing that looked like it could be a child's toy.

"They were," I said. "I saw them."

"You don't believe," he pointed out slowly.

"Hard not to when you are speaking a language you don't know and then the people talking to you disappear in a flash of light."

"They wouldn't show themselves to you," he said looking a little insulted. "You are making this up to tease me."

"No," Kaija said from the door, "they were behind us talking about you... talking about Vále too. Then they went *poof*," she said. I was thankful for her interruption, for her telling him what she saw. I didn't want Arttu to think I had been teasing him about his faith. I would never hurt him that way.

Arttu nodded and looked down at the stove. "What

did you say to them?"

"I asked them to bless your new arena, to let the spirits of the fans who have gone on before settle in the new arena as well," I said to him.

"And they said?"

"That it was easy enough, but you had never asked."

"But I did," he said, looking stricken. The look on his face made my heart sick.

"Maybe not in the right place?" I said tipping my head up for a kiss.

"Maybe," he said bending down to kiss me.

After we stepped apart, Arttu slipped the carving back into his pocket, and we rejoined the party. Everyone was celebrating, and everyone drank too much except for me and Arttu. I got the feeling he was protecting his house from his friends, and I was just following his lead. I can be as much of a stereotypical drunken Irish-American as he can be a stereotypical drunken Finn, but somehow that night it just felt wrong. After his friends left, all in cabs except for Vále and Kaija who were staying the night, we tidied a little, and he unlocked his nook. He stepped inside, pulling me along with him. He knelt and started lighting the candles.

"This one is for my grandparents," he said gently. I knew his grandparents had a large hand in raising Arttu.

"This one is for my father, wherever he is." I was surprised by that. Arttu had never known his father.

"This one is for everyone who has—ah—gone before?" It was rare that he couldn't find an English word for something.

"Ancestors?" I asked.

"Yes," he said, turning to a few more candles, their holders more elaborate and set up higher than the others.

"These are for the gods and goddess."

He lit them and then took out the small bear carving, setting it out on the table. "I want to thank you for being there for me and for my team… and seeing us through this game," he said in English. I had never heard him pray in English. I had never been in his altar area. "Branna said you came to her, and I thank you for that. It would have been…distracting if you had appeared to the team, but I feel you with me, always. Please bless our team's new home. Bless our skates, bless our hands, bless our eyes. See us safely home."

He looked at me out of the corner of his eye, as if expecting me to say something. I thought about the game, the big men, the speed, the sharp skates, the aggression, the pucks and even the sticks. Everything in hockey could be a weapon. The only thing keeping anyone safe was a few pounds of padding, good eyesight, quick reactions and dumb luck… and maybe the will of the spirits of a rink or even the Hockey Gods. I looked up at Arttu and then at the carved bear on his altar. It still seemed to glow gently. I formed a prayer and flung it with all the strength my soul possessed towards that bear, but the words passing my lips were just a whisper, just a hint of noise. I had to have faith that his Gods would hear me.

"Bring them safely home," I said, "Bring them all safely home."

The End

About the author:

Elizabeth Inglee-Richards is a writer of urban and suburban fantasy. She loves writing about fairies, werewolves, witches and what have you, all set in the modern world. Her work is mostly set in Delaware or Massachusetts, the only two places she knows well enough to set fiction.

She lives in the second smallest State in the U.S. with way to many pets including birds, turtles, cats, dogs and sheep. She has seen two well-loved arenas come down, the Spectrum in Philadelphia and the Boston Garden.

Her blog is:
www.elizabethingleerichards.blogspot.com

ELIZABETH INGLEE-RICHARDS

Salting Dogwood

by Quincy Allen (Colorado, USA)

July 17, 1918 – Hemphill, Texas

ime is a funny thing to a ghost. It stretches and bends and squats down in hot times like wax. It can fold over on itself or even break when the world is cold. That's how Harriet Truth's ghost knew it was just about time to move on. It was the promise she'd made to her daddy that held her to earth when the Lord's light called her, but what pulled at her now came from someplace else.

Her ghost flickered and shimmered beside old Preacher Johnson, listening to him speak kindly of a lamb taken too soon and a woman who had already known too much loss. Her mamma's crying was hard, and this, the second funeral in ten years. It was a long, drawn-out wailing full of agonized sobs and a bereaved askance hurled at Heaven and He who ruled it with such apparent indifference. The cries pressed in on Harriet like fresh-dug earth on a coffin. Her mamma kneeled between the old grave and the new. She'd cried the same way when they buried Harriet's daddy after the lynching. Daddy's headstone was small and plain and not even paid for by the county like it had been for most of the others. Harriet stepped in front of her mamma and traced fingers over the 1908 of her father's stone and then the 1918 of her own. It was just one more 1918 added to the millions carved into wood and stone in the aftermath of the great influenza epidemic. Those ten years had passed quickly, her promise clouding over everything.

With a fold of time Harriet returned to those two dark weeks full of burning crosses and tightened nooses. She stood in the middle of that last, black night when white shrouds dragged her daddy out of the house, lit the house aflame and set daddy in the nearest blackjack oak waiting for someone to cut him down. Daddy had screamed and told mother and child to run out the back as fast as they could. Daddy would be the last of the nine killed. Mother clutched daughter, hidden in the woods till sun-up. Then they returned to the ash of their small home and discovered what had been left in the blackjack out front. Her mother had gone running and screaming to get help, but that was the spot where Harriet waited, looking up at her daddy, her hand resting on his still boot. That's where she made her promise.

The murder of a white man set it all off. Most around Geneva knew Hugh Dean. He was a peaceful man, not inclined towards the antipathy to blacks that was day-to-day in East Texas and much of America. He'd been shot to death in Rockhill church right there in Geneva, and rumor had it that the six black men who ended up in the Sabin County Jail were responsible. A few nights after their arrest, a mob of over a hundred came, some in white, some not, and most carrying torches. The first five were hanged, and the sixth was shot trying to escape. Two more black men were hanged the following night outside of Hemphill. The next night they got Harriet's daddy. He was the ninth man guilty of being black. The whites in East Texas all figured justice had been served and forgot the whole thing.

Time folded in on Harriet again, taking her back a few days and revealing the truth. It was Dean's affable nature that did him in. Harriet stood inside Rockhill church surrounded by white shrouds. Morning sunlight hit the congregation through stained glass, painting rainbows across a hood-pointed, white canvas. It wasn't Sunday, and there was no preacher. At the pulpit stood a man in red who hollered into the sea of white like a hurricane building up into something terrible. He reminded Harriet of a dragon, eyes all aflame.

"My brothers! I've heard that the town of Geneva is not pure!" He was a thick man, but strong, in his late twenties, and his malevolent eyes almost glowed beneath slim eyebrows of black. The congregation denied the accusation, but they knew the truth. "What's more, I've heard that one of our own, a white man, has taken to treating those mongrels like they were more than animals!"

In one voice they shouted "Dean!"

The dragon's voice quieted almost to a whisper, but the fire in his eyes grew ten-fold. "My brothers, I have a plan that will allow us to rid Geneva of the traitor and set many fruit in our righteous dogwood tree! All I will say is that when you find the traitor's body, find dogs to collar for the crime, and the Klan will serve up its justice. I will return when they are caged and rid Sabin County of the impure." He paused, taking a long deep breath, and stared down at upturned hoods framing bright, hungry eyes. "ARE YOU WITH ME, MY BROTHERS?" he screamed.

A chorus of unified, bloodthirsty hatred bathed him in its heat as the congregation shouted "YES!"

Another fold set Harriet in a lavish downtown Houston office days later. She stood just inside a closed door, the backs of three men faced her, and a thick man with black hair sat concealed behind a desk and an upraised newspaper. She heard a satisfied chuckle from behind the newspaper and then watched it slowly descend, set upon the desk like a hard-won trophy. The face exposed was that of the dragon, but the fire in his eyes shone as nothing more than a simmering spark waiting to be rekindled.

"Gentlemen, Dean is dead," the dragon purred. "Murdered in Rockhill. Six have been arrested and await us in the Hemphill County Jail. Send word and gather the flock. We will make our way to Hemphill tomorrow night and meet out the justice of the Klan."

The vision faded before Harriet like smoke exhaled into a breeze. The dragon's voice shrank to a distant whisper. The haze was replaced with the peaceful silence of her own grave after the last tear was shed, the last mourner departed. She kneeled upon the fresh earth covering her coffin and traced a finger over the date carved into her headstone once again. Harriet shuffled back across her grave and thrust her arm down through the cold, loose earth. She didn't have to search. The postcard came up out of the earth clutched in her hand, and she stared at the picture.

On the night the first six had met Klan justice, someone in white took a photograph of their dogwood tree and its grisly fruit. A few days later the Harkrider Drug

Co. in Center, Texas made a postcard out of it. Such postcards were common in those days. Lynchings were something people bragged about, and folks bought and sent them to friends and family showing what they'd seen, even boasting they'd been there or taken part. It wasn't the first such postcard Harriet had seen, nor would it be the last, but it was the only one she kept.

Harriet had been sick for a week before going on to the Lord's grace. She had seen plenty go before her as a result of the sickness that swept around the world. On the fifth day of coughing, knowing what was coming, she asked her mamma to get the postcard out of her secret box under the bed where she'd kept it safe for ten years. At first her mamma fought her, cursing the card and threatening to burn it, but Harriet, laying in feverish sweat and coughing thick globs of death, was suddenly very serious.

"Mamma," she said, "I needs that card... to remind me of the promise I made to daddy. And I wants you to bury me with it." Another coughing fit took her, and hot tears scorched their way down her face. "Promise me."

With tears of her own, her mother made the promise with her eyes closed and a hateful heart then handed the card to Harriet. Harriet took the card carefully in her hand, staring at the tree and the men in it. She flipped it over to the poem on the back. She'd never learned to read, but she'd heard the poem enough times to remember it. It was entitled *The Dogwood Tree*, and she recited the words to herself so her mother couldn't hear:

> *This is only the branch of a Dogwood tree;*
> *An emblem of WHITE SUPREMACY.*
> *A lesson once taught in the Pioneer's school,*
> *That this is a land of WHITE MAN'S RULE.*

> *The Red Man once in an early day,*
> *Was told by the Whites to mend his way.*
> *The negro, now, by eternal grace,*
> *Must learn to stay in the negro's place.*
> *In the Sunny South, the Land of the Free,*
> *Let the WHITE SUPREME forever be.*
> *Let this a warning to all negroes be,*
> *Or they'll suffer the fate of the DOGWOOD TREE"*

Slipping the postcard in her apron, Harriet's ghost felt a tug upon her soul and drifted through silence to her next resting place to await her opportunity.

*   *   *

March 27th, 1925 – Indianapolis, Indiana

Madge Oberholtzer locked her office door and walked down the hall of the Indiana State Department of Education building. For three years she'd been teacher and administrator of the literacy program for disadvantaged children of any race. Her shoes echoed off tiled floors and stone walls as she headed towards the ladies' room. It was because of her job that she'd met David Curtiss Stephenson.

Stephenson had caught her attention back in January at the annual State employee's dinner. He'd done his best to sweep her off her feet, with a fire in his eyes that stirred something within Madge, but the stirring wasn't amorous. It was attraction, like bees to honey, but bereft of desire. He was a few years older than her, heavy-set with a shock of black hair covering his head and slim eyebrows over narrow, calculating eyes. He was wealthy, very powerful and deeply involved in politics. He'd been instrumental in helping Jackson win the '24 Governor's election only a few months earlier. He courted Madge throughout dinner and, despite having no actual interest in the man, she found herself accepting his offer for another date that turned into a third. He was courteous and polite, taking her to expensive restaurants in his chauffeured Cadillac, and yet she felt nothing for him.

When she was in her teens she wanted nothing more than to marry and have children, but her fever during the great epidemic seemed to have burned the dream right out of her. From that moment on, all she had cared about was teaching children how to read. And yet, in the back of her mind there was a strange sense of waiting for something, and she wondered if Stephenson was it.

Things had gone badly at the end of their third date. The conversation had turned to more personal matters, and Stephenson mentioned with bravado that he was the recently anointed Grand Dragon of Indiana and leader of 250,000 pure, white souls. Her stomach turned, and that's when she'd told him about the nature of her students. She'd expected him to explode, to scream and curse her, but he hadn't. He'd looked at her with a wicked little smile, as if he'd known all along, and his eyes sparked like the devil himself was dancing inside his skin. She'd excused herself, boarded a trolley and ignored his calls and messages for almost three months.

And then he'd called, only a few hours ago. Madge had been seated in her small office grading papers and preparing for her next class when the phone rang. She normally didn't take calls until after her last class. It was as if her hands belonged to someone else. She watched them put down the papers, pull the candlestick phone-stand towards her and lift the small receiver off its hook. The receiver to her ear, she leaned in to the mouthpiece, her mouth shaping words that weren't hers. "Indiana State literacy program, this is Miss Oberholtzer."

"Please don't hang up."

Recognizing his voice stirred within her a feeling of immediate disgust. His speech was slurred, albeit slightly, as if he had been drinking, which surprised her since prohibition was well respected in Indiana. She felt the urge to simply slam the receiver down, but something stayed her hand.

"What is it you want, Mr. Stephenson?" Her question came through toneless and cold.

"My reasons are professional not personal, I assure you," he said in his firm, silky-smooth Texas drawl. He'd told her when they'd first met that he was raised in Houston.

"What could you possibly have to speak with me about in a professional sense?" Her own curiosity surprised her.

"I'm glad you asked. The truth is I was speaking with Governor Jackson this morning. We both believe that someone of your distinct qualifications and demeanor would be ideally suited to a new position he's creating."

"Forgive me if I'm not a little suspicious, Mr. Stephenson. We're very different people." She didn't hide her distaste.

"True enough, to be sure, but that's the reason the Governor thought of you. This position is something for the good of the State. Would you be disposed to come discuss it this evening? I can send my car to pick you up."

She wanted to refuse, to tell the wretch that she had

no interest in anything he or the Governor—whom she knew was also Klan—had to offer, but she heard herself saying, "Certainly, Mr. Stephenson, as long as your intentions are of a professional nature. You may have your man pick me up at five o'clock."

"Thank you, Miss Ober..." She hung up the phone and stared at it as if she'd never seen one before. She wracked her brain for some explanation as to why she would have conceded to his request. It was impossible, and she couldn't imagine what possessed her.

An image floated up out of her thoughts like cloudy mud when you step into a still pond. Madge had a vision of Stephenson, but it didn't come from her memories, and it wasn't in Indiana. The memory was ghostly, faded, smoky, like a dream seen through a dirty mirror. Stephenson wore crimson and screamed into an ocean of pious white hoods spotted with strange patterns of color. His eyes were that of a fiery dragon, and he breathed smoke.

The vision faded, and she found herself standing before the ladies' room door. She shook her head, trying to clear the frightful vision, and walked in. She stepped up to the sink, turned on the water and stared at her reflection. The face seemed almost foreign to her, and a chill coursed its way through her body. She leaned down, splashed her face with water and lifted her head.

It was not her own face looking back at her, but the face of a teenage colored girl in a plain, thread-bare dress of gray covered with a dingy apron. It should have surprised Madge, but it didn't. She merely stared at the face and knew the girl's name was Harriet.

"I's sorry for what I done to ya," Harriet said apologetically. "You died of the sickness same as me. But

I made a promise, and the good Lord is helping me keep it… through *you*. Don't you worry though. It's me that'll bear what's coming. I'll take it all. He can't hurt me no more than he already has."

"Why?" Madge asked, not comprehending but knowing deep down this was how things needed to be.

"Cause I made a promise."

Harriet pulled a postcard out of the pocket of her apron, extended her hand through the glass and placed it on the sink between them. The photograph on the front shocked and appalled Madge, but she'd heard of such things. Through the mirror her eye caught streaks of bright light come down from a window behind Harriet. Madge reached down to pick up the postcard, and for just an instant their fingers touched, sending an icy-cold shock through her. Madge squinted her eyes with the pain of it, and her mind swirled as she pulled her empty hand back. When she looked again, she saw the card on the other side of the mirror in Harriet's hand.

In an instant Madge understood everything. She turned her head and looked at Heaven's light streaming down behind her. Without a word, she turned, walked into it and was gone.

Harriet turned away from the mirror and stared down at white hands. They were smooth, soft and nothing like any hand she had ever felt before. She ran her tongue over someone else's teeth and breathed air deeply into someone else's lungs. A sad smile spread across her face, and she steadied herself for what was to come. Without another thought she walked out of the ladies' room and through the front doors of the building. She slipped the postcard into a postbox just outside and strode towards the waiting Cadillac like a soldier heading off to war.

Stephenson's man Earl Gentry helped her into the car, and she could smell the whisky on his breath. Gentry was an obese man, his gut spilling over his belt, and the cheap brown suit he wore was threadbare and spotted with food that hadn't made it to his mouth. He was silent as he drove through the city, but Madge could feel the tension, almost like heat streaming off of the man, pouring into the back seat and wrapping itself around her. They arrived at Stephenson's mansion and parked around the side of the house, between the back door and the four-bay garage.

Gentry nearly dragged her out of the car, forcing her through the back door roughly and shoving her into the kitchen. She rubbed her bruised arm as she met the steely gaze of Stephenson and the sidelong glances of two other men. Shorty, the regular chauffer, stood off to the side and looked at the floor when his eyes met Madge's. He was small, almost puny, with slack shoulders and eyes weary with a lifetime of denigration. Earl Klink, a massive, brutish bodyguard, stood tall and had traces of malice and a brutal hunger in his eyes. Madge's skin felt almost infected wherever he looked.

They'd all clearly been drinking. There was an empty bottle of illicit whisky lying on its side on the kitchen counter, a full one sat next to it and a half-full one was in Stephenson's hand. His eyes were alight with drunken fury.

"Reject me, will you?" Stephenson hissed and took a pull from the bottle. "Do you have any idea who I am?" Stephenson reached out his hand, motioning for Gentry to hand her over. Gentry shoved hard, and Madge stumbled into Stephenson's iron grasp. "I *AM* Indiana!" He glared down at her with a dragon's eyes. He set the bottle down and slapped her, his fury carrying a lifetime of senseless rage with it. The force of it pushed her into Klink's arms, and he slapped her across the other side of her face. She stumbled into Shorty who refused to meet her gaze and pushed her back towards Stephenson. Her face ached, and stars danced before her eyes.

"Please..." she whispered.

Stephenson's face split into an evil sneer. "What you need is to loosen up a little." He tightened his grip on her arm, forcing a yelp from her, and then thrust the open whisky bottle into her mouth. It burned like nothing else she'd ever tasted before. Over and over again he repeated it—slaps and burning whisky poured down a raw throat. Finally, she simply blacked out.

When Madge came to, she was lying on a bed somewhere in Stephenson's house. Her body was numb from the alcohol, but she could feel his presence, as if she were sitting too close to a pot-bellied stove. She opened her eyes to see the dragon staring down at her, framed in a moonlit window. Its eyes glowed with a hatred that seemed boundless as they burned into her. She knew what was coming and would have dreaded it, but she'd been waiting for it for a long time and had long ago resolved to endure it all.

With Madge's voice, Harriet Truth uttered a prophecy to the evil that prepared to inflict itself upon her. "The law will get their hands on you," she said with an easy and stoic confidence.

Stephenson laughed mercilessly and boasted, "I *am* the law in Indiana." And then it began. The dragon loosed its rage upon the lamb. It beat her first then bit into her again and again like a rabid animal. The rape lasted hours and was as filthy and bestial as a dog tearing into carrion. She never cried out, never gave it the satisfaction, which only seemed to spur him on into further atrocities. Hours later, after it had been quiet, Stephenson's men came in and found them both passed out. Fear gripped them when they saw what the dragon had done.

*   *   *

Madge woke up to morning sunlight in a hotel room she didn't recognize. Someone had dressed her in her torn, bloody clothes, and her whole body was alight with pain from the bruises and bites and rape. Stephenson wasn't around, but the other three men were. It occurred to her that they couldn't have gotten her into a hotel without someone saying something unless it was owned by the Klan. She was utterly alone.

Klink, seeing that she was awake, turned to Shorty. "Watch her, runt," he said with obvious venom. At first Madge thought the big man's disdain was meant for her, but Shorty winced at the word *runt*. "We have to figure out what to do next." Klink opened the door and passed through it with Gentry close behind. The door closed quietly, and Madge looked into Shorty's eyes.

"Why are you doing this?" she asked, desperate pleading in her voice. Shorty remained silent, but she watched an internal conflict wax and wane upon his face. "Are you going to kill me?" Her tone was flat, fatalistic.

Shorty was silent for a few seconds, clearly pondering the question. "I'm not," he said with a stoicism that kindled within Madge a glimmer of hope.

"So why are you doing this? They clearly despise you. Why work for such despicable men?"

"The Klan," he started, and he closed his eyes and shook his head. "They took me in... made me one of them." She thought she saw moister welling in his eyes. "Sometimes being part of something terrible is better than being nothing at all." Shorty turned to the mirror above the dresser and stared at his own face, a deadpan face except for eyes full of fear and a lifetime of regrets. "At least, that's what you tell yourself." Shorty wiped his eyes, sniffed once and then turned to stare at Madge. His eyes were now empty, caverns full of a cold distance that filled her with a twinge of pity for the man.

"Can I at least clean myself up? I need bandages and some... things... feminine things."

The bedroom door opened and Klink stared in. Shorty turned towards the door and straightened his shoulders. "She needs bandages... and *lady* stuff...." Klink gave him a dirty look and cast his eyes to where Madge lay. Perhaps for the first time he realized what his master had done. There was no trace of sympathy, not a shred of decency, but he seemed to realize that one of two courses lay before him: kill her or let her go. He grunted an affirmation and glared at Shorty with the same loathing as before. "Fine. But I'm going with you. We don't want her getting away before we figure out how to handle this." He turned his gaze back to Madge and narrowed his eyes as he stared into hers. "You try to run, and you'll think what Stephenson did was a waltz compared to what I do to you. And this whole area is Klan. They won't lift a finger to help you. You understand me?" Madge nodded. "Then move your ass. Let's get this over with."

Klink followed them closely, like a vulture circling a wounded animal in the desert. Shorty ushered her out of the hotel to a Klan drugstore just around the corner. Bandages, alcohol, cotton balls, she gathered what she needed to clean herself up. As they drifted from one aisle to the next, she deftly snatched a box of mercury chloride tablets when Shorty was looking the other way. She paid for the goods, staring into the face of a clerk who wouldn't meet her gaze.

Back at the hotel she retreated to the bathroom, cleaned herself up as best she could and stared into the mirror. It was Harriet's face there in the glass, and none of the marks showed on her shining, dark skin. The time had come. She poured six of the mercury tablets into her hand, cupped her other hand under a running faucet and downed them, chasing them with cold water. All three men had stayed in the other room while she cleaned herself up. She went to the bed, laid down and waited. The mercury didn't take long to send her into agonized contortions. It burned, and every ten or fifteen minutes another wave of pain doubled her over. At first the men thought she was faking it, trying to draw attention, but they knew they were safe in a Klan-owned hotel. She begged them to take her to a doctor, but it wasn't until she started coughing up blood that their faces went pale, realizing they'd run out of time. Madge curled up into a ball, lying half in and out of consciousness, her eyes closed and her breathing short.

"We ain't got no choice now," Gentry said fearfully but with deadly resolve. All three men stood around the bed where Madge lay in agony. "Shorty, you're gonna have to do it."

Shorty stared at the fat man, looking him up and down. Madge saw perhaps just a glimmer of spine.

"I'm a Christian, Gentry... God fearing. I ain't going to Hell for killing an innocent white woman, no matter what you or Stephenson says. *You* do it."

Gentry turned to Klink. "That leaves you."

"Go to Hell, Gentry. I've been in the joint, four

years, and I'm not doing a lifer rap for anyone. Besides, all we gotta do is wait. She ain't gonna last long."

"Well, we can't let her croak here," Gentry said, rubbing the back of his pudgy head.

There was a pause as Klink and Gentry exchanged glances. During Madge's assault, it had been the alcohol talking and given them backbone, but now they squeaked and squirmed like rats in a trap. It was Shorty that saved her in the end. She never did know why. Maybe it was a lifetime of abuse. Maybe he just had more humanity than the rest.

"Lemme take her home," Shorty finally spoke up, "let her die with her family."

"Are you out of your mind?" Klink asked.

"We can't leave her here, and dropping her off to die someplace is the same as killing her, Klink. If we try and help her, we can tell the judge we did everything we could. She's the one who took the pills, and you said yourself, she won't last long. Even if she does say something, it's our word against hers."

Klink and Gentry both considered Shorty's reasoning, cowardice winning in the end. Klink looked at Gentry who merely shrugged. "Yeah... I guess you're right, runt." Klink stared at Shorty and shook his head. "Take her."

At noon Shorty gathered up Madge's unconscious body, put her in the car and drove her home to where only the Oberholtzer's tenant Mrs. Schultz was present. He told the old woman that Madge had been in an automobile accident, and then he left in a rush without leaving his name, confident that Madge would not live long.

But Madge didn't die. A doctor was sent for and a story told... a story that spread. It didn't take long for the outrage and the arrests.

*　　　　*　　　　*

April 13th, 1925 – Indianapolis, Indiana

Madge's mother stared down into her daughter's pallid, sweating face and prayed for a second miracle, this one seven years after the first. Back then it had been a week of hell, starting with a cough that quickly turned into thick, throat-tearing heaves full of yellow and green that threatened to shake her weak, feverish daughter to pieces. Madge had gotten caught up in the influenza epidemic of 1918 and ended up lying in that very same bed. Back then the same doctor had said exactly the same thing as he said only a few hours ago: there was nothing more he could do, and the Oberholtzer's should begin making final preparations.

Her mother remembered the moment of the miracle like it was before her eyes once again. Madge hadn't coughed for hours. Her cheeks glowed with the burning hue of deadly fever. Her breathing was thick and labored while her mother sat beside the bed and clutched her daughter's hot, sweaty hand. Then Madge went into a fit of convulsions and fierce coughing, as if a devil were trying to rip its way out of her body. It subsided. Madge lay back in the bed, her face calm and her chest still. Her mother screamed in despair and then felt the presence.

The curtains flickered, even though the midnight air was still. She felt a chill and sensed something at the foot of the bed. A shift of air brushed past her check, and Madge's matted hair quivered across her forehead. Madge took in a long, sucking breath, her chest heaving once, followed by a long exhale, then her breathing returned to normal. Her mother couldn't believe her eyes. She laid her hand on Madge's forehead and found the heat gone. Madge's cheeks were losing the angry hue of fever. Madge opened her eyes the following morning, and everything went back to normal.

So there her mother sat and prayed for a second miracle, not the least bit guilty for the asking. A knock on the door brought Madge's mother back to the present and all-too-real fear of losing her daughter.

"Come in," she said, her voice sounding stronger than she felt.

A thin, clean-shaven man stepped in, removed a faded brown cap off of short black hair and tucked the cap under his arm. "Mrs. Oberholtzer?" he asked. He wore a simple brown suit with worn elbows, and his black shoes were dusty and unpolished. He had a green bow tie that seemed to dance over his Adam's apple when he spoke. A fountain pen was tucked behind one ear.

Madge's mother cast a questioning glance at the man.

"My name is Henry Walker," he offered. "I take statements for the courts."

Realization flashed into her eyes. "Mr. Walker! I'm so glad you're here." She lowered her voice to a whisper. "The doctor says that we don't have much time."

"I'm sorry, Mrs. Oberholtzer."

"She's still asleep, but…"

"I'm awake, Mr. Walker." Madge's voice drifted up from the bed as if from a great distance and through dense fog.

"Miss Oberholtzer, I'm sorry I disturbed you, but

I've come to take your official statement." He paused, his eyes focusing on the gaunt, black-and-yellow bruised face that stuck out from the blankets. "I can come back later if you're not up to this."

"No. I'm afraid I don't have much time." She winced, and Walker watched an arm slide up from under the covers, push the blankets down and beckon him. He had to swallow when he saw the bruises and bite-marks that painted the white skin in a mottled pattern of tormenting abuse.

Henry turned to Mrs. Oberholtzer and saw tears rolling down her face. "I'm sorry...." she started, closing her eyes and turning her face away. "I can't hear this again... it's too...." Her body shuddered with sobs. She covered her face with one hand, grabbed the doorknob and rushed out of the room. Walker heard her burst into violent sobs as she ran down the hall. He swallowed again, pulled a small, black notebook out of his pocket and sat in the chair next to Madge. He looked at her with tender eyes that recognized suffering and wanted to do something about it.

"How are you feeling?" he asked out of habit and then wanted to kick himself for the stupidity of it. The embarrassment on his face gave him away.

"Don't worry, Mr. Walker. It's okay. How I feel isn't important anymore. What is important is that you're here. This is the last piece," she said and tried to sigh. She got halfway through it, and her whole body winced with deep pain. The agony seemed to last for several heartbeats, and her face twisted into a grimace like something was tearing at her from the inside. "How about I just tell you what happened," she managed when the pain abated slightly.

She began the tale.

He nodded, pulled the pen from behind his ear and started writing as she spoke. As her story unfolded, Walker found himself filling with fury and sorrow and even shame for being a man, for it was men who had committed such evil. Madge finished, wrapping up with his entrance into the room. She let out a long breath full of relief and despair and satisfaction, all impossibly mixed together, but genuine nonetheless.

"How did you endure it?" Walker asked finally, full of horrified sympathy.

"I knew what was coming from the moment he first grabbed me," Madge said. Harriet had known what was coming from the first moment Madge Oberholtzer saw the fiery eyes of David Curtiss Stephenson. "I guess I just turned my back on it all while he did what he did… it was as if I wasn't there."

Life passed from Madge's body that night, with her father looking down and her mother weeping while she held her daughter's hand. The cries turned to a long, drawn-out wailing full of agonized sobs and screams of bereaved askance hurled at Heaven and He who ruled it with such apparent indifference.

*   *   *

September 15th, 1925 – Indianapolis, Indiana

"Stephenson! You got mail!"

Convicted of second-degree murder, Stephenson sat

in his cell with a blank stare on his face. All he could think of were the men, *Klan,* who had turned their backs on him. He thought of how he would roll them over and bring them down with him. A guard's hand stuck through the bars and held out a postcard. Stephenson stiffly reached out, snatched it and peered down at the photograph. The Hemphill dogwood image brought back memories that warmed him, and it was enough to put a smile on his face after months of frowns and scowls during the trial. He flipped it over. The smile disappeared, turning to agonized shock. The poem on the back was not as he remembered it.

You were the root of the Dogwood tree;
A heartless soul of white supremacy.
And though once taught in the Pioneer's school,
This land is no more under the white man's rule
The Red Man once in an early day,
Was told by whites to mend his way.
Yet this lamb, by God's eternal grace,
Has shown you truly the dragon's place.
Across this land, a place to be free,
Let true, blind freedom forever be.
Let this a promise to all evil be,
I am salt in the roots of your dogwood tree.

A single sentence was scrawled awkwardly next to the poem in a child's scrawl, and a signature.

I got you.

Harriet Truth

ᗷhe End

Author's Notes:

Harriet Truth is a composite of many. She is the spirit of Harriet Tubman and Sojourner Truth, but she is also a tribute to every person who suffered so horrifically at the hands of white men and had the indomitable courage to make a stand, including Madge Oberholtzer, who faced evil with a courage most couldn't comprehend.

The multiple lynchings in 1908, possibly the largest mass lynching in American history, did indeed take place. After Hugh Dean was shot to death, six blacks were arrested by the county sheriff and incarcerated in Sabin County Jail in Hemphill, Texas. On the first night, the prisoners were taken from the jail by a mob of roughly 150 men and women brandishing torches. Five of the six were hanged in a nearby tree while the sixth was shot trying to escape.

Over the next few nights three more black men were hanged by similar but smaller mobs. Not only were no whites brought to justice, but their actions were celebrated by the good, white people of Texas. As proof of such vile celebration, the postcard described in this story is also real. Apparently such postcards were commonplace in the aftermath of Klan lynchings across the US.

The influenza epidemic of 1918 killed millions globally. It's been speculated that its widespread nature was a result of birds carrying it across the world. The speed with which that little virus decimated our numbers certainly lends itself well to the notion of an avian-borne killer.

Finally, the kidnapping, rape and death of Madge Oberholtzer as well as the downfall of the prominent David Curtiss Stephenson (born in Houston, Texas only 80 miles southwest of Hemphill) is also true. The Ku Klux Klan had been reborn around 1915, and it gained both momentum and membership throughout the twenties.

According to my research, in the spring of 1925, Klan membership under Stephenson was either 35,000 or 250,000 strong. Reports conflict and the difference may be between Indiana membership and membership through the 22 states under his control. His trial and conviction shed light upon the evil of the Klan. Rats abandoned the sunken ship in hordes, and by 1928 only 4,000 members of the Indiana Klan remained. Stephenson had been the root of Indiana's dogwood tree, and the death of Madge Oberholtzer was enough salt to bring it down for good.

It was Billie Holliday who sang, "Southern trees bear a strange fruit." As a culture, each and every one of us should take any steps necessary to forever pour salt upon the roots of dogwood trees when we find them sprouting in our midst and ensure that they never bear such horrible fruit again, regardless of race, color or creed.

About the author:

At an early age Quincy Allen had the intention of becoming an author. Unfortunately, he was waylaid by bandits armed with the age-old phrase "So you wanna be a starving artist the rest of your life?" As a result, he ended up a slave to the IT grind for 17 years, maintaining his sanity with motorcycles and music. Now in the midst of a mid-life career change, he's been published in *Penny Dread Tales Volume One* and *Short, Fast and Deadly.* He's written three episodes for the Internet radio show *RadioSteam* and has short stories coming out in *The Scribbling Ibis, Tales of the Talisman, Spirit Legends* and *Best Served Cold.* He is a finalist in the Rocky Mountain Writers Association *Colorado Gold Writing Contest,* he's working on editing several anthologies and he works part-time as a tech-writer to pay the bills.

You can follow his writing travails at www.quincyallen.com/quincy-allen.

Battle of the Resurrected Foemen

by Henrik Ramsager (Sao Paulo, Brazil)

It was a day to be glad to be alive. The sun had settled late the night before and rose with the whistling meadowlarks early the next morning. The presence of a warm sun brought with it a feeling of optimism for the new day in the small Wyoming town. Such a feeling was good for business, and nowhere was this more apparent than at Mrs. Broadhurst's bordello. By early afternoon, brisk business was afoot.

At two minutes to two, a stranger in town entered the bordello. Mrs. Broadhurst herself, smiling in expectation of an addition being made to her moneybox, greeted the newcomer.

"Good afternoon, sir. You're new in town, aren't you? Welcome to my humble establishment, where all your needs, whatever they may be, will be seen to."

"Morning, ma'am," said the dark-haired visitor without removing his hat. "As a matter of fact, I've just come from next door where I was hoping to see a Mr. Potbury. Weren't no sign of him, but there was a note on the door saying I could leave a message here if I liked. So I've come to do just that."

"Oh," said Mrs. Broadhurst, her smile evaporating into a disappointed frown as she contemplated the deprivation to her earnings.

"Any idea when he might be back?" asked the stranger.

"He's probably out on call somewhere. He could be at the mortuary. He seems to spend a lot of his time there, but there's no telling. Tell you what," she added, her smile returning in full bloom, "while you're waiting, wouldn't you like to avail yourself of one of my girls? There's hardly a stranger comes to town who don't eventually find his way to my door, either through personal recommendation of a satisfied customer or in answer to our advertisement over at the Gold Label Saloon."

The stranger scratched the back of his neck as if in contemplation of the offer. "Well, it wasn't on my mind when I come in here."

"Come now," persuaded Mrs. Broadhurst with a wink. "Our rates are more than reasonable considering the quality of the service."

"Now that you come to mention it, I guess I wouldn't mind after all. There are worse ways to spend my time."

"That's the spirit," said a pleased Mrs. Broadhurst. "Right this way, sir."

The tall stranger followed the proprietress from the entrance room into the parlor. The heavy scent of competing perfumes and tobacco lay in the air like a fog bank. Along the far wall was a row of chairs and a divan with a faded pattern. Here three ladies in frilly evening attire lounged and chatted in soft voices. One of them glanced up quickly then returned to her conversation, perhaps eager to make the most of her time before she might be called away by the newly arrived client.

"There now. Didn't I tell you there'd be something good to choose from?" beamed Mrs. Broadhurst proudly. "Just look at the variety of cleavage."

As if that was an agreed-upon signal, all three ladies now looked up at the potential client with sultry eyes. There was a momentary awkwardness while the visitor debated whether to let his eyes drop for a closer look.

"Any particular kind of girl you're looking for?"

"No—except that I'd favor one with some contour to her backside," replied the customer, lowering his voice so as not to be overheard by the ladies.

"That'll be Miss Henrietta."

"She's not too inexperienced, is she?"

"No, you needn't worry on that score. She's known as a seasoned artisan among the local clientele, and not a one of them ever issued a complaint against her."

"Where can I find her?" asked the client, searching eagerly with his eyes among the three ladies before him.

Mrs. Broadhurst smiled the smile of contentment she reserved for moments such as this when she felt that the transfer of cash payment into her hand was imminent. "She's with a client just now but should be done with him any minute. In fact, she's overdue now. That just goes to show you the sort of dedication you can expect when you're in Miss Henrietta's company."

"Well, she sounds like the one for me then."

"I'm sure you won't be disappointed." Thinking over what she'd just said, Mrs. Broadhurst added a moment later, "Mind you, that's not a guarantee of any kind."

"I'll take my chances."

"Fine. That's settled then. I'll give them another five minutes, and if they're not out by then, I'll tap on the door. As soon as she's finished in there and ready for you, I'll bring her out. I always offer clients a chance to look over what they're getting before they commit."

"You run a first-rate establishment here, I can see," observed the client.

The stranger was invited to sit down in the "customer's seat" by the inner doorway that led to the boudoirs.

The minutes ticked by. Two of the painted ladies started a card game. The other, who was on the divan, leisurely smoked a cigarette at the end of a long cigarette holder. Her other hand held a Japanese fan—a gift from a grateful client who admired her nether contours.

Mrs. Broadhurst remained standing by the door leading to the entrance hall, tapping her foot impatiently as if measuring the minutes. The clock on the wall showed that five minutes had now passed. She was on the verge of seeking out Miss Henrietta when a bell jangled. Someone had entered through the front door.

"Ahh," exclaimed Mrs. Broadhurst, eager at the prospect of welcoming an additional client arriving with ready cash.

Mrs. Broadhurst was just reaching for the handle of the door that led to the hall when it opened suddenly from the other side.

A small, meticulously dressed, precise-natured man with a receding hairline stood in the doorway.

"Oh!" said Mrs. Broadhurst at sight of him.

"Good afternoon, Mrs. Broadhurst. Good afternoon,

ladies," he said to the others. "Hope I'm not intruding. I just stopped in to see if there were any messages for me while I was out."

"Well…" began Mrs. Broadhurst.

"Ah, you must be Mr. Potbury from next door," interrupted the stranger, standing up and crossing the room to Mr. Potbury.

"Now just a minute," interjected Mrs. Broadhurst, coming between them. "What about your appointment with Miss Henrietta?"

"I reckon that'll have to wait till another time," replied the stranger. "Thank you all the same."

A speechless Mrs. Broadhurst watched as the two headed out the door together a minute later.

Just then Miss Henrietta showed up in the doorway leading from the back rooms. "Goodbye, Billy darling. Remember to ask for me again next time you're in town," she cooed to the client with her. The client thanked her and, with a parting kiss on his cheek to remember her by, was out the door.

Mrs. Broadhurst was aflame with anger. The moment the door was shut behind the client, she laid into Miss Henrietta. "Didn't I tell you to always finish on time with a client? Half an hour is the absolute maximum. If you'd only finished up and come out two minutes earlier, you'd have had a new client. It was all arranged for you, but he had to go."

"I'm awful sorry, Mrs. Broadhurst," she replied. "I guess I lost track of the time."

"You guess you…." began an incredulous Mrs. Broadhurst before stopping short. "Have you ever heard of such a sorry excuse in your life?" she asked, speaking venomously into the air to no one in particular.

"I'm sorry, Mrs. Broadhurst," repeated the girl, who seemed to have no new or additional excuse to offer.

"Every cent of that money you just lost me is coming out of your wages," growled Mrs. Broadhurst with a finger raised in scornful finality.

"Yes, Mrs. Broadhurst," muttered Miss Henrietta in a sad voice as she lowered her eyes in submission.

Meanwhile, Mr. Potbury and the stranger were just arriving at Mr. Potbury's office.

"Here we are," said Mr. Potbury to his prospective client. "Won't you be seated, Mr.—I didn't catch your name."

"I'll come to that when I come to that," replied the client curtly as he took the seat indicated to him.

Facing the chair the stranger had taken, with a big desk between them, was another chair, which Mr. Potbury now sat down in.

"Can I offer you a smoke?" said Mr. Potbury, holding out a cigar box.

"Thank you, no," said the other.

"You don't mind if I indulge in one myself?"

The stranger shook his head. "Mr. Potbury," said the visitor, coming straight to the point, "how familiar are you with your local history?"

Having just struck a match, Mr. Potbury was partaking of the first few virginal puffs of his cigar. Withdrawing the cigar, he deliberated a moment on the question. "As familiar as anyone who wasn't reared here. It was just a few years ago that I settled in this town."

"Then I take it you've heard about the 1823 expedition east of here?"

"Wasn't that the expedition that ran into Indian trouble and was slaughtered to the man?"

"That's right, although for Indians it was seen as something other than a slaughter. From their point of view it was an unwanted encroachment into their territory."

"As I recall, the expedition was said to have collected quite a bit of gold before they all perished."

"Right again. It was either buried and forgotten somewhere or else came into possession of the Indians. But the subject of missing gold, however tantalizing, is not why I'm here."

This disappointed Mr. Potbury, though he kept it to himself. "I confess that I'm at a loss as to how all this has anything to do with my services as a...."

"It does—more than you can guess."

"Oh?"

"I'll tell you everything I've come to tell you, Mr. Potbury, but first I need to satisfy myself that you can guarantee my confidentiality—that is, even if you decide to turn down my proposal."

Mr. Potbury released a wreath of smoke up into the air and watched it rise toward the ceiling. "Mister, I've never yet turned down a client that I was able to help, and even if Satan himself were to walk through that door with a proposal, whatever he had to say wouldn't go beyond these walls. I pledge you my word on that."

The visitor, hearing this, began to relax in his chair and feel more at ease with the man across from him. "All right then. You were wondering what my name was," he carried on.

"You don't have to tell me it if you don't want to."

In answer to this, the stranger removed his hat and set it down on a corner of Mr. Potbury's desk. From behind his head fell a braided ponytail held by a leather band. The stranger crossed his arms. "The name's Proud

Toe."

"Proud Toe?" repeated Mr. Potbury. "You're an Indian, then? You could have fooled me. In fact, you did fool me." Mr. Potbury tapped some of the loose ash from his cigar into a tea saucer. "If you don't mind a personal remark, Proud Toe, you look—and sound—more white than red."

"That's why I was chosen to go out into the world as a representative of my tribe. I'm their eyes and ears, able to move freely among the whites."

"You're not a full-blooded Indian, then?"

"My mother was a white Irish schoolteacher from Baltimore and, later, Kansas City, as genteel as my father was savage. That is, savage by your standards."

"You're putting words in my mouth now."

"All right. Savage according to the opinion of most white-skins. My father was a Cheyenne—not a chief exactly, but high in standing."

"Where do your sympathies lie, then? Strictly with the Indians, I take it?"

"That's right. Our way, the way of the hunter, the tiller of the earth, the fisherman and the warrior—a part of nature and never against it—is the true way, the only way. All other ways are false to our way of thinking."

"I can respect that, even if as a white man I don't fully comprehend it... or prescribe to it as a way of life that's suitable to me," commented Mr. Potbury, giving voice to his initial thoughts, even if, upon reflection, he probably would have kept them to himself.

"Then there's hope for you yet, white man."

"By the way, are you sure you've come to the right man? You realize I'm a necromancer, right?"

"I know who you are, and that's why you're the one

person that can help us."

"And just how might I do that? By raising someone you know?"

"Not just anybody. A while ago I referred to the 1823 expedition."

"And I'm still waiting to hear how that ties in with your needs," Potbury said.

"What do you or any other white man know about that expedition? Only that they all came to a bad end. But as a Cheyenne I can tell you how they died. They were defeated by a single man."

"A single man? All thirty of them? How is that possible? He must have been a devil of a sharpshooter."

"He was no sharpshooter," Proud Toe said proudly. "His weapon was not the musket or the bow and arrow or even the tomahawk."

"Yet he killed all thirty of them single-handed? Then he must have taken them unawares one by one with a knife."

"Nor even a knife. Anyway, his name—not that you're likely to have heard it—was Thunder Foot, so named because the earth was said to rumble with noise when he walked. He's a legend among my people, and we'd like to have him back."

"You're saying that you want me to raise this person? For what purpose? So he can go out and kill some more people?" Potbury asked.

"No. We only want him resurrected so he can defend our people against the renewed invasion of whites who come into our sacred lands in the Black Hills."

"I've heard about this new illegal encroachment. That's what the lust for gold will do to men."

"We have no desire to go on the attack. Had our

ancestors wished it, they could have pushed out from the Black Hills with the Great One at the head. Your not having heard of Thunder Foot is evidence that there was never any intent to advance beyond our territory."

"I'd be taking an awful risk. If the authorities ever got wind of this, there'd be no end of trouble for me. I might even be arrested."

"No one else need know. Besides," added Proud Toe, "your incentive would not be unsubstantial."

"This caught Mr. Potbury's attention as no words had before. "Substantial? Just how substantial were you aiming to make it?"

"Five hundred dollars in gold, delivered upon proof of a successful resurrection."

Mr. Potbury's mind raced with the possibilities of what he could spend five hundred dollars on.

"I'll admit, you've succeeded in attracting my interest. Big Toe, I'm tempted to take you up on your offer."

"I didn't doubt that you would be. And it's Proud Toe."

"Sorry. I was always bad at remembering what people call themselves. You have the remains?"

"Yes. They can be found at an old Cheyenne burial site overlooking Longfall Canyon."

"I see. Well, that's something anyway. Would have been impossible to resurrect your champion without his remains."

"Does that mean we have a deal?"

"Tell you what, I have to sleep on it. Come back in two days... on Wednesday... and I'll have your answer for you."

"Fair enough," answered Proud Toe, getting up to

leave.

"One more thing before you go. Since I'm out of guesses, would you mind telling me how this Indian Hercules of yours killed all those men of the expedition?"

The visitor paused halfway to the door and looked back over his shoulder at Mr. Potbury. There was just the subtle trace of a smile on his face. Or perhaps it was a grimace.

"That's easy to answer. He rent them apart limb from limb."

On that note, the visitor pulled up his ponytail and tucked it back under his hat. Then he calmly strode out the door, leaving a speechless Mr. Potbury with a great deal to consider.

*   *   *

The next day two military men rode into town and made straight for Mr. Potbury's office after receiving directions from someone loitering outside the barbershop. When a feminine voice called down to the soldiers from Mrs. Broadhurst's balcony, they continued to trot past the bordello without so much as a glance her way. To all appearances they were in town strictly on business. When they came to Mr. Potbury's office, they dismounted and hitched their horses to a post. Dusty after their long ride, they both slapped trail dust off their uniforms as they made their way up the walkway to Mr. Potbury's office door.

A knock on the door yielded immediate results in the form of Mr. Potbury himself. "Good morning. What...ah, Colonel, isn't it?... can I do for you?"

"You go by the name of Potbury?"

"None other."

The officer turned to his companion and said, "Lieutenant, see that we're not disturbed and that no one listens outside the door or side window."

"Yes, sir," answered the young lieutenant crisply with a salute as his commanding officer pushed past Mr. Potbury then shut and locked the door from within.

"Sit down, Potbury," ordered the colonel, gesturing toward Mr. Potbury's chair.

"Just a minute now. What's this all about, Colonel? In my own office, I'm used to a certain...."

"You'll find out soon enough exactly what this is about," interrupted the colonel, himself heading for the visitor's chair across from Mr. Potbury's desk.

"You mind if I smoke?" asked the colonel upon taking his seat.

"Go right ahead," offered Mr. Potbury, who took it for granted that the officer would proceed to smoke whether he minded or not.

"I've been dying for a smoke," remarked the colonel as if to himself. "My mother taught me never to smoke in the saddle or when out strolling. Said it was unseemly."

"I understand," replied Mr. Potbury, at a loss for anything else to say just then. He, too, now took his seat.

The colonel rummaged through a multitude of pockets, his frown of disapproval all the while growing. "It appears I'm fresh out, or else suffered a loss on the trail," lamented the colonel.

"Have one of mine," said Mr. Potbury, turning and sliding his open box of cigars in the direction of the colonel.

"These look expensive."

"Don't let that stop you."

It didn't. The colonel took up a choice-looking cigar

and brought it to his nose for a sniff. The expression on his face showed that he was pleased with the product. The look of pleasure quickly dried up, however, as he searched his pockets in vain for a match.

"Allow me," said Mr. Potbury, displaying a lit match and bringing it to the end of his guest's cigar.

"Much—hmm—pfumph—obliged," said the colonel as he began to puff on the cigar. "Ahh—that's heaven, or as close as I'll ever come to it," he added as he leaned back and, to Mr. Potbury's mind, made himself feel more at home than propriety dictated.

Mr. Potbury got up to open the window so as to let out the smoke.

"I'm afraid I'm going to have to ask you to leave that window closed," objected the colonel, "to ensure our privacy."

"Sorry," said Mr. Potbury, retracing his steps back to his chair.

"Say, you got anything to drink? I feel as though I got sawdust down my tongue and throat."

"Just some cold coffee," proposed Mr. Potbury.

"That would really suit me just fine."

Mr. Potbury found a spare cup and set it down on the desk before the officer. Then, bringing over the coffee pot, he filled the cup to the brim.

"You want anything to eat with your coffee?" asked Mr. Potbury, who, in the short time he'd known the colonel, seemed to have gained some insight into the workings of his mind.

"Mmmm," said the colonel as he withdrew the cup of coffee from his lips. "You've read my mind exactly. I'm just about famished. We'd have brought more rations with us than we did before setting out from the garrison, but we didn't plan on taking a wrong turn and going near thirty miles out of our way 'fore we finally ended up here."

In answer to the colonel's call of nature, Mr. Potbury brought over a cloth-covered dish from a side table and set it down on the desk next to the coffee cup.

"I was saving this mince pie for my lunch, but I reckon you have a more urgent need for it than I do," said Mr. Potbury. Along with the dish, he laid out a knife and fork on the table.

As he uncovered the pie to the delighted eyes of the colonel, the officer remarked, "That's most assuredly a sight for sore eyes." He started to say more, but as he immediately fell to stuffing his mouth with a generous slice of the pie, the words were lost.

"Here, let me help you," said Mr. Potbury, who'd alertly noticed some stray crumbs descending from the colonel's chin and took it upon himself to undo the colonel's bandana and convert it into a bib, which he tucked into his front shirt collar.

"Much obliged, Potbury," said the colonel, who continued to eat as if he'd only just discovered food.

Noticing the colonel looking about as if in search of something, Mr. Potbury prompted him: "Could I interest you in some fried potatoes and corn to go with that pie, Colonel?"

The words were like music to the officer's ears.

"Mmm-mm!" he said as his eyes grew large at the prospect of the suggested addition being made to his plate. "Mumph obliged."

"Give me a few minutes," said Mr. Potbury as he headed for his stove along the wall and pulled out a pan from a small, low cupboard. "You might like to ease up some on that pie in the meantime," he advised over his shoulder. "Then you'll be able to eat your side dishes at the same time."

"Mmm-umph," agreed the colonel. "Byw whu way, you got any swuh or pmprumph?"

"How's that?"

"Swuhl or pehwer?"

"Salt or pepper, you say? So happens I've got both right here," said Mr. Potbury, reaching down for two shakers. A moment later he crossed back to the desk and set them down. While he was at it, he also lifted his guest's plate and laid out a place mat so as to protect the finish of his desk. "Another minute and the potatoes will be ready," said Mr. Potbury, noticing the hungry-eyed look the captain was giving him.

"Much obliged," said the colonel again, having followed Mr. Potbury's earlier advice to suspend his eating of the pie.

"You can have the corn now at any rate," offered Mr. Potbury a minute later. "Don't worry about your potatoes; they'll follow shortly."

"Aaah," said the diner when everything was assembled together before him. The soldier rubbed his hands together in anticipation.

"You're welcome," returned Mr. Potbury, taking his exclamation as thanks.

His cooking chores done with, Mr. Potbury retook his seat opposite his guest, who was now going at his meal full throttle like a Union Pacific locomotive.

The colonel, for all his chewing, was a slow eater, so it was some time before he had finished his meal. When the last morsel of food was off the plate, the colonel patted his stomach with satisfaction. "You're a good cook, Potbury."

"Thank you, Colonel," replied Mr. Potbury as he cleared the desk.

Once he'd taken his seat again, the colonel looked him over with careful attention to detail, something his former appetite had gotten in the way of.

"So," began the colonel, finally getting down to business. "I understand you're a necromancer."

"You understand right."

"Aren't you curious as to why I'm here?"

"I figure you'll tell me when you're ready to. I don't believe in rushing people."

"Why do you think I'm here? Can you guess?"

"I don't know. Maybe you have a general or someone important you want raised. Maybe you'd like to add George Washington to your outfit."

"Are you mocking me, Potbury?"

"No, sir, not at all. I'm just speaking straight to you the way I'm accustomed to."

"Because if you mock me, it's the same as mocking the entire army of this territory."

"I'm sure it is."

The colonel exhaled, then suppressed an after-meal belch. "You mentioned that you like to speak straight," he said, moving on. "Good, because that's what I intend to do. First of all, have you or have you not been visited by a member of the Cheyenne Nation in the last twenty-four hours?"

"Yes."

The colonel's moustache bristled. Whether it was from indignation or from gratification at getting an admission out of him, Mr. Potbury couldn't say.

"And have you or have you not struck a bargain with said Indian?"

Mr. Potbury was tempted to answer no to avoid further trouble, but a plan had been formulating in his mind ever since Proud Toe's visit.

"Yes," said Mr. Potbury, meeting the colonel's eyes level with his own unblinking eyes. "Our transaction has been completed. The Indian who visited me paid me generously for my service."

"About now is where you ought to say how ashamed you are of yourself and how you intend to reverse your spell or incantation or whatever the hell it is you call it," snorted the colonel.

"Ashamed? I don't follow you, Colonel. I simply raised someone at the direction of a paying client. I don't discriminate on the basis of the client's skin color. Gold has only one color, and that's the only color I concern myself with."

"You mean to say you don't know who it is you brought back to life?" roared the colonel in a voice that could wilt flowers. "I find that hard to believe. I only don't break your backside at the end of my foot because you gave me a meal, and I'm indebted to you for it."

"Instead of shouting at me," challenged Mr. Potbury, his own voice rising with anger, "maybe you ought to tell me who exactly it is I wasn't supposed to raise, because I sure as hell don't have any idea."

The colonel opened his mouth to bark again at Mr. Potbury but stopped himself. "Upon reflection, I do believe there is a chance you don't know. I'm willing to give you the benefit of the doubt for now, Potbury."

"Well, that's something at least."

"The Indian you so wisely raised," continued the colonel, his voice tainted with sarcasm, "was none other than Thunder Foot. Ever hear of him?"

"No."

"Neither had we until just recently. It seems he's some kind of mad-dog engine of destruction with the strength of twenty men."

"That so? And how'd you learn that I made a deal to resurrect him?"

"Never mind. The military has its ways."

"Why is the military taking an interest in this anyway? You think this Indian will attack one of your forts maybe?"

"Not exactly. The fear is that civilians will come to harm, and that's where the army comes in. Our job is to protect civilian lives, no matter where the threat comes from."

"What makes this particular redskin so much of a threat?"

"We've had our scouts and spies out, and from what I understand, he can't be beat. No bullet can penetrate his hide."

"You don't really believe that, do you?"

"Whether or not I believe it is irrelevant. The important factor is that the Cheyenne believe it. Just imagine what someone like this Thunder Foot could do for their morale. He would be the biggest threat since Kicking Big Bear. With him at the head of a war party, they might just about be unstoppable. And other disaffected tribes might just join under their buffalo-head banner. They could sweep every homestead and town between here and Deadwood and probably wipe out whatever forces we could muster to oppose them."

"I see. So that would represent quite a threat to anyone who's not Indian. I'm sorry I raised him then. If I'd known I would have refused."

"All we need from you, Potbury, is your assurance that you'll undo what you did. Then you'll have no more trouble to fear from us."

"Put him back in his grave, you mean? I'm sorry, but it can't be done, Colonel."

Mr. Potbury expected an imminent explosion, but none was forthcoming.

"You're not angry then?" asked Mr. Potbury a moment later.

"I haven't the time," answered the colonel. "Any other day and I might have had you trussed up and delivered to the stockade. But, frankly, we have need of you."

"Oh?"

"In the event that I was unable to undo the resurrection of Thunder Foot, I was authorized to make you a proposition."

"What sort of proposition would that be?"

"What we want is this. We want you to raise someone to oppose Thunder Foot. We're willing to pay you handsomely. As this is a priority case, we're even willing to exceed by fifty dollars what the Indians paid you."

"You have my interest, Colonel, but there's just one problem. Who in this wide world am I going to raise who has the remotest chance of being able to stand against Thunder Foot?"

"Ever hear of a hell-branded mountain of a man named Zachary Sachs?"

"Sure. He used to live in Deadpan Gulch back in the early mining days of that town, didn't he?"

"That's right. Some say he was descended from Big Joe Montferrand himself, who lived up north in Montreal before the time of the Revolution. Went by the name of Zachary Sachs, as I said, or Great Zachsach as he was known to be called. He was said to be stronger than any two oxen put together, if the legend is to be believed. He was certainly a freak of nature."

"I thought he was just that—a legend."

"He's real enough." The colonel sat back comfortably in his chair, feeling more than a little satisfied that he had, it seemed to him, piqued Mr. Potbury's interest. "We managed to locate his grave a while back. So…"

"So?"

"You think you can resurrect him?"

"Colonel, I can resurrect anything that once lived, provided the remains can be found."

"Then I'm happy to say that we have a deal, Potbury," said the colonel, rising to shake Mr. Potbury's hand across the table.

*   *   *

The sky was a mix of swirling powder and blue fading into a flaming expanse of red. Herds of bison roamed on the open prairie in every direction. A logical exception was the area containing Longfall Canyon, with its harsh terrain of jagged rocks and treacherous rapids coursing through the basin. Near the edge of the canyon wall was a hill. At the high point of the hill was a half-forgotten Cheyenne burial ground, previously imperceptible to the eye of anyone who did not know it was there. Right beside a rotting medicine pole lying on the ground, a hole was newly dug.

A quarter mile away, in the amber-headed grass of a

low hill, crouched Mr. Potbury, an associate of his named Zeke Harbinger and a dozen military men. Likewise crouching out of sight on another hill equidistant from the wooded cliff was the Indian contingent.

"Do you see anything yet, Lieutenant?"

"No, Colonel," answered the lieutenant. "There's no sign of anything or anyone yet."

"Hand me those field glasses, Lieutenant."

"Yes, sir," replied the lieutenant, passing the glasses to his superior.

Holding the glasses before him, the colonel studied the burial mound and surrounding area. "Well, Potbury?" he said at last, putting the field glasses down and looking at Mr. Potbury next to him. "Yonder is where you arranged for Zachary Sachs and Thunder Foot to have it out. You sure you raised them proper and that they know where the location of the confrontation is to be?"

"As I said to you before, Colonel, Thunder Foot is already out there atop that hill. You just can't see him yet. Last time I saw him he was sitting under a cottonwood tree in sight of his own grave, meditating and preparing himself for his re-entry into this world and this time period. He knows that Zachary Sachs is on his way to him. When Sachs arrives, Thunder Foot will show himself sure enough."

"And what about Sachs? You sure he'll be able to find his way to this spot?"

"Sure I'm sure. As soon as I took charge of his remains, I brought them to the ridge next to the burial hill and resurrected him there."

"Why don't I see him then?"

"He's behind the ridge. If you were to go there right now, you'd see him stretched out. He's still in a daze—

half asleep, you might say—but I whispered instructions in his ear for about an hour that he is to confront an Indian warrior atop the nearby hill."

"You think he got the message?"

"He got it all right. He answered me as if he were talking in his sleep. He said that as soon as he got up, he was going to crush that Indian's bones and then carve a top hat out of him to wear in town on a Saturday night. He also said something about being a half century behind on his drinking, and that his favorite drink was coffin varnish."

"Ha. That sounds like our boy," said the colonel, well pleased. "He'll sure give that Injun a lacing." Then, striking a sourer note, he opined, "Sure do wish I could get me an up-close view of Sachs, just to satisfy myself that it really is him."

"Like I said to you, Colonel, that's the last thing you'll want to be doing. If you go buzzing around there now, there's no telling what sort of hell might break lose. Maybe you don't need to worry too much about Sachs, but if you start toward him and that Indian sees you, he'll come for you, sure as my granny had a backside too wide for the doorway. My view is he's a killing automaton. You can ride away from him—jingle your spurs all you like—but he won't stop till he gets whichever white man comes first into his sight. Your horse will tire and die before he gives up—and that'll be never."

"Damn it! Oh, damn it," said the colonel suddenly.

"What is it?" asked Mr. Potbury, alarmed.

"I got this uncommon urge for some bacon grease just now. This always happens when I'm going into battle or something else is about to happen that has me on tenterhooks."

"Hold on! I see something now, to the south-east!" cried the lieutenant, looking through the field glasses again.

All eyes followed an uneven row of pine trees skirting southward along the back foot of the hill toward the low, flat ridge not far from the edge of the abyss. It was there that a figure walked out from behind the ridge in the direction of the burial ground on the hill.

"It's him. It's your champion all right," declared Mr. Potbury.

"Things are heating up now. Things are certainly heating up now, by jiminy," said the lieutenant, excited at the prospect of viewing the fight to come.

Meanwhile, over at the Indian contingent, they were no less excited and confident in the chances of their champion winning the day.

"There he is! There he is! That's our man all right," said the colonel, who had just requisitioned the field glasses again. "Will you look at the size of him! Glory be!"

Before them was Zachary Sachs in all his might. Even at this distance, it was apparent that he was no common mortal. One of the soldiers estimated that he was at least ten feet in height.

A challenging roar—a howl—echoed as the legendary man-mountain shuffled forward toward the Indian burial hill and his date with destiny. So heavy was he that each step of his resounded on the ground.

The challenge was quickly answered. A ferocious growl like that of a bear boomed across the battlefield. In the next moment Thunder Foot, coming from behind the base of the hill, walked into view. As expected, the legend lived up to his name. With each step he took, a great pounding sound—louder even than that of his opponent—was heard, like the sound of thunder that crackles in the heavens. A momentary shudder went through the ranks of the white contingent when they saw that he was a head bigger than Sachs, standing perhaps twelve feet in height.

A cheer went up among the Indian contingent as their champion spotted his adversary and lumbered toward him. His limbs were like the limbs of the tree he now stopped alongside.

"What's he doing?" wondered the colonel aloud.

In the next moment, the colonel's question was answered. Wrapping his mighty arms about the tree, Thunder Foot, to the amazement of the onlookers, both white and red, uprooted the tree and cast it aside. It was a magnificent display of brute strength.

Not to be outdone, however, the white champion pulled at the nearest tree and also uprooted it before throwing it to one side.

There was now no doubt in the minds of both groups of onlookers that they were looking upon two legends out of the past, and that the confrontation to come would be an epic battle to be told to their children and, later, retold to their grandchildren.

The battle began. Perhaps to show his prowess, Thunder Foot kicked at a large boulder near the edge of the canyon. With a low rumble it fell into the canyon. The sound hadn't begun to fade before Sachs was charging his opponent. Thunder Foot met him head on. Mighty blows were struck against Thunder Foot's chest and face, which he returned in kind. The blows were heard all the way from where the two camps of watchers observed. There was a great deal of loud stomping and repositioning of the combatants. They seemed slow on their feet, but perhaps this was to be expected, as they were so big and heavy and, besides, probably hadn't fully recovered yet from their recent resurrections.

The fight was short-lived but intense. Little was offered in the way of variety: repeated blows to the head and upper body, and at the same restricted angles. Neither seemed to be much affected by the battering, despite the sounds of loud impacts, which would seem to indicate that a great deal of force was being absorbed. The two fighters seemed evenly—even perfectly—matched.

Then finally something new happened. The two closed at the same time, locking arms about each other's massive necks and shoulders, and did what might have been taken for a dance-hall sidestep under other circumstances. Seemingly paying no heed to the perils of the cliff, they simply stepped over it simultaneously and disappeared from sight. An animalistic bellowing and the dislodging of colliding rocks sounded as their immense bodies fell to the bottom of the canyon.

"Good God! Did you ever see the like!" shouted the colonel. Those in the company of the colonel stood up. At first they hesitated to go forward, fearing that one or both of the fighters might have survived and was about to reappear at the cliff side.

"I think it's safe enough to take a look now," advised Mr. Potbury. "Either the jagged rocks below did them in or they were lost to the rapids."

Before they set out, Mr. Potbury made sure to collect his fee from the colonel, who, satisfied at the results of his work, readily complied. Placing the sack of money in one of his saddlebags, Mr. Potbury, along with Zeke Harbinger, moved out on foot with their horses in tow. Halfway to the edge of the canyon, they joined the party of

Cheyenne warriors.

"Proud Toe remain on hilltop. He keep out of sight," explained the old Cheyenne chief to Mr. Potbury. "Not good other white men see Proud Toe. He must continue watch white men careful in white-man disguise. He say you not give identity away. Give word."

"Yes. I promise never to reveal his identity so long as I live," said Mr. Potbury.

"Potbury is good white man," said the chief. "All Cheyenne proud this day. Thunder Foot slay mighty white warrior. He show no fear. Stand up for Cheyenne."

"I'm glad to see you're satisfied with the results. I'm just sorry that Thunder Foot had to die as well."

"Honor best served in death."

"Well said."

"Now...gold promised for Potbury. Take," said the chief, gesturing for a young, one-feather warrior to hand Potbury his money in a bison-skin bag tied with a leather string.

"In gratitude and friendship, I accept your payment," said Mr. Potbury in a humble voice before pocketing the bag in his other saddlebag.

"Here," said the chief, holding out another smaller bag. "Cheyenne people give one hundred dollars gold worth as extra. You take."

"No," dismissed Mr. Potbury. "I'll take only what was pledged and no more."

"You are good," said the old chief, embracing Mr. Potbury. "Very good," he added with emotion like a father to his son.

Mr. Potbury, his associate and the Cheyenne warriors proceeded to the cliff edge where the others were peering down at the canyon bottom. Having seen enough—which was nothing—they were already getting ready to depart.

The Cheyenne, even with their keener sight, could see no sign of the two combatants.

It was not many more minutes before the military men and then the Cheyenne had withdrawn. This left just Mr. Potbury and Zeke Harbinger at the canyon edge.

"So, it looks as though you pulled it off, Elijah."

Mr. Potbury shook his associate's hand. "It looks that way, Zeke. Well, the wheels were set easily enough in motion once we made sure that army scout in town— Ambrose—overheard us conversing about resurrecting Thunder Foot. He wasted no time in getting the information to the colonel.

"Everything seemed to work according to plan. Those hollow trees we set up loose in the ground last night had everyone from the chief and colonel to the bugle boy fooled. Though our two "combatants" looked ungainly and awkward, no one was able to tell that each giant was really just a man sitting on the shoulders of another man and dressed in padded clothing. Lucky for us, neither toppled over. Had they done that, they wouldn't have been able to get up again."

The associate looked over the edge of the cliff. "It looks like the four of them dropped safely to the nets that were waiting six feet below, and I see the nets have already been taken in," observed the associate. "If they'd somehow missed the nets, we'd have heard it."

"That reminds me," Potbury said, "Colt, you all right down there?"

"Everything's fine down here," came the sound of a muffled voice from the hole that had been dug into the face of the cliff wall opposite to where the nets had been. Brush grew just over the entrance, rendering it invisible to anyone from above.

"Fine," said Mr. Potbury. "You boys sit tight till nightfall and slip away then. Best not to take any chances now when there might be someone still looking our way. As discussed, we'll all meet up at my office about this time tomorrow when we'll hand out your share of the money."

Mr. Potbury and his associate moved away from the edge. His companion remarked, "Don't you feel bad about cheating both your clients, Elijah?"

"Not me. The bottom line is what I always have my eye on. I'm just surprised they ever thought I could reanimate dried-up old bones. It's tough enough raising a newly deceased person. Anyway, it seems to me everything turned out for the best, and not just for me. This way, both sides got what they wanted and bloodshed was avoided."

"I suppose there's something in what you say, but now there won't be any resurrected legend to stop those gold prospectors coming into Cheyenne territory."

"You're right about that, but even if there had been ten Thunder Foots to wreak havoc, they'd still have come, and there would have been a lot of bloodshed. The prospectors coming no matter what the obstacles are is something the Cheyenne hadn't considered. They'll continue to come so long as there's gold to be found."

"By the way, besides the four men who played the giants, there was also the sound-effects man on the burial mound; that's a lot of men to keep a secret. Aren't you afraid one of them will spill the beans someday?"

Mr. Potbury considered a moment. "Well, they'll have a lot of money to help them keep quiet. Besides that, I gave them one other incentive."

"And that is?"

"I told them if they ever told a living soul, then I would resurrect them after they died and make them my undead slaves."

The associate shuddered. "Does that apply to me too, Elijah?"

"Don't you worry, Zeke. We've known each other too long for any threats to be taken seriously."

The two men mounted up and began to urge their horses through the cliff's wooded tract and across the prairie. They were bound for the trail on the other side that would lead them back into town. Their first stop in town was the bank where the clerk was sure to be startled at the sight of the biggest deposit he was likely to see for a while.

The End

About the author:

Henrik Ramsager, a cat owner, has recently appeared in *Cutlass and Musket: Tales of Piratical Skullduggery*, *Midnight Showdown*, *Six-Guns Straight from Hell* and *Evil Dragons*. He was the first place winner of the 2010 Rogue Blades *Discovery* anthology contest.

Till Death Do We Part

By Kit Campbell (Colorado, USA)

here was blood on my wedding dress. At least, I assumed it was blood. I wasn't about to reach out and stick my finger in it to find out for sure. But there it was, smeared down the brilliant white like a river, so clear I could make out the handprints.

There were heavy footfalls outside the room, the sounds of someone running up the stairs and down the hall. I could tell without looking that it was my fiancé, Loren, coming in answer to my scream.

His breath caught as he entered the room behind me. Part of me wondered if he should be here. After all, the groom was not supposed to see the wedding dress before the wedding, but with the amount of crimson covering it, it was no longer recognizable.

"Gwen...?"

I swallowed around the lump in my throat. "I'm leaving," I said. I took another look at the ruined dress, fighting back tears. It had been perfect, but like so many other things lately, it had been twisted and corrupted... a warning.

Loren shifted his weight, staring at the dress. "When will you be back?" he asked quietly, as if he was afraid of the answer.

"I'm not coming back." It hurt to say it, but I couldn't take this anymore. "I love you, I really do, but this is only getting worse. If you want me to come back, you know what you need to do." I turned, careful to avoid looking at his face so my resolve didn't crack, and moved purposefully through the house, collecting only my car keys and my coat before I was out the door.

*   *   *

To say that I didn't see it coming is an understatement. This sort of thing doesn't belong in the realm of normal life. So when I met a nice guy and dated him for a few years before he got down on one knee and proposed, my only thoughts were of fancy parties and a long life filled with happiness.

Loren and I got along so well—had a lot of habits in common—and he always laughed at my lame jokes.

It was perfect... or, at least, it seemed perfect.

I ditched my tiny apartment and moved in with him. Loren had a newer house, full of light and angles and contrasting colors. It radiated with happiness. I was happy. Loren was happy. My cat Ceci was happy, as there were sunbeams everywhere. It was a dream come true, as horrible and clichéd as that sounds now.

The first sign of trouble was Ceci. She began to follow me around the house, making sure I was always in view and meowing piteously if I was not. She would stop and stare at random corners, tail flicking. She'd never shown any sort of nervous behavior before. I called the vet, but he told me sometimes cats got weird as they got older, so I wrote it off as some sort of quirk.

Then the noises started... sounds of someone coming down the stairs when I was home alone, cabinets opening and closing by themselves. Once I swore I heard the door immediately behind me open, but when I turned to look, it remained closed.

This always happened when Loren was out, so I chalked it up to being a combination of nerves and the house settling. Houses settle, right? Maybe it was some soil thing. Anyway, noises never hurt anyone.

I didn't think much of it for several more weeks. The creaking didn't increase in frequency, and while Ceci would no longer come into the bedroom, her newfound sense of unease didn't seem to be getting worse.

One night Loren and I sat down on the couch and laid on the coffee table some wedding planning books I'd gotten from my sister. As we chatted about possible dates and locations, the hair on the back of my neck and my arms began to stand up, as if it were cold, but Loren seemed not to notice at all. I kept looking up into the corner. It felt like someone was there, staring at me. I caught bits of movement out of the corner of my eye when I looked away, but no matter how many times I looked up, there was nothing there except a vague feeling of dread.

"What do you keep looking at, honey?" Loren asked after he'd watch me repeat this process God knows how many times.

I just shook my head and focused on what we were doing, ignoring the presence in the corner. What made it worse, however, was that I could see Ceci just down the hall, her attention fully on that same corner. If there was nothing there, both my cat and I were having the same joint hallucination. Just the same, I wrote it off. Some sort of weird electromagnetic field. I'd heard somewhere that such fields could mess with your head, and some people were more sensitive to them than others.

Loren cheerfully continued on, leafing through a book and pointing out things he liked, completely oblivious.

The next morning I found the books scattered everywhere. I scolded Ceci, but as I began to pick them back up, I found my name scrawled on the back of one in handwriting that was barely legible. It looked how I might write with my left hand, out of practice and without real flow.

I stared at it for a long time. I hadn't written that. It wasn't Loren's handwriting, and I doubted Ceci had acquired the ability to properly hold a pencil. The writing utensil in question I eventually found under the couch, broken in half.

Things moved after that. It wasn't just noises anymore. Now cabinets would be left open, especially where you were most likely to hit your head on them. The wedding books would never stay in any sort of pile. If I put them on a bookcase, the next morning they would be on the floor. If I left them on the floor, they'd be spread out between the couch and the kitchen. Things that were carefully put away—necklaces, car keys—would end up on the floor of the coat closet.

And it wasn't just that. Oftentimes I would feel that presence, and it seemed to be less and less happy each time. Ceci began to hiss at nothing at all, and I found myself looking over my shoulder and spending more time outside of the house where the atmosphere was, well, safer.

At night I would wake from a dead sleep for no good reason and think I saw shadows moving. I was becoming grumpy and irritable, but how do you approach your fiancé—a perfectly nice, normal guy more concerned about whether you had a good day and how his favorite baseball team is doing than anything else—and ask him if his house is haunted without coming off like a loon? He wasn't home when a lot of the stuff happened and didn't seem to notice when it did.

Besides, I wasn't convinced myself. Ghosts were something you scared your friends with around campfires and read stories about under your covers at night to give yourself a bit of a thrill. They did not lurk in new, modern construction, which was probably not built on an Indian burial ground. There were plenty of logical explanations: overactive imagination, forgetfulness, wedding jitters, extremely ingenious and devious cat.

I kept things to myself.

Wedding plans progressed. I offhandedly brought up selling the house and moving somewhere else, using the old "new starting point for us to build our lives together" line, but Loren was happy where we were. I began to wonder if I had early onset dementia or schizophrenia or something. That was just as likely as some spirit from beyond hiding my keys.

In fact, I was seriously considering going in for a psych eval when something happened that changed my mind. At this point, the date had been set, a location had been chosen, attendants had been asked. Loren and I had spent the evening before looking at invitation designs online. I got up to go into the kitchen—I don't remember why, to get a drink or something like that—but I will never forget what happened next. As I slid my mug into the microwave and closed the door, a spoon flew out of nowhere and collided with the cabinet, inches from my head.

In the door of the microwave, beside my own reflection, was the image of another woman, fury written across her features. I spun around, but I was alone in the kitchen. A glance back at the microwave showed she was gone. I bent down, retrieving the spoon. It was bent from the impact with the cabinet. I was lucky it hadn't been my head. Not only that, but the spoon was ice cold.

That spoon didn't throw itself. I squared my shoulders and went into the living room. Loren looked up from the couch, smiling at me, though the smile faded as I approached. "Gwen? What's wrong?"

"Has anyone ever died in this house?" I felt silly even asking it, but wasn't that how ghosts were made? Something unfinished tied them to a location.

Loren stared at me, which did nothing to help. I twirled the spoon between my fingers while I debated retreating to the kitchen, except that woman could still be there, flinging deadly spoons. I pinched myself discreetly to see if I was asleep, but no such luck.

"Died?" Loren said eventually. "Not that I know of. Why?"

He seemed uncomfortable, but I had a freezing spoon in my hand that had been lobbed at my head by an unseen entity. "Do you ever get the feeling the house is, oh, I don't know, haunted?"

"Haunted?" He gave a feeble laugh. "Can't say that I have. Why?"

I was tempted to list off everything I'd noticed, but instead I murmured, "Never mind," and went to retrieve my drink.

Things died off for a bit after that. I'm not sure why—whether that spoon had taken all her energy or what—but we returned to random sounds and a neurotic cat, and I began to think that perhaps I had imagined it after all. Planning went so well without my books being shoved about that by the time the holidays rolled around, most of the big things were scheduled, and we were on to details like decorations and favors. Loren's parents invited us over to spend Christmas Eve with them. I'd met them a few times at various events, but this was the first real family sort of thing I'd been invited to share.

Loren's parents lived in a sizeable house in an upscale neighborhood. I couldn't help think that perhaps that's why Loren had a house of his own at his age and in this economy. His parents were very nice to me, taking time to ask me questions about myself and show me things they thought were important.

After dinner his mother had gotten out a photo album and was flipping idly through, pointing out pictures to me as they appealed to her, when I got the shock of my life. In one photo, the same woman I had seen reflected in my microwave stood next to Loren, smiling as she wrapped both arms around his shoulders.

"Who is that?" I asked.

"Oh, that's Diane," his mother replied.

"And who is Diane?" I managed to ask without sounding like an idiot.

"Loren's first wife. Surely he's told you about her? She died years ago in a car accident."

She continued on with her album, but I could no longer follow. After all these years, Loren had never told me he'd been married before. So what did that mean? Did he see her too, reflected in microwaves? Or did he just have an idea who it would be if someone was haunting the house?

I made it through the holidays without bringing it up, but I think everyone thought I was either sick or high the entire time.

I managed to wait until mid-January around noon on a Saturday when, hopefully, Diane would not be lurking. "When were you going to tell me that you were married before?" Perhaps not the best way to lead in, but straight to the point.

Loren looked for escape, but I think he took in my hands on my hips and decided it would not go well for him.

"I don't know," he said. "I felt like I should tell you early on, but there was never a good time, and then as things got more serious, it felt awkward that I had never brought it up, so I just...didn't."

"Do you see her too?" It wasn't the logical way to go, but who was I kidding? It's what mattered most to me. I wasn't crazy. The house was haunted, and not just by anyone, but by my fiancé's *dead wife*. Who, judging by the fact that my wedding books were, once again, scattered from here to Kingdom Come, was not so pleased that I was moving in on her man.

"I... well." Loren scratched the back of his neck. "How to answer that? I *think* I see her, out of the corner of my eye sometimes, but nothing concrete, nothing that couldn't just be my imagination." He stood, taking my hands. "Gwen, darling, I'm sorry I didn't tell you about Diane. I don't like to think about it. She died not long after our wedding, and we'd had a fight, and she'd gone out...and then she never came home."

I took a deep breath. "She needs to go. You need to help her pass on."

He didn't seem convinced. "I'll try," he said.

"She needs to go *now*." I said.

"Gwen," he said in a placating voice, "we don't even know if she's really here. And if she is…well, if she wants to be, is it really so bad?"

"I hate to tell you this, but two's a couple, and three's a crowd."

He sighed. "I don't want to hurt her."

"She's dead, Loren!"

We agreed to disagree, but the next day I found my wedding dress. I don't even want to think where the blood came from, especially when it had seemed to drain her so much with the spoon. The dress was a warning, and I was beginning to feel the same way—it was her or me, and I suspected I was losing. It's hard to fight against guilt.

I went to my mother's house and told her I just needed a place to sleep for a few days. Loren called after a few hours, but I didn't answer. I hid out in my old room and read some old books, feeling very blue. Was it so much to ask that my fiancé pick me over a ghost?

The thing was, I knew she wouldn't just go away. Things had gotten worse the closer we got to the wedding, and I couldn't believe she would give up. She had eternity on her side.

I realized I had left Ceci behind. Poor cat.

What were my options? I could try to send Diane on to the other side myself, though I couldn't count on Loren for any support, and I doubted she would listen to me. There were ways to force a ghost out, so I had heard, but if Loren wasn't even able to ask her to go, I couldn't imagine that would win me any brownie points.

I drifted in and out of sleep all night. Nothing disturbed me, but that was part of the problem. It was like I was expecting it. I finally dropped off early in the morning and awoke to Loren sitting on the edge of my bed.

"I thought it over," he said. "You're right. If she is there, it's selfish of me to not let her go, and I shouldn't lose you because of her. So I'll ask her to leave."

A short time later I was dressed, and we were back in the house. Ceci came running as I walked in, ducking behind my legs. Things were in a worse state than usual. Papers and books were scattered across the floor, and the curtains had been partially pulled down. If I didn't know better, I'd have thought we'd been burglarized.

Loren squared his shoulders and stepped into the middle of the room. "Diane," he said, "I want you to listen to me."

I stayed near the door. There seemed to be no difference in the room, but I could feel something in the air change that sent shivers down my spine.

"Diane, I don't know if you realize it, but you've passed on. You're dead. You've been dead for years. You need to move on. You need to go into the light."

The papers on the floor were rustling, and I could hear the cabinets in the kitchen opening and banging shut, like someone throwing a tantrum. The lights began to flicker. I scooped Ceci up and backed further into the corner.

"Don't stay here, Diane." Loren continued to talk to thin air, ignoring the growing chaos around him. "It's time for both of us to move on. Don't stay here because of me. I can take care of myself."

The coat closet door opened and slammed shut. I

jumped, clutching the cat to my chest. Above Loren the light bulb fizzled and died, and I could see Diane reflected in the sliding back door where there was no one in the room. She didn't seem at peace; her reflection was yelling and gesturing violently.

Loren looked more serious than I'd ever seen, his hands curled into determined fists as his dead wife swirled disorder around our living room. As I watched, one of the wedding books picked itself up off the floor and tore itself in half. "I love you, Diane, but this is no longer your home. I release you from your hold here. You *must* go."

As soon as the words were out of his mouth, everything stopped, books and paper halting their midair dance and plummeting to the floor. The curtains gave up their fight and succumbed to gravity. I caught a split second view of Diane smiling, but then she was gone. I let Ceci down slowly. She meowed and ran off, but it was a more playful run of old, not the fearful one she'd adopted lately.

I took a step forward, but even the feeling of the house had changed, resembling that of when I'd first moved in, when we were all happy. The relief was almost palpable. There were no creaks, no phantom footsteps. All was quiet.

We cleaned up the house. I slept through the night with no invisible visitors, and in the morning, my wedding books were where I'd left them.

Best of all, when I went to check on my wedding dress, the blood was gone, no sign that it had ever been.

I gave Loren a kiss on the cheek as I went out to go to the bank. "See, that wasn't so hard, was it?"

The answering smile was almost worth the last several months. "Thank you, Gwen. I needed that as much as she did."

"See you in a bit," I said and left.

I climbed into my car, turned the key and started down the road. A good song was on the radio. I turned it up and sang along, relishing my newfound liberty and the peace at home. Maybe I would bring home some flowers to help brighten the place up even more.

The air shifted abruptly, and a chill ran down my spine. Out of the corner of my eye, I thought I saw something move. I looked up into the rear view mirror.

Diane's reflection leered back at me.

The End

About the author:

Kit lives in Colorado with her husband and her increasingly neurotic cat. By night she torments the internet with landsquid and folding plesiosaurs. Occasionally, there is writing.

Shadow of a Black Cat

by Gerri Leen (Virginia, USA)

The black panther prowls, its cries carrying across the ground it covers, making those who hear it peer out of curtained windows and check that the doors are latched up tight. Horses and cows, locked in barns for the night, move nervously in their stalls.

In a town far south, a woman pauses at her dressing table, notices how insubstantial her room seems, how airy the corners, how evanescent the gaslight. She closes her eyes and focuses her will, imagining the room as it once was: elegant—the height of fashion in a house that was the model of sophistication, in a town that was one of the richest, busiest places in the region. Thurmond, West Virginia: her home for such a long time.

The big cat stops for a moment. He senses the fabric of the world shifting, feels the force of his mistress's will. He hears the wail that means the huge, roaring thing is coming. Loping easily, he makes his way to the rocks that overlook where it will pass. It appears out of the mists as if called.

The cat sniffs. There are no humans on it. And somehow the cat recognizes the wrongness of the thing, how out of place it is.

But this is not unusual.

The cat leaps aboard the rushing thing, lands on a cold, hard surface, like the rocks of the river he races past. He skids but stops before he slides off. Heart racing, yowling in triumph, the cat rides the roaring thing toward the woman who calls him, who brought him to life.

The woman finishes her hair, securing the last bit with a pin her husband has given her. It's a panther, black and sleek, and its eyes were emeralds that gleamed, but she has willed them to become topazes, and they shine copper now. She murmurs a word, calling on the spirit of the cougar as her grandmother taught her to do long ago, before her father took her away from her mother's people and told her never to mention she was part Shawnee.

There are no black cougars, but she needs one, and so one has been born. He prowls now where the Shawnee once hunted, brought to life by magic and will and terrible desperation.

She's been working on this for decades, and tonight, finally, she has remembered the words of her grandmother, Shawnee words that will bring the cat home and release her.

Her door opens. Her husband looks in on her. "Aren't you ready yet?"

She can see the outline of the doorframe through him, but he slowly solidifies. He is holding his gloves, slapping them hard into the palm of his hand.

Her back twinges with pain. Each slap of the glove finds an echoing mark from his riding crop. The blows were delivered methodically, as if he got no pleasure from hurting her.

That he can still hurt her, even now when they are both dead, is the worst of the wrongs she has been dealt.

"Mkateewa," she whispers, naming the cat. It means black in Shawnee, black like the New River that rushes by the town. She intends it to mean darkness and death and deep, swiping claws. She rises, ignoring the pain in her back as muslin slides over torn skin.

Her husband turns from her, as if in disgust. If there were still a town to go out to, he would be solicitous, gentle and tender in public, the best of all possible spouses. No one would ever know what happens behind these walls.

What happened—tenses are such a problem when you're dead.

"A black cougar was seen wandering the town," she murmurs as she rises.

"There's no such thing." He does not seem to realize that she is wearing one in her hair.

He definitely does not realize she has conjured one, that even now she can feel her cat riding the rails to this grand junction of lines and tracks.

There is no such thing as a black cougar. It is a satisfying thought. Only the unreal can free her from the inescapable. It is a puzzle she has put together.

The pin pulls her hair as she turns to look out the open window. She sees the town for what it really is, a faded, desolate place at night.

She hopes that after tonight she will never see it again.

The cat feels her pull. Even though the rushing thing frightens him, he stays on it, ignoring the vibrations and the trail of vapor that carries back to him a tangy scent smelling of things human. He hears the howl of a whistle, like the cry of a hawk, only louder, not quite the wail of a dying rabbit, but close in its ability to pierce the night.

The cat shivers, and he feels a warm touch on his fur. He hears her say "Mkateewa" and knows it is his name. He feels at once in two places, a small cat on this huge, rushing thing and an even smaller feline, clinging to hair that smells of sweet grass and berries. He sees a man, sees something white flapping in his hands.

The woman flinches with each flap, and the cat yowls in anger. His claws come out, pulling the hair tight, and he feels her pain.

The river turns white and wild. He hears it as he roars by, the wind carrying the sound of water hitting rocks, of owls hunting the darkness, of night swallowing up things that should not be.

But he is protected. He feels her will around him and around the rushing thing that should also not be. Sage smoke seems to carry them forward, the beat of a war drum matches his heartbeat, and her hand touches him again, in that second place, where she carries him with her, so high up. The cat digs into the hair again, but soon he will claw other things.

The woman flinches as the pin tears at her hair. It hurts more than she expected, but she consoles herself that it will hurt her husband even more. They walk slowly, death holding them back, keeping them from arriving at the door. Her husband doesn't know he's dead. She isn't sure why he doesn't know, but he thinks this is life, never questions, just fades away and then reappears for his nightly ritual.

Something...*other* controls this, but she can end it.

"You were lucky to find me," he murmurs. "Most men wouldn't put up with your past."

Her past.... Her father was a coal miner. He died in the mines, left her tied to the town, trying to pay off his debt. She was beautiful. She thought the fine gentleman who wanted to rescue her was her salvation, but he had only spotted the perfect victim, one who would never, ever leave him.

She thinks that if she had left him, he'd have hunted her down and killed her, but then she might have been free. If she had struck back at him, had shot him or stabbed him or poisoned his food, maybe whatever holds her here would have let her go.

But they died together, their beautiful house burning down around them, the locks fusing in the heat, initiating some hellish bargain to trap them together forever.

She hears the train coming, feels the pin rip a bit more in her hair.

The cat sees a huge thing crossing the river. It is like a hollowed-out log that a cub would crawl through, and he crouches as low as he can, growling as the rushing thing leaves the earth and flies through the air, into the log, over the water.

The log is not solid, and he can see the water through it. He begins to panic, but then the log is gone, and he sees a building. He leaps off the thing, feeling her near him.

The pin clatters to the floor, and the woman can smell the sweet grass of her grandmother's fields. She can hear the beat of her cousins' drums. She can see smoke curl like from the pipe her grandmother's brother smoked and knows it is the sacred dust that her impossible cat is raising as he rushes into the woods toward where the house stood before it burned.

Her husband bends down. The pin stabs him, and he sucks at his finger. Then he frowns. "Weren't these emeralds?"

The cat smells her. She is things old and things young and things hurt. She smells like the sacred doe that will never be caught, like the warrior who sits under the sun and waits for the coming dream. She called him forth. She holds his soul.

His soul lies on the floor. His soul has just stabbed the man she hates.

She smiles. "They were emeralds. They are something very different now."

To the cat, the man stinks of the rushing thing, of oily, dark places that smell close and dangerous, and he jumps through the open window to get closer.

The woman laughs as her cat lands on the floor near the fireplace. His eyes glow copper in the gaslight. His fur is blacker than jet, than coal, than the dark heart of her husband.

The cat does not hesitate. Hatred fills him, and he leaps, landing hard on the man. He sinks his claws into unreal flesh. He bites into veins that hold no life. He shakes the corpse of the dead man and tears at it until there is nothing left.

The woman sinks to the ground as her husband disappears—not fading out this time as he's done so many times before, but burning from the edges in, like a parchment held to a candle flame.

She can hear his screams as whatever hellish bargain he's made is finished.

The cat walks over to her, sniffing her, rubbing against her, marking her as his own. She smells good, and he allows her to pet him, even though she is making strange sounds, and his fur is wet from where she sets her face against him.

She forces herself to let Mkateewa go. "There are no black cougars, my great one. Not till now." She stands and, with a vicious stomp, breaks the pin in two. The vessel that holds the cat's soul is broken, and he is no longer under her control.

Yet, he does not attack.

The cat is confused. Her smell has changed, but he has ridden the rushing thing to get to her. He has crossed the broken log to save her. He lies down next to her feet and rests.

The woman smiles as she watches him lying so peacefully, but there is little time, and she has no desire to tarry in this ghost of a town. "My beauty, you must finish this before you become too real to kill me."

Her will is strong. He feels her calling him. Her touch on him is lighter now. Like the spring breeze through the leaves.

She bares her neck to him and closes her eyes. Her back no longer stings. Her husband's lash can never touch her again.

The cat lunges. She tastes of the downed elk, of the deep woods and mountain trees that give way to rock and snow, of bear and wolves and ravens that cry loud and long.

Her hands twist in his fur, and then she is gone.

He sees her fade. Like fog over the river. She is light and full of warmth, and he rolls in what is left of her until she is truly gone.

The house around him disappears. He lies in rubble, in a place that barely smells of anything human.

In the far distance he hears a ghostly wail, not quite the sound of a hawk, not quite the squeal of a dying rabbit. He pads away from the rushing thing that would carry him back to the mists.

The woman is gone, but he keeps the name she gave him. He is Mkateewa, the black cougar. He should not exist. He does anyway.

The End

About the author:

Gerri Leen is celebrating the release of her first book, *Life Without Crows*, a collection of short stories published by Hadley Rille Books. She has over fifty stories and poems published in such places as *She Nailed a Stake Through His Head*, *Sword and Sorceress XXIII*, *Return to Luna*, *Sniplits*, *Triangulation: Dark Glass*, *Footprints*, *Sails & Sorcery*, and *GlassFire*. Gerri lives in Northern Virginia and originally hails from Seattle. Visit http://www.gerrileen.com to see what else she's been up to.

E-pistles from the Gods

by John B. Rosenman (Virginia, USA)

IAGRA – ONLY $1.99 PER DOSE!
Lost the joy of sex? We're here to help you!
BE A STUD AGAIN! HERE'S HOW . . .

Granger grumbled as he scanned his morning spam. If only romance were so easy. His doctor had prescribed every pill and potion on the market for him, and nothing worked. Therapy had proved equally useless. When it came to sex and self-confidence, he was a dead battery, psychically drained by too many painful and humiliating relationships. He'd even had matchmakers in his congregation try to improve his love life, but each encounter had turned out to be a nightmare. Granger knew of fellow pastors who had married church secretaries and choir mistresses. Why couldn't he do the same?

MY NAME'S CINDY, AND I'M INTERESTED IN A HOT DATE!

"Un-unh, honey. You won't get it from me," Granger said. "Just ask any woman who ever went out with me."

His junk mail promised everything from "*Online Ordination*" and "*Genuine Replica Rolex Watches*" to "*Immediate Delivery*" of drugs and the chance to quit his job and make $200,000 a year at home. Granger shook his head in disgust. The only thing missing was the Nigerian Get-Rich-Quick pitch, and the day was still young yet. Despite all the spam blocks and filters he'd used, the Enemy's electronic excrement continued to pour in, befouling his inbox. Even the most sophisticated, cutting-edge programs he'd employed hadn't worked for long. Since the cost of reaching millions of customers was almost zero, spammers had an irresistible incentive to be resourceful.

Not, of course, that Granger ever parted with any cash or tried any online dating services. No, no, *never!* Despite his loneliness and limp libido, he still had his spiritual standards and would never sink so low as to pay for feminine companionship.

This dirt, this detestable, digital dung—it clogged up his machine as never before, and it required more and more time to winnow the chaff from the wheat. Some of the latter came from his parishioners seeking answers for their problems. As a preacher, Granger tried to serve his flock, and he was sick of the endless garbage, especially the porn that corrupted the young and weakened the nation's fiber. Just yesterday he accidentally summoned an obscene set of graphics that made him choke. If the government didn't clamp down soon, things would get completely out of control. Indeed, for some time he'd had a feeling that the Internet was on the verge of some terrible calamity. He didn't know what it was, but . . .

Several new bits of dreck came in. Granger lifted his finger, prepared to delete them.

ZEUS WANTS YOU!!!

Caught despite himself, he clicked on the message. What was this? He stared at the image of a majestic, white-bearded man in flowing robes who cast a lightning bolt in his direction. Flaming words announced his message.

WE OFFER A GREATER SELECTION . . . MORE BANG FOR YOUR SPIRITUAL BUCK! . . . WHY SETTLE FOR MONOTHEISM WHEN POLYTHEISM HAS DOZENS OF GODS TO CHOOSE FROM?

Frowning, Granger moved his cursor to the next message and opened it as well. At once he pulled back in shock and revulsion. A lurid, full-color picture showed a tentacled, Lovecraftian horror. Unmentionable eyes stared directly at him.

FORGET CHRISTIANITY . . . CHUTHLU AND HIS DREADFUL 'OLD ONES' WILL COME DIRECT TO YOUR DOORSTEP AND PUT THE BITE BACK IN YOUR WORSHIP!

Granger rose in disbelief, almost tipping his chair over. What kind of messages were these? He heard shouts and went to the window. Peering down, he saw a handsome youth in battle armor stride down the street as neighbors gawked. The youth held a spear cocked above his shoulder and was ten feet tall.

Ten feet tall?

Granger wiped his eyes and looked again. No, not ten feet, closer to twelve. What was happening to him? Was he going mad? His alarm increased when the figure halted and looked up at him, blond curls stirring in the breeze, so handsome, yet the face looked sly and impish. The face started to change, to *melt*. Then, within seconds, it reformed. Granger's mouth fell open. No, it couldn't be!

Outside, Granger's own face stared up at him, complete with acne scars and a receding chin. The creature smiled mockingly. "Loki, the God of Trickery, wants *you*!" the youth shouted and shook his spear.

Granger retreated quickly, his heart pounding. He *must* be mad... imagining things! That *thing* couldn't actually be out there, could it? But then he remembered the weird messages on his monitor: Zeus and Chuthulu... now Loki. Could there be a connection?

He sank to his knees. God in Heaven, he had expected something bad to come from the Internet, but hardly *this*! Was it possible that gods—all the divine or hellish beings humanity had ever conceived—had somehow taken form and were now using the Internet to invade and recruit? If so, it would be the ultimate commercialism! An image suddenly filled his mind of people throughout the world innocently clicking on these new messages and opening doors for all sorts of gods to enter this realm. Gods would pour through like a plague. They would be a new, more terrible kind of virus, a Pandora's Box that could never be closed.

More shouts came from outside. This time he heard high-pitched screams punctuated by riotous laughter. Their meaning was now inescapable.

Monstrous invaders from the Internet were on his

street.

Murmuring a prayer, Granger raced from the room and flew down the stairs. Please God—or gods—let him be wrong!

But he wasn't.

Reaching his front lawn, he was just in time to see an improbable procession approach. A gross, nearly naked man rode a white ass and sang some crude song. Granger saw him raise a wine cup and empty it in a single gulp. Even more amazing, the rider was accompanied by a rowdy crowd of centaurs, satyrs and nymphs, not to mention drunken young men and women who pawed each other and drank from bottles and wineskins.

"The Romans called him Bacchus," a stunned voice said, "the Greeks, Dionysus."

Granger tore his gaze away and recognized his neighbor Heller, an anthropology professor at a local college.

"What?" he asked.

Heller nodded at the fat man who was laughing uproariously. "The god of wine," he said. "According to legend, he seduced innocent youths and virgins with the grape."

Bacchus's booming voice drowned him out. Granger tried to make out the words, but it seemed to be some kind of Latin chant. If only he'd studied the language more in the seminary!

Suddenly the god's words changed into English. "DRINK!" he shouted. "DRINK AND DRINK AND DRINK SOME MORE! CELEBRATE AND COPULATE! COPULATE AND MULTIPLY! HELP THE SPRING CROPS TO GROW! ENJOY THE VINE'S SACRED FRUIT!"

His words caused a frenzy among his followers. Granger saw couples rip off their clothes and race to lawns where they rolled naked on the grass, following Bacchus's instructions. Nor was that all; some of his middle-class neighbors pressed forward and received flasks from the wine god's hands.

"DRINK!" he exhorted, splashing wine on the street as he drunkenly waved his cup. "BE AS FRUITFUL AS THE PREGNANT VINE!" He belched then roared with lusty, infectious laughter. Seeing the god hold out a goblet of wine to him, Granger pulled back, resisting the temptation. But Mrs. Holsom, a pious member of his congregation, elbowed him rudely aside and moved toward Bacchus.

"Stop! It's a sin!" Granger clutched at her, but she shook him off and claimed the prize. Glancing about, he saw that each of these fools had surrendered to this false, pagan god, this drunken abomination.

A shrill woman's scream split the air.

He swung to Heller who was drinking wine. "Did you hear that?"

"W-What?"

"Never mind!" As Bacchus and his retinue passed, Granger ran down the street in the direction from which the scream had come. Whoever the woman was, she sounded as if she was in deep trouble, and he knew he must help.

As he ran, people scampered excitedly in all directions, drawn to this or that supernatural attraction. Between some houses he glimpsed a tall, birdlike creature on the next street: an ancient Egyptian god, perhaps?

Swinging left at the intersection, Granger felt a massive, winged shape pass overhead. He looked then tore his eyes away. Horrible! Granger raced on. These creatures could be all over the world by now. What did they want? But he knew the answer. The gods wanted the same thing any salesman wanted. They wanted you to buy their product, to lay down your worldly goods for what they had to sell. But there were important differences. Unlike standard hucksters, the gods *were* the products, and they wanted you to fear and worship them, perhaps even offer sacrifices to prove your loyalty.

And if you refused them? Or swore loyalty to another god, perhaps a competitor? Weren't most gods inherently jealous and, in their own way, possessive?

The woman's scream sounded again, much closer. He redoubled his efforts, entering the local school's baseball field. He noticed it was ringed by a crowd of people, all gazing up.

He slammed to a halt and looked skyward to see a gigantic, dragon-like creature.

Descending.

Toward him.

Granger staggered back, narrowly escaping the lethal talons as they came down. Unlike Bacchus, this god was awe-inspiring. It looked like a plumed serpent with shimmering, multicolored scales. Bright feathers blazed about its neck and head.

"Watch out!" someone screamed, pointing at the bulging turf at Granger's feet.

Granger darted sideways just as the ground erupted. A giant with a bear-like face rose from the earth. The face was striped yellow and black. Of more interest, though, was the beautiful, half-naked woman the monster clutched.

She screamed.

Granger gulped. It was the same scream he'd heard

before, but now he realized it wasn't from terror. No, judging from her lustful expression, it was another emotion entirely.

The giant set the woman down. Her breasts heaving, she danced excitedly about, watching the two gods in fascination.

The gods pawed the ground, flexed their muscles and squared off against each other. They charged, clashed, grappled, howled and leapt apart. The serpent fanned its wings and neck feathers in warning. The bear-faced giant gnashed six-inch fangs.

Coming closer, the crowd *ooohed* and *aaahed*, laughed and clapped their hands. Granger saw several parents raise children to their shoulders so they could see better. The huge combatants circled each other. The serpent released a hellish squawk, his opponent, a guttural roar. They braced themselves, pawed the earth some more, preparing to attack. Then they straightened, threw their hands up into the air and sent thousands of sparks skyward. A moment later dazzling, rippling sheets descended. Granger reached out and caught one. It was a poster, a full yard square, and it bore bright, garish lettering.

QUETZALCOATL – God of the Wind and the Master of Life,
and . . .
TETZCATLIPOCA – God of War, the Sun, and the Moon,
Cordially invite you to witness the renewal of their bitter and ancient enmity at their Brand New Temple, this city's Coliseum, on Saturday at 8:00 pm.
See . . .
The Master of life bring rain and fertility,

E-PISTLES FROM THE GODS

The gift of fire,
And open the Earth's treasure chest of gold, silver and
precious gems!
See . . .
His dreaded adversary, the Master of Discord, tear out the
bleeding hearts of virgins to satisfy his ravenous appetite,
Rape Queztalcoatl's delectable nieces and turn man
against man in bloody, greedy war!
FREE DOOR PRIZES! FREE REFRESHMENTS!
PLUS A FREE DRAWING
For the Ladies . . . 10 free diamond bracelets!
For the Men . . . 10 free brand new SUV's!
Come One . . . Come All!

All across the field Granger saw people catch the posters and read them. An excited jabber rose. Children squealed, jumping up and down.

Come One . . . Come All!

Then something happened. Granger saw the two towering gods flicker, as if about to vanish. Quetzalcoatl's plumed head actually did. Then both gods were whole and solid again, as real as he was. *Only they weren't, were they? At least not quite,* he thought.

Spotting the mayor's assistant nearby, Granger raced to him. "Godwin," he said, "we've got to turn off the power!"

"Huh?" Godwin clutched the poster in both hands and studied it closely. "A free SUV! I wonder if it's an Explorer."

"Godwin," Granger pressed, "we've got to stop this."

Godwin's eyes skittered away from his. They

focused on the two gods as if hypnotized. "Twenty free prizes," he crooned in ecstasy. "Holy cow, maybe my wife can win one too."

Granger raised his hand then hesitated. He was a man of God and hated violence. Still, he had no choice.

He slapped Godwin then shook his shoulders. "Listen to me! It's an invasion. These creatures came through the Internet, and if we don't stop them, they'll take us over!"

"Unh," Godwin said. "Don't you think you're over-"

"No, I don't!" He resisted the urge to slap him again. "Listen, you've got to listen! I just saw these two flicker. That means they're dependent on power, on electricity, and the connection isn't completely stable. If we can turn it off . . ."

Sanity struggled back into Godwin's face. "The power plant. I'll call, tell them to turn off the city generators!"

"Do it now! And contact other cities too!" He watched Godwin pull out his cell phone then remembered something. He had left his computer on! Who knew what celestial or demonic con artists were about to cross over? He thought of Zeus and his lightning bolt.

ZEUS WANTS YOU!!!

Turning, he broke into a run. Three blocks to his house . . . two . . .

He reached his house at last and dashed up the stairs, determined to turn his computer off. No false god was going to come out of his machine.

But when he burst into his study, he gasped.

A beautiful, *nearly naked* blonde sat before his computer. She wore only high heels, bright red garters, and black, fishnet stockings that accentuated her sleek, alabaster thighs.

Granger's heart climbed into his throat.

The woman swung toward him on his chair. "Hello, Granger," she said. Her sweet voice was like a caress.

He swallowed, trying not to gaze at her exquisite, peerless body. Such lush breasts, such sculpted legs. "You . . . you're Venus, aren't you?"

"I prefer to be called Aphrodite," she said. "Either way, it's the Goddess of Love, at your service." She smiled and coyly teased an erect nipple. "Incidentally, we deactivated Godwin's cell phone, so he never got through to the power plant."

"It's too late, isn't it?" Granger said. "You've harnessed the Internet and crossed over."

"Yes," she said, "we're everywhere. It's a glorious new age. *We* will conquer you, and *we* will be in control. Forever. And here's an epistle for you. You pious preachers have had your chance. No more hymns or hosannas, hounded heretics or holy wars. Now it's *our* turn, and we'll do a better job than you ever did. From now on, it's going to be harmony rather than hate, happiness instead of holocausts."

A great roar split the city and rattled the house. Granger rushed to the window and looked out. Two colossal figures perhaps five hundred feet tall were locked in fierce combat about a mile off. As he watched, buildings crumbled and people screamed.

"Maybe it's not a glorious new age at all," Granger said. "The problem with you gods is that you're too greedy. Like salesmen everywhere, you don't like competition." He turned back to her. "Sooner or later, you'll attack and destroy each other."

She smiled. "Oh no, *we* won't. *They* will."

"They?"

"The boys."

It took him a moment to get it. "The male gods?"

"Yes. We—the goddesses—came up with the plan. Only we made them think it was *their* idea to use the Internet to open up a new market." She laughed as more roars sounded. "We'll just let the boys duke it out amongst themselves, and then, when they're all bloody and beaten, *we* will take over."

"These goddesses... who are they?"

Her smile turned wicked. "Why, all the divine females you humans ever imagined, from all times and places. From fruitful Freya and Isis and Oshun and Amaterasu to warlike Kali and Sekhmet and Oya and Macha." She winked. "We're taking over, Grange my boy. Taking over *everything*."

She rose from the chair and slinked toward him with a seductive smile.

He threw up a hand. "Stop! I... don't want what you're selling."

She raised her eyebrow but obeyed. "How do you know, Granger?"

"I just do. You're wasting your time." He nodded toward the window. "None of you junk gods can sell me anything, no matter how hard you try."

"But I'm not selling, Granger," she said. "I'm giving." She glided toward him with feline grace. "And I don't even ask you to believe in me. I'll believe in *you*."

He backed away in confusion. He must not be ensnared by her and led astray. "Nice try," he said hoarsely, "but it won't work. Truth is, I believe in a better god, a *much* better, truer god." He glanced at her tantalizing body, feeling as if he had narrowly eluded her spell. "My g-god doesn't need such ch-cheap tricks."

She crept closer, her lovely green eyes fixed on his. "Your god may be good," she purred, "but give me a chance. Are you completely happy, Granger?"

"Yes. Yes, of course. What-"

"Tell me about women." She licked her lips, watching him.

"Women?"

Her hypnotic gaze seemed to probe his soul. "Tell me, Granger." Her voice now had a dark, husky tone.

He swallowed. "I've... uh, had a few bad relationships."

"How bad?"

He trembled, determined not to say any more. But his lips opened as if conjured. "The last woman really hurt me. I . . . I'm impotent. I've tried for years, but nothing has helped. Pills, therapy, it's all been useless."

Aphrodite's eyes caressed his body, making him feel naked. "Do you know why I came to *your* house?" she asked, her voice dark music that stirred his blood. "It's because I like a challenge."

"Forget it," he said thickly. "It... would be a waste of your time."

"Maybe you haven't tried the right woman."

"Oh yes, I have. I've tried everything."

The goddess reached out and touched his arm. It felt like fire. "I can make you whole, Granger. I can turn you into a new man."

He swallowed. "It's no use," he said, feeling a strange fever surge through his body, reminding him of something he hadn't known in a long time. "I'm impotent, I tell you. Totally. Nothing can help me."

She frowned then dropped her gaze below his waist. He saw her eyes widen in surprise. "Are you sure?" she said, moving to embrace him.

The End

About the author:

John recently retired as an English professor at Norfolk State University where he designed and taught a course in how to write Science fiction and Fantasy. He is a former Chairman of the Board of the Horror Writers Association and has published approximately 350 stories in places such as *Weird Tales, Whitley Strieber's Aliens, Fangoria, Galaxy, The Age of Wonders*, and the *Hot Blood* anthology series. John has published over a dozen books, including SF action-adventure novels such as *Beyond Those Distant Stars* and *Speaker of the Shakk* (Mundania Press), *A Senseless Act of Beauty* (Crossroad Press), and *Alien Dreams* (Drollerie Press). Shorter books include *A Mingling of Souls* and *Music Man* (XoXo Publishing), *Here Be Dragons* (Eternal Press), *The Voice of Many Waters* (Blue Leaf Publications), *Green in Our Souls* (Damnation Books), and *Bagonoun's Wonderful Songbird* and *Childhood's Day* (Gypsy Shadow Publishing). Recent developments: MuseItUp Publishing contracted for three novels, *Dark Wizard; Dax Rigby, War Correspondent*; and *Inspector of the Cross*, and two stories, *More Stately Mansions* and *The Blue of Her Hair, the Gold of Her Eyes*.
http://www.johnrosenman.com
http://www.myspace.com/291520102

https://twitter.com/Writerman1
http://www.facebook.com/home.php and
http://s631.photobucket.com/albums/uu31/jrosenman

Read an interview at:
http://www.milscifi.com/archives/arc-JohnBRosenman.htm

A Heart Full of Love

by Anne Marie (Colorado, USA)

rowing up I longed for the day I would become a man. For when we are men we're allowed to wander into the human world. Until that day, it exists only in legends and stories told at darkest night by those who have witnessed it. Now that day is here, and I don't know what I long for, because becoming a man also means being bound to a girl in marriage. Why have a wife when I don't know if I want to grow up at all? I'm too young. Even after sixteen summers, I'm too young. The ceremonial drums that indicate my boyhood has passed are thrumming through the village. The sound calls for me and me alone. They echo the beat of my heart.

Women and children are always kept away from this ceremony, though I never bothered to ask why. It's a conclave of men and the initiate. Still, we children know something of what occurs inside the Okizi House. We know the stories—passed down from our ancestors—of the sacred pot. Every woman in our village has in her possession a sacred pot. It's meant to hold her husband's heart while he's gone. In this way, the men can't die alone and far from home. Our fathers, when they are home, are cold and stoic. They don't smile or laugh as the boys of our village do: another reason I want to stay a boy. I don't want to lose the spark that lights me up inside like a thousand campfires.

"Estofis," my mother calls. She's beautiful, though worn by time. "We must go."

Why should my mother be made to take me to the ritual? Shouldn't my father, brave and strong, lead me himself? He could explain what was coming as we walked to the beat of the drums. But they—the Elders—make our mothers do it. Is it because this is the last time we will truly love our mothers? For without our hearts, how can we ever love anyone at all?

She takes my hand. Her firm grip tells me all I need to know. I would follow my mother into Elkv's domain if she led me. My father may be my leader and guide, but my mother is my life and soul. Our two figures throw long shadows in front of us. The beginning part of the ceremony must be held in exact twilight. It's the only time that the Great Spirit walks among the Men of Maka. Only he can protect me from certain death.

The drums are louder when she opens the long flap of the tipi. "Take with you, my son, all the lessons I have taught you. I will never stop loving you."

"Thank you, Mother." I reach to embrace her. She holds me close, tight, and releases me too quickly. Only the smell of her, like golden astrea growing wild on the hillside near our village, lingers in the air.

I enter the tipi alone and shivering. The flap shuts behind me. From inside I can hear her tying the long leather thongs. My mother will remain at the entrance. If anyone or anything endangers those within, she will kill them without hesitation, for all the men of our village are at their weakest here in the Okizi House. Their hearts and our magic source are here.

My eyes are drawn to the center of the tipi where a deeply dug pit filled with ashes, stones and new logs roars with fire. The wood burns red hot, crackling when the fire hits an air pocket. The ashes stir up and float above me like feathers of a newborn chick on a summer's breeze. The air is thick and smoky with sage that wraps around me and seeps into my pores. Sweat beads at my forehead and runs down my shoulders and along my spine.

I have worn only what is required of me: darkly woven pants. The women of the village began weaving them the night of my birth. Each strand of hand-dyed cotton was touched by an elder woman. Each strand contains their wishes and hopes for my future. Each strand is meant to prove I'm ready to become a man and join the Elders with my father and his father.

It's then that I see I'm not alone here. A hum begins among the men sitting around the fire. They're masked, hiding their identities from me. My father is among them. He's required to lead the ceremony, but I can't yet tell which one is him. The hum crescendos into *messa di voce*. The pulses intensify and fade, only to start the process over and over. One voice spins and winds among the others, and I know it belongs to my father.

The sound soothes me. It puts me into a kind of trance. My vision wavers. In the eerie light of the flickering fire, a girl comes into view. At first I believe it's an illusion brought on by the smoke and fear. She's dressed in the ceremonial garb of marriage, her silhouette darkly outlined by the firelight. Her long black hair is sleek and plaited with beads and bones. When she steps closer, I see a smile that lights up her face. It could melt a thousand winters. My heart swells with every step she takes closer to me. Even the small scar that draws a red line from her mouth towards her ear endears her to everyone who looks at her. Her name is Pakpvketv.

She's a few years younger than I am. This girl has been the object of my friends' and my fantasies for many moons. I knew she neared the age of marriage, but never did I think I would call her wife. Her father and mother lead our people, meting out honor and punishment as is required of them. I shudder a little, knowing that great things will be expected of me... and of her.

Pakpvketv reaches her hand out, breathes my name, "Estofis," like a word of power... like magic. I take her hand in mine and feel the heat from our bodies entwine like lovers. It takes only seconds to know I will belong to her until my dying day. The sparkle in her eyes tells me she feels the same way. Gently, hesitantly, she moves even closer, the scar on her face softening as the firelight halos her head.

My fingers stroke that line. Her eyelashes flutter closed. I bend down to kiss them. Before I'm allowed to claim her mouth with my own, I'm pulled from her. She releases my hand, and I look down, disbelieving I touched her at all. Her smile remains, though it is tinged with regret. The strong hands that hold me push me down to the ground. They bind my arms above my head. My legs are restrained by the masked men who have not stopped their trance-inducing chant.

Someone pulls a thick glove woven with serpent magic onto Pakpvketv's delicate hand. Slower than I can remember anyone moving before, Pakpvketv reaches down into the fire and removes a knife. Its long blade burns white hot. The hilt of it must burn too, but the glove protects her flesh. The smell of pliable metal awaiting the hammer sizzles in the air like a stolen kiss, too hot and dripping with desire.

Lines of paint are drawn onto my exposed chest. The sensation of fingers on my skin lulls my fears, and I can't explain why I bend to their wills. Have I lost myself to Pakpvketv's smile already? One of the men—probably my father—places the sacred pot near my side. The light from the fire reveals its pattern. It matches that of my pants. My father began to paint my sacred pot the night I was born. I'm too busy wondering at how one man could be so intrinsically connected to the village's elder women to notice that Pakpvketv is standing next to him, the knife's fiery glow illuminating her face. He's whispering something into her ear, and she's nodding while a tear escapes her long dark lashes and falls down her cheek. The chanting makes it impossible for me to hear anything, but I know what to expect.

But it's all I can do *not* to focus on the glowing knife as it is lowered closer and closer to my painted flesh. I don't feel the first slice. It's the stench of burning flesh rising to my nose that makes the pain a thumping, burning, living thing. If I were not becoming a man today, I would scream. If I did scream, the chants of the men would drown out all my intentions. Realizing this, I do scream. It's not manly. It's not becoming. It's all that I have left.

Pakpvketv moves the burning hot iron from one side of my ribs to the other, just below my breastbone and through layers of skin, tendon and muscle. Once done, she hands the knife to a man who disappears with it. The snakeskin glove is removed. I'm afraid to watch what she'll do with that delicate, sienna hand. Her soft hand slides into the incision she has so deftly made. It pushes up past my lungs. The slithering feel reminds me of an eel. The pain makes me retch. I feel a tug at my heart. It beats in time with the drumming until it stops all together.

She wraps her hand easily around the organ and pulls once more. My traitorous heart disengages ventricles and arteries, which close like a salamander's stump when a limb has been torn free or eaten. Their purpose is fulfilled after sixteen summers of joyful boyhood. In the hole where my heart should be, Pakpvketv places something that pushes against my lungs and sends ice through my veins. The men continue chanting, masking out my screams into the gathering dusk.

After that, I pass out. When I wake in the Okizi House, there's no burning fire pit. There are no men in masks. There's only Pakpvketv. She wears a simple brown shift. Her hair is still plaited with bones and beads, but she's wound the plaits around her head and off her neck. To me she looks like a younger version of Earth Mother. Remembering that she's my wife, a swell of pride fills me. For a moment I'm terrified that I can feel such things without a heart.

"Estofis," she says. Her hands are clean, sitting atop the sacred pot in her lap. "Husband."

I sit up. A noise like that of dried snakeskin being rubbed together follows. My hand moves instinctively to the slash across my chest. It's still there. The raw edges are like charred wood: blackened and rough. Though there's no pain, the cold stoicism must not be far off. I grimace at this.

"Wife," I reply, reaching for her before I become empty.

That radiant smile returns. If I had a heart, I would say it leapt. My heart now sits in the sacred pot, but something inside me does turn over. The earth moves when she is near.

"We don't have much time before the ritual is complete," she says. She places her sacred pot—for it no longer belongs to anyone but her—on the ground by her side. Instead of standing, she walks on her hands and knees towards me.

The girls of our village must be taught what they're expected to do before the ceremony actually takes place. It's only the men that are left in the darkness of boyhood. Pakpvketv takes me places I have never been before physically or emotionally, especially when I'm above her and her hair is loose, fanning out around her head.

Our first union is over quicker than I would have liked. The thing that keeps me from shame is the knowledge that we're bound together now for eternity. She sleeps beside me. Our chests rise and fall in perfect unison. I place my hand over her breast. The sturdy thumping of her heart brings me peace in the absence of my own heartbeat.

In the morning I will wake with her at my side. She'll be my wife, and I'll be her husband, but the perfect serenity of this first night together will have vanished as quickly as morning dew.

The End

About the author:

Anne was born and raised in Colorado where she currently resides with her beagle Brody. She's a servant of folklore and mythology from around the world. She loves great white sharks, languages and the impossible. Currently, she's working on a YA paranormal that involves most of the above. You can follow her on Twitter: @annemariewrites.

Shadow Games

By L Young (Auckland, New Zealand)

*M*anus jolted awake from another nightmare, his sister's pleas still echoing in his head. It was still dark. Looking around through the bars of his prison wagon, he saw the convoy had halted at a crossroads. Tightly packed trees lined the road, their scent reminding him of his home in Britannia.

Across from him his fellow captive Durano rubbed his eyelids. "We in Corvem?"

"I don't know," replied Manus, watching Laxus, his owner and his trainer, jump off the lead wagon. Laxus glared at the unpaved crossroad before them. "So we're lost?"

Despite being bigger and heavier than the short, rotund Laxus, Tiberius wilted under his tirade. "They were your directions."

That shut Laxus up. He peered around the darkness, as if expecting to be assailed by bandits. "These damn backward provinces and their roads. We'll have to wait till morning. The magistrate will not be happy at our late arrival for the games."

"Can I help you?"

The female voice in the darkness caught everyone's attention. Manus watched a short, hooded figure—a basket in one hand and a lantern in the other—step into the torchlight. She set the basket down and drew back her hood, revealing a plump, pretty face with a small, slightly up-turned nose and a head topped with tied-back red hair.

Laxus smiled. "My dear, wherever did you come from?"

"My master has a villa just down the road," she replied. "Your men are gladiators?"

"The best," replied Laxus. "Culled from the most brutal races in the Empire."

She smiled. "My master's a big admirer of gladiators. I'm sure if your men put on an exhibition fight for him, he'd be happy to provide lodgings for you."

Manus repressed a sigh. Still drowsy, the last thing he wanted was a fight.

"That'd be most helpful," replied Laxus. "We're on our way to Corvem but somehow got lost."

The girl nodded. "These roads are confusing to outsiders."

"What are you doing out here alone?" asked Laxus.

She patted her basket. "I'm on my way home."

The excuse sounded phony to Manus, but Laxus appeared to accept it at face value. "Of course.... I'm sorry, I didn't get your name."

"Alke." She gestured down the road. "Shall we go?"

"Lead the way."

Alke guided the small convoy down the road. While Tiberius took the reins, Laxus walked beside Alke. Manus recognised that look. If the girl was lucky, her master kept her close, if not, Laxus would be doing all he could to convince him to let him have her for the night--a deal that would no doubt involve Manus and his comrades shedding more blood.

The villa shone out in the darkness. It was more impressive than Manus expected, being at least two stories tall and surrounded by a large, stone wall. The wall encircling the compound appeared incredibly smooth, making it impossible to climb to freedom. An imposing wooden gate, overseen by a watchtower, marked the entrance. Beside the gate a pair of guards watched their approach. The men were dressed in a simplified form of the Roman Army's scaled armour, topped by a Greek style helmet that covered much of their face.

Alke left Laxus' side and whispered something to them. The guards signaled the watchtower, and the gate was wheeled open.

Manus sat up as the convoy manoeuvred itself into a massive stone courtyard. To one side stood a tall arena-shaped building, and on the other sat a squat prison-like building. Positioned between both stood the villa, its fine marble furnishings and statues indicating its owner's wealth.

The wagons had barely halted when a tall man with short black hair and a finely trimmed beard stepped out of his home. His well-built physique was evident even under the loose folds of the purple toga. The man clapped his hands together and made his way down the short flight of stairs. "I am Adelfred. Welcome."

Manus' ears picked up at the Germanic sounding name, and he could tell Laxus was equally surprised. Maybe the man was an exiled tribe leader living off the

Roman purse, but as far as Manus knew, only Emperors wore such garments.

Overcoming his surprise, Laxus bowed as low as his body allowed. "I'm Calus Laxus of the House of Laxus. Thank you for the welcome."

"It's an honour to meet such a famous gladiator owner."

Laxus preened. "You've heard of me?"

"I keep track of all the Empire's best fighters," replied Adelfred. "Even out here."

Adelfred cast his eye over the carriages. Though used to being treated like cattle, Manus found himself unnerved by something in Adelfred's gaze. Tapping on Manus' cage, Adelfred said, "You have some magnificent examples here. I'll enjoy seeing them fight."

"Your slave did mention a small exhibition match in return for lodgings," said Laxus.

Adelfred laughed, patting Alke on the head. Manus saw the briefest of frowns cross her face. "I fear she has misled you. All fights here are to the death."

Laxus raised his hand. "I'm sorry. I appreciate the accommodation, but I can't afford to have any of my fighters killed." He smiled thinly. "At least not without compensation."

Adelfred slapped him on the shoulder. "I would expect nothing less from a true Roman. Turious!"

A dark skinned man stomped forward holding a massive wooden box. Adelfred opened it to reveal a small fortune in gold and jewels. "If any of your Gladiators survives a fight in the arena, this is yours."

While all Manus heard was the statement, *if any of your men survive,* all Laxus appeared worried about was the box. Once again Manus felt like an ox being taken to slaughter.

Laxus raised an eyebrow. "How do I know you will honor your agreement?"

Adelfred's hand lashed out, wrapping around Laxus' throat. Tiberious and Laxus' other men moved to grab their weapons, but Adelfred's men grabbed theirs just a bit faster.

"You question my word, Roman? If I wanted you dead, you would be. Unlike your people, when I make an agreement, I keep to it."

He dropped Laxus to the ground. "All this gold is yours if your men survive, but if they fail." He muttered something incomprehensible, and lightning sprang from his fingers, enveloping Tiberius and Laxus' other guards. Their burnt corpses tumbled to the ground. As the smell of charred flesh wafted back to them, Durano crawled to the far side of the cage muttering, "Damn, damn, damn."

"That's no way to die," replied Manus, feeling bile rising to the top of his throat.

Squealing, Laxus ran for the gate, oblivious of the fact it was already closed. Two of Adelfred's men intercepted him, dragging him kicking and screaming back to their master.

"What are you?" said Laxus.

Adelfred laughed. "The man offering you a fortune. My deal is still open, dog."

Laxus paled. "Who am I to refuse?"

Adelfred slapped him on the shoulder. "I knew you'd see things my way. Come. You can watch the battles with me in my arena."

As Laxus was led away, the gate to the large building on the left opened, and Adelfred's men escorted the wagons forward.

"I don't like this," said Durano, shaking his head.

Manus forced a smile as they entered the tunnel, its darkness closing in on them. "Easy. You have to keep your wits."

Under Alke's watchful gaze, the guards ushered the gladiators from their wagons. Manus warily got up from his resting spot as they wheeled open his cage door. Leaping down, he slowly took in his new surroundings, but the grey stone of the chamber revealed nothing. He felt the wooden end of a spear being jabbed in his back. Reddening, he spun around and got the sharp end pointed at his face.

"Move!" growled the Guard.

Manus frowned. *You'll get yours soon enough*, he thought.

The guards herded them into a row then, with liberal jabs to their sides, escorting them to another room filled with cages of various sizes. They were guided to the largest cage where wooden seats lined the wall. Manus noted the dried blood staining the floor. As the last gladiator entered, the guards brought in several of their wooden trunks containing their armour and gear, minus their weapons.

The men helped each other strap on their armour. By unconscious consent no one spoke about what was going on. Talking about it would mean acknowledging it was really happening. They took their seats silently and wondered what awaited them in the arena.

One by one Alke led the gladiators out into the arena. Normally all one heard was the cheers of the crowd, but here they heard the screams of the fighters and other sounds that defied description. So far no one who'd left had come back, leaving just Manus and Durano alone in the waiting area. That might mean nothing, thought Manus—or everything.

As he often did before a bout, Durano tapped his feet repeatedly. Manus tried to calm him. "Easy, mate. Don't want to wear yourself out before the fight even starts."

Durano shook his head. "How can you be so calm?"

Manus smiled, "I'm not calm my friend. But there's no point in worrying till you get out there."

"I'm fine once I get out there. It's the waiting I can't stand."

The arena door opened, and Alke returned. She pointed at Durano. "Your turn."

Manus extended his hand. "Remember to leave some for me."

Grasping it in return, Durano forced a smile. "No promises."

Durano disappeared into the tunnel, leaving Manus alone with his thoughts. The walls began closing in on him. In the dark, stark images flashed in his mind of his brothers and father lying dead on the ground, their entrails sprawled around them. Their deaths were bad enough, but their failure on the battlefield had left their homeland wide open to the Romans and Roman depredations. He remembered seeing his younger brothers and sisters being taken away. He'd vowed to find and free them. But even in those rare moments when he allowed himself to imagine the thought of buying his freedom or even escaping, it wasn't long before he wondered where he would even start.

The door opened, and Durano stumbled back inside. Sweat shining from his bald head, veins popping from his tensed up muscles, he was covered in blood and sporting a dazed war-worn look in his eyes. Even on his worst days in the arena, Manus had never seen him look that bad.

"Are you alright? What's out there?"

Durano shook his head. "I don't know what it was."

Manus wanted to ask more, but Durano sported a glazed look that didn't invite questions.

"Lucky last," said Alke.

"What's going to happen to him?" asked Manus.

"He'll be looked after. I promise."

She sounded sincere. Slightly mollified, Manus spared Durano one final glance. The door opened up, and they made their way into another room filled with weapon racks. Usually there were guards, but here it was just the girl. Alke gestured for him to take a weapon. He picked one out, a standard Roman gladius, the weapon he'd become most used to in the arena. Tightening his grip on the sword, he said, "I don't suppose you'd be any good as a hostage?"

She laughed softly. "He'll simply kill us both."

Manus tried to sound uncaring. "You think that scares me?"

A wistful expression came over her face. "There are worse things than death."

It was a fact Manus had become well acquainted with in recent years. "What are my odds?

Her smile disappeared. "Just remember, whatever you face out there can be defeated if you keep your head." The door to the arena opened up. "Good luck."

Manus took a deep breath and made his way out of the tunnel. The arena was massive yet stark with its emptiness. As he crossed the threshold, night turned to day. "By Taranis," he muttered.

A single spectator box occupied by Adelfred, Laxus and several slaves looked out over the killing ground.

Adelfred's voice echoed down to him. "Fight well, Gladiator, and you will receive riches beyond your imagination. Fight poorly and your reward will be equally fitting."

The massive door on the far side of the arena creaked open. Manus' eyes widened as his opponent edged out.

It looked like a beast from stories his father used to tell. Covered in shiny red scales, it resembled an overgrown lizard. Manus estimated it to be at least twenty feet long and six feet tall. He made a quick prayer to Taranis and hoped for once the god was listening.

The beast turned its spiked, oversized head at him, studying him with its large golden eyes. Roaring, it charged. Gripping his sword, Manus advanced to meet it. When it was just a few feet away, he leapt on its head, wincing as he felt a spine stick into his leg. Scrambling up its back, he stabbed his blade into its spine, blood spurting out.

Its long, snakelike tail twisted up and wrapped around Manus' chest, trapping one of his arms. He slashed down, cutting the tail in half. As the tail released him, he fell to the sand and rolled to his feet. Jerking his head around, he saw the beast bearing down on him. He dived beneath its head, and the ground shook as it galloped over him.

Rolling to the side, he swung out his blade, slicing into its back leg. As it collapsed, he dragged himself clear to avoid being crushed.

Breathing deeply, Manus cast a critical eye over the beast. Its tail and back were bleeding profusely, and without its back leg, it didn't have enough strength to carry itself. It crawled several feet towards him before slumping to the ground.

Manus locked eyes with it. The beast let out a wailing noise, as if begging him to spare its life. He looked up at the spectator box. Clapping his hands, Adelfred boomed. "Excellent! Finish the beast."

Manus turned back to the wailing beast. Something in the beast's eyes stayed his hand. It was like him— trapped in a life it didn't want or ask for. He tossed his sword onto the sand. "No."

Even from where he stood, Manus saw Laxus' face pale. That alone made the act worth it. Adelfred's face remained blank. After several seconds he replied, "You have spirit, gladiator. I'll enjoy seeing you fight again," he smiled, "when you've recovered from your injuries."

He raised his hand. Lightning burst forth, and Manus' world vanished in a mist of fiery pain.

Consciousness returned fleetingly. Pain lancing through his body, he remembered seeing Alke through a reddish haze, standing over him with her eyes glowing as she muttered in some unknown language. She suddenly noticed him watching her, and he blacked out.

He shot up from a nightmare, sweat running down his face. The smell of herbs was thick in the air. As his eyesight returned, he saw he was in a large stone room alongside several identical but empty beds, medical supplies stored in alcoves in the wall. He flexed his arms and noticed that all the old scars lining his leanly built body were gone, including his slave brand. Running his hand through his brown hair, he realised even that felt cleaner, and he no longer felt back pain from all Laxus' beatings.

"Good, you're awake."

He jerked backwards.

Sitting a short distance away, Alke said, "Sorry. I didn't mean to scare you."

"You startled me," croaked Manus defensively. "You didn't scare me."

Smiling knowingly, she said,"Would you like some wine?"

"Please." She got up from her chair and poured him a cup. "Thank you," he added.

"One of the few things that makes contact with Romans bearable."

Manus noted the bitterness in her voice. "How long have I been out?"

"A whole day." She ran her fingers along his arm, and he found himself shuddering. "You had a lot of burns plus other older injuries, but they're healed now."

Manus raised an eyebrow. "What are you? A witch? Demon? Spirit?"

She laid a hand on her chest. "Do I look like a demon?"

Manus shrugged. "I've never seen one, so how would I know?"

"Adelfred channels some of his power through me for things he's too busy to do—like bringing you back to life."

Manus put the cup down. "I'd hoped it had been a nightmare."

She circled him. "Dreams end. This could go on for much longer."

Manus tried to focus on something else. "My friend. Is he alright?"

"He's sleeping off a jug of wine in his cell as we speak." She narrowed her blue eyes. "From your accent you are from Britannia?"

Manus nodded. "The Ordovice. We tweaked the Roman's noses once too often, and they responded by cutting off ours. My father and brothers are dead. The rest of my family was taken as slaves."

A pained expression came over her face. "I'm sorry. I've lost family to the Romans too."

Manus hadn't spoken to a woman in any depth since his capture, and he had to remind himself to be polite. "Where are you from?"

"Germania, once upon a time." She gazed at him, reminding him uncomfortably of Adelfred's gaze in the courtyard. "May I ask you something?"

Manus nodded.

"Why did you spare that beast?"

With her stare burning into him, Manus debated how truthful to be, but he saw no reason to lie. "I saw a little of myself in the creature, trapped in a fight not of its making. It was already defeated. Why I should kill it?"

She relaxed. "An unusual trait in a gladiator."

"The Romans made me a gladiator. I didn't choose it."

"Still, Lucuis would have appreciated it."

"Lucuis?"

Her face tightened. "A friend. Adelfred turned him into that beast." She looked away. "When you left, Adelfred finished him off himself. At least he's at peace now."

"I'm sorry."

Taking a deep breath, she replied, "He's been dead to me for a long time."

He rose from his bed and decided to take a risk. "Can I ask you a question?"

She smiled, "Don't worry, I won't tell."

He swept his hand across the infirmary. "What's going on here?"

"Let me show you." She stepped forward, placing her hand on his head.

Pain shot through him. When he opened his eyes he was no longer in the infirmary. He stood in the middle of a village much like his own, people happily going about their business. The familiarity brought a dull ache to his heart. Then the screaming began.

There was a flash, and the image changed. The buildings were ablaze, and dead bodies littered the ground. Roman soldiers moved purposely around, herding the survivors into slave columns. He saw a Legionary push a young woman to the ground. Manus ran to stop him and passed straight through the soldier as if he was a spirit. The image changed again. The buildings were now charred ruins, birds picking at the dead bodies and the Romans gone.

"No!"

Manus spun around and saw Adelfred enter the village, tears streaming down his face. In his dark brown cloak, Manus thought the man looked like a druid. He thought he saw someone standing behind him, but the figure was blurred. "I should have been here," he muttered. "It was my job to protect them."

Looking up at the sky, Adelfred screamed, "Dark Gods! I offer you my soul if you give the means to punish the Romans as they've punished others."

Dark clouds gathered above, and a burst of light struck Adelfred. Manus was thrown back. He shook his head and found himself back in the infirmary.

He looked down at the floor, taking a moment to settle himself. Seeing another village devastated by the

Romans was like rubbing salt in his still raw wounds. Finally he looked up. "What was that?"

"I have some limited power of my own." She gestured to the infirmary. "This started as a means of punishing Romans. Now it's just an excuse to watch fights. Everything you see here exists because of him. He killed all the people here and brought them back to serve him."

"If he can bring people back from the dead. Why didn't he bring back his village?"

"Not part of his deal," replied Alke.

Manus slumped down, running his fingers through his hair. "And I thought my old life was bad."

"This life has its benefits. Wine, women, food and, as long as you keep him entertained, you can't die."

He shook his head. "I'm sick of fighting for others' entertainment. I vowed to find my family—that's all I care about."

After several seconds of silence, Alke said, "What if I could get you out?"

Though suspicious, Manus decided he had nothing to lose. "I'm listening."

Despite the two of them being alone in the room, she lowered her voice. "I have an escape plan, but I need a distraction to keep the guards busy."

"You were outside before. Why not make a run for it then?"

Alke shook her head, red hair flying. "There's nowhere he couldn't find me, but if my plan works, that won't be a problem."

He crossed his arms. "What's the plan?"

"I can't tell you. Adelfred can be very persuasive in a *pulling your fingernails out* kind of way."

He raised an eyebrow. "You could be planning to escape and leave me to face Adelfred's wrath."

"When I brought you back. I mixed some of my essence into you."

"Which means what?" asked Manus, a sinking feeling in his stomach.

"I die, you die."

Manus shivered at the idea of being beholden to her. Finally he said, "So you say, but if none of this is real. How do I know I died at all?"

"Step beyond those walls without me, you'll find out soon enough." replied Alke. "If it makes you feel better, name a price and I'll give it to you when this it over."

"Oh yes, I feel much better now."

Alke shrugged and turned to leave. "Very well. Enjoy your new life."

Manus grabbed her arm as something occurred to him. "Wait!" He studied her. "Can your powers help me find my family?"

When she hadn't answered for several seconds, he said, "Well?"

Alke nodded. "Yes of course. If that is what you want."

"So how do we proceed?"

She reached into a hidden pocket in her dress and handed him a gold key and a small dagger. "This will unlock any door here. I need you to create a distraction, while I carry out my task."

He rubbed the key between his fingers. "What sort of distraction?"

"As long as it attracts a lot of attention, it doesn't matter."

"And where do we meet up?"

"We'll meet up when they catch you."

Pulling out the dagger, he replied, "I wasn't planning to get recaptured."

"You will, and we'll meet up then. Just don't be scared."

Putting on a show of bravado, Manus replied, "I've already fought a monster and come back to life. What's there to be afraid of?"

She raised a red-gold eyebrow. "There's always something."

"I can see we're going to get along great," said Manus as he extended his hand. "Good luck."

After a second's hesitation she took his hand. "You too." She moved to the door. "A guard will come in to escort you to your cell."

"One last thing," asked Manus. "What is Adelfred to you?"

She paused by the door. "Nothing anymore."

It was obvious she was keeping something from him. They were connected in some way. Maybe they were family or lovers or Gods. He didn't know. *Let her have her secrets*, thought Manus. It was only fair since he had his own. He had no intention of keeping to her plan.

Most of this was beyond his understanding, but he understood duplicity. Whatever game she played with Adelfred, he had no intention of being caught in the middle. Much as he wanted to believe she could help him find his family, he couldn't judge her sincerity, so her promises and claims meant nothing. He would escape and find his family himself

What Adelfred had done to him before had been painful enough. He didn't want to go through it again. If he could escape now, he intended to, and to Hades with her distraction.

A tall guard entered the room. He was armed with a spear and has a sword hanging from his belt. "Let's go."

Manus gave him an apprising look. "An old champion are you?"

The guard ignored him. "Move."

Manus raised his hands submissively. "Just asking. You sound like a Thracian. Thracians have quite a reputation."

"Still good fighters?" replied the guard.

"No, can't fight for shit," replied Manus. "The only reputation they got is for sheep shagging."

Reddening, the guard rushed forward. Manus grabbed his arm and jabbed the dagger deep into his neck, blood running over his fingers. The guard stumbled for several seconds before collapsing to the floor.

"Stupid Thracians."

He quickly removed the dead guard's armour and uniform and gave himself a quick examination. Splatters of blood dripped down the armour. Up close the guards would recognize he was not one of them, but in the dark he hoped to pass unnoticed. Hiding the dagger in his gauntlet, he warily opened the door. The tree-lined pathway stretched out before him, though still dark lamps lit the way.

Hearing footsteps, he elected not to test his disguise and eased himself back into the shadows where he watched two guards march past. They moved with a casual competence. Too casual, thought Manus. They may have started off as fighters, but years of guard duty can dull the skill of even the best soldiers. His own tribe had taught that lesson to the Romans many times. Too well in the end, he thought ruefully.

He waited several seconds after they passed before continuing to the prison chamber. He slowed as he got closer to the entrance. Two men stood guard. He peered up at the watchtower that looked out over the entire settlement and noted that no one was on duty, which seemed strange. Manus mentally shrugged. With a sorcerer in residence, they probably didn't have too much to worry about. Hands behind his back, he carefully withdrew the dagger.

He felt their eyes linger as he approached. "Evening, lads." He grabbed the nearest man, jabbing his blade into his throat.

As the guard went down, Manus swung around and rammed the blade into the eye socket of the other man's helmet. Pulling the blade free, he scanned the area for any more men. Fortunately, it was clear.

He unlocked the door and advanced inside, ready to deal with any loitering guards. The corridor was empty. Letting out a breath, he grabbed the nearest body and dragged it inside. He returned for the second and deposited him beside the first. Hopefully, Manus thought, they'd go unnoticed until he had accomplished his task.

He made his way toward the prison proper. The strong smell of animal dung hit his senses. His confident stride slowed to a shuffle as creatures peered at him through the bars. He couldn't begin to name even half of them. It was as if someone had cut up a group of animals then randomly reattached the parts. He saw a beast with the head of a bird and the body of a bear, while in another cage a lion with the body of a snake yawned at him.

In the next cage a massive beak slammed into the bars. The cage's inhabitant, an eight-foot-tall bird, squawked angrily at him, its feathers flying as it tried pecking at him. Manus jerked back, knocking into the bars on the other side. Something slithered over his shoulder, and he jumped away as it began hooting at him. "Bollocks," he muttered.

Forcing himself to stay calm, Manus moved quickly away from the cages. He pushed the images of beasts aside and focused on finding Durano.

Gradually the animal cages gave way to the human ones. The men inside looked to be in various degrees of drunken stupor, but Manus was surprised to see how well furnished the cells were. They had finely crafted chairs, woolen rugs and comfortable looking beds with even more comfortable looking women inside them. Then he saw the bars and reminded himself that for all their comforts they were still cages.

In his heart he would have tried to release them all, but he knew many of them wouldn't want to leave. Incomprehensible as it was to him, some people liked being slaves. Durano might feel the same way, but he had to try.

After walking past several cages, Manus finally found Durano's cell, and thankfully he was alone, snoring away ungracefully. He opened the cage and leaned beside him. "Durano?"

Durano's eyes shot open, but he smiled at Manus' appearance. "You son of a whore. You missed out on some party."

Clamping his hand over Durano's mouth, he whispered, "Quiet. I'm escaping. Are you in?"

Durano laughed. "I'm not going anywhere. This place is great."

"You didn't look that enamored before."

"That was before I saw what life was like here. Wine, women, and he can bring you back if you die." He jabbed Manus' chest. "You're proof of that."

It was not something Manus cared to be reminded of. "Don't be stupid," he hissed. "Adelfred is a sorcerer. Whatever games he's playing, it won't end well if you stay."

"My risk," replied Durano.

Manus studied him. Durano was a grown man. If he wanted to stay in this otherworld, so be it. "Very well. Good luck."

Durano grabbed his arm. "I can't let you leave, Manus. If you anger Adelfred, he could take it out on me. I can't let that happen."

Manus spun around, kicking Durano between the legs. As he doubled over in pain, Manus punched him in the face. The Gaul fell, blood flowing from his nose. Manus grabbed him a headlock, cutting off his air until he was unconscious. "And I can't let you stop me."

Manus ripped strips out of the blankets and used them to tie Durano up. Then he lifted him up and dropped him back into bed. Sighing, he took one last look at Durano and departed. He walked past the dead guards and opened the door. In the moonlight he saw the gateway and the freedom it represented.

Manus felt a slight twinge of guilt at not following Alke's plan, but he'd had his fill of taking orders from others. Besides, if he succeeded, she'd get all the distraction she wanted.

His confidence grew the closer he came to the gate. The watchtower was still conspicuously empty, and he doubted the small gatehouse held more than three or four men inside, plus the two men loitering beside the gate. It would have been good to have Durano's back-up, but he'd faced worse odds in the arena.

He was just a few feet away when a loud ringing echoed across the compound. Manus doubted it meant anything good for him. Drawing his sword, he charged the two guards. Ducking under the first man's swing, he impaled his sword into his chest. He swung around just in time to avoid the other man's blow. The guardsman was fast, constantly changing the angles of his attack. Parrying his blows, it took Manus a moment to figure out his pattern. Feinting left, he brought his blade down upon the man's arm. As the arm fell away in a bloody mess, he finished him off with a slash to the chest.

Manus turned around to see three more men emerge from the gatehouse. He smiled. "Who's next?"

One guard raced ahead of the others. Sidestepping his attack, Manus slashed his blade across the man's back. He ducked under the next man's swing and jabbed his blade into his throat, blood spraying out onto the courtyard.

Manus leaned back as a sword jabbed at his face. Diving down, he rolled to his feet and thrust his blade into the man's leg, his blood splashing across Manus' armour.

He stood facing the villa and watched as a dozen more men charged towards him... more men than he could handle. He fled towards the gate. He grabbed the heavy wooden block that locked it, and he threw it aside. Ignoring the pain in his back, he seized the gate's iron handle and pulled it open.

His brief run for freedom stopped immediately. There was nothing beyond the gate but a swirling red cloud. As he looked on, the swirls coalesced into shapes. He saw a spirit woman wave at him. A wolf like cloud floated by him then snapped at him, its jaws coming within inches of his face. Manus jerked back as other animals started hovering near the gate.

Manus was ready to risk much for freedom, but he wouldn't go willingly into that. He slowly turned around to see a dozen guards surrounding him in a semicircle, anger in their eyes and swords at the ready.

He was tempted to charge them and end it now to avoid Adelfred's wrath, but the sorcerer would probably bring him back anyway, and he wasn't in the mood to be stabbed to death. Tossing his weapon down, he raised his hands. "Looks like you got me, lads."

They rushed forward, pummeling Manus with the hilts of their swords. After several minutes they stopped, leaving him groaning on the ground. Before blacking out, Manus felt two of them grab him by the arms and begin dragging him.

The next words he heard were from Adelfred. "Can he fight?"

"Give me more time," replied Alke, "and I can have him back at his peak."

"Can he fight?" repeated Adelfred.

"Yes."

"That's all I require."

Opening his eyes, Manus saw he was in the middle of a large atrium, two guards standing at his side. Alke knelt beside him, sorting through what he assumed was a bag of medical supplies. She gave him a faint smile, but whether it was one of knowing superiority or support he couldn't tell. She whispered, "Good work."

Still in pain, he muttered, "Thanks."

She patted his hand and got to her feet. Across from him stood Adelfred and Laxus who was rubbing his hands nervously.

"I must apologize," said Laxus. "This one's always been a problem."

Adelfred grabbed Laxus' head, twisting it until it snapped. "But he is no longer your problem," replied Adelfred as Laxus dropped to the ground.

"So much for your deal," said Manus.

Adelfred laughed, but there was no cheer in it. "Deals with Romans never count." He looked down at Manus. "I enjoy a man with spirit. Let us see if you are as spirited with your next fight."

A masked man entered the atrium, clutching a sword. He removed his mask. It was Durano, his expression glum but determined.

Manus looked over at his friend. "Why?"

"This is my chance," said Durano. "I'm not letting you take it from me."

"He's using you."

Durano shrugged. "Nothing new there."

Adelfred stepped between them. "Here's the deal, Gladiators. This is a fight to the death. True death." He smiled. "If Durano wins, he gets to stay. If Manus wins, he gets to leave."

Manus wondered if a single word was true. He glanced at Alke, but she looked away. He wouldn't be getting any help there. His blue eyes burning with fury, he said, "Fine, but when this is over I want a fight with you."

Adelfred studied him. "Why?"

"If my friend dies, then so do you," growled Manus.

Durano laughed, but it sounded hollow to Manus' ears. "You're the only one dying tonight."

Manus winced at the words.

"Such confidence!" replied Adelfred. "It's a pity you

have to die. However if you win, I'll give you your fight."

A sword materialized in Adelfred's hand, and he tossed it to Manus. It was the standard Roman Gladius, which wouldn't have bothered him too much, except Durano was armed with a longer Celtic sword. He glanced over at Adelfred who smiled. *So much for a fair fight,* thought Manus.

Manus gave it an experimental swing. "It'll do."

Adelfred stepped away. "Begin."

The pair circled each other. They had sparred many times, with the outcomes coming out too equally for Manus to be confident of victory.

Durano charged, swinging his blade. Manus parried the blow. Durano followed up with a series of fast thrusts that Manus only just countered. Spinning on his heel, he sidestepped Durano's next thrust, jabbing his blade at Durano's throat, but the black haired giant was fast. Even as Manus was mentally celebrating his victory, Durano moved out of the way. "Won't get me with that old trick."

"Then I'll have to try some new ones," said Manus.

Durano charged again, and the pair engaged in another bout of thrust and counter thrust. As Manus desperately beat off another jab at his throat, he knew he would have to think of something quick. He was tiring, while Durano appeared fully rested.

Durano saw it too. "Give up Manus, and I promise a quick death."

Through ragged breaths Manus replied, "I'm just getting warmed up."

He followed that up with a series of stabbing thrusts, but Durano successfully countered each blow. Durano then twisted around, almost decapitating Manus with a backhand slash.

Manus slipped, falling to the ground. He recovered just in time to block Durano's finishing blow. He kicked out at Durano's leg. As Durano stumbled, Manus dived out of the way and rolled to his feet. He stood up, plunging his blade into Durano's chest.

Manus tossed his sword aside and caught the falling Gaul. He lowered him to the ground and took Durano's hand. "I'm sorry, comrade."

Coughing up blood, Durano replied, "I am too.... Had to try." Then he slumped down.

Manus got to his feet, frowning. "You owe me a fight."

Adelfred narrowed his eyes. "Indeed. Are you sure you don't want to rest first?'

Manus shook his head. "The sooner I'm out of here the better."

Adelfred shrugged. "So be it. Alke, hand me Durano's sword. Someone competent should get some use out of it."

Leaning down, Alke picked it up. She paused before handing it to him. "Hasn't there been enough blood spilled today? Surely you've had your fill by now?"

He slapped her hard on the face, leaving a red a mark across her pale skin. "I've warned you before about questioning me."

Manus stomped forward. "Don't you lay a hand on her!"

As Adelfred's guards moved to intercept him, the sorcerer smiled, "Well Alke, it seems you've caught the attentions of another gladiator. Instead of killing him, maybe I should turn him into a beast like the last one."

"No!" Alke cried.

With a strength belied by her stature, she plunged the

blade into Adelfred's chest. His face contorted in a mixture of shock and pain, Adelfred stared down at the sword. Alke jerked away as if just realising what she had just done.

Manus jumped as the two guards began screaming and clutching their heads. One ran up to him, grabbing his shoulders. As he stared into Manus' eyes, his body turned to dust. Manus began frantically wiping the dust off him.

Adelfred fell to his knees and looked up at her. "How?"

Tears streaming down her face, Alke pulled out a small gold amulet from her bag. "I took your invincibility away." She kissed him on the forehead. "Goodbye, father."

Adelfred's flesh began melting from his face, running into pools on the floor. Within seconds his body had become a mound of flesh and bone on the ground. Manus felt bile rise to the top of his throat and vomited onto the floor.

"He was a good man once," said Alke. "I never wanted to kill him, but he gave me no choice."

"The amulet?"

"When he offered his soul to the Dark Gods, they gave him this. It gave him immortality. It's taken me years, but I finally figured out a way to remove its power." She narrowed her eyes. "With your distraction, I was able to enter the sanctum where it was held and alter its enchantment."

Manus stumbled as the ground shook beneath him, and the walls began crumbling around him. "Now what?" he sighed.

"Without my father to sustain it, his world is dissolving." Noticing his nerves, she took his hand. "It'll be over shortly."

Manus found his nerve wavering as the world around him collapsed, and the marble beneath his feet disappeared until there was only grass. When he looked up they were in a field surrounded by trees.

Manus looked around slowly. "Where is everyone?" The guards? The slaves? The beasts?"

Alke waved her hand. "Gone, just like the buildings. It was father keeping them alive. Without him they head to the afterlife that should have long ago claimed them. If it wasn't for me, you would have joined them."

"I guess I should thank you," replied Manus.

"It comes with a price. Everything from the Gods does," replied Alke. "Unfortunately, if you get too far away from me, you'll die. You're lucky your escape didn't work, or you'd be as dead as them."

Manus felt his chest tighten. "So I've merely swapped one master for another."

"I prefer partner." She paused then said, "Thank you for defending me."

Manus realised that for all her power she was facing as uncertain a world as he. His concern abated slightly, and he said, "Thank you for saving me a fight. I'm not sure I could have won. I'm just sorry Durano couldn't be saved too."

"I'm sorry, but the enchantment I put on the amulet hadn't finished its work."

Manus nodded, and an awkward silence descended between them. Finally he said, "What about our deal?"

"I want to help you...but."

Manus wondered what else she was hiding from him. "If this is going to work. You're going to have to start giving me straight answers."

Alke face flushed. "I can only guide you in the direction of your family. Pinning them down may take a while."

Manus gazed at the rising sun. It was never as easy as you hoped. "Well it's a start."

She threaded her arm through his. "Then follow me."

The End

About the author:

L. Young was born in Auckland, New Zealand and currently resides there with his family.

Squatter's Rites

by Frederick Hilary (Euboea, Greece)

here are many strange people that shelter in the dilapidated ruins on the edge of this city. Almost all are destitute, and not all are alike. Some used to be dukes and some believe themselves dukes, thus making a heaven of their hell. Others clothe themselves in tramp's garments and yet secrete tins or wads of money in hidden nooks, enough perhaps to buy them a comfortable house in a respectable suburb. Yet others, their vain sight blinded perhaps by poverty, have gained the prophet's ability to discern eternal truth or the astrologist's ability to read fates in the stars. I myself have run into such types at one time or another, but strangest of all was the Arcadian god whom I found sheltering on the roof of our half-finished apartment block.

My father-in-law had started building the apartment block years ago, but the work ground to a halt when the woman in black from the hovel next door pronounced a curse on the project. Widow or witch I did not then know, though I inclined towards the former. Years had gone by, and the place had stood amongst the doctor's offices and leaning apartments, a skeleton, three floors without outer walls and a top floor that looked up indifferently to either autumn clouds or summer stars.

My wife and I used to climb the railless stair and imagine what each room might be like finished. In each there was the usual pile of junk: animal or human waste, heaps of rubbish, rusty cans and nails, plastic bags that hung from the refuse piles like streamers on carnival day. On the exposed top floor lay a mattress that had somehow been dragged up there and served as a bed for the Albanian refugees who arrived fresh from the purges in Kosovo. They sometimes fled when we reached the top, but more often they just looked at us with eyes that could not be challenged, their looks saying more than words could... that they were beyond feeling sorry or aggressive. The god of the oak woods, when I found him there that last summer, neither ran nor held his ground. He used his spells or magic (whatever the appropriate term might be) to blend in with the refuse, just as a nature spirit might merge with the oak bark or with the green bushes. But while nature gods can take the form of nature and dissolve quickly out of human sight, they cannot do the same with man-made decay. Thus it was that I saw him, and our commerce began.

I was alone that time, for my wife was nearing childbirth and resting in our rented basement apartment. It was a ritual of mine to look the place over on my way back from the office, though what squatters I found I never had the heart to turn out.

"Who are you?" I asked as I discerned the outline of the creature against the heap of rubbish. I thought him a ghost, but since I have talked with the ghost of my great aunt through a medium, I am not especially afraid of ghosts. In fact, I wondered whether this shimmering, seemingly incorporeal form might not be another of my relatives ready to impart inconsequential secrets of the afterlife.

The being did not answer at first. The form shimmered more than before, as if making a last effort to disappear into its surroundings but then materialized fully before me with a sound remarkably like a sigh. I could only gasp at what I saw. It had the form of a goat-footed god, animal-hoofed below, legs of mossy brown hair and a naked torso above, muscular and youthful. His hair fell in tight ringlets about his fine brow, and his eyes were unlike any human eyes I have ever seen, for they did not simply reflect the light but shone with a light that was of a different, younger sun. His face was not handsome in the way that men's faces are handsome and women's faces are beautiful. It was an ideal and therefore beyond desire, in a way that human faces never can be, for their beauty never inspires reverence, only eros.

"I am Faunus, of the oak woods that were," he said, and so saying slumped down on the stained, dust-covered mattress. A puff of dust rose up as he sat, and I thought for a second that he might disappear, like in the smoke of a magician's trick. But it was just the dust clouds that had blown in from Africa and settled on everything, and he remained, sitting cross-legged on the mattress and rhythmically flexing his fingers, as if playing an invisible set of pipes.

I did not know what to say to this and asked whether he was, in fact, some kind of spirit.

"No. You would say that I am some kind of god, if you had to put it into your language. I am a nature god, a satyr of the woods, a being from a time when all the world was green and good and things did not decay and the sun did not measure the ebb and flow of generations. You have heard of Arcadia?"

I thought about pastoral poems, about the fragments of verse I remembered from my literature degree, where Pan roamed quite tamed through Eighteenth Century gardens disguised as Arcadian woods. I nodded doubtfully.

"Arcadia was my home long ago. Though when there is at first no time and then time begins, one cannot speak in terms of length at all. The gods of Olympus sported and played, just as we fauns and dryads frolicked in the groves and meadows, and none of us, from the Thunderer down to the lowliest wood sprite, cared for what might come after. But some force greater even than Zeus had set in motion the decline and decay that is the dynamo of all history. Gold diminished into silver and silver into bronze. Bright turned to dark and unmingled light to shadow, and before we could wake and rally ourselves, the whole thing had become clay and mud... and man had his day. We did not die—we are not made to die—but we diminished ourselves and retreated into the ever shrinking quiet places—the green places."

"This place isn't, if you'll not mind me saying, exactly green, is it?"

"We only come forth when there is some task to do."

"What task?"

The faun tilted his head to one side and lowered his eyes, so as to say he did not mean to share his task with me. "This building belongs to you?"

"It belongs to my wife's family, actually. It isn't

finished yet."

"That is plain enough to see. It is better so, at least for me, for I have been able to shelter here for many months now and have even seen you before, and your spouse. Though last time I managed to make myself the colour of those rusting tin cans with greater efficiency. I suppose you will want me to move on?"

"What's the point? You may as well stay. There is no work being done anymore. It's stopped for years now. My father-in-law believes that the old widow next door put a curse on the place. She said that she did not want the shadow of a big apartment falling on her leaning hovel there. So no further work will be done."

"And did it come true?"

"That's the funny thing. We scorned her at first, but then the company we'd employed to finish the work started going through financial difficulties. My father-in-law's shop began to lose customers, meaning that we couldn't pay the workers. The architects pulled out of the project—all explicable, every bit of it, yet all working towards the fulfillment of the curse. Work was abandoned eight years ago. All because of a curse, if you want to believe it."

I went to the open edge of the floor and looked down on the old woman's house. It was indeed a kind of hovel, made of mud and brick, with a roof of such dense ivy that it looked like a garden growing on top.

"That's the witch's house," said the god from behind me. "Do you believe in witches?"

I turned to him. "Well, I don't know. A few moments ago I didn't believe in gods. I am starting to think about quite a few things. Didn't really buy the whole witch's curse story, even though I'm not what you call a skeptic. Who knows?"

"Well, I do. The old lady is indeed a witch. It is true that your apartment will never be finished, and that she has in fact put a curse on you. Curses work through nature, through cause and effect and coincidence. And they see that their task is carried out. The end result is the same. I do not care for curses myself, nor for magic that interferes with the natural course of things. Still, I must concede that in this case it is probably for the best. After all, what is this little decaying skeleton of a house compared to the dreadful ruin of the apartment building it would become. It is for the best if even one dwelling goes unfinished, for they have all contributed to the disappearance of the green spaces I have loved."

"You think so? My wife and I are expecting a child. This building was intended to be her dowry, our little nest egg. We need somewhere to live."

"And where do you live at the moment? You are not, as I, sleeping under the stars, I take it?"

"We are renting, I'll admit. But the money'll run out one day. We'll never get this place finished."

The god came next to me and looked down at the witch's house. I had to step aside, for the beauty of his presence, ever more stark in the bright sunlight, was too much.

I crossed to where he'd been sitting, to the mattress, and planted myself down on it, making my own little puff of dust in the process. The god went on looking down at the house, and as I watched him, in profile, I noted that, even in that perfect face that knew no lines of trouble or of age, there was nevertheless something alien playing upon it, the ghost of some sort of desire.

"What is it? Why do you look at it so?"

The god went on staring. "It is nothing... nothing that can be profitably spoken about."

There seemed some puzzle behind those words, and I laboured to work it out. "You spoke of a task earlier. Why have you come here, to this run-down place, when your proper place—even in the world as it is—is the green woods? What are you looking for, Faunus?"

"You ask too many questions, human. Accept what the witch has done to you and go back to your wife."

"And what has the witch done to *you*?" I do not know what prompted me to say it. There was something in that look of his—in the longing that was plainly there— more out of place than upon any human's face. I knew that he was troubled by the old woman, and that he too sought something and wanted some business finished. So I asked him, and it appeared at once that I had cut to the root of things. He turned to me and gave me a pained look, so that the beauty of his face sank to a mortal level, lines of displeasure creasing an expression that was naturally sublime.

"What business is the witch of mine?"

"I might ask the same of you. All right, then, supposing I believe that old lady really is a witch. What can I do to lift the curse?"

"The witch must lift it herself, under pain of death."

"And what is to stop her from placing another?"

"That is for you to riddle out."

"Help me, then, and I will help you. But first, you must tell me in what way I can help you."

The god paced around amongst the rubbish. I saw his fingers flex again and nimbly play invisible pipes. He opened his mouth and pursed his lips and brought breath from his god's lungs and played notes upon invisible reeds, but of course no sound came. Then he said, "Gods do not need the help of men. Men call upon gods, even lesser gods, for blessings. They bear to us libations, and throw offerings upon the eternal fires, and sometimes we incline to listen and sometimes not, as the whim takes us."

"Very well, then," I said. "I will go into the witch's house and get her to lift the curse, even without your help. But should I come out again, do not expect me to aid you in return."

The god was silent. I left him to his ruminating (as it seemed) and went down to the witch's door. Her house was a rundown cottage with an ivy-covered roof and clay and mud walls. There was a little window only on the front side and no other means of letting in light, for on the left and right side there were bare walls, and at the back the cottage was blocked by a rising set of apartments. Ancient and decrepit, it was out of place among the surrounding buildings, even though our building too, in its unfinished state, looked something of a ruin.

I expected the door to be locked, but when I tried the handle, it opened easily and quietly. It was a small door, striped, with flaking green paint, and it seemed eager to let me through into the dark space beyond. As I peered inside I saw that there was no internal source of light, no candle or lantern as might have been befitting such an old looking place, let alone any electric light.

Apart from the light from the open door, there was only a thin, watery shaft of light shining down in the darkness at my right, coming from the little window. This illuminated—this is perhaps not the right word, since it did no more than provide a faint impression—a wooden dresser taking up the far wall of the room, in which the plates were all cracked or broken completely, and one of the shelves tilted down diagonally.

I stepped inside the cottage, looking for something to wedge against the door, so that it would not shut me in darkness, and easily found something that would serve: a broken piece of shelving, the floor being littered with all kinds of bric-a-brac. The house was worse than our unfinished apartment block—it looked long-abandoned. The smell was stifling: ammonia and animal droppings mingled with damp and mold. There could be no person alive in here, surely—witch or not.

I tried to remember when I had last seen her. She had been standing at her door sometimes when Tanya and I came to visit the apartments and dream our dreams. Watching like some carrion bird, her face twisted with malice. How long ago had that been?

I stepped over broken fragments of china and ornaments. To the right was the kitchen area. I could see it cast weakly from the window light, but to the left was utter gloom. I thought about the smell and realised that I could discern the stench of decayed flesh. She was dead, then, surely. Did this mean the curse would be lifted? Wouldn't it be right now to call the authorities and report her passing? I imagined myself on the phone: "I'd like to report the death of a witch. How long has she been dead? From the state of her place, I would say several years. Still, she managed to put a curse on us and watch us from her doorway, even though her body had long decayed and her soul gone to whoever claimed it."

I felt the looming darkness to my left. There was something too deep about this darkness, too obscuring, making it impossible, even with the light that fell in from the door, to make anything out at all.

I felt something or someone grip my wrist, tight, with

hard, brittle, bony fingers, so that I suddenly cried out in shock. The fingers pressed down, and I felt a searing pain.

"Tell him I've had enough. He can stop watching me now."

The voice came from right next to me, though I could see only darkness. I looked down in terror and found that I could not even see my own hand where it was fixed in the vice-tight grip. There was a thick, knotted darkness there. The voice was like the darkness somehow, so thick it could not be penetrated by any other sound.

I was too terrified to speak. I have never been brave, not even squaring off against colleagues in the office. To have my hand grasped by a witch was more than I could endure, and it was a wonder I kept myself from fainting.

"Tell him it was because I loved green, growing things... just as he did, once. I loved what they did. They sprouted through the ceiling, so that even the roof became a garden. All used to be verdant life once, here in this grey desert, but I never learned to play the thing enough. I wanted to turn all these horrid surroundings to green gardens, to virgin paradise. I wanted green shoots to spring up from the cracks in the concrete and vines to entangle the walls and at last overcome them, to turn them to rubble and let the rubble blow away like the desert winds from Africa. I wanted it all to go back, but I never knew to play the notes properly. This house is all I managed. Or not quite all, perhaps. It was me, too. I should have been dead years ago. Perhaps I was. The music gave me life, even my aging body, just like a young, green sapling. It straightened my stoop; it sent green blood flowing through my veins, but it has grown harder and harder to sustain it. The notes no longer come. My breath isn't there anymore, so I have stopped playing, or trying to play. I watched you from the roof, heard all you said. Now I am giving it back to him. Make sure he gets it. Your curse will be lifted as soon as my soul flies away."

She let my hand go. Before doing so, however, she pressed something into it, something made of wood. I stepped back out from the gloom of the entranceway, still in shock, and looked at what I was holding. It was a set of panpipes. Then I knew what the god had been seeking and what power had kept the witch alive. I knew what I must do at once, for even though she had not stipulated as much. The lifting of the curse, it seemed to me, was the bargain she had struck for the pipes' return.

Faunus moved on once I had given him the pipes, just like the other refugees. I looked down a last time from the stark skeleton of our apartment block and saw that the ivy green roof of the witch's hovel had become just a patchwork of decaying wood. The place was a ruin, just as it seemed when I entered.

The witch was right about the curse. Suddenly, just after that day, everything seemed to fall together, and work commenced. My father-in-law managed to get the bank loans he needed, and the place is now finished. They have knocked the old hovel down. The neighbourhood is much more up-market now. There used to be a tree on the roadside opposite our entrance hall, but it's been cut down. We have a little garden at the back, though, and I grow my own vegetables sometimes. There are new apartments all around us, hardly any green at all, so I think the witch wouldn't have wanted to live on in any case.

They removed her body, I suppose, though it wasn't from any call I made. I wonder how long she had been dead. Perhaps the body had died some time before, even though the magic of the panpipes gave life to it even in its decayed form.

As for Faunus, I suppose he has retreated to the last green spaces that are left. I try to look for him sometimes, when I'm out in the countryside, but I suppose that a nature god can blend into the woods and grasses much better than he can into a heap of refuse. I don't think I'll see him again. My eyes no longer notice the growing things among the grey. They no longer discern the refugees that blend into the dullness and the void of this metropolis, like the shadows of forgotten gods.

The End

About the author:

Frederick Hilary lives in Greece where the myths and landscape provide a constant source of inspiration for his stories. His taste for the numinous was first sparked by reading *The Lord of the Rings* as a teenager, and he particularly enjoys reading and writing stories that feature encounters with the supernatural. He has been published in various places online and in print, and his website can be found at http://frederickhilary.weebly.com/

⑨he Saga of Anna Belgermaine

by Carole Hall (California, USA)

After my great-grandmother's funeral, sitting alone in the Cape Cod house where she had lived all her widowed life, I came across a carefully folded, handwritten manuscript in a secret, spring-locked drawer in her cherry wood cabinet. My loose sleeve had activated it quite accidentally, and it slid out smoothly, almost into my hands with its offering.

Anna Belgermaine had been a remarkable woman, graceful in the extreme and quite beautiful even as very old age came like a thief in the night to steal her loveliness. The black and white photograph of her a young woman displayed an elegance that brought a smile of pride to my own face as I lifted it from the Steinway piano. When her beloved husband Charles died in a factory fire, it seemed she grieved alone for the rest of her days. Her two sons, Ben and Jacob, had scattered to the ends of the earth and were not heard from for many years. I found their obituaries in the same cherry wood cabinet as the following manuscript—for want of a better word—that I am about to offer you.

For years I had been busy with the extraordinary events of my own life in Boston: climbing the corporate ladder of a prestigious arbitrage firm, losing a husband to divorce in the process (all unaware of his many dalliances and peccadilloes until it was far too late to rectify). Perhaps I had indeed sacrificed him to my own career prospects, for I did not even have occasion to see my great-grandmother as often as I might. But I kept in touch by phone, nonetheless, and it was not until after her death and in time for her funeral that I managed to find my way back to her lovely, three-story, white painted house in Cape Cod where I now sit.

After many days of sorting, invoicing and admiring her belongings and treasures of all sizes, I was advised by her solicitor that I had indeed inherited everything as her sole surviving relative.

"You have the lot, Mrs. Jordan. Lock, stock and barrel," he had said. It would eschew me from a life of servitude to others, if I wished. It was only then that I finally came across this tale written in poem-like rhythm that gave me pause to reflect on what she was trying to impart. At the first hasty reading I glimpsed the passionate woman that my great-grandmother must have been. Finally, with much more yet to accomplish in the rearranging, and at first thought emptying of this marvelous old house, I brought my portable SONY radio into the large, beautifully furnished salon. I switched it on to my favorite classical music station to send the silence away and tried to make sense of what she had left behind and thought so precious as to have hidden it for many,

many years.

   As the sun began to set across the gray Atlantic Ocean, I poured myself a glass of her exquisite moscato wine and began what she had laid down on paper in her own flowing handwriting. She did not have much formal education and, indeed, at fourteen years of age, was already deemed an adult. Her missive was not without flaws, yet it was filled with passion. She had not been given to flights of fancy, I was sure; her wealth had proved substantial. It was enough to last all her days in the extreme lap of luxury through thoughtful stock market investments, which she herself earned and practiced diligently. So madness played no part in the brain of this woman. What then had really happened? Or did anything happen at all? What was she trying to tell whomever found this? She was not a writer, no other such literature existed anywhere, not a scrap of anything else, just this tale about... well perhaps you can puzzle it out. I have spent many hours trying to decipher it and reached no conclusion.

I woke to find the morning gray and still
Unborn and waiting on the rim of time
As if a sleeping God must now bestir
To touch the wind and bid the daylight shine.
The lake and wood beyond my windowpane
All colorless beneath a heavy sky
The world in awful semi-balance held
And so within my stagnant mind was I.
With quick dispatch I thrust aside all thought
And would not touch the new day with my hands
I turned to capture yet again my dreams
But sleep had fled and drained her kindly sands.
Beyond the door and hard stones at my feet

A flirting wind plucked at the frocks of trees
A startled bird arose in cackling flight
Across the hill came the stinging scent of the sea.
Now the sun in hesitant splendor rose
Like a Phoenix from a corner of the land.
Charting its irretrievable passage home
Beheld by God and guided by his hand.
I walked toward the top road and the cliffs
Unseen, unmindful, unaware
Heard the mighty drum roll of the sea
And saw a rabbit slip a poacher's snare.
As if in one accord the pewter sky
Now became a hundred scudding clouds
Stark gray and silver, just beyond my reach
I stood in awe and cried aloud.
All corners of the compass as far as I could see
The morning stretched and yawned and reached
Girded its loins, appointed the day
And startled me with its beauty into sudden speech.
"O God! If you can fill this barren world
And move me with your wondrous poetry
For pity's sake, I beg, reach down
And from the mists of life pluck me!"
As if in sadness for my desolation,
The clouds began to weep soft, salty tears
To bind the gaping, painful wounds of life
And by their moisture wash away my fears.
I stood now on the cliff and watched the sea
Singing its timeless song to the ears of the shore
Then saw the Stranger make his narrow way
Over the craggy rocks and across the sandy floor.
At first I thought to flee, then heard the wind call
And bid me gently wait

I could not pull my eyes from his wind-braced back
As I watched the manly splendor of his gait.
He stumbled, I gasped from startled throat
He climbed the rocks all slick from Spindrift Sea
The wind tore at his dark and dripping hair
And then he paused to look straight up at me!
All Time became as nothing, as still could be
The world stepped back, then shuddered out of sight
Sucked in the valley of his depthless eyes
My simple beating heart took wing, then flight.
Stayed by an unseen hand I dared not move
But watched his firm ascent to firmer land
My world became a wondrous, welcome thing
As he reached out and grasped me by the hand.
Oh! Splendid life, all magically you soared
To drive all aching fears away
While now he lingered softly by my side
And brought a newfound meaning to this day.
Ah! Yet my hungry heart drank full its fill
Stirred the smoldering embers of my soul
I worshipped at the temple of his Man fire
And did not notice as the eve grew cold.
For then the twilight slipped a covering grace
The daylight ceased, as gently did the sun
I turned my happy eyes into the west
But then looked back to find him strangely gone!
All like a stone my heart grew dead in me
With frantic eyes I searched both sea and shore
Unable to believe yet knowing in despair
That what I'd found and loved was now no more.
In silent dread I walked the passage home
Closed tight the door and set the fire aglow
Recaptured all the wondrous, happy hours

And saw again that Stranger far below.
Now I turned to think of who and why
And whence the one who'd stepped into my world
I heard the wind fling pebbles at the door
And then the rain its bevy earthward hurled.
All night I stayed before the blazing hearth
The darkness deepened then the dawn began
The first bird called - I did not heed,
My thoughts all with that nameless man.
Towards the village common I did wend my way
In search of happy human company
Drank deep of red and mellow vintage wines
And listened to a tale they told to me...
"One hundred fifty years have come and gone
Since the sailor kissed his love and went to sea
Vowed by his breath and life on his return
To wed her by the Village Wedding Tree.
The days swung into months her vigil kept
Upon the cliffs eyes eastward to the sea
While Alan Dunn fought weather round the Cape
And cursed the fates that would not let him be.
Hard ice on scuppers wind to freeze the eyes
Hailstones from Hell and pitch black morning skies
Bark and timber of the ship did tear
And Cape Horn laid her heavy ballast bare.
The monstrous seas swept past the oily deck
To wrench the hapless seaman standing there.
Yet, still she kept her lonely vigil calm
Though suitors richly sought to tempt away.
Then day-by-day despair and hope did flee
While Alan Dunn lay dead beneath the sea.
At last she wed the Squire all on a mad March day
So they say, in these lonely ocean parts,

When the great North winds of winter blindly come
That a specter climbs the rocky granite cliffs
Out of Cape Horn comes the ghost of Alan Dunn.
The maiden heard the tale with beating heart
And sped her marriage bed for the road to the sea.
Called her dead lover's name with anguished cry
And hurled her body into the cruel sea."
Ah! silently, my breath scarce moving me,
I saw again the dripping man who'd come.
Embraced me with his timeless, welcome arms,
And I had loved immortal Alan Dunn!
I dare not speak of what I know to be
Though memories come to haunt and make me sad,
My ghostly vision must remain untold
For lest my neighbors think that I am mad.
So close the door and keep the hearth aglow
And age alone before the cherry firelight.
I'll turn my ears from whispers in the wind
And lock my soul against the winter night.
Anna Belgermaine. October 21.

The hairs on the back of my neck stood up as I laid the manuscript down on the table. I wouldn't think anymore today, I thought. Leave well enough alone, for now.

Some days later, as the sun shone down in warm splendor, and a breeze came up from the ocean, I found myself taking extraordinary comfort from the house. There were, all told, nine bedrooms, two of them large suites with accompanying bathrooms, a formal dining room, a totally enclosed glass salon, a large kitchen, a study or library and various odd little rooms filled with green plants. One, a sunroom, was glorious, with tropical palms and a velvet-covered divan on which to just sit and enjoy. I found myself utilizing it most afternoons, watching the sun turn the clouds the color of wedding ring gold and leave the heavens to slip slowly into the sea.

And so it was the sound of the sea that lulled me to sleep and woke me gently at dawn. Previously I had thought of selling everything quickly, closing and putting the house on the market and returning to Boston, yet the more I pondered the less I liked the idea. What was my hurry? I curled up on the easy chair on the veranda with a cup of tea each morning and enjoyed the feel of my ancestor's domain. Selling it now bordered on sacrilege, I felt, so I dallied. I found a delightful leafy wood to wander around and a small lake nearby.

On the sixth day there came a timid knock on the front door, and I opened it to behold a small, dainty woman standing on the stoop, hands clasped together.

"Sorry to disturb you, missus, and there's awful sad I am to hear of Mrs. Belgermaine's passing, but I was wondering if you needed someone to keep house, if you be staying on, that is."

So, it seemed, word had got around, I thought, and was almost relieved to see a friendly inquiring face after so much solitude. Indeed, I would not be able to keep this formidable house clean without help, but was I staying on?

"Please, yes, of course I will need help," I heard myself earnestly reply.

"Come back in the morning, and we'll get started getting this old house back into some kind of shape. What is your name?"

We spoke for a few more minutes, discussing salary, viewing the many dust-clothed rooms together, getting to feel comfortable with each other, and it was settled. I hired Marjorie at once, and she smiled with obvious pleasure.

It was that small woman that cemented the thought I had been sequestering in the back of my mind. Yes, I would be staying on it now occurred to me, without a doubt. I decided in a heartbeat that here I would make a new life. I sent a quick wire to Boston, terminating my employment. Keep the severance pay, thanks for the memory. I returned to my apartment in the Boyle district to pick up essentials, including my magnificent Siamese cat Cassandra, and a drive back and welcome to my new Cape Cod home, all courtesy of Anna Belgermaine.

After a few more days, the will probated, and my bank balance grew portentously. Something else was on my mind. It was the manuscript, of course. Since reading it countless times, it had managed to lodge in my curiosity like a bur in a dog's fur. Why had my great grandmother written it? What did it mean? Running around in my mind was also a quote from Shakespeare's play *Hamlet*: "There are more things in heaven and earth, Horacio, than are dreamt of in your philosophy."

It was a little over a month later that I made the friendly acquaintance of the nearby village fishmonger.

"You'll not find fresher fish in all of Cape Cod. Comes straight from the fisherman's catch this morning, it does."

There was the baker, whose bread and morning buns delighted the tongue, and the grocer, John Jones, who took an instant liking to my being a new customer.

"Come around and meet my wife. She'll be fair tickled to meet a relative of Mrs. Belgermaine. There's a proud lady she was, to be sure." It was of the baker that I inquired if there was a library close by.

"A library? Aye, not three miles that away. Mrs.

Bernard's been librarian there since afore I were a boy in short pants." He pointed in the direction I should take. "You be a reader, then?" He scratched his graying thatch of hair.

I was impetuously tempted to disclose the contents of the manuscript I had discovered but quickly thought better of it. I needed to do preliminary research, but about what I wasn't yet sure. I was beginning the process of feeling my way down a dark, ghostly passage without a spark of light, yet knew I would have to traverse it and keep my own counsel in the meantime. So I nodded, "Good day," and presently took my leave.

The librarian was indeed as old as a withered apple, her hair white and scarce upon a tiny head, but her smile beamed wide and generous, and so I found myself totally at ease.

After a few opening questions and answers, mostly how I had come to be in the Cape and would I be resettling, that I finally broached the subject.

"Did you ever have occasion to meet Mrs. Anna Belgermaine?" I inquired after introducing myself as her great-granddaughter. There was no one but the two of us in the library on that sunny morning. It was a small library stacked from floor to ceiling with books, many bound in fine leather, which I surmised had been given as gifts. Some I thought would be quite rare. It was a lovely place to pass the hours.

"Yes, indeed," replied Mrs. Bernard, now studying me with intelligent blue eyes. "Why, she was here many times. One of our best patrons."

"Was she, by any chance, doing research on any particular subject?" I edged around, not wanting to show my hand. By voicing it, I knew we had probably come to the same conclusion. Had there been any record of a sailor named Alan Dunn living in these parts a century and a half ago that had been lost at sea? Is this what Mrs. Belgermaine had also come searching for?

Mrs. Bernard clasped her weathered chin in her hand, deep in thought, but I could see she was observing me closely.

"There had been a time, years after she lost her husband in that awful fire, when she came almost all the time trying to find reference to some sea-faring tale. Quite anxious she was. When I could find nothing of note here, we enquired into Boston's great library, and I think she found what she was looking for. After that she seemed calm."

"What was it she found?" I asked, holding my breath now. "Was it a fable she found?"

"Why no," said Mrs. Bernard. "no fable at all. It was a true ship right out of Cape Cod called the *Frances Gray* that got herself sunk over in Africa with all hands. Dreadful tragedy, but then we've had many a ship go down with lots of hometown boys. The other ship was a hundred and fifty years past, no one to even remember that one, I'm thinking. I don't know why she was in a blather about that particular ship."

"Was that it?" I asked. I was reaching the end now. My own great-grandmother had done all the research for me long ago. What if I mentioned Alan Dunn and something else came to light, and I found myself on forbidden ground? How much did this sweet librarian know? Had Anna Belgermaine confided in anyone at all? I was beginning to think that she had not made mention of this event, that it was beyond her comprehension. Therefore, it could not be realized by anyone, so she had recorded it the only way she knew fit and hidden it away for the future.

"What do you mean?" Mrs. Bernard countered, but underneath I think I heard, "Best leave things be now."

With that unspoken advice I already gleaned the answers. Something unworldly had happened to my great-grandmother, not a fable but an inexplicable happening all those years ago. Perhaps the librarian had enough knowledge or intuition to put two and two together, perhaps not, but she was gently warning me to pry no further into a mystery that could never be solved. Taking my leave, I felt the little old librarian's eyes following me out the door and as far down the street as she could see me.

I have inhabited this house for over a year now. The four seasons have come and gone, and I have made friends of my neighbors and townsfolk. Marjorie has become a friend as well as a great help in my magnificent house on the Cape.

"I don't know how ever Mrs. Belgermaine kept her place clean, so big it is. But then, after her husband passed, it seemed she wanted nothing but to be here alone, poor lady."

I took the opportunity to repaint my home a brilliant frost white so she stands out like a beacon. Fishing boats coming back into port tell me she can be seen for many leagues, and somehow that is a comfort to me.

"Your house guides me back home better than any lighthouse," said Thomas, the gentle fisherman I have been seeing. He is a kind man, and we spend happy hours together. Like my great-grandmother, I find myself standing on the high cliff, watching the boats far below as they cleave through tall ocean waves. Perhaps I'm watching for something else too, if everything else will ever be just right, but perhaps I'm just daydreaming. I haven't told anyone about the manuscript—until now. I'm not sure I ever will. I put it back in the secret drawer in the cherry wood cabinet. Best leave some things alone, I'm thinking. I don't put much stock in the netherworld or ghosts either, but it's winter again, and the wind flings pebbles at the door as I lay awake in this great bed with Cassandra tight by my side. And I can hear the voice as it comes back to the house, and it's calling me.

The End

About the author:

I'm a native of the United Kingdom, now living in California. I've had fifty-two short stories published, live with my best friend, a massage therapist, and three Siamese cats. I began reading at five years of age when mother refused to read the end of fairy tales, telling me, "You have to find out for yourself," so I did. I'm working on a second novel, with the first one awaiting a publisher.

Shadows Lost

by Kevin R. Quirt (Ontario, Canada)

Rachel would have fallen asleep on the observation table if it were not for the wires pressing into her scalp. She couldn't remember the last peaceful night she'd had, but she fought sleep whenever she could. Sleep always came with the nightmares of frantically searching for her crying baby, never able to find her.

The dextromethorphan would be taking effect soon, and her lab assistant Pete would be activating the tiny magnetic clip glued behind Rachel's ear to stimulate her angular gyrus. She ignored the lab machinery's various beeps and flashes and waited for any sense that her experience was about to begin. Even if the experiment failed again, waiting for it to happen allowed her to think about something less painful, for a while at least.

A sensation like diving into a wave overtook her, and she embraced the feeling and left her thoughts behind. The cascade of energy over the periphery of her senses confused her. Had she just been propelled forward, or did the world take a giant step back?

Quiet now, the motion stopped, but her senses continued to hum with a crispness that informed her she'd never left the room. She'd only left her body.

Rachel opened her senses and saw her body beneath her. She could see every fiber on her black jeans and how the folds of her sweater flowed into one another effortlessly. The steady beeping of the electrocardiogram reverberated through her, letting her know that her heart, though distant, wasn't strained by the high DMX dose. She listened to the scratching of pen on paper from the EEG. Each swish of the mechanical pen oscillating back and forth sounded like a tight turn with skis through snow.

It's real, she thought as she reveled in the new sensations. She'd read the reports of out-of-body-experiences and wondered what people meant when they said they could sense everything when they left their body.

After years of research and trials, her experiment was a success: the elicitation of an OBE through magnetic field brain stimulation in a controlled environment. She thought she'd be more excited. She looked around at the test equipment Pete had put in place. Standard ghost-hunting fare: a thermal scanner, an EMF reader and a motion detector. She didn't agree with the choice of equipment, but her backer, an avid believer in the paranormal, insisted.

Get to work, she thought and started the mental checklist of actions to perform while the OBE lasted: try to activate each detection device in sequence, twice, then move into the observation room where Pete was sitting and read a randomly generated, five-digit number off his computer screen.

Rachel took one more look at her body and coasted over to the detection equipment. She moved around each one and watched their needles sit idle until she moved on. The number generator was the key to the experiment. She had a 1-in-100,000 chance of guessing the number that the computer generated. Pete wasn't even supposed to look at it, to remove any possibility of an ESP interaction instead of an OBE. If she successfully reported the number, that was good enough proof for anyone that her experiment had worked.

With a thought she was through the wall and into the observation room. She took a moment to let the new sensations envelop her and stopped suddenly. Her senses were telling her one thing that couldn't be possible; there was a Rachel already in the room.

She stared at the other Rachel, who was spying over Pete's shoulder as he looked at the readouts from the equipment. Pete took no notice of either Rachel and leaned his heavy frame forward. His chair let out a groan that would normally have sent a shiver down Rachel's spine. His stomach popped the buttons holding his lab coat together, exposing his black *The Prodigy* t-shirt. The hefty rave-fan yawned as he gazed over Rachel's body in the other room.

"Who are you?" Rachel asked. The entity had her old, curly hairstyle. Rachel had stopped using all hair products when she found out she was pregnant.

The duplicate turned to Rachel and flashed annoyance at being disturbed.

"What are you doing here?" Rachel asked with more force. "Why do you look like a younger me?"

The other Rachel turned back at the readouts and answered, "Actually, it's you who looks like an older me."

Rachel felt fear rise inside her. Was this a ghost? Was this whole experience a hallucination? Why was it interested in watching her body?

My body!

Rachel backed away from the duplicate. She began to panic, wondering if she could figure out a way back into her body before the entity could steal it—if that's what it wanted. But it just stood there, staring at the data outputs.

The chair creaked again as Pete sat up. He looked through the window into the observation room and spoke into the microphone. "Anything happen?" he asked into the room where her body lay.

Rachel felt the world stop when she heard a voice reply back.

"I might've fallen asleep for a second," her body responded. "I think I zoned out for a bit. Nothing else."

Rachel flashed back over her body and was stunned to see it sitting up on the table. Her body reached under her shirt to remove the ECG lead wires from her chest. If Rachel had been in her body, she would have done the same thing to keep Pete from trying to do it. You make the mistake of sleeping with one of your lab assistants, and they all think they are going to get some. The body let out a sigh as she removed the wires from her scalp. Rachel could see the annoyance on her body's face because the wax used to hold the EEG wires in place was sticking to her hair.

Rachel tried to jump into her body but found herself on the other side. Both she and her body looked up as Pete entered the room to wrap up the loose wires from the equipment.

"We'll try again tomorrow," Rachel's body said.

"Can't," Pete replied. "My shift at the hospital starts tomorrow night, and I still need to study."

Rachel kept trying to fly into her body as it argued

with Pete about the importance her of research versus the pressures on rave-loving medical students during their internship.

"Why do I need to be here? Why can't you sit in the booth for a while? Hire a few patients to be your guinea pigs? You have the funding now. I was crazy to take this job. I'm done!" Pete yelled as he stormed out.

Rachel's body let her assistant leave without a peep. Both Rachels knew Pete's couldn't afford to turn down the extra cash, and changing subjects at each test event would just introduce another uncontrolled variable. Rachel watched her body glance at the data outputs and toss them on the desk before it slumped back on the table. Rachel forgot how tired she'd been before she left her body. She could see the body was still feeling it as it surrendered to a nap.

Rachel kept trying to return to her body. She tried lying within it. She tried screaming at it, as if she were trying to wake from a nightmare. Finally, she rested beside her sleeping body, feeling its deep, steady breathing. She took in everything her new senses told her. Try as she might, she could sense nothing wrong with her body, except that she wasn't in it.

A light snore let Rachel know her body was not going anywhere for a while. She turned her attention back to the observation room. Even through the wall, she could tell the other presence was still there.

Rachel's thoughts carried her into the room where she saw the other being, still leaning over Pete's chair, staring at the now unchanging screen.

"What are you doing?" Rachel asked.

The entity looked up and spoke in a tone reminiscent of an observation during an experiment. "You've been able to maintain pattern integrity for a significant period of time after termination of body contact."

"What do you mean, 'termination'?"

"You're responsive to environmental stimuli and capable of expressing frustration over your lack of comprehension of your current situation. I wonder what's causing your strength of coherence."

Rachel wanted to slam her duplicate against a wall to force her to talk sense.

"What was your last thought before you left the body?" the younger duplicate asked.

"None of your business," Rachel snapped back. "Answer my question. Who the hell are you?"

The duplicate paused before answering. "Your pattern carries a higher than expected degree of emotionality. That could explain the length of your coherence, but it's also making you difficult to interview." The duplicate smiled. "I'm the Rachel that the body produced during the first OBE experiment over two years ago."

The Rachel? That made no sense. "The first OBE experiment was a failure," she replied. "Nothing happened."

"That's what the Rachel currently in the body thinks happened today. She has no clue that she, on a consciousness level, is less than an hour old. Actually the first experiment, and many since, were successes," her younger duplicate responded. "My experience was similar to yours. I achieved a coherent consciousness outside of my body, but my biological brain moved on and generated another consciousness before I returned, so I could not reintegrate. I watched my body get up and move on without me. It took a few more observations before I realized what was going on."

"Which was?"

The duplicate smirked. She wanted Rachel to realize that she'd figured out more from the experiments than Rachel had. The duplicate reminded her so much of herself from two years ago, so competitive and focused only on her research.

The duplicate tried to explain in a manner that the newly separated Rachel would understand. "Consciousness outside the body is like the sand castles we used to build at the edge of the ocean. Every wave of sensation threatens to carry more and more of the structure away. If the consciousness doesn't have enough focus to hold itself together, the castle will dissolve into the sand."

Rachel had always hypothesized that consciousness was generated by the brain but could function independently of it. She'd never considered that if a consciousness left the brain, the brain might just move on and create another consciousness. Rachel shared that memory of building sandcastles. Mom would fret that she was building them so close to the water, but the water's edge had the best sand for building. She hadn't thought of sandcastles in years and was surprised she could think of them now. Memory is built into the biological structure of the brain. Since distant memories are called into consciousness but are not necessarily part of consciousness, she hadn't expected long-forgotten memories to be carried from her body. But she could see each castle she'd built in her mind's eye. These memories had to come from somewhere. Maybe there was some connection between her and her body yet.

"You didn't seem surprised that I showed up during the experiment, but you did seem surprised that I stayed,"

Rachel said.

"A consciousness coherence-pattern usually manifests during these experiments. Most dissipate within seconds, some after a few minutes. It seems to depend on their level of focus at the time of their departure from the body, which brings me back to my question. What were you thinking of just before you left the body?"

Rachel didn't want to answer the question. This should have been the one person she should be able to tell anything to, but she knew that this manifestation of her consciousness had been released from her body before she even got pregnant or lost Annie.

"Do you know what happened to me," Rachel paused, "after you left the body?"

"After I left, there were six more experimental events. Manifestations were produced in five of them. There was a break in experimental events during your pregnancy, and they resumed two months ago with an increasing frequency of one or two per week. You are the first manifestation since the experiments resumed, likely because Pete hasn't told you he's cutting back on the DMX dose so he can steal it for his raves. I was so happy to see you get back to my work. I have to admit, I was pretty angry when you took over my body and decided to take a hiatus."

"It was not a hiatus! I was pregnant, but Annie...died, less than an hour after she was born."

The younger Rachel's expression flashed a hint of annoyance. "That event would have caused a strong emotional response in you. Were you thinking about Annie when you left your body?"

"I haven't thought of anything since! That's why I'm here all the time. I need to think about something else for a while." Rachel paused, feeling guilt over her words "something else for a while."

"The focus of attention on the loss of your daughter has allowed you to maintain your coherence. Interesting."

Rachel thought of throwing her head back and in an instant was staring at the ceiling. "Interesting," she repeated. "I was thinking of how much I miss Annie. I can't stand it." She turned back to the duplicate. "Were you there? Did you see anything when she died? Do you think she could have manifested like us?"

"I wasn't there, but it's possible. Newborns are almost entirely instinctual. I guess if Annie was focused on a particular need when she died.... My focus is tied to my work. I can't maintain integrity outside of the lab."

"The maternity ward is only two floors up!" Rachel responded, surprised a version of her could show as little interest in Annie as the father.

"I told you I can't maintain my integrity outside of this lab. It's too closely linked with my work. I've tried to leave to study some of the patterns that lasted long enough to leave the room, but I lose focus and start to feel myself being washed away." The duplicate stopped to compose herself. "I think we have an opportunity here. You've been looking to work to help you move past your daughter's death, and I've been sitting here for years as nothing but an observer. Now that we are together, maybe we can help each other out and take some control over this situation."

"Do you think I can go back?"

"No. The experiences the body undergoes in the few seconds it takes for a coherence pattern to leave changes the brain's biological template just enough so that the consciousness pattern can't reintegrate. The brain, missing its consciousness, just creates a new one. Since the new consciousness has the same biological brain structure, it comes to life with memories that give the new Rachel the impression that she already lived a lifetime."

The duplicate's theory made sense. The only reliable cases Rachel had heard of OBEs involved people deeply anesthetized or dead for a few minutes. No new experiences to mess up the brain's template during the return.

That also meant that she could never go back.

She wanted to talk more about Annie, but the duplicate seemed satisfied with the information she'd received and turned back to the computer monitor.

"Look how your brain waves peaked. I've seen it every time an OBE is produced, but this peak is huge. I wonder if the death of the baby made you so emotional that your sympathetic nervous system was working in overdrive and reinforced your pattern. This is amazing. I never took emotion into the equation before. I couldn't have figured this out without you. I thought you were throwing away my career when you took over my body and got pregnant, but you really came through! Glad to have you back on the team, Rachel."

Rachel stared at this leftover from her earlier self with pity. It was soulless. Seeking answers, but missing all the important things.

Was Rachel like her? Only a shadow of a personality? Too much of an emotional wreck to realize she'd left most of herself behind on the table?

"I can't do this...I can't stay here like this."

Her younger self muttered but did not look away from the screen. "Christ. If the only thing holding you together is the pain of losing your daughter, then you have a miserable existence to look forward to." The duplicate looked up. "Why don't you make one more contribution to science to help us both out? My experience outside the lab has led me to believe that if you let your senses go, you can disrupt your pattern and lose yourself. If I'm right, you don't need to be outside the lab to do this. How about we put my theory to the test and see if we can put you out of both of our miseries."

Rachel thought about her duplicate's words for a while and knew she did not want to live as an empty shell of pain. Without caring to say goodbye, she let her senses inhale and felt herself expand to fill the room and beyond. She could hear the cold clicks of nurse shoes in the hall outside the lab and the polytonal emissions of the communal TV in the geriatric ward upstairs. With a thought, she could see the flickering lights reflecting off the contoured faces, sleeping or staring at the TV. Her thoughts became less important as her senses took paths of their own through each of the wards. The hospital felt almost completely inside her now, although she was so diffuse, there was little of Rachel or her pain left. The sensations washed over her, offering to carry pieces of her away into the noise. She started to let go of herself.

I guess this is what it's like when a copy dies, she mused. Her senses were touching almost everything in the hospital, too much for her to focus on. It wasn't scary or overwhelming, just easy to get lost in. She figured this is what losing coherence was but didn't care. There was nothing for her in this existence. She hoped the new Rachel had better luck letting go of the anguish from Annie's death than she did. She threw herself into her senses, hoping to bury her pain.

Crying.

Rachel's consciousness jerked back together. She was alone in the observation room, beside her sleeping body. The duplicate was probably still in the other room, staring at the screen. Her senses were still like dancing vines through the hospital, sending her a hush of white noise. One of the tendrils sent her a sound that cut through the snow of sensation: crying—above her. The cry was unmistakable. It was the same cry she heard in her dreams of Annie.

Rachel looked at her body and folded herself around it in an embrace. She hoped the new Rachel would understand that everything was going to be better now.

She shuddered as she followed the sad sound through the geriatric floor and up into the maternity ward. She rose into the operating room, and she ignored the caesarean that was going on. The noise wasn't from this room. Of course it wouldn't be. Annie had died in the ICU while Rachel was being stitched up. Rachel only held Annie after she died.

Rachel narrowed her senses out of the operating room and into the ICU. The walls between the rooms dissolved, along with everything else, into a dusty white background: everything except Annie. She encircled the crying baby and let out a cry of her own. Her heart filled, holding her daughter for the first time, but it also broke when Rachel realized Annie must have been crying here all these months.

"Waiting for Mommy," Rachel tried to whisper to Annie.

Annie's crying slowed as she rested in her mother's embrace and let out a sigh. Rachel felt the pain that bound them together evaporate, and she held Annie close as both shimmered into the white background.

* * *

In the lab the newest Rachel woke from her nap with a yawn. The sleep had definitely helped. She hadn't felt this good in a while. She sat up, stretched and tried to remember what the weather was supposed to be like this afternoon. It'd be nice to get some fresh air. As she walked out of her lab, she thought about the nap and whether a sleeping subject would work better.

The End

About the author:

Based in Ottawa, Canada, Kevin Quirt writes speculative fiction in between the learning experiences provided by his children. A psychology major, Kevin's fascination with the human mind is explored using fantastic circumstances. You can learn more about Kevin at http://smartasamouse.blogspot.com/.

KEVIN R. QUIRT

Voices on the Wind

by Terry Phillius (Colorado, USA)

Swift Eagle crouched at the far end of the clearing, leaning over a fresh pile of grizzly scat. He got on all fours and sniffed it, the steam rising into his nostrils. Behind him, hiding behind a small, shivering grove of aspens, intently watching Swift Eagle's every move, crouched Ben, tightly gripping his .50 caliber muzzleloader.

Swift Eagle picked up a firm black turd and squeezed it between his thumb and forefinger. He stood up slowly, his raven-black hair glistening and shimmering in the fresh, morning sunlight.

Muscles and sinews rippled underneath his skin as he straightened and pulled an arrow from the quiver resting against his dark, tanned back. He nocked it with his left hand and held the arrow tight against the bowstring with his right. He lifted his head and began sniffing the air, hoping to get a scent of the bear both men had been tracking since sun-up. The cool, spring breeze carried nothing but the pleasant smell of wild, mountain blossoms.

There was no trace of the ursine killer that had taken the life of a brave guarding the tribe's ponies during the previous night.

Ben stood up as quiet as a panther and checked the load of his rifle. Levering back the hammer with a quiet snick, he nodded to himself, certain it was ready to fire. As Ben searched the trees surrounding the clearing, he watched a great, dark-plumed eagle glide over the clearing and rest in the top of a weathered pine just beyond where Swift Eagle stood.

Although his back was turned, the sound did not escape Swift Eagle's sharp ears. He looked up and watched the giant bird settle in the top of the tree. For long moments he did nothing. Then, with a slow, deliberate movement, he grasped the nocked arrow and placed it carefully back into the quiver. Ben could say nothing, for he didn't want to scare off the grizzly or alert it to their presence, but he was bewildered. He knew as well as Swift Eagle that the bear was close by, *very* close by. He could think of no reason why his friend would be so reckless.

The eagle made a quiet squeal, and Swift Eagle looked up at the bird, nodding his head as if he suddenly understood something. Ben took a step into the clearing and cast questioning eyes at the Cheyenne across from him. Swift Eagle turned to Ben and smiled, holding up his right hand with the palm outward. Then, sudden as a lightning strike, there was a crash in the trees behind Ben. He spun at the commotion—a moment too late. He was bowled over before he could even see what was coming at him, let alone get his rifle raised to fire. All he saw was a huge, dark brown flash pass over him as he tumbled into the tall summer grass of the clearing.

The bear, aware that she was being followed, had doubled back on the two men, trying to stay downwind of them to hide her passage. Guided by a force not her own, she ignored the first man and headed straight for the other who's scent had been plaguing her dreams for weeks. To suddenly see him had deeply affected her down to the core of her spirit.

Although Ben couldn't see it, Swift Eagle never made a move as the grizzly approached. His face was calm as the charging beast ran straight for him. As Ben got to his feet, shaking off the dazing blow the bear had inflicted upon him, he turned to see the bear thunder into Swift Eagle's calm, motionless form. Swift Eagle screamed as it knocked him to the ground, and he flailed his arms helplessly as the enraged grizzly raked across his chest with vicious sweeps of deadly claws. Ben raised the rifle that had miraculously not left his hands, aiming it just behind its front leg. He swore once under his breath and slowly squeezed the trigger, his body twisted heavily with the tremendous recoil of the .50 cal. The deafening boom shook the entire valley, echoing back and forth many times off the sides of the hills stretching up and away from them, reaching up into a cloudless sky.

There was an inhuman growl of agony as the bullet ripped through skin, muscle and bone, burying itself deeply into the pounding heart of the grizzly. She turned to face what had caused her so much pain, and through blood-shot eyes she saw the man standing there amidst a billow of smoke quickly drifting away on the gentle breeze. Three steps were all she could manage before she collapsed in a heap in the middle of the clearing. Blood pounded in her ears as she lay motionless, watching the man walk slowly up towards her. She could feel no motion within her chest, and she knew that her time had come. A blossom of blood erupted from her mouth, and she shook violently as life fled from her body.

Ben watched the bear blow its last breath out onto the tall, now blood-damp grass. With a shudder across the length of its body, it released its bowels as the spark of life abruptly left it.

"Clever son-of-a-bitch," Ben said as he walked past the dead form of the grizzly. Walking up to the broken shape of Swift Eagle, he said, "Why the hell didn't ya keep that arrow nocked? Ya could've at least slowed the bastard down!"

"Bitch," Swift Eagle corrected with difficulty and a fit of painful coughing. He lay on the grass covered in his own blood and drew in deep, heavy breaths, wincing at the pain flashing across his chest. He could feel that most of his ribs were broken from the weight of the bear, and there were deep furrows in his flesh from the powerful tearing of her claws. He gazed up into the eyes of the eagle above him and smiled weakly.

Swift Eagle spoke to Ben in the tongue of his people. "Help me get to the tree my old friend." He coughed once and spat out a mouthful of blood. "It is my time. I must tell you something before I pass on to the next cycle."

"Tell me somethin'? What the hell are ya talkin' about?" Ben moved up to Swift Eagle and, placing his rifle in the grass, dragged his mortally injured friend up to the tree, leaning him against the trunk.

Swift Eagle said, "You are one of the People. You have been for a long time. I'm moving on to the next path, just as I was told by the Old Ones in my dreams. That is my destiny. The presence of the eagle here and now showed me my time had come, and I am glad that you are the one here with me. For it is to you that I can now begin to tell The Tale and bring you into The Circle. Until now I did not know if we would be able to hunt with each other in the hereafter. Now I know."

"Tale, what tale? This ain't no time for tellin' stories. I gotta see if I can bandage ya up so's I can get you to Running Wolf to be fixed up proper, so there ain't gonna be no here-after, not for quite a spell."

"No. You will not have to do that. Here is where I will die, and here is where my spirit will become one with the Great Spirit." Swift Eagle was racked by a fit of painful coughing, and the blood seeped even more quickly from his wounds with the exertion. Ben could see Swift Eagle's pulse as it flowed thickly out of his wounds. "Long ago the Great Ones made a Circle, and in my dreams they told me that was where I would go when I passed out of the life of this world. Listen, my friend. Listen to the wind. Do you hear them?" Swift Eagle placed a bloody hand on Ben's arm.

"Hear what? I don't hear a damn...." and then he heard. There were voices on the wind, and although he couldn't understand what they were saying, he knew they spoke.

"Those are the Old People, Ben. They are my ancestors, and now they will be yours as well. You must take me to the Great Circle—the voices will lead you— you must take my body there and build the stones. Promise me. I can't tell you the Tale here. I don't have time. But from there I will be able to speak to you in your dreams as the Old Ones have spoken to me for so long." Swift Eagle coughed again, harder and more labored than before, a trickle of blood formed in his nostrils and slid its way to his chest. The pulse of the blood seeping from his wounds was much slower than before, almost gone.

"I swear on my life. But where the hell is this Great Circle? I don't know the way."

"Listen to the voices dancing across the breezes of these hills. They will guide you better than ever I could," Swift Eagle said smiling. He closed his eyes for the last time.

Ben sat there for quite a while, watching the life flow ever slower from his dying friend. And then the pulsing stopped completely. Ben stood up, and there was a deafening shriek from the eagle still perched in the top of the tree. As the unearthly sound finally stopped echoing off the valley walls, Ben watched in amazement as a shimmering, ghostly-white mist rose out of Swift Eagle's body and drifted into the air. The eagle spread its wings, as if it had been startled by something, and the misty-gray form floated straight up at the eagle and flowcd into its body. It let out another shriek, but the sound was different this time—surprised. *Almost human*, Ben thought to himself.

"I'll be damned," was all Ben said as he watched the eagle fly off to the west.

*   *   *

When I moved into my cabin on the hill—the cabin that had belonged to my grandfather—my then-wife-now-ex couldn't understand it. She was born and bred in the city, so she had no wish to spend any time up here among evergreens, wind and silence. Our friends had told me that moving up here was the final straw. In their letters they scolded my need for solitude, that it was what forced her to file for the divorce. Time and time again they had written, telling me that if only I would come down off the hill, I might be able to get her back. As painful as the loss was, leaving was something I just couldn't do. Not then or now. The Secret had brought me back to the hill. I had been born up here, it's true, but there was more up here than pine trees and fresh air. At the time my wife had accused me of being a social misfit, because I wanted to stay up here "in the middle of nowhere," as she used put it, and do my writing. She was wrong. They were all wrong.

I hadn't come up here to be alone. This had been a magic place for me. The Secret surrounded the hill—and the hills surrounding it—a secret that my grandfather and Mr. Ashley had passed on to me. I had never even told my wife The Secret, for it was an old thing of the mountains and the past, something she would never believe, let alone understand. But I now had a chance to pass that secret on to my son. In the settlement set down by her lawyer—I had chosen not to have one—I was not allowed to see my own son for more than one week a year. My wife said that she wanted her son to be a part of her world not mine, and up here there would be no place for him to play, no friends for him to be with. I couldn't argue with her.

Our friends had said that I caved in too easily. They wrote to me that if only I had gotten a lawyer, if only I had fought for more time with him, I would now know who he was. I hadn't seen him since the divorce. That was sixteen years ago. Once the divorce papers were signed, she moved to southern California to raise him in *their* ways. She and her new husband were both capable parents, and through letters from old friends I discovered that my son was indeed happy, doing well in school and now preparing for college. It was never my place to interfere with that process, but he was eighteen now, and they all told me that I had missed out on the fragile years of his youth, that I could never get those years back, and he would never really be my son. In some respects they were correct. I couldn't get the time back, but I had a gift for him they would never understand—ever.

I had chosen to stay out of his life for his own sake. It was better for him to grow up in a place where he could more easily be a part of the world that was preparing to receive him, but the time had finally come. It was now time to impart to him what had been imparted to me so many years ago. If he wished, he would be able to carry The Secret to his children and beyond into the formless mists of the future.

Shortly before his eighteenth birthday, I wrote him a letter telling him who and where I was. It was brief, but it must have sparked in him some interest about the man who had sired him. Maybe he was at that age where he wanted to know who he was, and knowing who I was would help him in that quest. He had written me roughly a month later, asking if he could come visit me. I suspect that he didn't tell his mother where he planned to go or even for how long.

She probably would have been furious. After all this time she would probably say that I wasn't his father anymore, that I had no right to bring him up here on the hill and force on him the disease or affliction she thought had destroyed me and our marriage. I had no intention of telling him anything he didn't ask about, so her fears were unfounded. But she had always been a bit paranoid about life—of living—so that's why he asked me in the letter to not say anything to anyone until he had a chance to break it to her after he returned. For her, if things didn't fit the world as she saw it, she became obstinate and confused.

So there I sat, rocking gently on my porch, watching the sun inch its way across the roof of the valley, waiting for him to arrive. A single hawk circled and soared above me, crying out almost like a small child, as if it was trying to get my attention, but my thoughts were with the pending arrival of my guest. It's an odd sensation waiting for someone who is my son but whom I haven't seen since his infancy. It's almost as if he really isn't my son, as if I'm waiting for a stranger to drive up the narrow dirt trail that leads from my home to the small mountain community fifteen miles below the entrance to the valley. What to say, what to do? How does one greet an expected stranger? I tried to listen to the hill for an answer, but nothing came.

The breezes gliding across the face of the hill were warm and full of quiet mumblings. They offered no answer as they slid through the boughs of the shivering evergreens. However, as I rekindled the dead embers of my pipe, there seemed to be an answer whispered here and there for me to catch, if only I were in the right place, listening with the right ear. Yet those whispers eluded my porch like children playing hide and seek in a deep forest. They were voices mingling with the greenery and life that covered the hill, voices that taunted and teased me, trying to get me out of my rocker and chase them once again amongst the wildlife scattered here and there around me.

As a child I was always taken by the voices, but as I grew older I learned to ignore them when I wanted to. In my youth I had been scolded harshly by my grandfather more than once for missing dinner because of the games I played with the voices. Many times I let them lead me all across the range to special places—and on several occasions the old place—but there wasn't much need for that these days. I had hopes that my stranger would also be entranced by the wispy voices on the wind. A smile came to my lips, and I drew deeply from my now glowing pipe. That would not be so bad, I thought.

The sun continued its journey across the valley and began sliding down behind the saddle made by Finley and Howard's Peak. As the hawk continued its lament in the sky above, I began to worry if my stranger would be able to find the hill. I'd made a map leading him to my home, but up here it was easy to lose one's way among the twists and turns of the range. This was not an easy place to find, even with a map. A knot formed in the pit of my stomach. I didn't have a phone, so he would have to find the place or wait for a letter to reach me from wherever he decided to wait.

Laughter played in the distance of the forest, laughter directed at my concern. For just as I was about to go down the road to wait at the entrance of the valley, the voices were interrupted by the distant hum of a motor echoing off valley walls, muffled slightly by verdant pines.

I stood to peer down the valley and saw the scattered glow of headlights threading their way up towards the hill. The knot in my stomach tightened even more. I stepped to the edge of the porch and leaned against the weathered log support of the overhang. All I could do was wait.

"He's coming, Mr. Ashley," I said quietly to the forest. "He's almost here." I turned my head towards a big pine standing a short distance from the cabin and watched a gentle, wispy puff of smoke filter its way up into the rapidly darkening sky. I could just barely make out the faint, pinpoint glow of his pipe underneath the tree. "What the hell am I supposed to say?" I asked, but I knew Ashley wouldn't answer me. He'd always told me that people had to solve their own problems.

It took ten minutes for the car to wind its way up the rough twists and turns of the valley. The sun had sunk behind the ridge when headlights finally bathed me in a hot glare as the car came around the last bend in the road. I squinted in the brightness and covered my eyes to avoid the glare. The car pulled up and the lights went out before he was fully in the rock driveway. He pulled up next to my Land Cruiser, and I could just barely make out the shape of a brand new Celica. When the tires stopped rolling, I heard a deep, booming rhythm coming from the stereo. But that too shut off, and the engine was cut. There was a long pause, as if he were deciding whether or not to get out of the car, but then I heard the click of a door, and the dome light came on. A shadow of a temporary plate taped to the rear window stood out harshly on the trunk.

For just a moment I had my first look at my son in over sixteen years. His hair was long, pulled back in a ponytail, and it was the same light brown color my hair had been when I was his age. Mine was darker now and graying in streaks. He wore a tank top with some sort of design on the front that I couldn't make out. Before I could make out any more details, he grabbed a bag from the passenger seat and stepped away from the car, closing the door quietly. The dome light went out, and I heard rather than saw him walk towards me. My eyes hadn't quite adjusted to the sudden darkness, so all I could do was wait for him to get closer before I could really see him.

"Watch out for the log, there." Just as his footsteps reached the spot I was talking about, there was the sound of stumbling feet.

"Shit," he said. His voice was young and strong. It

was a man's voice, but full of youth, and it suddenly saddened me like never before that I had missed out on sixteen years of his life.

"Mr. Johnson?" His voice wavered slightly, as if he wasn't sure if he was in the right place and I the right person.

"Will. Call me Will. And yes, it's me. I was expecting you a little sooner. I hope you didn't have too much trouble finding the place, William."

"It's a long story.... Well, not that long, and it's Billy," he said.

"Sorry about the dark," I replied. "I should have had a lantern going."

He paused just at the base of the porch steps expectantly. "I've got some more stuff in the car, should I go get it?" he asked. I still couldn't make out more than his form in the dark, even with my eyes adjusted.

"Naw, let's get it in the morning. You must be starved. Come on inside and I'll start a pot of coffee. Do you drink coffee?" God, I hoped he did. I really didn't have anything else besides water and tea.

He walked up the three steps and stopped in front of me. For an awkward moment it looked as if he didn't know whether to hug me or shake my hand. Then he held out his hand stiffly. "Sure, black, but do you have any sugar?" I clasped his hand and shook it firmly. Good grip.

"Yes, but it's the unrefined kind. Have you ever had that?" I thought I could just barely make out his eyes rolling in the darkness.

"No, but that's okay," he said. Behind him I saw a faint glow of match-light beneath the pine tree.

"Come on in and I'll get us some light." I turned and opened the door to my home. It suddenly occurred to me that what I called home would be quite rustic to someone who had probably spent all of his life in the city. "Just wait by the door until I get a lamp lit."

"Lamp? You don't have any electricity?" There was a simple confusion in his voice. He probably felt like he had stepped into *The Twilight Zone* and walked out into the dark ages. I moved into the cabin and easily wove my way through the sparse furniture.

"Well, I do, just not for lights." I found the lamp and heard him set down his bag. I pulled a match from my shirt pocket—one of the advantages of being a frequent pipe smoker—and, opening the lamp, lit it. A warm glow, gently seeping into nooks and crannies, filled the interior of the main room, and I heard an intake of breath behind me. "It's not much," I said, "but it's pretty comfortable once you get used to it."

The room was sparsely furnished. There was a well-worn bearskin lying in front of the fireplace to the left of the front door. In the middle of the room sat a kitchen table, an old, tottering thing made of oak. Around that were three ancient, hand-made chairs that looked unstable but were actually very sturdy. The 'kitchen,' a simple affair with a small sink, inadequate counter-space and some pale green cupboards, took up the corner to the right of the door. Beyond that sat my desk—the only modern furniture in the whole cabin—and upon that rested my laptop and printer. There were two rocking chairs in front of the fireplace on either side of the bearskin, and on the back wall on the right side of the door leading to the bedroom hung a pair of old, muzzle loading rifles. On the left side of the door was a modern, lever action 30-30 and a Colt .45 dangling in a shoulder holster.

I paused and was again plagued by the knot in my

stomach. Once I turned around I would be faced by my son. Holding my breath, I turned to him.

Legalize Hemp.

That's what his shirt said: *Legalize Hemp* and a big green leaf in the center. It crossed my mind that he was probably trying to make some sort of statement. Or maybe he was testing how I would react. I was certain that his mother would not approve. She had always been down on cannabis. *"Never tried it, never will,"* she would say. He was standing in the doorway with the door halfway open, and a gust of wind ruffled his long hair slightly.

I didn't say a word about the shirt. "Come on in Billy, have a seat." I motioned to a chair at the table. There was no expression on his face at all, but he closed the door behind him and sat down. The old wood creaked as it took up his weight. He was wearing faded blue jeans, and he had on leather sandals with dark brass buckles. I noticed that he wore a pendant on a leather string with a yin-yang on it hanging out of his shirt. His eyes were bright, taking in every corner, every detail of my cabin, and as I looked closer, I noticed that he had his mother's eyes. Dark brown they were, and they shone just as much as hers had. His gaze stopped at my computer, and a puzzled frown came to his face.

"Like I said, I do have electricity, just not for light. That's how I've earned my living over the years." I walked over to the window and pulled out a meat pie I had baked that afternoon. "I've got solar panels and a storage battery array behind the cabin for the computer. Would you like some meat pie? It's fresh."

He hesitated a moment and then said, "Sure, that sounds good. To tell you the truth, I'm starving. I haven't eaten since this morning. I spent the entire day driving all across these mountains trying to find this place."

"Damn it. I'm sorry about that. I should have made the map clearer." Suddenly I felt like an idiot. I placed the pie in front of him, looking into his young eyes, expecting to see irritation. I was surprised to see him smiling.

"No, it's not your fault. I let myself get too distracted by the scenery and missed the turn. I actually had a good time. I've never been to the Rockies, at least not like this. All I've seen are the hills outside of L.A. I'm glad I got the chance to look around. You've picked a beautiful place to live."

"I didn't pick it. I was born here, and you've actually been here before, you just don't remember it. It's more than beautiful, Billy, it's *mystical*. There's not another place like it on Earth, at least that I know of."

He gave me a quick "You've been up here too long" look, which almost immediately disappeared, and then he said, "I believe you," which he obviously didn't. He leaned over and smelled the pie, inhaling deeply. His eyes closed and he exhaled. "Mmmm, that smells great. What's in it?"

I smiled back at him and turned to get the plates, forks, and a knife. "It's probably better that you don't know. It's your great-grandfather's recipe, as least he's the one who taught it to me, and most of the stuff in there you won't find in a grocery store."

He laughed lightly behind me and said, "You're right. I don't want to know. My mom...um...mom tricked me into eating squid because she didn't tell me what it was. She said it was whitefish. When I found out what I was eating, I almost had to run to the bathroom and toss my cookies. It would have been okay if she'd let me know beforehand."

"That's just like your mother." I put the utensils on the table and sat across from him, making the old chair protest loudly as I placed my weight in it. The chairs had been made by my grandfather before my father was born, so I had good reason for keeping them around. My grandfather had always said, *"Keep anything older than you that still works. Respect your elders."*

"Your mother did that sort of thing to me all the time," I said. "I remember once...oh hell, this was before you were born... I remember we were at a cafe in downtown Denver. She tried to get me to eat eel. I didn't try any, the damn stuff looked like giant black and gray boogers dipped in butter." Suddenly I saw that night as clearly as I saw Billy sitting in front of me. "In fact, that was the night we..." I was overcome with sorrow and a feeling of loneliness I hadn't felt in a long time. The hill let you forget a great deal when you wanted it to. Sarah and I had always thought that it was on that night Billy was conceived. We had gone for a long drive towards Estes Park, and on a hillside in the autumn moonlight we made love.

"Will? Are you okay?" he asked. Billy was reaching for the pie with the knife in his hand.

I sniffed and rubbed my nose lamely. "Yeah. Yeah, I'm fine. It's just something I hadn't thought about in a long time. It's nothing." I handed him a plate. He served us both, and we began eating.

"This is great!" he said. "Please don't tell me what's in it till morning. I'd hate to have to run to the bathroom and hurl this up and waste it. I've never tasted anything quite like it."

For the next few minutes we busied ourselves with the eating of fresh baked meat pie, an experience I would recommend to anyone whose company I enjoyed.

"Where *is* the bathroom anyway? Through that door?" He pointed to the back of the cabin with his knife.

I shook my head and tried to talk around a mouthful of pie. "The shitter is around the corner of the porch to the left about twenty meters." His head snapped up in mid-chew, and he looked at me like I was a bit touched in the head. Then he slowly began chewing again. There were only the sounds of cutlery tapping against old plates, the sometimes loud chewing of a bit of gristle that had escaped my careful eye and ministrations with a knife and the occasional gulping of moist pie. It was a very comfortable silence, one I had forgotten how to appreciate in my years of pseudo-solitude.

Billy put down his knife and fork and looked me square in the eyes.

"Do you miss mom?" His question surprised me. There was a hint of accusation in his voice, but only a hint. I really couldn't blame him. I didn't know what Sarah had told him over the years, but I was certain it couldn't be good.

"That's an easy one. I do... or at least I did." I put a chunk of the pie in my mouth and chewed thoughtfully, partly because it was a pretty uncomfortable subject, but mostly to buy myself some time. One of the advantages of living alone in the mountains far away from anyone who could possibly bring up painful memories is that it becomes easy and quite routine to deliberately forget whatever you want to. My memory had become a sort of patch-quilt with some of the pieces missing, or more accurately, cut or torn out. As gramps had always told me, *"If there is nothing to remind us of what we wish to forget, things get conveniently forgotten."* I swallowed and took a deep breath.

"I'll tell you the truth. I haven't really thought about your mother for a long, long time." His eyes narrowed slightly. This was obviously something he had thought a great deal about, long before ever coming up here. "It was easy for me to forget all the things in my life that were painful, but now that you're here, I have to fight off the memories. It's almost as if I'm drowning in them. I do miss your mother, more than she or any of our friends would ever imagine." There was an unspoken accusation behind his eyes identical to the one his mother used to use on me. "I know what you're thinking, and no, I didn't come up here to run away from her...or you for that matter."

"Then why did you come up here? How could you just leave mom and me?"

So that was it.

"I wasn't running away from you or your mother. She and I just wanted different things out of life, and I knew that she would have no trouble finding someone more than suitable to take care of you and her." I paused for a moment and searched his face for what he was feeling. There was a bit of anger, but not much. Mostly it was curiosity and confusion. "Your parents don't know where you are right now, do they?" I asked knowingly. I raised an eyebrow and watched as his cheeks flushed crimson.

He turned his head and looked out through the front window to avoid my gaze and said, "No." But rather than turning back to me as I assumed he would, he did a double take and looked intently out towards the big pine—Mr. Ashley's pine.

I followed his gaze, but from where I was sitting I

couldn't see the base of Ashley's tree. I had a feeling he might have seen a pinpoint of light in the darkness out there.

"And if she did know, do you think she would be happy about it? Would she approve?" The question sat in the air between us for a moment unanswered, and then I continued, "Or would she insist that you stay at home or go someplace else, anything but come up here to see me?" He shook his head, as if to shake off a dream, and then turned back to me.

"We both know she'd be pissed off, and she would probably do whatever she could to get me home," he said defensively.

"Then why are you here? What brought you up here *'into the middle of nowhere'*?" I tried my best to imitate her "annoyed and confused" tone as much as possible, and Billy laughed as he immediately recognized it. "Why did you come to see me, Billy?" I had him.

"It was just something I had to do. You are, after all, my father. I wanted to know who you are, find out about where I came from. But that's different. What has that got to do with you abandoning mom and I."

Anger flared up inside me. "I didn't abandon anybody!" I snapped. I took a deep breath to control the sudden burst of emotion. "Your mother was the one who walked out on me. She filed for divorce. She got the fancy lawyer to get custody rights. She was the one who took you to L.A. where she knew that I would not be able to see you. Did you know that she got her lawyer to allow me only one week a year of visitation rights?" His eyes grew wide at that. I guess the city let people forget things too. It figured. "It was her, Billy, not me. I didn't fight her and her lawyer, because I thought it would be easier for you to grow up with your mother and whomever she decided to marry. And I was right. You've grown up into a fine figure of a man. I'm proud of you, and I can't tell you how happy I am to see you after all this time. I won't say I'm free of fault. Quite the opposite. The divorce is as much my fault as it is your mother's. But the point is that *we* were to blame, not just *me*."

The look on his face had changed, but I couldn't read it. He stood up, and the chair squeaked as it slid across the floor. He walked around the table and stopped right next to me. I stood up, and before I could say anything, he grasped me in a bear hug. For a moment I felt confused and a bit awkward, but then the past washed over me, memories and regrets, and it hit me hard that this was, indeed, my son. I began to notice hints of the infant I had known so many years ago as my baby boy. I hugged him back as hard as I could, and I could feel tears welling up in my eyes. "I'm sorry, son. I'm so sorry I missed out on your life. I'm gonna' make it up to you, though. I promise."

"You already have, dad. Just seeing you. You already have." We spent a long time like that, which was a good thing, because it took some time for me to get control of my tears. I imagine he had the same problem, because every now and then I would hear a sniffle. Finally we separated, and he went to stand in front of the bay window.

"How about that coffee?" I asked, "It'll only take a minute... well, a few anyway." I moved over to the cupboard and got out the old pot that was as old as the cabin.

"Hunh? Oh, yeah. That'll be fine." He kept staring out the window, apparently fascinated by something.

I busied myself with getting the coffee ready, and

every now and then I would gaze over my shoulder and look at him. He didn't move. He just stood there gazing into the night. Occasionally he would look in the direction of the big pine, but he didn't say anything.

"Coffee's ready," I said after a few minutes. He turned around and smiled, but there was something hidden behind the smile, something that was a question—about the pine—but it hadn't formed in his mind yet. I knew it would, eventually.

*   *   *

With the song of a hawk filling the daylight, we spent the next three days getting to really know one another. I told him about growing up around the hill and what his grandfather was like: a kind, quiet man with a big heart and a love of the wilds. I had spent most of my youth growing up on the hill with my grandfather, because my father would disappear for weeks at a time, walking through the woods, following the whispers on the wind. I guess my dad really wasn't much of a father, and I told Billy as much. Then it occurred to me that I had turned out much more like my old man than I ever realized. Whether it was fate or conscious choice, I had no idea, but the parallels were there, and it bothered me quite a bit. I also told Billy about going to school in the town fifteen miles distant, how I managed to get accepted to college on a writing scholarship and then met Sarah in my senior year.

"What about *your* mother?" he asked.

That stopped me dead in my tracks. The mountains had let me forget about my mother as well. Suddenly, it came back to me. "She died." I took a draw from my pipe and continued. "I was only three or four at the time." I searched my memory for what she had died of, but there was nothing there. I drew a blank.

"What happened to her?" he asked.

"I don't remember." I looked out the window and thought I saw a puff of smoke filter out into the bright morning sunlight. "I guess neither dad or gramps ever told me that. Or if they did, I can't recall. Isn't that funny? I have no idea how my own mother died." I felt a smile pass my lips, but it was a sad one. "Not funny at all, I guess," I said wistfully. The hawk punctuated the emotion with a quiet peal from some distant treetop.

Those first three days were perhaps the happiest of my life, even more so than the happy years with Sarah. And in that short time I got to know my son very well. We only spent the nights in the cabin. Once the sun was up, we were out in the forest or down by the creek exploring the place of my birth and upbringing. I showed him some of the places that had been special to me as a child... and still were I guess, but I deliberately avoided being led near the Old Place, no matter how hard the voices tried. It wasn't time yet. In the evenings, after we had eaten and I sat in gramps' chair on the porch smoking my pipe quietly, I would catch Billy glancing at the big pine or listening to the wind as it slid through the evergreens. I'm almost certain he saw the shadow of Mr. Ashley at least a few times, but if he did, he never said anything about it. He would just keep trying to catch glimpses of the smoke gliding up into the evening sky or the sudden, brief glow of a pipe.

On the morning of the fourth day, I got up and discovered that Billy was not in bed. That surprised me, because I was usually the first one up. I put on some shorts and walked through the main room onto the porch. Billy was already sitting on the porch with a small pack lying next to him, and he was in gramps' chair smoking my pipe. I smiled, for I knew that he had heard the voices. I think he had been fighting them since he arrived. Or perhaps his upbringing in the city hadn't really allowed him to fully hear the words. Either way, he was listening now, and I guess he was ready to follow the voices. I knew where they would lead him, but I didn't say so.

"Going for a hike?" I raised an eyebrow and smiled broadly.

"Yeah. Are we the only ones up here on the hill, dad? I keep hearing voices, but they're really faint." He looked very perplexed, and his curiosity was getting the best of him.

"Well, it depends on how you look at it. There aren't any other *people* up here besides us. No one in the town ever comes up without an invitation. We all respect each other's privacy around here." Again he looked perplexed... and a bit expectant. We both knew that I hadn't really answered his question, or had made the answer more complicated than the question itself, but he didn't push the issue. He seemed to know, just as I had so many years ago, that answers would come soon enough.

"How much food have you packed? You'll probably need enough for two or three days."

"That's how much I packed, but how did you know?" Again he was confused and even a little afraid. I silently cursed the city for teaching him fear. He was just now learning to listen with his heart, with his very spirit, and he didn't know how to deal with it.

"A lucky guess," I said simply. "Are you ready to go?" I knew the answer to that question as well.

"Yeah, I was just waiting for you to get up. I didn't want you to worry about me, but this is something I feel I need to do. I've never even been camping with mom and da...um...Jack before. I can't explain it, but it's as if voices I can't really hear are calling to me. I probably sound pretty crazy, don't I?" He stood up and picked up the pack.

"You're not crazy. It's part of the hill. You can't really ignore the voices when they choose you. You have to trust in them and follow where they lead you."

He hoisted his pack and slid it easily onto his muscular shoulders, stepping easily to the edge of the porch. He handed me the pipe, which was still smoldering. "Here you go. I hope you don't mind, but I always wanted to try one of these. I like it."

"Hang on a minute," I said as I took the pipe and placed it in my mouth, taking a full draw without inhaling. I blew the smoke out and then walked back into the cabin. "I have something for you that I had hoped you might be interested in."

I went back into the bedroom and rummaged in the bottom drawer of my dresser to reveal a tight bundle of red cloth wrapped with a leather string. Walking back out through the kitchen, I paused and picked up the leather tobacco pouch that had been given to me by my grandfather. It had a circle within a circle seared into the flap, and there was a cross splitting the whole thing into quarters. Around the perimeter of the circle there were thirty-six points equally spaced all around, with arrows pointing in the four directions. Looped through one corner of the pouch was a leather thong with a hawk's claw and an eagle's feather. The pouch was ancient but looked as supple and new as the day gramps had given it to me.

There were just a few more creases. I opened the pouch and smelled the fragrant aroma that seeped up to fill my nostrils. There is nothing quite like the fragrance of fresh tobacco.

I walked out onto the porch, handed Billy the pouch and bundle and said, "I had hoped you would take an interest in pipe smoking, so I kept this for you." He took them with a look of curiosity on his face. He began untying the leather string and, after removing the brittle stuff, unfolded the red cloth. In the center of the bundle was a hand-made pipe. The bowl was dark brown and smooth. The stem was also handmade, but of a different, lighter wood than the bowl. Its surface glistened faintly with the oil that had carefully been rubbed into it so many years ago, and as Billy stepped off the porch into the sunlight, it appeared to be faintly faceted with the irregular cuts that had been shaped in its creation.

"That was made by your grandfather on one of his walkabouts. He gave it to me, but gramps had already given me this one, so I asked my father if it was all right for me to give it to my son, if I ever had one. He told me that pleased him, so I've saved it all this time, hoping that you would want it."

"Thanks." He looked in the bowl and noticed that there was none of the black charring that he had seen in mine. "Hey, it's never been used."

"That's right. A pipe should only have one owner, and the first person to smoke it should be the one to keep it. Since it was going to be yours, I figured I'd better leave it alone." He looked at the pouch. I stepped off the porch into the sunlight and said, "That belonged to your great-grandfather. It's yours now, and I hope that you too will be able to pass it along when the time comes. It will keep you smoking for as long as you have it. Just don't ever empty it before the sun comes up." He gave me a funny look when I said that, but I didn't clarify the statement. "You'll also need these." I fished in my shirt pocket and pulled out a handful of wooden matches. "Not much good without matches. The days of rubbing two sticks together are gone. And remember, don't inhale, just draw it into your mouth and let the taste please and warm you."

He placed the matches in his shirt pocket and looked at the circle and cross on the flap closely, examining the talon and feather as well. Without another word, he slipped the pouch and pipe into a deep pocket of his pants and started off towards the trees. He stopped beneath the big pine and looked around the base. He walked around it once, looking for something, and then looked back towards me with a questioning look.

"I'll tell you when you get back," I said with a broad smile. Just then the wind picked up and ruffled his long, untied hair. He lifted his head into the wind and appeared to be listening. I, too, listened to the wind, and I could make out the voices I knew he was listening to. "Follow them, and they will lead you to the Old Place." He turned to me once again and nodded his head. Then he turned and began walking through the forest. I watched him through the trees as long as I could but lost sight of him quickly. "Listen to the wind, boy. Hear it," I whispered. I saw a hawk sail over my head, flying in the same direction as my son. *Good omen*, I thought. The messenger will always speak to you, *if you're willing to listen.*

I began remembering the walks I used to take, and then the memory of my own first journey to the Old Place came back to me. I was twelve. Dad was on one of his jaunts, and gramps was sitting in his chair on the porch, smoking his pipe. I was under the big pine, listening to Mr. Ashley talk of the days of trapping and the games he would play in the woods with the Cheyenne. His voice floated out of the past....

"I 'member a day when Swift Eagle and I were tryin' to sneak up on one 'nother down the valley. We just come back from hunting spikes on the flats and were overcome with the romps, just like a young buck findin' his legs. Swift Eagle was always a might better than me when it come to that sort o' stuff. I guess practicin' from the first day you was born lends you a little edge over a white man...." And he suddenly stopped and tilted his ear towards the wind. He puffed quietly on his pipe, and the smoke floated around his head despite the slight breeze. "Do ya hear 'em, boy. Listen close."

"The voices? I hear them all the time," I said. I looked into the wind to try and see the faces hidden in the forest.

"I know ya hear 'em, but can ya hear what they're sayin?" He looked at me expectantly.

"I've never tried before. What are they saying?" I stood up and dusted the pine needles off my overalls.

"You have to listen yerself. They say different things for different folks. Now listen." I turned my ear towards the voices.

"No! Not with yer ears, nitwit. Use yer heart. Close yer eyes and *listen*." He took another puff from his pipe and closed his own eyes.

I closed my eyes and let the voices move across me. I had never tried to listen with my heart, but after a moment, I realized what he was talking about. The heart. Listen with the heart. It was as if I had been deaf the first twelve years of my life, and suddenly I could understand the voices.

They didn't speak in words. You couldn't hear words with your heart, but they did speak. Life. They spoke of life, the life of the hill, and the life of the valley and the life of everything. They spoke of mountain winds as old as time and the infinite life that was perfectly intertwined with it to make the intricate tapestry that is Mother Earth. They spoke of animals and people, rocks and trees—everything. They spoke of how that tapestry touched the spirit and wrapped it, carried through this life and every life.

And then the voices changed. They called to me. I never have really understood how it works, but I could feel them beckoning me into the forest. My grandfather slipped up next to me as quiet as an owl and placed an old, hand-tooled leather pack at my feet, already packed.

"He finally listened with his heart, didn't he, Ben?" my grandfather asked. His voice was gruff but kind. At the time I had no idea how he knew I was going on a journey. I looked into his eyes and suddenly realized that he, too, could hear the voices, far better than I could. All his wisdom, all his caring, it all came from listening to the voices.

Mr. Ashley took another thoughtful puff. "Yessir, he hears 'em now."

"You need to follow the voices, boy," my grandfather said as he picked up the pack and held it out for me to put on. I slipped my arms through the straps and let it settle on my narrow shoulders.

"Where will the voices lead me, gramps?" I was slightly frightened, but I trusted my grandfather with my life. I knew that he would not let me walk into anything dangerous.

"You'll see soon enough. It's not for me to second-guess the voices of the hill. Just keep listening with your heart and trust them as you trust me." He slipped his hand into his pocket and pulled out a pipe. "Here, it's time you tried this." It was shiny and new, and I had never seen anything as beautiful in my entire life. "I made this for you. It's never been used, the way a gift like this should be. Take care of it, and it will last forever."

"Thanks, gramps. I'll keep it forever." I pocketed the pipe and turned off into the forest.

"Listen to the voices, boy. Hear them," Gramps yelled to me through the forest. And faintly, just faintly I could hear Mr. Ashley whisper the same thing.

I wandered through the forest from that afternoon through the night and into the next day. I didn't sleep, not even a rest. All I did was let the voices lead me through the forest. More than once I saw an outcropping of rock, or a house-sized boulder that I had seen only hours earlier, but still I let the voices lead me to where they wished—across the hills.

The one thing I had learned in my first twelve years of life was to trust in the words of Mr. Ashley and my grandfather. They had never led me astray before, and to this day they haven't let me down. The voices led me through brambles, over rocky ledges and up nearly sheer cliff faces, but I followed their lead. Only now, after years of going there, could I lead someone else to the spot without the wind to guide me. After a day and a half, I reached the top of a hill quite distant from the hill my grandfather's cabin sat on. I couldn't even hear the river up here, just the wind speaking to me.

Atop that hill had been placed a Great Circle. The moment I saw it I knew it was an Old Place, just as Mr.

Ashley had spoken of during his reminiscence. Never did I imagine that I would be allowed to actually see an Old Place, like the ones in Ben's stories, but here it was.

Almost at the apex of the hill was a circle of interlocking, white stones so perfectly placed that they must have been carved to fit one another. The stones matched up upon their edges to leave almost no distinction between one stone and another. Within that circle was a circle of small skulls—the skulls of animals: birds and mammals alike. Again, there was a symmetry that was inspiring. Bisecting the paired circles was an evenly measured cross with points spaced around its outside like the points on a compass. Here and there around the circle, scattered randomly across the top of the hill, were piles of black stones no more than a foot high with bits and pieces of fruit, corn, bones, and feathers, and there was even a small drum placed against one. All of it looked as if it had been placed there only yesterday, but I knew that most if not all of it had to be hundreds of years old. There must have been forty or fifty of the rock piles adorning the hilltop which was devoid of trees except for a single, great pine resting thirty or forty yards straight west. And there was an eagle's nest in the top of the tree.

I suddenly felt the weight of an unfathomable past flood across me like water passing over the head of a drowning man. I was overwhelmed by the past contained within the Great Circle, and for a moment, just a moment, I lost track of myself and understood the lifetimes that the circle held in place. People—men, women and children— all surging across the face of the hills, listening to the beat of their own hearts and the voices on the wind. I suddenly understood the wisdom my grandfather possessed. I didn't have the wisdom myself, but I knew the source of it. From here, a focal point of all life, there was an understanding of mankind and what he is all about, how he relates to the world around him.

I spent four days there, going without food for the last two, listening to the voices and memorizing what they had to say. To this day I can still remember all the things I was told: a lifetime of words, a million lifetimes of words, all compressed into the span of several days. This was the connection, and it would haunt and guide me forever. It was an understanding that I would have to give myself up to till the day I died. The price of such an understanding would be to try and pass on this knowledge to the next generation: passing it on just as Swift Eagle had done for Ben Ashley, Ben Ashley had done for my grandfather and my grandfather had done for me.

My thoughts returned to the present, and there I sat, rocking gently on the porch of my grandfather's home, waiting for my son to return and tell me what I already knew. For three days I sat there, waiting for him to return, only getting up to give in to the natural urges of being alive. And I too listened to the ageless voices riding the winds.

*   *   *

I was dozing quietly in Gramps' rocker when I heard a rustling in the trees behind the cabin. I let myself come out of hazy unconsciousness and sat upright in the chair. My pipe was resting in my lap, so I began to repack it from the leather pouch I had made as a boy. There was no sign on the flap, but there was a long arrangement of hawk's feathers running down a strip of deer hide laced together with a handful of colorful beads. The pipe packed easily, and after making sure it was tight enough, I drew a match from my pocket, struck it on my thumbnail and lit the tobacco, drawing deeply. My tongue tingled, and I felt warm all over. Just then Billy came walking around the corner, smoking away thoughtfully at his pipe. He smiled as he spotted me on the porch.

He was dirty, his jeans spotted with green and brown, and there was a tear in them. His hair was pulled back in a ponytail again, but it was obviously unwashed. There were streaks of dirt on his face and forearms, and the left sleeve of his shirt was ripped up the seam to his shoulder. I looked at him and just started laughing.

"Sometimes..." he said, smiling, "sometimes those voices have a bad sense of humor. They led me into places where a mountain goat wouldn't go." He started laughing as well.

"I know. You'll have to tell me about it someday, but not for a while. You need time to think about what you've seen and what you dreamed." He didn't have to ask me how I knew he had noteworthy dreams while he was there. Just then a small, red-tailed hawk flitted down from behind the cabin and landed in the top of the big pine. It was the same one that had been flying around since Billy arrived. My son looked at the bird for a moment and then nodded to himself, as if he had made a decision that had been puzzling him. Maybe he had seen an omen in the bird just as I had.

"I do have to tell you about a dream I had while I was at the Circle, or at least part of one. Tell me, dad, when was the last time you were up there?"

The question surprised me. "Oh, hell. It's been ten or twelve years. There just hasn't been a reason to go. Why do you ask?" He moved around to the front of the porch and walked up the steps tiredly. He slipped the pack—now noticeably smaller than when he left—off his shoulders and placed it on the floorboards. Then, with a bit of effort, he lay down and propped his head on the pack.

"One of the dreams I had was for you, dad," he said as he closed his eyes.

"About me, you mean," I corrected.

"No, dad..." He opened his eyes and stared at me deeply. "The dream was *for* you. It wasn't meant for me, I was just supposed to tell you about it when I got back." He closed his eyes again and seemed to be trying to remember something. He started speaking again after a moment.

"Childbirth. Grandma died while trying to give birth to your little sister. They both died."

The flicker of a memory flashed through my mind when he said this. I remembered a winter night when I was three. Mother was swollen and screaming from the bedroom. Dad had told me to stay out in the kitchen while he and Gramps tried to deliver a baby, but something was terribly wrong. She had been screaming for a long time, and then she suddenly stopped. Gramps came out of the bedroom after a little while, and there was a funny look on his face. He looked very sad, but behind the sadness there was something else, a coldness, but one that wasn't unkind.

As the image floated across my mind's eye, the knowledge of the past forty years allowed me to realize what had been hidden behind my grandfather's eyes. Acceptance. Saddened acceptance of life...and death. The memory spoke to me.

"Come on, Will," gramps said to me as if he were

there once again beside me. "Let's go for a walk in the moonlight and frost." He placed his tan, wrinkled hand on my shoulder and led me firmly out the front door. The air was cold, and it bit into my face and hands as we stepped onto the porch. He lifted me onto his shoulders when we reached the bottom step, and his boots crunched into the brittle, icy snow. Without another word he started walking down what would eventually become the road up the valley. Just before we were out of sight of the cabin, I turned around and saw my father carrying a bundle out the front door and behind the cabin. He had a pack across his shoulders.

There was a tightness in my stomach. I didn't understand what he was carrying, but it filled me with dread.

"Look at the moon, boy. What do you hear?" He tilted his head up, and we both gazed at the bright form suspended in the dark night air. The light from the moon cast an eerie, bluish glow across the snow, and the trees looked black, blacker than the night.

"Listen to the wind, boy. You're mama's riding the wind now."

Never would I hear a more beautiful way of telling a child his mother has died. He was right, though. As we continued down the valley, I thought I heard my mother's brilliant laughter dancing through the trees, and with it there was a small, more quiet laughter, that of a child. The wind picked up, and my hair danced across my face. To this day I swear I heard a gentle woman's voice say "It's okay, Will. We're alright." It was the voice of my mother. But that didn't take away the sadness that had suddenly filled my heart. My grandfather laughed a little just after I heard the voices speak, as if he had heard them too, and then he wept for a long time.

"Down, Gramps. I walk," I said. He easily lifted me from his shoulders and placed me beside him. We walked most of the night, and dad wasn't back when we returned to the cabin. He didn't return for eight days, and what had happened was never mentioned.

Billy's voice broke my reverie.

"Anyway, a dream I had was about her, but it wasn't her," he said, pulling me up out of the past I had so easily forgotten.

"Wasn't her?" I asked. "What do you mean it wasn't her. How did you know who it was?" I leaned forward in the rocker as he sat up.

"She was a hawk, dad, but she spoke to me. She said it was okay to remember. It was wrong of your dad to never speak of it. She wanted you to know that your grandfather wanted to get it out in the open, but your father insisted. She wants you to go to the Old Place some time. She wants to talk to you, but she can only do it from there. She isn't strong enough elsewhere, and she said you were finally ready." He looked again at the hawk in the trees, and suddenly it leapt from its perch and sailed swiftly over the cabin.

"I'll be damned," was all I said for a long while. I guess that hawk *had* been a good omen. We sat there in silence, each thinking of our own memories. It had always bothered me that I had never dreamed of my mother or heard her voice. But then it occurred to me that she had not lived in the valley as long as myself, my father or Gramps. I had always thought that she had not been here long enough to form a connection with the Great Circle. I guess she was as much a part of the Circle as the rest of us, she just didn't have as strong a bond with the place.

"What is this place, dad?" he asked, relighting his pipe.

"I've been waiting a long time for you to ask me that question. You must swear never to tell a soul about this place without good reason. Normal people won't understand the hill, and they would eventually corrupt it. You must also, however, promise to tell your sons or daughters if they ask the same question you just asked me and you think that they can keep The Secret as well. Swear it."

"I do swear, dad. On my life." He raised his right hand as he spoke.

Just then a puff of smoke drifted from beneath the big pine. "Perfect timing, Ben, I said. "Perfect timing," Billy turned his head and watched the smoke float into the afternoon sky and dissipate.

"What is that, dad? I've seen the smoke and something glowing since the night I got here. At first I thought there was a fire, but it wasn't, so I thought I was imagining things. Then I thought I was hallucinating, because I never saw anyone there. But there is someone, isn't there?" He kept looking at the base of the big pine as he spoke.

"Ben Ashley. That..." and I pointed the mouthpiece of my pipe at the tree, "...is Ben Ashley. He was a trapper in these parts, among others, in the early eighteen-hundreds."

Billy's head snapped around, and he looked at me first as if I were joking. When I didn't say anything, he looked as if I were crazy. "You can't be serious," he said totally astonished.

"Tell me, before you came here did you ever have a bird speak to you?"

"No."

"Have you ever let voices on the wind lead you through a strange forest to a circle of stones and skulls?"

"No."

"Have you ever seen smoke rise out of nowhere in the middle of a forest where there is no fire?"

"No," he said again.

"Well then, accept that this place is like no other that I know of on Earth, although I suspect there must be others being kept secret. Accept the fact that this place is magical...or spiritual...whatever you want to call it. How much tobacco have you used since you left?"

"What?" he asked confused at the abrupt change of subject.

"How much have you smoked? Open the pouch and tell me what is left."

A curious look crossed his face, as if that were something he had wanted to ask me. He pulled the pouch from his pants pocket and opened the flap.

"It's full!" His voice carried the bewilderment he had been ignoring during his journey to the Old Place, but now that he was directly faced with it, he couldn't understand it. "This was half-full last night, I'm certain of it. I remember telling myself that I was probably smoking too much, and I didn't want to empty it like you said. But I swear this thing should be empty by now."

"Doesn't make sense, does it?" I asked as a broad smile touched my face. "You'll find that what makes sense where you came from just doesn't quite fit here, and vice versa. "Tell me, where is the Circle?"

"It's..." he twisted as he sat there, moving a pointed finger in several directions, and then a confused look crossed his face. "It's.... Damn it, it's..." His face screwed itself into fierce concentration, but the way to the Old Place just wasn't in *his* memory.

"You'll find that the only way to get there at first is to listen to the voices. It takes years to know in your own head where it is. I'm not sure you could find it with a helicopter, not if you searched for the rest of your life. You have to follow where the voices lead you...wherever they lead you." I stood up, and my joints popped from sitting for too long. "Come on, I'll introduce you to an old friend of the family."

He stood up, but he hesitated when he realized I was walking towards the big pine. "Come on, son," I said, "there's nothing to be afraid of." Just then the breeze kicked up and we both heard the squeal of a hawk high above the valley, riding the updrafts and flowing thermals. He reached a decision internally and stepped off the porch, stepping into stride easily next to me. Another puff of smoke was carried off by the breeze, and as we approached, we saw dimly in the shadow of the noon sun the wispy figure of a man dressed in deer hides, sitting with his back against the tree.

Ben had almost no color to him, and we could easily see right through him. Billy gasped as the apparition came into view. And old muzzleloader was next to Ben, and he was pulling deeply on the end of an Indian-style pipe. From the end of it dangled a long string of feathers and small bones. Around his neck he wore a heavy string of huge bear claws that would match the fur in the cabin, and his knee-high moccasins were deeply inlaid with colorful beads.

"Hello, Ben. This is my son. Billy, this is Ben Ashley." For a moment the figure didn't move. Another billowing could of smoke floated into the air. Billy was standing more behind me than next to me, and I could sense the tension he was feeling.

"Ain't nuthin' to be 'fraid of, boy. Nuthin' here but what's left of a tired old man. Spent most of my life trekin' 'cross these here hills...better part of sixty years. Now I gets ta rest. The place is home...for so many people ya couldn't imagine. It's like heaven, I rekon. Lemme' tell ya' how it is. Swift Eagle 'splained it ta me just after he died. Long time ago, long before the whites ever really come to this country and mucked it up, this whole land was pure. It belonged to The People. Now a couple o' their Great Ones had visions o' what was comin', so they made this place. Here The People live forever, and I guess it sort o' carried over for anyone who lived here and could hear the voices o' The People. Ya see, the Old Place is a center, and around it spins the lives of all the people who lived and died here afore us. Ya remember that nest in the top o' that pine west o' the Circle?" he asked my son.

Billy moved from behind me and stepped uneasily up to Ben. He gulped twice as he stared down at the pale figure sitting before him. "Yes, sir. I remember. There wasn't anything in it though. It was empty."

"Swift Eagle must a' been huntin' somwhere's. That's his nest. Just before he died this big eagle came swoopin' out o' the sky and landed in a tree over us. See, we was huntin griz a couple hills over from here. Damn son-of-a-bitch circled 'round us and jumped me and Swift Eagle. Tore him up pretty bad 'fore I could get my Hawking spun around and take a shot. I nailed her clean, but Swift Eagle was done fer. We sat there, an' he told me the beginnin' of the Tale, just like I'm gonna' tell you in time. Surprised the hell outa' me when Swift Eagle's spirit just got up outa' his body and jumped right into that there eagle, but I'll tell ya right now, I got myself religion—Indian religion. So, I gotsta pass on the tale, keep the Circle flowin'. I'm the teller now, since Swift Eagle can't or won't do it. I ain't sure which. So that leaves me. Have a seat, son."

Billy sat across from Ben just as I had done so many years ago. For three days Ben and my son sat there talking. Billy would get up in the morning, eat and then go out to the big pine. He only came back in to eat and sleep. Everything else he did out there. The Tale would take a long time to tell, years as a matter of fact, and after it, Billy would be able to stay here if he chose to. Swift Eagle had let Ben into the Circle when he died, and I guess Ben had been told the rest of the Tale while he was on the other side.

On the evening of the third night of the Tale, I was rocking on the porch, smoking my pipe and really listening to the wind. There was something there, and I had to hear it. The voices were trying to say something, but it had been a long time since I had listened with my heart, and I couldn't quite make it out. I knew it would come to me though. It always did. Billy walked up from the big pine just as the sun was dropping below the saddle, and there was a curious look on his face. I watched as Ben stood up and faded into the forest. Billy seemed to be sad about something.

"What's wrong?" I asked as he stepped up onto the porch.

"I've got to go. My time's run out for now, but I'll be back as soon as possible. I think I want to move up here with you, dad, but I have to get some things settled back at mom's." The fact that he didn't call Sarah's place "home" gladdened me.

"Do what you have to, son. But there's no hurry. You have plenty of time to come up here. You ought to go to college, see what they have to offer. Then visit here in the summertime. Maybe you could finish out the summer here after you clear things up with your mother. We can build you your own cabin, or make this one bigger. It's about time I started having people up here. I've been alone too long. Who knows?"

"I don't know about college, dad, but we'll see. Maybe it would be good for me." He turned his face into the light breeze blowing down from the head of the valley. "Have you been listening to the voices?"

"I've been trying, but I'm a little out of practice. It's been a while. I'll hear em' though. I always do." He smiled as he turned back to face me, like he knew something I didn't, but he didn't say anything. After a short while, enough time for both of us to smoke our pipes, we both went inside and turned in for the night. When I woke in the morning, the covers were balled up on the floor, so I must have had a restless night, but I felt as if I slept fitfully. I don't remember any of my dreams, but I know I had many of them. I did have the sense that my dreams had been crowded with people though.

For the second time Billy had risen before me. I got dressed quickly and walked out onto the porch. The wind was blowing fairly hard as I walked out, and Billy was sitting in the rocker once again, smoking his pipe. And for the second time, there was the pack at his feet.

"I thought you were leaving," I asked.

"I am," he said. "The car is already packed up and ready to go," he smiled.

"Then what is the pack for?"

"Listen, dad."

Suddenly I could hear what the voices were saying. The old sensation of their call hit me. It had been so long that I had forgotten what that felt like. I looked down at my feet and smiled. When I had gotten dressed, I had put on my hiking boots rather than the leather moccasins I normally wore around the cabin. "I guess I did hear them last night, I just didn't know it." He stood up, hugged me firmly and then walked down the steps and moved towards his car. He turned back halfway between me and the car and said, "Thanks, dad. I'll write you as soon as I get back, and I promise to come back this summer and all the summers after that. I've decided to go to college after all."

"What made up your mind for you?"

"A hawk told me in my dreams last night that I should go. Once I heard her at the Old Place, I guess it was easier for her to reach me."

I picked up the pack and walked down the steps as well. Just as my feet touched the grassy earth, there was a peal from high above, and in the early sunlight a hawk circled high above our heads.

"Good luck, dad," he said with a tear running down his cheek. "I'll see you soon." With that he walked to his car, got in and drove off. I watched the dust cloud stirred up by his car for a while as he drove down through the trees. Then, wiping a tear from my own cheek, I hefted the pack onto my shoulders and listened for the voices.

There was another peal from the hawk, and then I started walking into the forest, letting the voices guide me once again. There was a bright flutter of laughter that sounded oddly familiar, and it danced through the trees like the playful little sister it was.

The End

About the author:

The first forty years of Terry Phillius' life have been an exploration of this existence and the Universe around him. Terry seeks literary expressions of the human and sometimes inhuman condition. With a strong connection to the natural world and a love of the outdoors, Terry's focus is on exploring the mind, body and spirit and the connections they have with the Universe at large. He's published one book of poetry (*Sphere of Seven Billion Gods*), short fiction in *Penny Dread Tales Volume One* and hopes to expand his writing credits in both short, novella and novel-length fiction. You can learn more about Terry at http://www.terryphillius.com/terry-phillius..

The Tardy Hand of Miss Tangerine

by Jon-Michael Emory (Colorado, USA)

Her departing gift to me—a beneficence, let's call it—was a tattoo of letters and numbers across my chest, taut as clothesline between the areolas, drawn in her own hand. It was done in a font so gracefully balanced and femininely stylized that it seems to flow upon gentle currents: willowy beginnings rolling into tighter lowercase, slanting a bit left, with the last letter's descender or stroke plunging down and finishing in a tight, grasping coil, much like the prehensile tail of a seahorse.

Wangari, it reads, *14 May 2021 Must Hurry,* followed by a methodical placement of eraser-size dots, all drawn by a lover who fueled this and other divinations with a diet of pulpy fruit.

It has been four years since she magically scored this riddle into my flesh, though it didn't begin *appearing* until five weeks ago, taking three of those to reach full maturity, its color now that of forest green in shadow. This happened just after the spring equinox, and having known her to be an avid botanist, I cannot entirely dismiss its blossoming along with the columbine and forsythia as coincidental.

Wangari. An exotic name that turns out to be Kenyan in origin, specific to females. And that date, curiously military in its orientation, is obviously portending some kind of event. Well, I should amend that present participle, as the date in question has already passed some months ago, long before it ever began appearing on my skin. And I've looked from earthquakes to sunspots, tsunamis to polar shifts, hoping to validate my suspicions that some kind of connection exists between that date, that name and something catastrophic or remarkably momentous. After all, those gifted with prescience seem never to waste their talents on things inconsequential, at least when committing their predictions to the written word, e.g., Nostradamus didn't burden his quatrains with frivolous market trends in aquarium fish sales or the recurring concerns of Little League umpires.

Then, lastly, there's *Must Hurry*, which needs no explanation, followed by that peculiar sequence of dots, appearing very much like Braille, at least in cursory examination: a dead ringer for the letter 'T' to be exact. Just picture two colons side-by-side, then jack the right colon up one space.

I had thought of Morse code, but those characters are normally laid out horizontally. There is a 'visual' way to learn that alphabet by superimposing each sequence of dots and dashes over its respective letter, achieving the desired dimension, but that method does not produce the configuration on my chest, not remotely so. Nor do they appear to be, or acting as, some kind of diacritical mark, those ancillary glyphs that hang over, under or between letters, normally used to change vowel sounds.

And to confound matters even more, this conundrum is in reverse image and needs the assistance of a mirror to become properly legible, just as your rearview mirror brings out 'ambulance' when it has been spelled out backwards on the hood of such vehicles.

Although all of her predictions (at least the ones I know of) manifested in this fashion, they are of course quite decipherable on their own, as a mirror just conveniently decrypts the communiqués with less fuss. Nonetheless, having it painted this way in my flesh heightens the intrigue, as it perpetually reminds me of a chronic anxiety from which she never recovered: her *catoptrophobia*, or fear of mirrors.

I had originally assumed this malady of hers to be *eisoptrophobia*, or fear of seeing one's own reflection, as my research into such anxieties revealed. I remain inclined, however, to favor the other term, as it seems more fitting; that her fear was of someone, or some*thing*, lurking inside those silver depths and not of her own countenance, as I had once seen her marvel over its distorted image upon a kitchen appliance.

Given those conditions, it was easy to assume why she chose to write her predictions in this backward fashion: they were simply an extension of this phobia, a kind of droll attempt at self-mockery (although I do admit this seems more like impaling oneself with fun rather than just plain poking).

Now, that remarkable resemblance I'd earlier mentioned to Braille, specifically to the letter T, needs some clarification at this point, as I was using those dots' *virtual*, or mirror, image to make that comparison. And just to be thorough, I determined that the *real* image did not have a twin in Braille—not that I believed Braille was going to emerge victorious in this matter, but it does raise a curious point.

As I mentioned, it happened over four years ago. We'd met our junior year at a small but notable college, its campus nestled in the shadow of some famous peak in Colorado. It had been a clumsy meeting, as I'd been nose-in-book, aimlessly strolling across the grounds, she just as engrossed in a fat, ripe peach—she'd not yet switched permanently to its smaller cousin—and we collided.

"Christ! Watch where you're going!" I snapped.

"Sorry," she said, not really sorry at all, pulp snot-smeared across her left, freckled cheek. Green eyes, strawberry blond hair bouncing just above the shoulders, blanched skin and an unhealthy thinness any runway model would have envied. She wore a simple, white cotton blouse, a sienna broom skirt wrinkled to a severe degree of geriatrics and a stack of Chakra ankle bracelets bouncing above a pair of worn leather flip-flops. Well, it was early autumn, and I remember thinking how suitably she imitated that season, not just in supple fibers and September hues, but with her eyes, a loitering omen there of harsher, unforgiving things ahead.

I had detected a mild, musky aroma, certainly not unpleasant, with just a pinch of vanilla extract and clove. She wasn't exactly earthy (she shaved her legs, bathed regularly, was not unaccustomed to stock cosmetics), but any highbrow distinctions were hardly forthcoming. Had I mugged her instead, I might have expected to find in her suede leather bag an ounce of hemp, the bra she had permanently removed, the peace symbol posing upon a variety of mediums and a program from a recent Jimi Hendrix concert. Forgive me, it's cliché, but it is the best fit.

As I bent over to retrieve James Joyce, she found her nerve. "Optometrists are nothing to fear, you know. I understand they're listed alphabetically in the yellow pages."

"Oh, you're a comedy major," I decided, brushing pine needles from my book, clinging statically to the Mylar cover. "I would have guessed something less funny, like maybe tent weaving."

Her peach lay nearby, traumatized. I let it lie. To hell with chivalry.

She looked at me then, an arrogant aspect far too poignant for those farm-girl eyes (I'd thought Minnesota given the slight nasal lisp in her accent, but it was Nebraska, she would tell me later). "Botany, actually," she said, swiping a cotton sleeve across her mouth, an indelicacy that she further aggravated by extending her sticky hand. "Name's Lisa. Lisa Coventry."

I took it, introduced myself as a member of the campus' literary club, then asked for a napkin. And there began the most bizarre affair in the history of affairs.

Two months into the relationship (sex had been fashionably early, and damned good, if you must know), we found ourselves one cold and blustery night at a hockey game. We had arrived late in the third, with our team down 5-1 against the Golden Knights, NCAA champions of the previous year. The Knights went on to win, giving our team the beating it'd come to expect by then, having maintained the worst record in its division for so long that it had become a source of pride. We stayed long enough to participate in booing our guys off the ice then went for a hot cappuccino at Margie's, a popular hangout just off campus, famous for its chocolate scones and jaunty ambience— a place that Lisa once said smelled of burnt umber, and one we would ultimately haunt.

It was in just this place where I first saw her intangibly impress words with her magic finger, right smack on the tabletop, third booth from the left as you entered. They were words that wouldn't appear until many weeks later; slowly at first, like the faint beginnings of a bruise, and would eventually achieve the same color—a foretelling that a much-beloved Presidential candidate would win election that November, just weeks away. And he went on to win, just as her writing predicted. He also collapsed behind his podium three and a half minutes into his acceptance speech and died later that same evening from what the doctors eventually identified as a subarachnoid hemorrhage resulting from a ruptured brain aneurism. She had seen that too, putting it this way: *Cole wins then loses big 2016.* Not quite as cryptic as Nostradamus, yet refreshingly more flippant than Jeane Dixon.

Unfortunately, that electoral calamity happened many weeks *before* her reverse cursive began showing on that shiny grey Formica.

A belated prophecy and bad timing is lethal, if not laughable, to the integrity of such things: tardy, just as she often was for class, dates, or to any function she'd been invited, or not. And it was this immature characteristic I found out of her many to be the most taxing. Even her periods were often late, which caused me more than a few restless nights, I might add, after we'd recklessly consummated our relationship.

She never discussed or said aloud whatever she was prophesying, each time remaining mum on those few occasions when I personally observed her finger conjure magic: magic postponed to a date so far ahead that my memory had almost forgotten that any kind of magic had been conjured at all... that first time, anyway. After the tabletop incident at Margie's, every crook, bend and unanticipated movement of her right index finger garnered my full and undivided attention.

I learned very quickly to never inquire about such shenanigans, as she volleyed every time with a stern shake of her head followed by an even sterner recital of that popular phrase "patience is a virtue," or some other colloquial offshoot just as obnoxious, adding lastly but with the greatest emphasis that frigidity wasn't just something meteorologists talked about.

Of course, she had sworn me to absolute secrecy; an oath I have steadfastly honored until the commencement of this personal account. She's gone now, but I'm sure there remain examples of her writing somewhere out there amid Colorado's alpine foliage: perhaps upon some park bench or fountain; on the side of a boxcar; the underpinnings of a bridge; the sun-blanched metal stanchion of a street light; all masquerading as puzzling idioms to the curious few and just plain old reverse graffiti to the rest. Although, to be quite honest, I believe they were mostly for my benefit, the inspiration that honed the faith that would be necessary in the end.

But if her credibility as a futurist languished in the untimely appearances of her prophecies, then by the same token it was rescued by their *indelibility*. Late one snowy evening I tried removing her penmanship from that tabletop at Margie's. I sat down with a paperback and ordered my usual double latte; then, when no one was looking, I went to work with a moist pad of smuggled steel wool. And all I got for my efforts was a lesson in the durability of laminates and one pissed off waitress who'd finally caught me when a condiment of raw unrefined sugar was sent crashing to the floor. I never so much as dulled Lisa's writing, which at that point was still in its infancy, what I would call its watermark stage, where the outline was developing more prominently than the meat.

Not long after my bungled scrubbing, perhaps even within hours, someone replaced that table with a less expressive one. I was never able to track its relocation, having to finally surrender it to the same fog-enshrouded realms that are bequeathed such items. After that I never reprised those efforts upon her other predictions, those that eventually surfaced in concrete, wood, marble,,, and, finally, flesh.

Lisa's nickname around campus was 'Miss Tangerine,' apparently coined during a previous addiction to that fruit, just shortly into her first year there. She'd gone on to abuse other orchards, most specifically of the stone fruit variety, but that tag stuck nonetheless and followed her around like a skulking dog. I suppose it was cute in the beginning, but saying 'Miss Tangerine' eventually felt less like an endearing moniker and more like a pending epitaph.

When we met, her quaint obsession with peaches was about to turn, lastly, and most viciously, to nectarines. At first I found her quirkiness almost ... well, endearing. I'd been around campus halls long enough to know that academia and above-average IQ's have a way of luring your more obsessed types. Take your pick, any prominent college is full of them, but it wasn't long into our relationship when I'd begun suspecting something more than just harmless eccentricity and finally recognized it for what it was: a severe, uncontrollable addiction—as nasty as any alcoholic's—whose equivalent of *delirium tremens* was an uncanny ability to inscribe future events across any available surface *in reverse image*, only to later appear as yesterday's headlines.

I distinctly recall my first visit to her apartment just off campus: a quaint, one room abode nestled within the cavernous interior of a Victorian mansion. It was just one of many such structures orbiting the college, each having been vigorously renovated to the specs of a honeycomb, accommodating the mostly-rich faction of college students, of which Lisa was an unpretentious member.

Tapestries were in abundance: a hand-woven assortment of verdure and floral motifs reminiscent of bygone times when pride motivated artisans to lissome heights. I remember well the sticks of incense, pungent and poking out like quills from their soapstone burners, each of those holders acutely Asian in its carved detail. Clove was dominant, but there had been another spicy fragrance that I could not readily identify.

"Frankincense," she'd told me. "It comes from trees of the genus *Boswellia*, native to Africa. Don't you just love that word, *Boswellia*?"

Eager to please, I might have mentioned that it was worth a second look.

"What's your favorite word?" she continued. "Mine's Alabaster... definitely my favorite word of all time. The way it just rolls off your tongue: has a kind of regal aroma. Do you have a favorite word?" she asked again.

I affected a pensive pose then nodded with absolute certainty. "Vagina."

"Really," she said, feigning serious interest. "How incredibly boorish."

"That's me," I agreed. "And what the hell is a regal aroma? I didn't know one could *smell* words, even those of noble descent."

She laughed and tossed me a wink that seemed out of character. "Where I come from, you can taste them, too. Wanna beer?"

So as not to appear overly affectionate for such items, I allowed just the appropriate pause before committing to an answer. And as she opened her refrigerator (one of those ancient, round corner things that always appear to be unnecessarily thick, and moody), a sight was revealed that made me forget to ask her about words and their alleged flavors. Save for the top shelf where only two more bottles of beer remained and nothing else, every square inch of the interior was crammed with boxes supplying only one kind of fruit.

"That's a shitload of peaches," I said.

"Nectarines," she corrected, handing me a longneck bottle. "They're good for you."

It was our first date, so she didn't get an argument from me, although I did caution her about the hazards one might face when overdosing on fiber.

She looked at me then, a film of desperation sliding down her eyes, where within rose unmistakable paranoia. "Do you ever get the feeling you're being watched?"

I shrugged, suddenly wondering if I was. "Not on any kind of regular basis," I said carefully, "but sure, I guess. Hasn't everyone at one time, or other?"

As if preparing herself for a particularly nasty draft, she slowly crossed her arms over her chest. "How do you feel about mirrors?"

I didn't laugh, and in the brief awkwardness that followed, I easily imagined the reasons behind her phobia, having assumed that it was her own reflection she wished to avoid, the culprit being some kind of self-esteem or alter-ego concern. After all, she was a wallflower who seemed quite comfortable in her solitude: a loner who preferred the company of others in measured doses. And textbooks are full of the kinds of psychosis associated with those who inflict their own isolation.

She remained immobile, her eyes fixed, expectant, as if just the slightest movement would crack the thin sheen of anticipation that seemed to have gripped her.

"So," I began my approach, "you have a fear of mirrors, broken or otherwise?"

She finally nodded her head, slowly, deliberately. "Oh, yes. They can't be trusted."

From then on the evening progressed (for me, anyway) from piqued apprehension to the most incredibly ambitious lovemaking I had ever, or since, been involved. The reason I mention this again isn't to satisfy some hubristic self-image, but that the most truly interesting thing was found as we lay in the afterglow. I saw on the windowsill of her dormer (and only) window a rather large translucent bowl, tightly lidded, inside of which rested what appeared to be a large seed of some kind. The window had been opened wide, as if she'd anticipated our fevered rendezvous with sylphlike breaths of fall air puffing against sheer lace curtains: curtains, I remember thinking, whose embroidered design boasted a dexterity no longer viable, a skill no longer taught.

From her bed I was able to discern some very thin objects attached to the seed but was unable to make out just what those objects were. So, to whet my mounting curiosity, I finally rose and strode over to the windowsill, those puzzling objects now well defined, glinting in the invading moonlight. They were sewing needles or things very similar: a handful of them, jutting out like alert antennae. I assumed that some kind of experiment was taking place, one obviously linked to her botanical studies, and inquired upon that theory, as I did the type of seed.

"Peach?" I guessed.

"Nectarine," she said then confirmed that it was most definitely an experiment and asked me to please not touch the bowl or its contents. She hemmed and hawed for an explanation, finally resorting to, "Look, darlin', it's pretty complicated. Let's just say that if you don't know what you're doing, then you're better off splicing genes with a chainsaw. The placement of those pins is fundamental to the experiment's desired outcome."

"In other words, don't fuck with it," I said, keeping my hands at my sides and noting the curious analogy.

She laughed. "I'm just saying that you don't want to get too rough and disarticulate with that alignment."

"And a curious one it is," I said, trying to sound erudite.

I returned to her bed, the experiment unmolested, then retreated without further delay back to the warm and comfy left side of my brain, forgetting about the strange pincushion in the Tupperware bowl.

On our very next date we found ourselves back at her place (it was always her place, as I never dared take her to mine, a bleak, windowless two-room landfill occupied by three young and excessively hormonal lads, none of whom ever saw the entrance of a finishing school, let alone its alphabetized curriculum). This second time I was more venturesome, giving extended scrutiny to what was, save for those wall hangings and a few meager attempts at furniture, a skimpy lifestyle, even for a college student. And a quick peek inside her kitchen cabinets confirmed what I had already begun suspecting: that processed food had become, for her anyway, a thing of the past.

I had also confirmed the absence of any mirrors and was once again forced to ponder the impasses one must face when boycotting those reflective surfaces. Although, in all fairness to Lisa, I should make clear that if any grooming misadventures had ever taken place, then I was never aware of them. Her countenance was always flawless, her wardrobes impeccably worn, however dated they might have been. Granted, she was plain, and if mirrors had not been banished from her walls, then I doubt she would have been bewitched by her own reflection, as Narcissus had been his. Rather, her buoyant innocence was her appeal, her beauty, and that selective naiveté that was surely intentional, a coquettish ruse to keep the rust off those girlish pretenses—qualities no mirror could ever pretend to show.

As previously mentioned, I do remember one incident in particular, late in our relationship. I had caught her bent over the kitchen counter in just her pajama bottoms, staring at her toaster of brushed stainless steel, her nose nearly touching that small appliance, and despite that intimate proximity I could still see the apprehension stitched throughout her posture. She was slowly and carefully swaying left to right, right to left, intently watching her carnival image, regarding it the same way a spear-toting aboriginal does a transistor radio.

One thing that I found especially odd was a stark absence of plants. As a student making such things her life's endeavor, I expressed mild concern that she was not at least attempting to torture a baby philodendron—if not for her own gratification then for the gloating satisfaction of those who, like me, killed everything that photosynthesized, including plankton.

Although I didn't believe it for a second, she ashamedly admitted that her thumb was quite a few shades this side of green, always had been, but that she would nevertheless attempt another go, if only to appease my artificial concern. "Maybe some *Dracaena sanderiana*," she pondered, "or a nice starter of *Sansevieria trifurcate*. Don't you just love that word, *Sansevieria*?"

I agreed that it had a special ring to it, all the while remaining convinced that there was probably nothing Lisa Coventry couldn't grow.

One standout curiosity was a fifty-pound burlap sack, the kind used to transport coffee beans from, say, Caracas to Starbucks USA, as evidenced by the logo of some weary, mustached Venezuelan bean farmer pulling an even wearier donkey alongside, the caption reading "Arabica, El Capitán." I mention this in detail only because I'd seen identical sacks hanging empty on the walls at Margie's, so I assumed that's where Lisa had gotten hers. She was an avid coffee drinker, and this sack, smoldering in a distant kitchen corner, appeared half-full, so I'd naturally asked her if she ground her own beans.

It was to no surprise then when she reached into the sack and pulled out a handful of seeds very similar to the one I'd seen in the Tupperware bowl.

"You're collecting peach pits," I said, not the least

bit incredulous, once again assuming that it was simply born entirely of her preoccupation with everything botanical.

"Nectarine," she amended, then giddily divulged to me her wish to one day take a truckload of these bags across country and retrace the steps of John Chapman, aka Johnny Appleseed, if not in actual measured stride then at least in devoted purpose.

She glowed. "Just imagine the provinces a single grove could produce."

I was then struck again with that nagging dread that I might have to very soon initiate a restraining order against this obsession-prone woman. She continued. "Did you know the peach is actually a member of the rose family? A peach is a stone fruit of the genus *Prunus*. It's also called a drupe. Did you know a coconut is a drupe? Neat, huh?"

I shrugged, thinking a drupe was something plants did when starved for water. "Can we go now?" I asked. Dinner, the evening's main attraction, was becoming less realized by the minute.

She referred to *P. persica*-this and *Armeniaca vulgaris*-that about hybrids, cultivars, plumcots and peachcots and cherrycots.... My hunger was reaching critical mass, and all I longed to hear was an overly ambitious waitress asking me if I wanted bacon and avocado on my cheeseburger. But Lisa continued unabated. "And that thing you refer to as the pit," she said, "is called the endocarp. It's also called the stone and actually protects the seed located within. Did you know the Chinese make intricate carvings from the endocarps? Have for centuries, back to the Song dynasty. Don't you just love that word, *dynasty*? Of course, most of the *hybrid* stones out there don't lend well to carving, as do the ones predating the 1940's. You see, to the Chinese the peach is a symbol of longevity. The fissures are magic, you know. Doorways into other realms."

"Say again?" This abrupt and unexpected shift from hard science to the mythic brought me back from the brink of incurious descent, a ledge whereupon I often teetered dangerously when in her company.

"They knew about the fissures," she said. "The Chinese. I believe their carvings grew from a more primitive ambition to unlock doorways. An old family secret. Yup, the first ones knew about the fissures."

I was then reminded of the seed in the Tupperware bowl, quite particularly those pins poking from it. When I started to ask, she hitched to a totally different rant. "Oh, did you know that the delicious Calimyrna fig has a symbiotic relationship with a wasp? This tiny insect actually pollinates its flowers!"

A typical day in the life of Lisa Coventry.

On that following Valentine's Day, I was made aware of another of her predictions through the curiosity of others as I witnessed a few students showing marked interest in a marble bench situated between the cafeteria and music building. Presented in her distinctive reversed style, this one actually rhymed: *Rio 42 gets his due 10/2.* And with this one I didn't have to jump on the information highway to search for clues, as the story of Samson Rio had saturated the media just weeks earlier.

Samson Rio, or "Rio Forty-Two" as the tabloid press liked to call him, was a serial killer of substantial ill repute, with bragging rights to the most vicious string of murders in California history. Forty-two women raped and killed, and in an extraordinarily short amount of time, with initial forensic estimates putting the reign of carnage at three months, start to finish.

An often self-described "Latin Lover," Samson Rio's pedigree was no more south-of-the-border than Woody Allen's. It was, however, a fun fact the media wasted no time in exploiting, as it tied in so well with his promiscuous, barhopping lifestyle and choice of victims. They were beautiful, Caucasian women of no set age group or hair color, their only shared commonality being that each had their own head, an attachment Samson Rio found burdensome, as he removed each and every one, stockpiling them all in a rented storage unit in a San Diego suburb.

Each head was found within its own monogrammed hat box, whereupon the lid of each of those containers bore a black checkmark next to any one of three available ratings: *Good, Very Good, Awesume.*

Rio was indeed a very troubled man, not to mention a bad speller.

On October 2nd, while awaiting his arraignment in the San Diego County Jail, Samson Rio was found face-down in the communal shower, his throat deeply cut (so deeply, in fact, that many agreed a decapitation had been attempted). How Samson Rio found himself in general population was the most asked question, but in the end, no one seemed too interested in finding out.

To quote one late night talk-show host who commented upon that matter, "Justice is very much like ejaculation: it's always welcome, premature or not."

Of course, this news had aged considerably by then, and I mention it in detail to show that there was no theme or premise to her predictions, only that they targeted events that significantly impacted the collective conscience, not so unlike those of her fellow soothsayers, either still living or long dead.

That marble bench, by the way, went up and missing almost as quickly as had the table at Margie's, within just a few days of its emerging memo's discovery. It was quickly replaced with another bench built of robust aspen, as if changing to a softer medium would discourage further mischief. I was later told it had been polished down and reconstructed, then transferred to the faculty lounge as a pair of *au courant* end tables.

Later that evening, as we were exchanging Valentine cards, I nonchalantly mentioned to Lisa that I had earlier happened by that marble conversation piece. She nodded her understanding and only said, "He was a bad seed." After careful deliberation I went ahead and asked her if that was her personal opinion or professional one. She only smiled and said, "Did you know that if you bounce a ball inside a moving train, it will fall back to you and not three or four rows down."

She appeared legitimately taken with this dilemma, and I explained to her the simple physics behind such trickery.

"So," she asked, a demure smile betraying her ignorance, "if you and I were to jump into the air this very second, the rotating planet beneath us wouldn't advance one inch before our feet returned to the ground?"

"Now you're catching on," I said.

"Fascinating!" she said, then immediately turned sullen and took my hand. "Will you be sad if *this* train ever stops?"

I told her that I would rather be sad than relieved, that it was never a good idea to take the train that far.

Although she didn't say as much, her eyes agreed.

Our last night together came less than a week later. We skipped Margie's and hit a popular Irish pub for drinks.

Although she would have an occasional beer or two, Lisa avoided alcohol in excess, I had supposed, for the same reasons most young females do: to maintain levels of self-respect and those most important reputations, a course less endeavored, if not downright avoided, by their sexual counterparts. At least that is the alleged justification for such restraint. However, that night, over more than a few gin cocktails, our conversations turned to religion as they often get around to doing in relationships. When I inquired about her faith-based affiliations, she didn't claim any mild or devout conviction to any Western or even Eastern creed, only saying this: "Have you ever seen a god trip and fall on a flagstone pathway?"

I admitted, somewhat regretfully, that I'd yet to entertain such a vision.

She leaned in, as if magnetically pulled by my growing bewilderment. "Well, I imagine it looks pretty much the same as when a mortal person does it. It's just *funnier* when you know it's a god."

"And how would I know that?" I asked.

"By the way they take *your* name in vain when cracking their knee!" she said, slapping her own.

"Oh," I said, somewhat relieved, "you were making a joke."

"Was I?" she said, swaying to the beat of the gin. "Look, maybe all I'm trying to say is that people should consider looking peripherally for their gods instead of straight upwards. You're not as likely to find them falling from the sky in fiery chariots as you are them squeezing sideways between fence rails or over the tops of low garden walls."

When one pluralizes a lower-case god then insinuates that those divine beings might be walking among us as common folk, I start getting a little nervous, as it flies in the face of my monotheistic upbringing. Well, 'flutters' in the face, is more like it, as I'm not solidly sold on that concept. At least, I hadn't been then, but I didn't reveal my cynicism.

I held up my drink. "A toast: to the Holy Father, Holy Mother—and may the authorities finally question them about their parenting skills."

She just stared at me, a startled sort of expression made more serious by the booze, I was sure. Then she said, "Makes you wonder if deific children are ever forced into creating imaginary friends."

I played along, offering that, yes, I supposed they probably were, but that those imaginary friends would most likely be far more substantive, more corporeal than those created from a finite mind, at least outwardly. That, given the unrefined skills of those juveniles, there would probably just be sawdust inside.

"Or," she giggled, "those gears and flashing lights like inside those robots from the old Twilight shows!"

I toasted again. "To gears and lights and robots who meet with tragic ends."

She twirled her ice. "Did you ever have imaginary playmates while growing up?"

I pretended to think about it. "No," I finally said. "I didn't have to. I always had an abundance of real flesh-and-blood friends, not to mention two older brothers."

"I didn't," she said, her eyes suddenly wide and glacial, as if something frigid had settled behind them. Then she warmed considerably and threw her arms around me. "Until you, that is." Then she kissed me and told me my lips tasted of the darkest shade of amaryllis and sounded far brighter than the reddest framboise.

In reflection I'm convinced that she had slipped the proverbial tongue, and that the alcohol was to blame, for it wasn't either her reputation or dignity she so much wished to maintain with a sober head as it was her *identity*.

Later that evening, in the glow of a dozen candles and a bouquet of lavender incense, the tip of her index finger danced across my chest, and I was sure she could feel the pounding of my heart... that her neighbors could feel it.

"What is it?" I asked, literally terrified.

"Ssshhhh," she whispered. "Patience is truly a virtue."

She vanished the very next day, never to be heard from again. She was last seen leaving the library late that afternoon, her image caught on surveillance tape. Library records indicated that she'd checked out *Wetland Plants: Biology and Ecology*, and *Freaks and Marvels of Plant Life*. Neither was ever found. Although there was speculation that she'd simply run away, the more accepted theory was that she'd met with foul play, probably by the likes of someone as devious as Samson Rio. This theory, mostly embraced by law enforcement, was never officially declared, for fear it might create undue anxiety, especially on campus, in the wake of the gruesome California murders.

I was, of course, a suspect and remain so to this day, at least in the eyes of a few detectives who never believed my alibi, even as my two roommates swore we'd been up all that day and half the night shooting tequila during a Three Stooges movie marathon (their obsession, not mine).

During the first days of the investigation, I only lied once to the authorities, telling them that I had only one item inside Lisa's apartment, but that I needed it as soon as possible, as it was a crucial science project. When they asked why it was being conducted at her place instead of my own, I explained that a primary ingredient was lacking at my windowless apartment: sunlight. Having earlier been there to question me, they knew this to be true and thereby let me retrieve it.

And to this very day that experiment sits inside my own refrigerator, in the same Tupperware bowl. I've never so much as touched that seed or its most curious protuberances.

After that, I went into a kind of emotional hibernation, coming out only to eat—which I did little of, especially staying clear of certain fruits—and study, which I did a lot of. I moved out from my basement quarters not long after Lisa's disappearance, having found a studio apartment within walking distance of the campus. I kept mostly to myself, retreating into an almost monkish devotion to school work. Time spent on the computer was for research only, and the viewing of television (although I was never a compulsive viewer to begin with) was a recreation I rarely, if ever, indulged. I had, in fact, left the only television I owned with my two grateful roommates, so any later glimpses of such things came inadvertently.

Eventually, four years passed by: a few of them slow-moving in a kind of dream haze, the rest dragging by like a crippled dog pulling itself across a long, cold patch of unkempt asphalt.

Then, six nights ago, I became sick. It started out earlier that day as a dull ache in my lower right abdomen and by dinnertime had become a persistent pain I could no longer ignore. Having no medical insurance, I drove myself to the local firehouse and had the paramedics check me out. An old friend of mine had once worked at that station. I was thankful that he was still there and working that evening: thankful not for his expertise in emergency medicine, as he wasn't able to help me in that respect, but because his was suddenly a familiar face in a world where so many things had slowly lost their identity, their color.

The three paramedics who looked me over all agreed that my condition didn't appear life-threatening, but that I should without delay get my ass over to St. Mary's Catholic Hospital, as it was not only the closest but wouldn't let a silly little thing like lack of health insurance get in the way of treatment.

I followed their advice and found upon entering the emergency room an attendance of the sick that seemed somewhat alarming for a late Tuesday evening. There was a lot of sniffing, coughing, expectorating... and lots of sobbing. And everyone was masked, including the staff.

Well, I'd told myself, it was, after all, flu season.

As I approached the admittance window, the receptionist handed me a mask then said, "By the way you're walking, I'd say you have a kidney stone." And, as it turned out, she'd been right. Three highly trained paramedics had argued between an angry appendix and acute gas, but it took a hospital receptionist just three seconds to nail it, my uniquely crimped stride the giveaway.

With the rickety hands of the infirm, I tied the mask around my face then presented my ID, all the while flinching and grimacing and apologizing for my state of indigence.

Poised over the admitting form she said, "On a scale

from one to ten, how would you rate your pain?"

"Forty-nine," I said.

The receptionist looked up at me, smiled and said (as did at least three other females throughout the rest of that debacle), "Now you know what a woman in labor feels like."

Taking this statement as an invitation to act accordingly, I leaned in as best I could and said, very calmly, "Then why don't you get off your sorry ass and find me some fucking morphine?"

From what I can remember, that simple request did not engender the same kind of compassion that is customarily shown those whose water, and patience, has finally broke.

From there my situation progressed to a draped cubicle where I was probed and prodded, all the while enjoying an intravenous drip of narcotics for my ever-increasing pain.

The next thing I remembered, the sun was up and I was down. Flat.

As I groped my way out of the anesthesia, I vaguely recall a tinny voice speaking from the edges of my bed: a female voice sounding not so unlike my own reedy thoughts until it uttered a word that had long ago become my obsession.

Wangari? Could that be right? Certainly not.

I fought to regain my wits. Had she actually said what I thought she did?

Muscling onto my elbows, I looked up at the television and became groggily aware of an attractive anchorwoman, her lips in synch with that voice, one that was coming from a portable remote attached to my bed, snaking between the rails. She was saying something about how epidemiologists from the Center for Disease Control had followed the chain of infection (what infection?) to a sandwich maker from some Bronx delicatessen and was now considering that worker, Wangari Turay, now deceased, to be the *index case*, or the first detected case, of the pandemic. She went on to say that Wangari immigrated to the US from Nairobi fourteen months earlier, but a search of customs records indicated that she had visited friends in Beijing, China just days before her death.

I'm sure the doctor who then entered the room saw me as a classic case of someone gracefully reentering consciousness: patient trying to sit up but listing terribly, eyes rolling and confused, mouth agape, drooling ever so slightly...

He was accompanied by a woman in white. I'll call her Nurse Viola, as she reminded me of a woman by that name who used to come in once a week and vacuum and dust my parent's house—a gentle woman who wore a ceaseless expression I often mistook for motherly concern, at least when it was pointed in my direction—the very same expression Nurse Viola was imparting. At least, that's what her eyes were indicating, as the rest of her face was covered by a white mask, as was the doctor's.

The doctor mumbled something akin to an apology as Nurse Viola reached over me and muted the television. Her eyes were kind, thoughtful, and I could tell she was trying to smile. "You appear to be coming around just fine," she said then raised the top third of my bed so that I could sit up without having to use my arms.

She then pulled back the covers, lifted my gown and inspected the sutures beneath a patch of white gauze taped to my abdomen. It was then that I vaguely recalled someone having told me the night before, while I was in a morphine fugue, that something had been found... something about exploratory surgery.

The doctor was standing between me and a window, outside of which I could now see an adjacent section of the hospital skirted by scaffolding whereupon dozens of workers in hard hats and white sterile suits were draping massive sheets of plastic over specific sections.

The doctor then turned from the window and said, "That's what they're affectionately calling it now, down at the CDC." He lifted a finger and pointed it in the direction of my chest.

"Wangari."

He turned back to the window, the grayness outside blanching his eyes to further degrees of concern. He continued. "On May fourteenth of this year, the CDC *officially* named the sub-type H18N4, that information having been publicly released in a memorandum to all hospitals and healthcare officials *just three days ago*. Now, I never paid much credence to prophecies or those who make them, and if that tattoo you're wearing was your only piece of evidence for such things, then my better sense would be telling me that you'd simply perpetrated a clever hoax. However..." He reached into his right smock pocket and withdrew a simple sandwich bag that he gently placed on my chest, as if it belonged there, right atop Lisa's divination.

"That's a peach seed," he said, "in case you weren't sure."

I had already picked up the bag and was staring incredulously at the specimen within. It looked to have been freshly cleaned. "Or, nectarine," I offered.

He shrugged. *Peach, nectarine, the ass end of a*

gerbil.... "Thing is... how can I put this... there were these nearly-microscopic strands of... fibrous tissue, these parallel fibers branching out of this seed and appearing to... to invade every organ in the vicinity.... I mean, the cavity was literally saturated–" He dropped his head, shook it then coughed a sound of strained disbelief.

"Go ahead, Michael," Nurse Viola said softly. "Just tell him."

He turned to me once again, nodded to the bag on my chest and said, "Let's just say that the lingering impressions of everyone in your surgical attendance are that this seed was not so much growing *inside* you... but rather you were growing *outside* of *it*."

My eyes had never left the seed. Stunned, I couldn't think of anything coherent to say. So, I said, "Did you save my kidney stone, too?"

He shook his head. "You eventually passed it. After injecting you with the dye, the X-rays did show a filling defect in the ureter, your stone, but they also detected radiopaque matter—that seed—in the same vicinity. I determined this to be a wonderful opportunity to go in and take a look-see, thinking it some species of cyst, and perhaps an accomplice in creating your pain, and the rest, as they say, is history."

The masks made it difficult to read their expressions, but there was absolutely no evidence that suggested either one was finding the situation the least bit funny.

"What kind of bug is this H18-whatever?" I asked.

"A sub-type of the influenza virus," the doctor sighed. "It's mean, and it's very, very fast."

"Once infected, what are our chances?"

He looked at Nurse Viola, as if she crunched those

kinds of numbers. "There aren't any," he finally said, heading for the door.

I inquired about a vaccine and received the same response, that there wasn't one.

At the door the doctor turned one last time, and said, "I'm still curious.... Why have the tattoo etched in reverse?"

I told him that the artist was a dear friend of mine from a distant past: an eccentric little genie from Nebraska who'd popped her bottle and liked to play Edgar Cayce in cursive, and that she suffered from a bizarre fear of mirrors and personalized her predictions to reflect that phobia, at least that was the theory, but I couldn't yet say just why.

I left out the magic, though the room certainly could have used some.

He thought on this a moment then offered, "Maybe from her point-of-view the ink *was* going on in a perfectly legible way." He paused, and even behind his mask I could see that he was smiling. "That is, if her perspective had evolved on the *other* side of the mirror." Then he turned and disappeared down the hallway, Nurse Viola in close second.

Above me, the news ticker was indicating the President of the United States and Congress had just agreed to begin using the military on a strictly limited basis to maintain order, specifically to help restore it in those outbreak areas of considerable population.

No one was calling it Martial Law just then, but it was still very early.

Funny, just when I'd given up hope of ever finding that catastrophe, that remarkably momentous incident that would finally make sense of the prediction on my chest, it sneaked up behind me.

I pressed the button that was to summon a nurse, any nurse, now confronted with the full realization that Lisa hadn't met with any foul play those many years ago, nor had she just voluntarily walked clean away from a promising life as so many others allegedly do for equally inexplicable reasons.

Nurse Viola returned, those maternal eyes dulled but still hopeful. "Something I can get you?" she asked while checking my IVs. "Refresh your water, perhaps?"

"Sewing needles," I said urgently. "I need at least seven." I was factoring in attrition due to clumsy fingers.

As she bent down to adjust my pillow, I rose as best I could to meet her, pulled open my gown, pointed to that prescient ink and said, "And you *must hurry*."

Within minutes she returned with a handful of those travel-size sewing kits one often finds abandoned in the covert side pockets of luggage. She placed them on the bedside table, admitting that the in-house pharmacy was full of such conveniences.

Each kit contained two needles, more than enough. All I needed was four, as I had finally realized that that sequence of dots did not represent any letter or number in Braille, any genealogical diagram or ancient Mayan symbol, but was quite simply a template. A guide, if you will, for the correct placement of four needles into the pit, into the fissures of the endocarp... into the very seed that had been taken from inside me.

My ticket to get back on the train I once rode with Miss Tangerine.

But I wondered, *Is the correct placement to correspond to the real image on my chest, or to its virtual one in the mirror?*

I chose the 'real' image, and have been relentlessly

working that sequence.

So far, I'm still here, all the while reminding myself that patience is a virtue.

It's been three days since my release from the hospital, and I write this for those few who might be left wandering in Wangari's wake. Just know that gods do indeed exist, and that, in the course of their mysterious ways, they, like us, often forget what their children are doing. It was just that fear that Lisa had for mirrors, afraid that someone behind those silver depths was looking for her, and they had been, because she'd gone way past curfew. And, finally, that there exists in the very back of my refrigerator, second shelf from the top, a large Tupperware bowl containing a pin-riddled seed. Should Wangari advance to every niche and corner, and to states of such unimaginable pain and suffering that the collective cry is for an immediate and global release, then simply remove one or more of those protruding needles from that seed.

That should have the desired effect.

And if I'm still here when Wangari comes knocking, then *I'll* do us all.

The End

About the author:

Jon-Michael Emory's stories have appeared in various zines and anthologies, such as *England's Fiction Furnace*, *Next Phase*, *Night Terrors*, *New Genre 2*, *Wired Hard III*, and *It Lives!*, another anthology by RuneWright.

ᎭHounded

by Lyn McConchie (Norsewood, New Zealand)

S he'd been running a long time, and she was tired almost to her death of it. The sheriff had promised a lot, she thought as she boarded the stage. For all his promises he'd done damn little, and for all theirs, the lawyers hadn't done much more.

"How far, Marm?"

"Nairnville, please." It was the end of the line, deep into the mountains and about as far from her old life as she could get. He'd find her there, she feared. It was only a matter of time. She'd broken her trail over and over, maybe she'd have longer free—and maybe she wouldn't, her mind added grimly. Big Jack Islay didn't like to lose.

In the seat in front of her, two elderly women were chatting. From their conversation they were neighbors on their way home from shopping in the city. Her ears pricked up as the subject changed.

"...cottage going begging and at a rent that low."

"Humph!" The snort was emphatic. "Middle of the forest an' mountains. You need a horse to get there, an' your neighbors'll be mountain folk. So he did it up nice. Who'd want to live right out there?"

"Oh, I dunno. 'S lonely, that I grant you, but the forest's real nice in summer." There was a pause. "Anyway, ole Bas never come to no harm, did he? Lived there fer nigh on twenty years, and he always said he never saw nor heard nothing. Reckoned the mountains was peaceful like."

"Peaceful, I suppose so. Mind you, the Ellices aren't the type to notice if anything was goin' on, and the old man wasn't one to see anything he didn't want to."

"Mebbe not. But Bas, he liked living there." There was a short chuckle. "He used to say anyone come by the main trail an' not knowing the short cuts, it took ages. Put them off. Not to mention having to pass the Langly's and the Merrin outfits and them not being friendly to anyone they don't know."

The stage halted for the women to leave, the ladies calling out cheerful goodbyes to most of the passengers. Chris peered ahead. On one side of the road trees crowded: tall, ancient but strong, oak, ash and thorn, something at the back of her mind listed. *Thorn?* she queried back. Hawthorn recalled old memories. When she was very young they'd lived in the country. Dimly she recalled the scent of hawthorn in bloom and the croaking of frogs on the pond. Her father had moved to Memphis for work. She'd married in the city—her mind shied away from that thought hastily.

The stage rumbled to a halt at the side of a village square: a shop, a church, a hotel and a school. She looked again, and a small, weary smile fought its way to her face: not a big hotel that was almost a tavern. They'd likely have three rooms upstairs. Two single and one double bedroom, all served by the one bathroom. But the rooms would be clean, the bath water would be carried up hot and the food would be simple but good.

"Nairnville, marm. You getting out here or you wanna come back with me to Knoxville?" She controlled an instinctive flinching at the driver's closeness. He meant no harm: a small elderly man with kind blue eyes and a broad smile, reaching for her small trunk. He lifted it down from the stage luggage rack, turning to look at her. "Want me to carry it for you? 'S a fair old weight."

Despite herself, her voice was flat. "Thank you, sir. I can carry it."

He nodded, stepping back to allow her to take it up. Chris dragged it up the boardwalk steps towards the shabby hotel. For a moment she stood watching as the stage doors closed. The driver lifted his hand to a couple of passers-by, then the horses moved out, and the stage rolled around the square and off along the trail down which it had arrived.

Chris picked up her trunk again, blessing strong muscles honed by years of hard work. She hefted the case across the road, dumping it by the hotel reception desk. A tall man came from the chattering bar to attend her.

"Single room, is it? For one night or a bit longer?"

"Single room and," she hesitated. "I'm not sure how long. Is it all right if I just say one night and stay on once I know?"

"Of course. Sign the register. Anything I can help you with?"

The women's gossip flashed into her mind. Without volition she found she was asking, "Are there any places to rent hereabouts?"

He leaned against the desk thinking. "Weeell,

there's Braslington House." He grinned. "Huge old place on the far side of the Douglas River. The owner died, the new chap's yet to arrive, and they want to let it until he does. It'd do fine if you've a fancy for twenty bedrooms and a kitchen bigger'n Jim Hooson's hay barn." Chris shook her head smiling.

"Didn't think so. Then there's the old cottage on Barkwell's land. It isn't bad, but it depends on how much company you want. Effie Barkwell'd talk the hind leg off a donkey, and the cottage is right by the house. She mostly lets that to the teacher when she gets here for the school year."

He took in the frown. "Not that one, then? Only one other I can call to mind. It's a long way from here, a good day's ride, an' it's been empty a while now, but the old man's son wants someone living there. He'd let it go cheap, but it wouldn't be suitable for a lady." Chris felt her pulse quicken. The women in the bus had said some of the same things.

"It belonged to an old fellow. Bas Ellice. He must have built it morn'n fifty years back. He died last month.

He eyed her doubtfully. "It's isolated. The nearest proper trail's a good two miles away. There's just tracks after that. Bas used to ride down here every two, three months to buy at the store, but he made nothing of that. You might feel different."

"I'd like to see it." Something about the place attracted her every time it was mentioned. Maybe the isolation. Jack couldn't just come driving up with his fancy carriage and his hard men at his back. They'd have to walk, and with a number of tracks, they could even get themselves lost. She smiled a little inside herself at the idea. Hitting the trees wouldn't do him any good. They wouldn't bleed and cry and do whatever he demanded.

The hotel owner was deliberating. "Miles Harman could show you over the place. He told me the lawyer said he should have the keys since Bas left him all his personal gear. Likely Miles will stop here for a drink later. I can let him know you'd like to ride out there, if you'd like me to tell him."

"If you would do that, please. I'd like to see it tomorrow, if it's convenient."

"I'll do that. Now Miss..." he glanced down at the register, "Miss Ross, you'll be tired being on that stage. I can do you a meal in the dining room, or I can send my wife up with a tray in an hour if that'd suit you better?" He saw the relief on her face. "All right then. Do you fancy a hearty meal or something lighter?"

"Light please." Heaven to have the choice, not to be told what she must do, the order emphasized with an upraised fist if she hesitated.

"Leave it to me."

She left it to him with gratitude, a feeling justified by the tray that appeared an hour later. Minutes after, Chris returned from a long, luxurious hot bath in an old cast-iron bathtub. The tray was borne by a large smiling woman who announced herself as "I'm Mrs. Moorhouse. My husband owns the hotel. Where do you want the tray, my dear?" Chris indicated the bedside table.

"It's very kind of you. It looks wonderful."

"You just eat up, dearie. You could do with something. You look as if you've been ill."

"I was in hospital." She heard her words and hastily added to them. "Appendicitis, but I was quite ill for a while."

"Ah," said Mrs. Moorhouse. "Nasty, that is. But I

mustn't keep you talking while the food gets cold." She left, quietly shutting the door behind her. Chris was left to consider the food.

Light meal or not, it didn't look as if she'd go hungry. The scrambled eggs were light and fluffy, the teapot full, and there was a stack of hot buttered toast. Chris ate then laid back on the bed, sipping her tea. Jack didn't like tea. She was expected to make powerfully strong coffee at all hours then be blamed for it when he couldn't sleep.

Outside the moon was rising. She heard the men downstairs in the bar laughing now and again, and someone sang something. Overhead, from the clear crisp sky, there came a long, drawn-out yelping Chris recognized as the cry of wild geese. In the bar below all sound ceased briefly. Then the rumble of voices began again. When Chris did sleep it was to jerk awake from a dream in which Jack moved towards her, cursing.

"Useless cow! Can't even give me a son without mucking it up. God knows I waited long enough!"

For once in her dream she defied him with the bitter truth. "It was your own fault. Couldn't even stop hitting me for a few months. You killed your own baby."

She lay awake until dawn, falling asleep again with first light, only waking mid-morning. She stretched while sun streamed in through the curtains, warming the room as it lifted her mood. She'd dodged for weeks, changing names and rooms, using the money her mother had left her and that she'd managed to get from the lawyers without her husband finding out. At last, just before she fled, she'd met the lawyers dealing with her mother's estate, making arrangements where they could send the bulk of the money. After that, she'd picked it up and run again. She knew Jack would have an eye out, what was his he kept.

But she'd broken her trail so long and so often, surely she could stay here safely for a while. Jack was a man of the city, for all he owned a ranch. He wouldn't think to look for her deep in the Smokey Mountain country, and if he did—she smiled briefly—he'd stand out like a fox in a hen house.

Chris studied herself as she dressed. She'd changed her hair color and style, lost so much weight as she criss-crossed Tennessee, missing meals, endlessly driving herself on, that she looked younger than the late twenties she was. At nine she descended the stairs to eat a hearty, belated breakfast. Mr. Moorhouse was waiting once she was finished.

"I talked to Miles last night. He said if you'd like to see the cottage, he'll be here at seven tomorrow morning with the buckboard, if that'd suit you?" She nodded agreement. "I'll let him know then."

"Thank you for your help." All her gratitude for unexpected kindness was in her voice, and he looked surprised.

"Nothing to it. Have a pleasant day."

Chris did. She wandered out first to see what she could discover. There was a stack of thin, poorly printed pamphlets in the hall porch. The place was just another tiny place, more off the beaten track than most. It had a history with few events of interest according to the leaflets.

The usual legends, the mountains hereabouts were supposed to be the haunt of a spirit that hunted evil men across the ridges with horse and hounds. Chris frowned then shrugged. Somewhere she'd heard that Scotts-Irish peasants had originally settled the mountains here. This tale would be a corruption of one of their ancient legends from the old country. It was all nonsense, probably some old local tradition. In a way she found that a pleasant thought, traditions still lingered in the mountains.

They'd lingered in Jack's family as well: a fist for any man who defied you, the back of your hand to any woman. Never forget a debt you owed—or that was owed to you. She owed Jack a life, the son she'd lost him, as he saw it. Chris shivered suddenly, although the day was warm. She'd told the Sheriff and her mother's lawyers once she was safe in hospital. They talked of invoking the law to keep him away from her. She's explained that no piece of paper would keep Jack away, and they'd spoken of the law's power.

Believing, she'd made a statement. They'd prosecuted, but Jack had good lawyers and a lot of friends, men of his own kind. They'd made her out to be clumsy, a liar, and the jury that knew nothing of her had acquitted. Jack went free, and for all the legal talk about how she'd be protected, they hadn't saved her. A wagon had come out of nowhere to run her down: a stolen wagon with a driver she'd recognized, but his alibi stood up. There was no proof and no safety there, so she fled early from the hospital where the accident had put her.

She shrugged the shadow from her mind. She was away from him. He wouldn't find her here, deep in the mountains where folk had no time for strangers. She went back to eat a late lunch and rest on her bed until it was time to come down for dinner. She ate well and slept unusually peacefully, a better sleep than she'd had for almost longer than she could remember. Mrs. Moorhouse came tapping lightly at the door at six the next morning.

"Miles Harman will be here in an hour, Miss Ross. I'll be putting your breakfast on the table this minute."

"I'll be right down." She flung a buckskin jacket about her shoulders. It would be cold within the trees' shade. She ran down the old creaking stairs to eat and wait. It was less than the promised hour when a lean old man walked up to her table.

"I'm Miles Harman." Christine rose to smile at the waiting man.

"Thank you for this, Mr. Harman. I'm most interested to see the cottage." He smiled back gently. Once in the buckboard, he talked about the small house they would see.

"It was well-built. Bas knew what he was about. Don't have many amenities as they say, but it's a good solid place. Small, mind. Just a bedroom an' a big kitchen with room for a dining table, no parlor. Water right into the kitchen though. It comes from the roof into tanks. That's why Bas put a real good roof on. You have to be careful though. If it don't rain, the tanks don't fill and you have to go down to the stream an' haul it back

"What about light and heat and a way to cook?"

Miles Harman grinned. "No problem there, marm. There's a good, big flat-topped wood stove with an oven on one side. She'll boil all the water you need an' then some. Ole Bas's son left the lanterns and lamp there as well. There's hooks to hang 'em on in the ceiling 'a both rooms, and there's a good table lamp as well.

"I'll need an axe for wood, and a small one for kindling?"

"All there," Miles told her briefly. "The boy didn't take much but his pa's personal gear." After that he was silent until they halted by the side of the trail, the buckboard drawing into a small layby cut into the forest edge. He hitched the horses and helped her down. "We walk from here."

They walked, along a narrow track that wound through great trees until a shape bulked against their background. Chris halted. *Bas must have believed in camouflage*, she thought. The cottage blended almost invisibly into its surroundings. Miles led the way to the door, opened that and waited for her to enter.

But Chris halted a moment, studying the trees about the house, the sunlight glimmering in patches across the ground. No lawn, just a small expanse of flat ground without real boundaries. The trees loomed above it all, sheltering, protecting, holding her safe from brutality and the fear she had lived with so long. Beneath them she would feel and hear little even of a gale. She fell in love as she looked up at the green foliage towering over her. It was as quick and simple as that.

She said nothing but turned, preceding Miles into the cottage. He'd told the truth there. It was well built, dry, and plainly furnished. She cared nothing for any of that. He showed her the two rooms, mentioned the quarterly rent—paltry—and added that if she chose to accept the place, the rent was to be paid to Mr. Moorhouse at the hotel who would hold it until young Ellice could pick it up. When he finally ran down she nodded.

"I can move in tomorrow. How much advance rent will they want? I can pay a year."

"Don't you want to think it over?"

"I'll have tonight. If you meet me at nine tomorrow morning, I can confirm my decision and pay Mr. Moorhouse."

"Very well, marm. I'll drive you back now. I can tell you anything else you want to know as we drive back."

Chris got out of the buckboard once they were

outside the hotel. "Thank you. I'll see you at nine." She waved as he drove away. Now, was the livery stable still open? It was a mixture of a place, odd bits of harness, an old pony trap and a corral with several horses and ponies standing half-asleep in the last of the sunshine.

She approached the owner. "That pony trap?"

"Aye, marm, belonged to Charlie up at Hooson's ranch. He built it outa bits. T'aint exactly standard like, but it's okay to drive."

"Is it for sale?"

"It is."

"I'll need a pony to go with it, but I want one broken to ride as well."

The man nodded thoughtfully. "I may have one. He's about fourteen hands, broke to ride or drive, an' he wun't be too big fer you, nor too small. But he's ugly."

Chris bit down a smile. She guessed which pony he meant at once. The beast was roman-nosed, an odd shade of grayish-brown and the small skirt of hair above each hoof said that there'd been a draft horse somewhere back in his ancestry. She haggled but closed the deal for both pony and trap and paid cash. She left with instructions that the pony was to be given a decent feed, watered and groomed. She also bought a sack of oats for him to be left waiting in the trap.

After that she went shopping at the general store, buying sacks of food, a drum of fuel for the lanterns and lamp, lengths of cloth to make dresses and a whole list of small items that would make her new life more comfortable.

Miles Harman arrived at nine am the next day, took one look at her new possessions and blinked. "That's Bas's pony."

Chris looked up in surprise. "He is? The stableman never said anything."

"Well, he is. Bas swapped him from one of the mountain folk an' called him Mouse. You could'a done a lot worse than buying him. He's a smart beast, sure-footed, an' he knows all the trails hereabouts." Chris smiled as Miles continued.

"That trap you got, that's a good buy too, you got a fair eye, marm. Couldn't git the buckboard in to the house but if you go the way I'll show you, you kin just about get that there trap in. Bas has a stable an' a shed by it where you kin put Mouse an' the trap. I'll ride along behind you with my buckboard an' haul some a' the heavier stuff you bought."

Chris waited only to pay Mr. Moorhouse before mounting the step of her trap and leading off down the trail. They forded the river, plodded up the narrowed trail, and once they reached a turn-off, Miles clicked to his horses and took the lead.

"This way, marm. His beasts pushed through brush onto a trail that had been invisible up until then, and Mouse plodded after them. The buckboard halted. "I can't go any further from here, marm. I'll unload what I have and help you pack it in."

Chris helped to load her trap with about a third of her goods and gear. Mouse moved off obediently, leaning hard into the breeching. It took another fifteen minutes before they came up on the house from the far side, and she halted the pony to look. Her house, her land, her refuge now. It took a couple of hours, but finally everything was under cover. Miles departed, leaving her with a wealth of good advice and information. Chris didn't even look after him. She was too busy making decisions as to where things should go and listening to the soft shushing of the trees.

In a week she had settled in. In a month it was as if she had always lived there. Let it be more than a respite only, she prayed. One day Jack would find her, but her mother had left Chris quite a lot of money, more than she'd realized until she met the lawyers: enough to keep her forever if she lived quietly, enough to buy this cottage if she could ever be sure that Jack had given up the hunt. A shudder savaged her.

The letter had come to the hospital where she lay after her so-called accident. The woman who'd brought it had known where Chris was and chosen not to give the letter to Jack. He'd never known his mother-in-law had died, although undoubtedly he knew by now. Still less had he any idea that the woman he'd disliked had left so much. Her first husband, Chris's father, had been poor. Her second husband had money. That came to her, and in the end to her only child.

Chris had sent a private message to the lawyers from the hospital, instructing them not to approach her husband but to wait until she contacted them again. Then, barely fit to walk, she'd fled hospital, the law that had failed her and the husband who wanted her back—or dead if she would not return. She'd left the hospital late that night, made arrangements with her lawyer, who was sympathetic, and run again.

Miles Harman had come back the day after she'd settled in here, a kind man and concerned for her.

"Miss Ross? Are you home?" She jerked upright from her single armchair.

"Come in." He entered, beaming in an almost proprietary way at her.

"Wondered if you could use the woodstove an' the lanterns yet. It's fall in another few weeks an' it'll be right chilly soon. I thought I could show you if you liked."

He meant well. Chris let him show her as he wished. She had the stove already lit from the previous night, but it was true she'd half forgotten how to use the lanterns. Jack had put in gaslights some years ago in their house in the city, and it was the servants who lit and used the kitchen stove. After he was gone again, she settled back in her armchair. He'd been right. The last few evenings had been chilly, but the lamplight glowed on the wooden walls of her home in a way that delighted her.

Miles returned again and again until he was sure she knew how to bank the fire to stay alive at nights, the best sort of wood to use and that she could use the axe and safely. Then she had to make it gently clear that she preferred her own company. He stayed away after that— with a half embarrassed anger he did not show. He'd liked the woman. Then she'd made him feel as if he was a bothersome old fool.

To Chris the forest and the mountains were timeless. In the silence and peace of the trees, she relaxed slowly, finding there was nothing to make her afraid here. She learned the scream of the vixen, the call of a hunting owl and to catch the occasional field mouse, freeing it outside again.

Mouse was turned out each morning in hobbles; he would come for a handful of oats each night and be barred safely within the stable. Chris wanted that to become a custom. There would be starving predators in the mountains in winter. One of her purchases in the store had been a rifle and a goodly stack of ammunition. She used the gun to shoot the rabbits that came to her small patch of garden and had rabbit stew to go with the greens.

For the first time in years, Chris could read all she wished. She'd brought books with her, purchased in Knoxville, and she read greedily in the evenings before she sought her bed. Winter drifted in so slowly it was a while before she realized it had arrived.

She knew it the day she drove Mouse to the village and found the river ford fringed with ice. That day she also found a book in the general store, traded in by some stage passenger. It was old, bound in shabby green with rubbed gilt lettering. She picked it up, examining the title with interest. *Folktales from England.* Chris bought it along with food and fuel. She still had ample, but if she was snowed in she would do better to have more than enough rather than too little.

She chose the book to read the following night and was soon deep in tales of strange events, a haunted church, the death of a miser, and... she stared at the title on the next page: *The Legend of the Hunter.* She read on with interest. When the story was done she closed the book to sit thinking. She dimly remembered hearing the name they'd said, and, oddly enough, it was the same name she'd heard muttered in the mountains. Chris snorted. Some twisting of old legends brought with the first settlers here most likely.

She noticed it was colder. The woodpile in the shed by the back door was getting low. She should walk down the track a ways and see what she could collect. It had been a full moon last night, even if she stayed after dark, there'd be light to walk home safely. She could take Mouse to carry any dry wood she found or haul a dry tree-trunk back if there was one they could move. There'd been an old dead tree she'd seen last week. Chris bundled herself into warm clothing, haltered Mouse, draped a sack on either side of him and set out, axe in hand.

Leaving the track, she meandered along between the trees, gathering and cutting until she had armloads of dry wood in each sack. She stopped abruptly when she heard a faint whimper. Jack had disliked animals. Chris had wanted a dog, but he wouldn't hear of it. Now the forlorn sound called to her. A puppy? Lost, starving, hurt or trapped. She called back, following the answering sounds.

She froze as she came in sight of the beast. No puppy, it was an adult dog, nor was it of any slight breed. Standing it might reach four feet at the shoulder. The heavy, powerful muscles curved in flowing lines under the smooth-coated pelt. It was gray, or to be more exact, Chris thought, a silvery color. The head was massive, narrowing only a little to heavy jaws. A Mastiff of some kind? Gold eyes stared at her. Then it whimpered again.

Would it savage her if she tried to help? How was it hurt? Could she leave it here, go for help? But she'd gone wood hunting in the opposite direction. It would take an hour to walk home. Bringing help back would take a day, and what if no one wanted to come? The dog looked at her.

"If I try to help you'll understand, won't you?" It wouldn't, but maybe the sound of her voice would help keep it calm. She moved in a little. "Poor boy. What on earth happened to you. Oh!" She could see a foreleg now, swollen twice the normal size, the swelling reaching far up towards the shoulder. "Oh, you poor dog. Don't worry. I'll help you." The swelling seemed to be getting worse almost as she watched. Maybe a snake had bitten the dog. She could deal with that she hoped.

"Just let me get Mouse to you." She was as quick as

she could be, leading the placid pony right up to the injured dog. "Now, let's see if we can get you across his back." It was difficult; the dog was not only big but heavy. Still, it seemed to appreciate she was helping. Chris forgot in her efforts any fear it might bite. Finally she had it lying along the packsacks. Abandoning her gathered wood to be retrieved another day, she moved as quickly as she could along the tracks until they reached her cottage.

By the time she had the dog stretched out on her hearthrug she was exhausted. She offered water, which the beast drank. That was good. Then, very gently she turned the grossly swollen leg to look at it. Half buried in the paw's pad she saw something protruding. That had to be it. The dog had trodden on something sharp, and infection had followed the wound. She patted it.

"I can see the trouble." It whined softly. "Don't worry. I'll look after you. I wonder who you belong to, someone who treats you well, I believe." It was so huge but so gentle. It had made no attempt to bite, even though she must have hurt getting it onto Mouse and off at the house again. Odd eyes. She didn't know a dog could have eyes of such a bright gold. She stroked the short fine coat, enjoying the softness.

"Okay, now, keep still." She was using her fingers, trying to get a grip on the thing sunk into the paw. "Ahhh!" Her fingers gripped. "Ouch!" She held up a finger from which blood oozed. The dog leaned forward in one swift movement to lick off the blood. "Don't get ideas." Chris patted him, then took another grip. This time the object slid smoothly from the puffy flesh.

She glared at it. "A quill. Don't you know better than to tease porcupines?"

She tossed the quill to one side, dressed the injury carefully then made the animal comfortable on the hearthrug with food and water. There went her own dinner, she thought ruefully, but tomorrow she could drive Mouse to Nairnville. They might know if a dog like this was missing. If not she could tell the storekeeper, and he'd pass it on to anyone who came asking. If no one claimed the beast, she'd like to keep him herself.

No one did, but he stayed only a short time. A few weeks later, on a bright moonlit night, she let him out when he was insistent. He never returned, and she wept. Winter went by, and apart from mourning the loss of the dog, she was happy. Spring is a time of renewal, but this Spring brought floods, Miles Harman again to see that she'd survived in her isolation and, late one evening, her husband, Big Jack Islay in his buckboard with his gun-slick driving.

Chris saw him first from the shelter of her trees. Dear God, somehow he'd found her, she wondered how he'd done that, but none of it mattered now. She had to get away. He hadn't seen her. If she faded back into the forest, she could be home in half an hour, grab a few things, her money, and make a run for it again with Mouse. The pony would take her through the mountains to one of the other small towns on the far side. There she could catch the stage.

Big Jack Islay kept his eyes busy. He'd been told where they'd have to leave the buckboard. After that they'd have to walk, but he had a map. He hitched the horses, pausing with his man to collect a couple of lanterns from the back of the wagon. It'd be dark any minute now, but if he waited some busy-body'd talk. She'd hear, and God knows it had taken long enough to find her this time.

If it hadn't been for a lawyer's clerk with his hand out and a man here who resented being sent away, he'd never have found her.

He started walking down the track. At the cottage Chris had leaped through the door, snatching up her money and other items she couldn't leave behind. Mouse, she must saddle him quickly. She heard footsteps then, stared out of the half-open door and froze in terror. He was here, she thrust the bills into her pocket and dived for the bedroom window in silence. It would take him a few minutes to realize she'd gone. It would have, but Jack had left his man to watch. He shouted. Jack replied, and as Chris ran they were after her, deep into the heart of the mountains.

"I don't like this, boss. There's some funny tales about the mountains hereabouts." The hired gun shivered briefly. It was freezing too, and the moonlight bothered him. There was something about that light. He remembered stories his grandda had told him, of great trees back in the country they'd left behind and tales of the wild lands and who hunted there.

"What are you babbling about," Jack Islay snarled. "She's getting away. After her! If I lose her this time..."

Above their hunt the moon rose higher, flooding patches of clearer ground with light. But under the trees it was flickering shadows. Chris knew the tracks by now. It was all that kept her ahead. She ran weighed down with her fear. She had the speed, but they had the stamina. She dodged, twisted and turned, but always they came back on her trail. She was tiring. Jack shouted furiously after her flying figure.

"Chris, stop. Stop, wife, or you'll be sorry." He cursed when she continued. Once he laid hands on her....

Ahead her foot caught in a tree root that lay across the path. She stumbled, slowing. He half-caught her arm. She wrenched free, leaping forward in a last gasp of speed, and as she ran she screamed for the first time. A short shrill cry of hopeless terror—and of rage at the man who had taught her that fear.

Above her a gap in the trees flooded the forest floor with silvery moonlight, and in that flood something appeared: a shape, itself a part of the glimmering moonlight. Chris did not slow. Whatever it was had to be better than the men behind her. It halted to look at her. She fell again, gasping, and it whirled to stand over her and from its throat came a wild belling cry—a summoning, one that was answered by others as Chris flung her arms about the shape.

"Dog!" He lowered massive jaws to lick her gently. From far up the track came a wild thunder of hooves, a horn blowing as it overlaid with savage music the growing clamor of hounds crying the trail. Jack Islay and his man halted then came on. Only a dog, and they both had pistols. Shoot it and get the woman away before the distant hunt reached them.

The dog was looking at him. Jack Islay shot, cursing the moonlight that affected his aim. The horn sounded louder. He stared incredulously as the hunt poured down the track towards him: a giant of a man on a black horse whose hooves spurned the ground they did not quite touch… a pack of hounds that raced before him, their eyes blazing golden flames. The horn sounded louder, bringing a hot gust of terror to take him by the throat. His man was babbling. Jack seized him by the arm, hitting him across the face.

"What are you babbling about, you superstitious

fool?"

"Herne! Oh, Jesus. Me grandda was right. It's
Herne the Hunter. She's called the hounds of Herne to
save her. *Look!*"

He pointed to where Chris knelt. Before her,
protecting, stood the dog. But this was no beast of earth
now. Its eyes flamed the same gold fire as those of the
pack, moonlight glowing silver fire along the muscled
flanks. It shifted, half in and half out of their world. The
huntsman's mount reared high. The rider's eyes fixed on
the two men. The horn sang as the milling pack turned to
look at them too, and with those eyes upon him, Jack Islay
broke in that moment. He ran, his man running faster
before him. The pack followed, the high wild music of the
horn urging them on. The prey was chosen. Let them
follow the prey. They did not see the rider turn back.

Chris knelt on the forest floor, her arms about the
great dog. Hooves sounded beside her, and she looked up.
The huntsman's face was strong, clean planes of bone
framing eyes that blazed down at her. Yet despite the
power, it was a face without evil. He would always deal
justice—yet that was his failing, she thought. Little mercy
showed in the lines, but the black eyes, which surveyed
her, were unexpectedly kind. He nodded once, his gaze
holding hers. Into her mind came understanding like a
blow.

Perhaps it had first been a test to see if she was fit to
share the mountains and forest with he who hunted here,
but the beast she had aided, a dog that in the space of a
moon had come to love her, had answered her cry. It had
licked the blood she had shed for it. The terror of the hunt
could never touch her. Justice was met. Ahead lay justice
for those who had dared to hunt her in one of the Hunter's

own forests. Hoof-thunder receded.

The dog urged her to her feet and walked beside her as she staggered back to her cottage. Now and again his tongue came out lovingly to lick her hand. She would not see Jack or his man again. They would run until they reached the buckboard. Then, with fear hot behind them, they would drive the horses like madmen until the buckboard crashed. They would die, the horn call still sounding its wild scream of justice in their ears.

Chris bought the cottage when the year's rent ran out. She lived there after that, accepted by the mountain folk who knew more than they found it necessary to tell. And if on moonlit nights she met a four-footed friend in the forest, if she walked and talked with one on two legs, who was there to speak of it?

But that was all to come. For now she could only stand at her door, one hand on the dog's great head as she listened to horn-song far away, riding the sky, the music of hounds singing back. The dog was gone when she lowered her eyes, gone to find his pack and the trail. There is a strange reality behind some legends, nor are they always bound to one place, for that she could only be thankful.

The End

About the author:

Lyn McConchie began writing professionally in 1990 with sales in that year to MZB's Fantasy magazine and several other genre markets. Since that start she has seen almost 300 of her short stories appear, many reviews, articles, poems and opinion pieces, and 23 books—with a further five sold. This year she was both the Sir Julius Vogel Award for Best SF/F book (Adult) of 2010 winner for her TOR Books fantasy, *The Questing Road*, and Best SF/F book (Young Adult) winner for her Cyberwizard (USA) fantasy *Summer of Dreaming*. *Cyberwizard* will have her short story collection, *Tales from the Marrigan Trade House*, and the sequel to *Summer*, *Autumn of the Wild Pony* out this year, while this year Kite Hill (UK) will also be publishing Lyn's collaborated alternate history novel, *Queen of Iron Years*. Lyn may be found on www.lynmcconchie.com.

Neville and the Gods

by Ed Cooke (Leeds, UK)

The old lady was not pleased with Thor, and Thor was absolutely livid with Neville.

Shamefacedly, helmet wings drooping, Thor retrieved his hammer from the greenhouse. Under his breath he thanked Odin for inventing mortality. If death didn't put an end to the old lady's tirade, she would carry on grumbling forever. He was wrong, not for the first time.

The welter of complaints ground to a halt with, "What have you got to say for yourself, young man?"

Thor's answer was a stream of obscenities unfit for the ears of respectable matrons. Since this particular matron was not conversant with Old Norse, he got away with it.

All she said was, "You'll have to speak a bit slower. I think my hearing aid is playing up."

She extracted the offending gadget and started to fiddle with the battery. Veteran of many a battle against gods, demons and everything in between, Thor knew an opportunity to retreat when he saw one. He bobbed his head in what he hoped was a deferential gesture and all but ran down the crazy paving to the front gate. He crossed the road and knocked so hard on Neville's front door that icebergs of peeling white paint caved and headed south.

Neville opened the door. He had been wearing that vest so long it was becoming a habit. "Oh," he said, "it's you."

Thor roared, "What in Valhalla's name did you make me do that for?"

Neville looked blank. Thor realised his mistake and repeated himself in English. Neville's expression did not change. He said, "You forget yourself. What god is better than Neville?"

Thor gave the ritual response through gritted teeth. "No god. No god is better than Neville."

Neville said, "Come in. Kettle's on," and went inside.

Thor followed him into the kitchen. It smelled of what chemical manufacturers deluded themselves was pine forest. Thor might be getting on a bit, but he still remembered what pine forests smelled like. Sometimes he dreamed of how he used to run through them, followed by a band of adoring worshippers wearing nothing but dirt. Neville's kitchen was usually an encyclopedia of dirt, but today it was spotlessly clean.

Someone came up behind Thor. He whirled and lifted his hammer. It was a tall, blonde Valkyrie, come at last to claim him in battle. If this was to be a fight to the death, why wasn't she wearing full armour? Why wasn't she wearing anything at all except a pair of rubber gloves? Then she walked calmly past him, and Thor noticed she didn't have any wings.

Neville said, "This is Eva. Eva, this is my friend Thor." Thor couldn't keep his lip from curling at the very idea of being Neville's friend.

The woman picked up a cloth and rubbed absently at an invisible mark on the worktop. She ignored Thor. Her eyes were riveted on Neville—yet there was nothing about Neville, balding and direly overweight, to interest the most sex-starved woman. Thor didn't suppose Eva's clearly rigorous diet extended to sex. What did this embodiment of perfection see in the collage of bad habits that was Neville?

"Have I cleaned everything, darling?"

"Not quite everything. Would you mind finishing the job?"

"Of course. I am so stupid. How do you suffer me?"

Eva knelt before Neville and gently lowered his stained jogging bottoms. Thor looked away.

"Would you like her to see to you, Thor? Afterwards?"

Thor swallowed. He had been with numberless women divine and human, and even the humans had been divine. The last time had been longer ago than he cared to remember.

"No, thank you," Thor said, struggling to keep his voice neutral. He and all his kin were already beholden to Neville. He didn't want to incur more debt and make things worse. Not that things could get worse than they already were.

The contract was a verbal one. Odin had wanted to get something in writing until Loki pointed out that anything with their signatures on it would find its way onto a tabloid front cover sooner than later. So they settled on an informal *entente*: call it a gentleman's agreement.

What were you supposed to do when you found yourself ensnared in a gentleman's agreement with as ungentle a man as Neville?

Eva was on her feet again by the time the kettle boiled. She made a pot of tea. Thor wondered how long it had taken her to hack Neville's teapot out from under its usual thicket of mould. He no longer wondered how she had wound up as Neville's handmaiden. He knew divine influence when he saw it. He said, trying to sound casual, "Seen Astrild lately?"

Neville hitched up his trousers and scratched his lolloping belly. His weight problem had only got worse since he hit on the idea of making Loki carry him wherever he wanted to go. "I thought you'd come to find out what the old witch over the road did to deserve a hammering."

"I was working my way round to that."

"She got off very lightly."

"Her tomatoes didn't."

"If you must know, she complained to Environmental Health about what Eva and I were up to in the front garden."

Thor snapped, "A woman like Eva wouldn't give you the time of day if you hadn't had Astrild's help."

Neville looked wounded. "Women are usually too shy to approach me. All Astrild needed to do was boost their confidence a little."

So the rotten swine had ordered Astrild to make this lissome Eva fall in love with him. That was low even for Neville. Thor was certain Neville was getting worse. "You shouldn't take advantage of us gods like this. It's immoral."

"Who are you to talk to me about morals? You must have fathered half the population of Norway in your salad days."

Thor thought this a conservative estimate but held his peace. Eva tore her eyes off Neville just long enough to hand Thor some Earl Grey in one of Neville's chipped mugs. Then she reverted to the doe-eyed gaze she did so well.

Without thinking, Thor downed the tea in one gulp. This technique was the only way to handle horns of mead, but it did not lend itself to hot drinks. Thor winced as the Earl rolled lava-like down his throat.

Neville smiled at Thor's discomfort. "Will that be all? It's just that Eva and I have been waiting for a sunny day like today. We're going to have so much fun in the garden that if Mrs. Tidbolt watches this time, she'll probably have a heart attack."

Thor crushed the empty mug in his mighty fist. Eva dived for a dustpan and brush—she must have bought them. There was no way Neville had ever owned such things—and began to sweep up the fragments. Once again, Thor found himself routed, twice in one afternoon. Since Neville had taken over, Thor suffered more indignities on a daily basis than he had had to endure in all his glory centuries combined. Then again, he was glad to be going. He certainly didn't want to stick around for further nauseating scenes of Neville in triumph.

Was it too much to ask, if the mortal was going to lord it over his rightful gods (strictly Neville had been born too far south to fall into Thor's catchment area, but Thor was prepared to stretch a point) that he should do so with common decency? Almost certainly it was. Thor had reviewed Neville's early life as recorded on the BetaMax tapes of the period in Valhalla's recreation room. It would have made a poor date flick. Many a plumber's acquaintance with the water closet was much slighter than Neville's; as a fat schoolboy he had spent most lunchtimes having his head shoved down boys' and girls' toilets.

The world of work had treated him no more kindly. The scent of unpopularity clung to him, as did the smell of the yellow deodorant blocks that colonised English urinals of the period. The only career open to him was as a toilet attendant for the borough council. It was while discharging his routine cleaning duties that he made his life-changing discovery.

So now that Neville had Thor and all the other *de jure* masters of the universe by the short and curlies, no one could really expect him to cut them any slack. The man had suffered, and now he was paying the world its cruelties back in spades. Thank goodness Freya hadn't lived to see her family wait hand and foot on such an oaf.

On the way out of Neville's house, Thor was disconsolate. He must have been, for only out of utter desperation could his brilliant idea have emerged.

He found Loki in his usual haunt. One of the sorriest signs of the gods' decline—though Loki would have denied it with his final breath—was that the Lord of Misrule contented himself with tossing spanners into the works of local government. These days Loki seldom left the council offices, save to accompany the Highways Department on an occasional site visit.

"I think I know how to get Neville off our backs," Thor said.

"I should have thought it was obvious to anyone but a knucklehead like you."

Thor didn't like Loki much. For a god who had once given birth to an eight-legged horse, he looked remarkably slender. These days the mead went straight to Thor's waistline and clung there, but Loki remained defiantly lithe.

"It is obvious," Thor persisted, "but seeing as you're the clever one, I want you to tell me whether there's any other way out of this mess."

"There isn't," Loki said. Thor was taken aback. He had expected Loki to niggle and qualify, to pick nits and hedge bets the way he usually did. To get a straight answer out of Loki was really something. Thor wondered why he didn't feel like glorying in the minuscule triumph. He cast about for something else to say, even though it was obvious that, having thought the unthinkable, he would now have to go and do it.

He turned to go. Loki said, "You do realise you won't be able to kill Odin unless he wants to die?"

"He was suicidal before. Since then, things have only gone downhill."

Odin: father to them all, but heavy hangs the head that wears the crown (Odin didn't actually wear a crown, but Thor liked the saying). Unbeknownst to the other gods, Odin had grown tired. There was plenty for a god to be tired of. No one really believed in any of them anymore, and their attempts to regain public attention had all fallen flat. Politicians explained away divine beneficence as the inevitable result of their own ingenious policies. Naturally their unbelief provoked godly wrath, but there was no shortage of terrorists to claim responsibility for Odin's fits of spleen. The net result was to crowd out the supernatural, which soon found itself with no outlet but cable TV.

No wonder Odin decided to top himself. It was just a pity that of all the public conveniences in all the world, he chose Neville's as the venue for his last bow.

The credulity that had made Neville a lifelong victim—he kept on believing that the other children really did want to be friends, even though he always wound up reunited with the U-bend—came up trumps when he found Odin on the brink of doing himself in. Upon learning that the sad old man sitting in the end cubicle was chief of all the gods, Neville's colleagues would surely have told Odin to get the effing hell out, because they were effing well about to close for the night and not about to miss tonight's *CSI Effing Miami* for the sake of some old nutter. Instead of which, Neville leaned on his mop and said, "That sounds like a tough job."

With those six words he endeared himself to Odin so much that the old fool forgot all about killing himself and told Neville magnanimously that yes, it was a tough job, especially seeing as nobody cared anymore. Neville said, "Oh dear." If he was being sarcastic Odin didn't notice. What Odin did was to pour out his life story, which must have wreaked havoc on Neville's evening television schedule. Since Neville was still there when Odin finished—the lazy slob probably slept on his feet through most of the saga, Thor reckoned—Odin was so absurdly grateful to Neville for saving his life that he promised Neville the gods would do his bidding. All he had to do was ask.

As mistakes go, Thor thought that made the *Hindenburg* and the *Herald of Free Enterprise* look forgivable. No sooner were the words out of Odin's mouth than Neville threw down his mop, never to lift it again.

The following month had been the busiest of Thor's eternal life. Everyone who had ever teased Neville, except those who were presciently ex-directory, found that their personal belongings came off worse in an encounter with the thunder god's hammer. Thor was caught in the act more often than not, since a seven-foot fellow rather stands out in suburbia. He could never justify his vandalism by admitting Neville had put him up to it. He had the shreds of his reputation to think of.

Odin realised his mistake, sufficiently at least to tell a few fibs about the extent of his powers. Some of Neville's wilder demands fell on deaf ears. "Your request for immortality cannot be processed at this time. Please try again later." But a god's word was his bond, otherwise what was left but anarchy?

Perhaps anarchy is preferable to murder, Thor thought as he approached Odin's modest semi-detached from the rear.

If you asked Thor to recollect all the indignities Neville had foisted on the gods, he would have shrunk from the task, stout of heart though he was. If you asked him to name the worst, he would have said without hesitating, "Making Odin live on his street."

Thor could hear Neville and Eva roistering in Neville's front garden, even from several hundred yards away. Thor had never written an *Art of War*, having been pipped to the post by Sun Tzu, but if he ever did, Rule No. 1 would be "Make sure you know where your enemy is. If he is screwing very loudly, this makes your job easier."

Except this wasn't an easy job, and Thor had no idea whether he would survive to put pen to paper.

Maybe there was a better way to put the world to rights. If Loki knew of one, he probably wouldn't mention it to Thor. He'd wait until the dust settled and quietly inaugurate himself as Chief God behind everyone's back. That was more his style than helping anyone to achieve anything.

Thor shrugged and kicked Odin's back door in.

The kitchen looked just like Neville's used to, before Eva set to work. Either Odin was too old to seduce the daughters of men these days, or else he took them straight to the bedroom without preliminaries. Thor hefted his hammer and stepped into the hallway.

The front room was occupied, as always, by Odin's extensive *Warhammer* collection. Thor looked closely at the arrangement of the figurines. He thought he recognised the battle Odin had recreated. It had been the talk of Valhalla for months afterwards. Those were the days.

Thor shook himself out of his rusty memories and climbed the stairs. Most of the floorboards squeaked, but it hardly mattered. Odin was neither so deaf nor so senile that he wouldn't be expecting Thor or one of the others.

When Thor reached the landing, he heard snoring waft out of what was laughably thought of as the master bedroom. It took more courage to step into that room than on to any of the battlefields he had known.

Odin lay on a divan patterned in floral damask. Thor stood irresolute at the foot of the bed. Odin's eyes twitched open.

"Wait!" Neville called from the foot of the stairs. How had he got in? He had probably made Odin give him a spare key.

Thor heard Neville puffing and panting up the stairs. The floorboards yowled in protest.

"Kill me," Odin whispered.

Neville loomed in the doorway, too short of breath from his run down the street to order Thor to cease and desist.

Still Thor hesitated. "But then these people will have

no god."

Odin's voice was a sigh. Thor had to lean close to catch his words.

"No god," Odin soughed, "is better than Neville."

Thor raised his hammer.

The End

About the author:

Ed Cooke works for the Methodist Church in York, UK. He writes lyrics for prog rock band *Voyager Project* and edits the Christian ezine *Rubber Lemon*. Both ventures can be found at their respective .co.uk domains.

Prometheus Released

By Kelly Dillon (London, UK)

aul's pen tip drifted a hair's breadth above marking the page as he scrolled down the long list of numbers, doing the calculations in his head. At the end he wrote the total in small precise hand—he wouldn't need to check the result, it was always right. It gave him an odd sense of pleasure to focus on the mundanities of simple tasks. It took his mind off... other things. Gods only know his younger years were traumatic enough to make this uncomplicated existence a blessing. Yes, the gods know that very well.

His brother may have been conscripted into carrying the weight of the world upon his shoulders, but not Paul, not anymore.

As he closed the accountancy ledger and returned his desk to meticulous tidiness, he saw movement out the window. An eagle, a large one, had landed on the handlebars of his bike chained to a stout pole on the footpath. So, they were trying again and were foolish enough to send *him*. He ignored the eagle's fierce glare that penetrated through layers of glass and polarization— his pens needed straightening before he could leave his desk for the day, and that took clear precedence.

Goodbyes in the office were perfunctory, the elevator ride down made in uncomfortable silence. His workmates respected him, of that he had no doubt, but they responded to an instinct so primal that they couldn't begin to rationalize it in their ordered world of numbers. If pressed, his colleagues might say that he just didn't fit, didn't feel like one of the team. What they were trying to say, without consciously realising it, was that he didn't feel like one of humanity. And they were right, not that it mattered. Paul wasn't so different. He ate, slept, did his work very well and occasionally had to chase eagles off his bike.

By the time he reached street level, people had stopped to stare, many holding their phones out at arm's length as a mechanical pulse of snapshots filled the air. There were mutters of disappointment when he eased his way through the small crowd to shoo the bird away with a flick of a hand that came close to connecting. As if the gesture had been for them, the gathering dispersed, although one couple lingered long enough to take a photo of him picking up his bike from where the thrust of wings had toppled it. That was about the closest to a divine visitation most people would ever experience, not that they would know it.

He briefly considered breaking his routine, doing something crazy like going to see a movie or playing a few rounds of miniature golf. But there really was no point, they would either hunt him down and cause a scene or wait in his apartment, and staying out late would only make him uncomfortable.

The eagle was waiting outside his door when he

arrived home, which relieved him slightly. The last time one was sent he'd tried opening the door, and it had snapped like driftwood—the cost hadn't been large, but the inconvenience was enormous. Not that they would understand such things, what use have they for human sensibilities like privacy and the value of personal property?

It scurried inside as soon as the door was open, and he "accidentally" stepped on its tail feathers, bringing a glare that held sparks and the tangible memory of another eagle poised threateningly above his exposed midriff. Once the door clicked shut, the bird disappeared in an absurdly theatrical flare of light that faded grudgingly to reveal an aging man with the weather-beaten look of a veteran.

Paul walked past him, unimpressed, headed for the kitchen.

"I would offer you a drink, but I don't want you to stay."

He heard the wind pick up ferocity outside in response, but the man managed to hold his tongue. Amazing, he was learning civility after all these years, just when Paul realised his own no longer mattered.

"Fire," he growled around a bushy beard.

"Yes, fire, it always comes back to that cursed Flame."

"Prometheus, we need you–"

"No! I am Paul. For all the indignities you have shown me, you can at least respect that."

"A name does not change the Titan. You are who you ever were, Light Thief."

"That time is long past and best buried. You may have bound my brothers into servitude and chained me beneath your torment for a time, Zeus, but by every other god than you I swear you shall have nothing more from me!" A spasmodic twitch lifted the hem of his shirt, revealing a mess of scar tissue on his belly above the liver. It looked like nothing so much as a desolate Martian landscape, crumpled and severe.

Zeus' eyes shied away from it, but a god was intrinsically incapable of showing remorse or admitting he had acted wrongly. Paul knew this and took the High Father's discomfort as the closest to an apology he would ever get.

"I paid my dues," he continued in a quiet tone, "day after day, more years than I can remember. And not one day of it did I regret, not for one moment did I wish to have left your fire where it was."

"Humankind should not have it. It was wrongly given and must be returned."

"Ha! Of course you would wish it, when my Flame warmed their civilisation until now each individual is on par with the power of Olympia. Have you seen these?" He held up a small black box. "They call them iPods. They're fantastic, and all because of my fire running through their circuitry. You would take all this from them and have them return to the hovel and the hearth, to soil their knees in the mud in their supplication of you."

"The flame that warms also burns. You believe you have given them a gift, but it is a poisoned one, and they shall soon destroy themselves with it. Am I to be seen as tyrant for protecting my children?"

"Tyrant, womaniser, patricida, shall I continue?"

"Insolent fool!" Zeus raised a fist, and deadly energies crackled from within, leaking from between clenched fingers.

Paul looked on calmly. Part of his mind reminded him that the news was on in twenty minutes. He always watched the news. Another part, a smaller part, shrieked at him for angering the Father of the Gods and conjured terrible predictions of his fate. Again, calmly, Paul took this part of his mind and shoved it into a deep dark box. It was the only way he had been able to stay mostly sane while the eagle gnawed daily on his liver. The gods were cruel in their punishments, but seeing them as petitioners now made every agonising day worthwhile. He had done that, his Flame.

"Do you still have the strength for it, or do your bones grow weak in the cold of the hearth?"

Zeus seemed beyond words. He had always been easy to goad, and Prometheus' nature had ever been to push the bounds in favour of humankind. He hadn't specifically spoken with the intention of inciting the elderly god to violence, but he was unsurprised when it came.

The first electrical blow threw him across the room to land awkwardly at the foot of his lounge. The effort had cost Zeus greatly, and he laboured to remain upright, both men staggering as if they were far into drink. Paul twitched from the residual sparks of lightning coursing through his body, but he faced the High Father proudly, defiantly, and then punched him in the mouth. Hard. He couldn't count the number of centuries he'd dreamed of doing just that, and he realised with a surge of satisfaction that it had been worth the wait.

Zeus, having landed inelegantly on his rump, starred up at Paul in disbelief as a small trickle of blood crept through his beard and dripped on his chest. At the sight of the fallen god, Paul's veins felt on fire, and his vision was cast over in shades of red. His people, the Titans, had warred with these Olympians from the dawn of the Age. It was his heritage, his birthright and his very great pleasure. But the battle furor collided with the trauma-born obsessive compulsions that now ruled his life, and both clawed for dominance. Zeus saw his hesitation and struck again, the lightning this time barely having enough force to push the Titan back a few paces, and he was still able to hold to his feet. But it had been enough to thrust him into a side table and disrupt the precisely arranged ornaments. Battle fury succumbed to the need to bring them back to order, and Paul suddenly wanted nothing so much as for Zeus to go, to leave him in peace so he could return to his routine and structured life. Even though it was clear the great god was beaten and unable to defend himself, meting out further revenge on this fading being now felt hollow. He turned his back and walked to the sofa, wincing a bit as he leaned down to pick up the remote and turn on the news.

"Please leave now." The Titanic rage of a few moments previous may never have existed, buried under the dominant human persona he had embraced to survive.

Zeus, even defeated, was not prepared to leave the matter be.

"Humankind knows not how to handle this power you have given them. They stand upon a precipice, and for their own good I will see them fall. Then they will return to us, and all will be as it was. You want to keep the fire? I shall make for them an inferno such as you have never known! Remember, once it begins, that I gave you this chance."

Paul ignored him utterly, engrossed in the nightly news, and the Father of the Gods stalked out. He clearly was too drained to return to his aquiline form but had enough strength to slam the door off its hinges. Paul pursed his lips in annoyance and mentally jotted down a reminder to contact the carpenter again.

But despite his resolve to not become involved, he found his dreams to be beset with horrific premonitions of the gods' revenge upon civilization—a civilisation that, thanks to Prometheus' stolen Flame, no longer needed them. They were hurting, rejected, and grew weaker by the day as racial memory faded and humankind pushed them further and further into the shadows of myth. They were desperate, and desperate men did dangerous things. And desperate gods? Unthinkable. More than once Paul woke with a start, drenched in sweat after seeing the whole world in flames, everything he knew consumed in one insatiable fire. Nightmares only, he hoped, and yet a god's vow could not be so easily disregarded.

Olympus itself may no longer have the power to wrest control back from the humans, but there were many underhanded ways the same could be accomplished. After all, it had taken the assassination of but one man to spark the First World War, and despite lessons since learned, world relations were little better now than in those days. It wouldn't take much to set superpower against superpower, and then... fire, missiles, destruction. Paul's ordered life would forever be disrupted.

It was unacceptable.

The gods had come wanting to spur him to action, and they had succeeded, but not as their pawn as they hoped. In the silence of the younger hours of night, Prometheus declared war on all Olympia.

Even resolved as he was, he found leaving his apartment difficult and wondered if he would be able to return. To have any hope at all he needed to abandon Paul and resume the Titan's mantle, to become Prometheus again. That part of him had never left, not really, but had been chained in his mind as surely as when he had been imprisoned beneath the eagle. There would be certain physical changes also, and it would be better no humans were in the vicinity during the transformation.

But finding land without people was not as easy as it had once been, and the sun's burning face was just starting to peer above the horizon by the time he had hiked far enough inside a nature reserve. He knelt and thrust his hands deep into the ground—for Titans, unlike Olympians, drew their strength from the very earth—they sank in smoothly, as if the rocks and dirt welcomed his touch. Power flooded into him, and a low cry escaped his lips. Too much too fast, and far too unused to it. The cry turned into a scream, and the elements roared in sympathetic passion. Winds whipped up, clawing rubble from the surface and turning it into deadly shrapnel while the ground beneath shifted and broke as fluidly as waves upon an ocean. And in the centre Prometheus was unharmed, if not untouched, for the outward manifestations of this energy were the barest shadow of what he fought to assimilate within himself. But he had mastered them before, for the better part of his long life, and that skill was not soon forgotten.

The tempest that had occulted his body eased, tamed, and as the debris fell like a curtain, Prometheus stood. He was taller now, both in stature and posture, the meek and ill-fitting accountant ceasing to exist, even though they shared the same features. Trees lay shattered around him as casualties of the recent chaos, and he gently lifted one out of his way, regretting the necessity of their sacrifice.

What would the humans ever make of this? At least none had been nearby to be caught unprepared in the vortex of primal energies.

"Brother, let me walk upon your path," he whispered to the sky, and taking a step, left the surface of the earth. It was as if he were climbing a ladder, but with each step the distance under his feet blurred and carried him unimaginable heights above the world. Humans, nor even birds could hope to survive here, as the air became thin and the temperature frigid. Eventually the brilliant light of the surrounding sky dimmed and retreated from the black of space. Prometheus stopped and turned, seeing his brother for the first time in eons. Even with the enhanced eyes of a Titan, Atlas appeared amorphous, a body of such delicate mist to bear so great a burden. As if he had grown beyond the size of any giant and, in so doing, had spread himself too thin. His back was bowed, and upon it rode the sphere of the earth, his two arms rising to wrap around it protectively. Tears sprang to Prometheus' eyes to see the shackles that bound his elder brother in position and allowed no respite. He was chained like a mule to a slaver's wheel, forever held in his circuit of the sun until his path must wear a furrow even in the very fabric of the universe.

"It has been long..." his brother's soft voice was carried on solar winds.

"Forgive me, I have not been myself, not for some time now."

"I shared the suffering your punishment brought, although I could do nothing for it. From here I feel... everything. But you are free now, and that thought does much to console me as I carry my own sentence."

"Would that I had the power to free you this moment,

dear brother. I would yoke Zeus in your stead, and we would spend the rest of our days making up for lost time. But although the gods have lost much, their edicts remain enforced with as much power as the moment they were uttered."

"Be at ease. I am resigned to my fate, and my task is not unrewarding. I carry all life through the procession of seasons. It is no small thing."

Prometheus bowed his head and felt a great surge of love for his elder brother.

"I have come to ask a boon."

"If it is within my power, it will be yours."

"I must again steal inside Olympus, but the gods are crafty and have hidden the entrance well after I was last there. Will you help me gain access?"

"Gladly, and I know the reason you have been unable to find the home of the gods. They have hidden it in the one place you would never think to search—inside me."

A hand the size of the moon drifted forward to cup him gently, and he was lifted towards his brother's opening mouth, hearing a whispered prayer of luck moments before he was swallowed.

Instead of the warm wetness he had been expecting, he found himself landed in a lavish banquet hall. The sudden halt made him pitch forward to his knees, hands ploughing into a rich burgundy rug softer than the fleece of a newborn lamb. Tapestries and exquisite paintings adorned every wall, most depicting the ancient battles of gods and Titans. One caught Prometheus' eye, and the scene caused him such strength of offense that under his glare it crumpled into coarse ash and slid off the wall like diseased flesh. That wasn't how it had happened, he had been there.

Chiding himself for the petty display of power, Prometheus crept silently down the empty hall, his vision overlaid with memories of the last time he was here. It had been brighter-lit in those days, and sounds of music and merriment had echoed from all directions. Now the harps and sistrums were laid down, the feast tables bare and lamps left cold. The gods would be huddled together now for comfort, not revelry.

Like a phantom from Asphodel, he glided down a corridor, his soft footfalls belying his great size. Ornate doorways led off from the passageway, many flanked by pristine marble friezes and Corinthian style columns, and the Titan surmised that they were quarters based on the personalized themes to each carving. He stopped briefly before one depicting Athena leaping, fully-grown and garbed for war, from her father's forehead on the day of her birth. Prometheus had been present, and it stirred an ache of regret that he had once—briefly—been treated as a friend to the Olympians. But no more.

The door in front of him began to open, and he froze, eyes darting for cover that didn't exist. He had only the time to take a step backwards before the goddess herself stood before him. She looked tired. Her once battle-bright eyes drooped wearily at the corners, and she held to the ebony doorframe as if for support. They locked eyes—neither spoke. The ghost of a sigh escaped her lips and she nodded, turning slowly to return to her room. Prometheus waited for the alarm to be called, for the warrior goddess to come bursting from her chamber as she once would have, resplendent in her gleaming armour. Instead, if he listened very closely, he thought he could hear weeping.

Had they fallen so far? Even subduing Zeus in his apartment hadn't prepared him for this—the Father of the

Gods must have borrowed much of what power remained for even that feeble display. Skulking through these corridors as a thief now seemed unnecessarily disrespectful. And yet he knew the things they had done in their long lives, and what they would surely do again had they the strength. The world had been their plaything once, until Prometheus had taken it from them. Well, now he would give it back, although not how they might wish it.

A branch in the hall he remembered led to an open courtyard, once the home of the fire. The last time he'd been here the light from it had nearly blinded him, and the heat had left him gasping for breath. Now the corridor was shrouded in shadows so thick he felt he might be lost within them. If even the smallest ember remained, there was no sign of it. No wonder the gods were desperate. This area—once the heart of Olympus—now seeped cold, the same chill as an open grave. It was infectious and had slowly worked its curse upon the Olympians over the centuries. He turned on it in satisfaction. Let it remain in the dark. It was serving a far greater purpose now on earth.

He almost left then, convinced that the gods were not long for life and would soon be scattered like smoke upon a breeze. Even with all the remaining power of this cold place, they could do no more than wail impotently as human civilisation flourished around them... without them. Zeus had been bluffing. And yet, for the companionship they once bore, he could not simply let them be dispersed upon the winds of the Age. Even the punishment the High Father had forced upon him, as unforgivable as it was, wasn't deserving of that. He would help them, in his own way, and they would hate him for it.

That thought alone set a warm contented glow through his chest. They would survive, perhaps eternally, knowing that it was the Titan Prometheus who had both saved and bound them. The irony was exquisite.

Mind set, he strode into the main feasting hall as if it were his by right. Olympians looked up at his abrupt entrance, their expressions migrating from surprise to hope and then fear. The lone lyre that had been playing trailed off uncertainly, its final note lingering in the air like a cat's mourning cry. Their attempts at leisure were abandoned; grapes fell forgotten from their fingers to roll a chaotic game of marbles across the smooth stone floor. Prometheus' gaze dropped to them momentarily, and he let a small private smile ghost across his lips. Only yesterday he would have felt the overwhelming urge to gather the errant fruit, but the very human Paul was gone, and nothing now restrained him.

"Friend or foe?" Hera called from her divan, although she was perched forward on it at such an angle that she merely looked awkward, not luxurious.

Zeus waved a hand to silence her, unwilling to hear the word that would seal their fate, but Prometheus had already spoken.

"Both."

The gods shifted nervously while Prometheus stood at his ease.

He left them hanging for a protracted moment before continuing, "Will you submit to what I have decided is for the best?"

Several deities began making questioning noises, but the thunder-like crash of Zeus' boot upon the marble floor stilled their tongues.

"No! We are the might of Olympus. We bend for no

man. And we will *never* submit to a Titan."

Prometheus' eyes narrowed slightly, but that was his only sign of disappointment. He had been sure that Zeus was too proud, but he'd still hoped that the others, given the chance.... But no, there would be no miracles for these gods. He had been prepared to do things the hard way the moment he stepped within their home.

"Then I challenge you, or any you would have stand in your stead. Gather whatever yet remains of your power. You will need all of it. Be warned, what happens to your champion happens to all Olympia. I will make sure of it."

"I stand for Olympus, as I ever have." Zeus suited his words by crafting a silver spear of lightning that he sent skyward into the shadowed recesses of the ceiling, "And I have laid low more than one upstart Titan in my day!"

"In your day," Prometheus repeated dryly.

As the two combatants closed the gap between each other, the remaining deities scurried out of the way, clinging to the walls as if they could witness the gigantean clash as mere paintings, unnoticed and undamaged. Prometheus could feel Zeus stretch out, siphoning power from his kin, the memory of their past, even the very stone of Olympus. He felt him drain them to their limit and still, despite the energy crackling around his glowing form, he could not begin to measure to his younger self.

With a report that sent tremors up the columns, a lightning bolt the thickness of Zeus" wrist flew towards the Titan's chest with deadly accuracy and intent. Prometheus snarled, not because of the attack itself—which would leave a lesser mortal nothing more than a smouldering ruin—but because of the god's predictability. They would not learn, would not grow! It was their inflexibility that had driven them to this lonely place, and even now, on the eve of their annihilation, they could not change. How different their existence might have been had they stepped down from their lofty thrones and worked with the humans rather than let their jealousy of the Flame keep them aloof.

He caught the bolt a glancing blow on the palm of his hand and deflected it harmlessly. Instead of counterattacking he stepped forward.

Zeus summoned the elements of his realm, always eager to rush to his aid. Wind and rain fused into a vortex that bore down on the Titan and threatened to tear him limb from limb. Prometheus folded his arms across his chest and bowed his head, creating a sphere of calm around himself that was little disturbed by the god's maelstrom. He stepped forward.

Sweat visibly forming on his brow, the High Father took half a step backwards and raised his hands. Shadows leapt from the chamber's recesses, merging together like ebony liquid and growing in both size and solidity. The dark sphere seemed to twist, unfurling like a flower, and a dozen writhing tentacles detached from the main body and focused on Prometheus. He recognised the apparition as Scylla, a primordial sea monster and scourge of ancient mariners, long since passed from the world of life but no less dangerous for being here now.

Before he could devise a plan of defence, he felt a weight hit him from behind, and heavily muscled arms wrapped around his neck. Ares, in aid of his father, had leapt upon him and sought to keep him distracted while the leviathan neared for attack. The ambush was a cowardly one unbefitting the god in his better days, and instead of throwing off the choking arms, Prometheus held tight. Held tight and increased his size, growing until he truly was a giant towering above them. And then he let go.

Ares fell, limbs flailing wildly as if trying to transform into something that would arrest his descent. But Zeus had all his power now, and the god was helpless. His body hit the polished floor with a sickening crunch. Prometheus didn't have time to check whether the war god had survived, as the shadow Scylla had become an immediate threat.

Tendrils reached out, clawing through the air for him, and one struck his head in a dizzying blow. For all the shadow she appeared, the creature was as solid as any other. And she was both fast and cunning, having spent her life deftly plucking sailors from deck tops and flinging them into the mouth of Charybdis, her hungry companion, if not merely smashing them against the rocks upon which she had perched. A tentacle wrapped around his waist despite his evasions, and then another, and another. Several sought his neck, and all his effort went into holding them back. His giant form was half obscured with undulating shadows, slowly constricting. Scylla's four heads, barely seen against the black of her body, shrieked in manic victory. He took a deep breath, his ribs creaking from the effort of holding it, and stepped forward into the monster's embrace. Like wrestlers they held each other in a primitive test of strength, for no other power could touch a creature born of shadows. He fell to one knee, lungs burning from that one final breath he'd snatched, but his grip never lessened. Scylla's muscles quivered, and one by one her tentacles unwrapped. Limbs that had sought his crushing death now frantically writhed for escape, wrapping around furniture, columns, or anything nearby to pull herself free. Exotic sofas crumbled into kindling, and a spiraling fault line appeared across the perfect column's surface. It broke away a moment later, raining down colossal shards that pinned two tentacles to the floor.

Scylla's laughs had transformed into yowls of terror, and then all sound cut off abruptly as Prometheus flexed and brought his arms together. Shadows melted from within his grasp, pooling on the floor at his feet before sullenly returning to their natural abode.

He stepped forward.

Zeus stood at his feet, barely reaching his knee but still radiating defiance. He squared his shoulders and spoke a word. Nothing happened. With an air of desperation he spoke again, pouring all his strength into the command. He grew perhaps a foot. Peering down from where his head nearly brushed the ceiling, Prometheus barely noticed.

"Kneel," the quiet command rumbled across the chamber, bringing down a further dusting of debris from the pillar Scylla had shattered. Even though it was clearly not directed at them, several Olympians huddled against the walls obeyed.

"I cannot stop you from doing as you will, you have won, I am defeated. But I cannot be made to bend knee."

"Kneel now, or I will summon the selfsame eagle that feasted upon my liver for centuries, and deliver you into its mercy."

Zeus heard the calm assurance, the ring of determination, and slowly the god dropped to the floor. Prometheus was satisfied.

"Gather close Olympians, I wish you no more harm than has already befallen you." He waited while they drew near, even Athena who had joined after hearing the sounds of combat cease.

"I intend to give the world to you, and to return the fire."

He heard a bitter laugh behind him and glanced

around to see Ares, bloody and obviously deep in unaccustomed pain, supported on either side by Hera and Demeter.

"But not as you wish it. This is the day gods die. This is the day you will be reborn as men. The Flame burns strongly upon the earth, and you will once more know its warmth, but never again will you dominate mankind as Olympians. From this point forward whatever accolades you enjoy in your lives will be earned, as all men must do."

"So you alone bear the power of a god and would rule in our place!" Poseidon said with frank dislike of the Titan.

Prometheus ignored the implicit accusation. "No, I will return to being Paul, which is all I wished before you disturbed me. Although Paul is now much changed, I think." He smiled at the thought of being free of the crippling compulsions to create order. Those issues had well and truly been dealt with here.

"Zeus has taken nearly all from you in his effort to repel me. I now take the rest."

What remained was pitifully small, but it was the difference between deity and human. He felt each shudder and mourn the loss as he drained it from them, but they would be the better for it in the long run. Like him, they would be able to live countless lives upon the earth, finally able to understand their charges instead of playing with their lives on whim. Eventually the experience might even make them fit to rule again; their incarnations becoming known as great men of history. Perhaps it had already happened with others—the world had forgotten many gods.

When it was done Prometheus lifted his face

skyward and whispered to his brother. "Let Olympus be expelled," he said. "Raze it to the foundations and deliver all within safely upon the earth. The resultant cyclone was immediate and absolute, and everything disappeared in a white haze.

Prometheus awoke first and found himself in the devastated crater of his earlier transformation. Men and women lay unconscious around him, and he could only recognise them as the past deities by the similarity of their features. Before they stirred he poured his amassed energy into the ground, returning the strength of a Titan to the earth so that it might be replenished. When they woke they would find themselves alone, human and sheltered in the shade of a giant tree.

The End

About the author:

Kelly is an Archaeology graduate with a Masters specialization in Egyptology, which has contributed greatly to her understanding of past cultures and their religious beliefs. Kelly's interest in world mythology has led her down various roads, resulting in her writing often, including strong historical and mythological themes. She has been published three times before, with another soon to be released, and is currently working on a novel detailing the rise of the Nephilim and fall of Angels.

9362620R0

Made in the USA
Charleston, SC
08 September 2011